AFTER INNOCENCE

"Fresh . . . extraordinary . . . an emotional roller coaster."
—*Publishers Weekly*

SECRETS

"Probably the best mistaken-identity book since Sandra Brown's MIRROR IMAGE."
—B. Dalton's *Heart to Heart*

"A love story that will dazzle readers with its insight into the human heart."
—*Romantic Times*

SCANDALOUS LOVE

"Brenda Joyce brings a woman's romantic fantasies to life. Emotional, poignant and highly sensual . . . passion at its ultimate!"
—*Romantic Times*

"The essence of romance!"
—*Affaire de Coeur*

The Rival

BRENDA JOYCE

St. Martin's Paperbacks

THE RIVAL

Copyright © 1998 by Brenda Joyce.

Photograph of the author by Sigrid Estrada.

All rights reserved. No part of this book may be used or reproduced in any manner whatsoever without written permission except in the case of brief quotations embodied in critical articles or reviews. For information address St. Martin's Press, 175 Fifth Avenue, New York, N.Y. 10010.

ISBN: 0-312-96621-0

Printed in the United States of America

St. Martin's Paperbacks edition / August 1998

St. Martin's Paperbacks are published by St. Martin's Press, 175 Fifth Avenue, New York, NY 10010.

10 9 8 7 6 5 4 3 2 1

This book is dedicated to Adam.

This book is also dedicated to the best friends a woman could possibly have: Anne Mohr, Wendy Mosler, Judy O'Brien, Carole Schuler, and Roberta Stalberg.

PROLOGUE

CAEDMON CRAG, 1746

What in God's name ails you, boy? Shoot!" the earl of Stanhope bellowed.

He squinted. The bevy of ducks just flushed from the heath by the hounds filled the cloudy gray sky, their frightened quacking mingling with the sound of their desperately flapping wings. He strained to see, but the mass of birds above him in the sky were oddly blurred. Beside him, his brother fired his five-foot-long matchlock rifle yet again, taking down what had to be his sixth duck. Garrick's palms were wet with sweat.

"Damn you, boy, shoot!" the earl, his father, shouted.

Garrick squeezed the trigger as sweat dripped into his eyes, blinding him. The huge rifle, held against his shoulder, went off, the blast almost rocking him off his feet.

"You missed!" the earl exclaimed in disgust.

Garrick lowered his rifle and wiped one worn wool coat sleeve against his face, leaning heavily on the butt of the huge gun. He was aware that his father had turned his back on him in profound disapproval, while Lionel, having finished reloading, took one final shot. Another duck came hurtling from the heavens to land on the heath with a thump.

The silence was now absolute. The frightened quacking of the ducks was gone, the guns silenced, the moors littered with the dead and broken birds.

"That was fine marksmanship, Lionel," said Richard De Vere, the twelfth earl of Stanhope. He was smiling as he slapped his eldest hard on his shoulder. "I daresay you are the best shot in these parts, even at your tender age."

Garrick wished he could disappear into the grim gray-green earth.

Lionel was laughing. He pushed thick, golden blond bangs out of blue eyes. Like his brother's, his hair was unpowdered, shoulder length, and pulled back into a queue. But that was where all resemblance between the two boys ended. Although younger by a year and a half, Garrick was already taller, and his hair was dark, his skin swarthy. Lace cuffs frothed out of Lionel's pale blue wool frock coat. Garrick's coat was brown, and the lawn shirt he had hastily thrown on that morning was plain.

"Father, fourteen is hardly a child, you know. If I could not shoot a duck by now, there would not be much hope for me, would there?" Lionel grinned.

Garrick toed the dirt of the heath where they all stood. The sky was gray and windswept. Wisps of clouds twisted, shifted, whirled. Although spring had come to most of England, it was hardly evident on the Cornish coast. The moors appeared stark, deserted, exceedingly unfriendly; the gorse had yet to bloom. The wind was raw. The sound of the violent surf, crashing on the southwestern coast of the peninsula, could be heard somewhere not far below the trio standing on the heath.

The earl of Stanhope, splendidly clad in a teal green frock coat and silver breeches, the long curls of his wig reaching his shoulders, agreed. "You were a fine shot by the time you were twelve, I do remember it well," he said, and he cast a disparaging glance at Garrick, who was twelve and a half years old.

Garrick busied himself with studying his matchlock, as if he might find something new and exciting on the barrel or butt of the gun. One of the spotted hounds came up to him, shoving its wet brown nose against the back of his hand. Garrick grimaced, pretending to be unaware of the dog. His father whirled. "And how many birds *did* you down, Garrick?"

Garrick was slow to look up. He felt his cheeks burning. He knew his father was fully aware of the fact that he had not hit a single duck. "None."

A hard silence greeted his words. "None," the earl said. "Lionel downed a good half dozen; you downed none."

Garrick met his father's blue eyes—the very same blue eyes as Lionel's. "That's right, Father," he said.

"Perhaps, when we return to London, you should stay behind—and practice your marksmanship," the earl said flatly.

Garrick shrugged, managing an I-don't-give-a-damn smile. The hound shoved its nose against his hanging hand again. Garrick could not help himself. He slid his palm over the smooth head of the dog. The dog could not soothe his jangled nerves. He despised hunting, and not because his damnable eyesight always seemed to fail him. He thought the sport excessively cruel, for he had always been fond of animals—his father said he was too fond. As if liking animals, even birds, made him less of a man.

"Father," Lionel said, no longer smiling, "remember the frost fair last winter? Garrick was undefeated in boxing— and only that farmer from Wickham outwrestled him. Does it matter if he cannot shoot?" He walked over to Garrick and grinned, throwing an arm around him. "And all the ladies like him better, too, although I'll be damned if I know why, as I am definitely the handsomer of the two of us." Lionel winked at him.

That was also a lie, but Garrick loved his brother for coming to his rescue—yet again.

"That will change; you're the heir." The earl of Stanhope eyed his second son. "Boxing and wrestling are hardly sports; they are suitable for peasants, Garrick," De Vere said rather coolly. He turned and waved at their waiting retinue. Immediately their horses were led forward by the liveried, bewigged servants on foot who were standing many yards away from them. The grooms rushed to see them mounted, while the kennel master fetched the setters and ordered his lackeys to retrieve the game. "I don't want you engaging in such sordid activities again."

The earl spurred his gelding forward. Garrick, stiff with tension, mounted, and he and Lionel followed more slowly. The rugged, rocky coast came into view, a hundred feet or so below them, on their left. The beach was hardly pristine, the sand stone colored, with big black boulders littering the surf. They rode not far from the cliffs, and just to their left were the stark ruins of a twelfth-century keep. The locals said it was haunted.

Lionel slowed his bay mount, as did Garrick. "Heed me well," he said, his voice low. "The next time we do a bit of shooting, why don't you say you're ill. Plead a stomach flu, for god's sake."

"As if he would believe me," Garrick muttered.

Lionel sighed.

Caedmon Crag came into view a few moments later, a three-story stone manor seemingly plopped down on a starkly treeless rise of land at the edge of the cliffs. Situated just a mile or so from the Norman ruins, it was a manor the earl rarely attended, and then only to inspect the workings of the Caedmon tin mine. A fortified stone manor, it had been built four centuries past and had hardly been modernized. Two towers guarded the walled entrance and barbican. The boys rode across the wooden drawbridge, which was never raised, through the domed entryway, and into the cobbled courtyard. The manor was set back a few yards from the barbican and outbuildings, its back to the perilous cliffs and the demanding sea.

It was suppertime, and the boys followed their father into the great hall, with its ancient weapons and pennants hanging on the walls and from the rafters. Their mother was sitting in front of a massive stone hearth at least twice her size, a volume of sonnets in her hands. Blond and blue eyed, she was a stunning woman clad in dark green silk and emeralds, but she did not smile. She looked at them all with a question in her eyes, rising slowly to her feet and laying the thin volume aside.

"It was a fine afternoon," the earl told her heartily. A

servant materialized with a mug of ale, which he accepted and drained. "Lionel has outdone himself, once again. I am very proud of him."

Garrick cursed silently because he could feel himself flushing again. His father could not be more clear, and it hurt. He felt all eyes upon him. Reluctantly he looked up, scowling.

The countess came forward. "I am happy for you," Eleanor said softly, her words almost melting together, kissing Lionel's cheek. Her gaze settled on Garrick uncertainly.

There was not much to say and Garrick said nothing, but inwardly he tensed.

"Garrick failed to make even a single kill," the earl said flatly. "I do believe he does his worst merely to displease me."

That was not the truth. Garrick met his mother's soft, sympathetic eyes and turned abruptly, heading back toward the massive front door, brushing thick black bangs out of his oddly amber eyes. He felt like shouting, "I am your son, too!" but he did not.

"Where do you think you are going?" the earl demanded. "Did I give you permission to leave?"

Garrick gritted his teeth and refused to answer.

He heard the earl say, as he opened the door, "His manners need vast improvement, madam. I am sorely tried with his behavior." And it was a warning.

He slammed the door closed behind him and ran.

He ran across the courtyard and back out through the barbican. Servants eyed him, but no one was very curious—they all thought him strange with his solitary ways, and he knew it. But I am not strange, he thought savagely, running harder now across the old, rotting wooden drawbridge and down the road.

Tears burned his eyes. He hated himself for being as weak as a child and told himself it was the wind, which was strong and high. He wished he were more like his brother, smart and strong and good at everything, and so well liked. He veered onto another path. He had no interest in going down to the village or even heading that way—he wanted only to be alone.

When the ruins of the keep came into view he slowed, panting, to a walk. The wind was stronger now, and it gusted in his face, causing him to blink rapidly. He was thinking about the dead ducks and his father. Did the earl despise him? Why could he never please him? Why did his father always point out his shortcomings? He had truly tried to make his mark, but for some damnable reason, the birds all blurred together when they took to the sky. He had tried his best. He always tried his best, even when accused of giving up. Damn it.

Sometimes he wished he were Lionel. Lionel was not just a splendid shot, he was a superb swordsman, too. He was far more adept than Garrick at both his letters and his numbers, and he was almost fluent in French, too. And Garrick was glad Lionel was so talented. He had been proud of his older brother for as long as he could remember. Lionel was the Stanhope heir, and Lionel was a hero.

Garrick kicked a stone off the path. It rolled and rolled, finally slipping over the side of the cliff, where it would eventually plummet a hundred feet to the sandy beach below. Perhaps he had to face the fact that he was never going to be like his brother—that the earl was right. He was, damn it, an embarrassing failure, and he was never going to please his father.

Pushing more hair out of his eyes, Garrick wandered into the keep. It was just a shell. The stone walls were broken, in places towering two or three stories high, in other places no more than five feet tall. Overhead, the sky was darkening. Underfoot, rocks and grass vied for control of the earthen space. Garrick stared at the section of charred black stone that had clearly been the hearth. He took a few deep breaths and wiped his eyes with his sleeve. He had not been aware before of his trembling, but now it began to lessen. He wiped his eyes again, sniffing. He could actually envision the Norman knights come over with William the Conqueror, standing in front of the fire, clad in mail and bloody from battle, warming their hands. Then he turned and walked over to an arrow slit, and he stared down at the stormy gray sea.

Waves pounded the shore. Plumes of white spray recoiled over huge, glistening black boulders, the sound deafening. The sky was ominously dark on the horizon, blackening. Garrick began to relax. He loved this wild, desolate place. He would not mind being left behind when his family returned to London.

"Garrick?"

He whirled and found his brother standing by the entrance to the keep. His queue had come undone, and Garrick pushed more wayward hair out of his own face. "What are you doing here?" he asked, but he was glad to see his brother.

"I should be asking you that," Lionel said with a smile. He walked over to where Garrick stood, and together they stared down at the sea. "A storm tonight," Lionel commented.

"Yes," Garrick said. "In a few more hours, there'll be good smuggling." He smiled. Everyone knew the locals smuggled under cover of either darkness or inclement weather. Years ago the boys had discovered a series of caves in the cliffs below the keep. In one of the caves they had found a dozen wet barrels filled with French brandy. For years they had played in those caves.

"We could sneak out after supper." Lionel grinned, his blue eyes alight. He toyed with a gold coin hanging on a chain about his neck. "Who knows what we might find if we catch the smugglers at their work?"

"We could," Garrick said. "If Father catches us, there will be whippings all around, even for you."

Suddenly Lionel's smile faded, his expression becoming very serious. He slipped the chain with the coin over his head. "You should take this."

Garrick looked at the offered coin. They had found it in the caves, it was Spanish, and Lionel had worn it for years for good luck. "I cannot."

"I want you to have it," Lionel said seriously. "Perhaps it will bring you luck, as it has me."

He shook his head, bent and found a stone, and threw it over the wall, toward the sea, as far as he could. Both boys watched it in its flight. "You found it. It's yours. Besides, you're the heir. God knows one day you may need good fortune."

"But I really want you to have it," Lionel said, very seriously now.

His tone made Garrick stiffen, and he stared. "It's yours. But thank you," he finally said.

"Very well." Lionel slipped the chain back over his head, found a rock, and flung it with all his might. His throw went farther than Garrick's had.

Garrick grimaced, found another stone, this one smooth and round, and put all of his concentration into the throw. He smiled when he saw that he had outdone his brother.

"Good throw," Lionel conceded.

The wind began to howl.

"They fired arrows, flaming ones, out of that slit," Garrick said.

Lionel looked at him, and both boys walked over to the slit. They peered through it and down the cliff. "How could invaders climb up here? It's impossible."

Garrick studied the cliff, which plunged down from the keep where they stood, into the frothing, raging sea. "It's steep, but not sheer. There are ledges for footholds. It could be done. Let's take a closer look."

"No. I don't think so," Lionel said.

"Why not? Surely you're not scared?"

"What would I be afraid of?" Lionel asked, but he was paler than before.

Garrick eyed him and walked to the other side of the slit, where the stone wall was broken and not even as tall as he was.

Lionel's eyes widened with alarm. "What are you doing?!" he cried.

Garrick climbed over the wall and stood outside of the keep on a narrow stone ledge that was just a few feet wide and a few feet long. Below him the cliffs plummeted jaggedly to the sea. It was a bit unnerving standing on the edge of the cliff, so far above the sandy beach, and heights did not usually bother him. But Lionel was afraid of heights, and Garrick knew it—even though he pretended not to.

"What are you doing?" Lionel cried again.

Garrick did not answer as it began to rain. He closed his eyes and lifted his face to the wild wind, feeling a sudden peace come over him. Yes, he liked this savage place, and that probably made him strange in his father's and even Lionel's eyes. No one else that he knew liked godforsaken south Cornwall.

Suddenly Lionel was standing beside him, having just climbed the broken wall. His face was white. "I am not afraid," he said. "But tell me, what is the purpose of doing this?"

The feeling of peace left Garrick, replaced with guilt. He should not have baited his brother, whose fear was now obvious. The two brothers stood shoulder to shoulder against the side of the keep, which jutted upward from the side of the cliff and the narrow ledge where they stood. At that moment, the wind howled again. A savage gust of wind knocked them both backward against the keep.

"It's raining. We should go home before it really storms," Lionel said.

Garrick changed his stance to brace himself more securely against the buffeting of the wind, and his foot slipped on a loose chunk of rock. It broke off and crashed down the cliff. "You go," he said. "I don't want to eat supper with them."

"And what will you do, stand out here on the cliffs in the middle of a storm?" Lionel asked with sudden anger.

"That's just what I'll do if I choose," Garrick said as angrily.

"Why don't you do as I do?" Lionel asked, turning and climbing back over the broken wall of the keep, to stand on the firm, safe ground inside the shell. "Why don't you pretend to agree with all that he says, but just think as you please? Why do you have to defy him? You can't triumph. He is the earl," Lionel said.

"I am not a stupid lackey, without thoughts of my own," Garrick snapped.

"You know what I truly think?" Lionel said harshly. "You are a fool, to butt heads with him at every turn!" He turned and stomped away. It was raining a bit harder now.

Garrick shivered, jammed his fists in the pockets of his rather frayed hunting coat, and leaned his back against the keep, hardly seeing the pounding sea below him. His thoughts about his brother, in that moment, were not kind. Lionel might pretend to agree, but in essence he was a puppet on a string, for he did as the earl wished him to do. Garrick could not, would not, live that way. How glad he was that he was not the oldest son.

Maybe he would stand out here all night, he thought defiantly. And if he caught an ague and died, maybe then the earl would finally realize that he had two sons, not one.

Either that or Lionel would just become even more precious to him.

The rain came then, in earnest.

Garrick turned, beginning to shiver from the cold, reaching for the keep's wall. He climbed over it, jammed his hands in the pockets of his hunting coat, and started trudging back to the manor. By the time he left the keep, he had started to run. The sky overhead had turned black, and the rain was incessant, a torrential downpour. Lightning blazed in the sky, somewhere over the ocean.

By the time he slammed the front door of the manor closed behind him, he was soaking wet and freezing cold and regretting having lingered outside. His father stood in front of the fire raging in the huge hearth, a drink in his hand, while his mother was seated in one of the upholstered, heavily carved thronelike chairs beside him. The earl flinched at the sound of the heavy door closing; his mother stood and turned.

"Garrick!" she exclaimed, rushing forward. Then she paused and said to a passing housemaid, "Bessie, go tell Larkin to prepare a hot bath immediately. And bring blankets at once!"

The earl had turned slowly and was staring. But the

countess cried, "Garrick, what have you done? Where have you been? You will catch your death!"

Garrick now hung back, reluctant to come forward. "I went to the keep," he said thickly, shooting an uncertain glance at his father.

"A brilliant idea," the earl said with open sarcasm. "Where is Lionel?"

Garrick, about to respond to his father's cutting remark, froze. "He left just before I did. Isn't he here?"

There was a moment of silence as both the earl's and the countess's expressions changed, registering some alarm. "He did not come in," the countess said. "Oh, he will catch cold, too!"

"It is only raining," the earl said bitingly. "I am sure that Lionel will be back at any moment."

The countess flushed and nodded. The housemaid had appeared with blankets, and she took one and wrapped it around Garrick. "Well, let's get you upstairs and abed. And Richard, let me know the instant that Lionel returns."

On the stairs, Garrick hesitated, a feeling of unease taking root within him. "Mother, he should have been back ten minutes ago. Something is wrong."

"Nothing is wrong," Eleanor said, her smile failing her.

But Garrick held on to the banister, unmoving, staring into the hall, past his father, at the solidly closed front door. Something was wrong, terribly so. He could feel it now.

"Come," his mother said, tugging on his hand.

Reluctantly Garrick obeyed, flashing one last glance behind him, dismayed and afraid for his brother.

They came with torches and lanterns, with horses and riders, with dogs. The road to the ruins was ablaze with light as the dozen men invaded the surrounding perimeter of the keep in the midst of the now steady downpour and the pitch-black night.

The earl whirled on his second-born. "Where?" he demanded. "Where did you last see him?"

Lionel had not returned. An hour had ticked by, but he had not appeared back at the manor. Several staff members had seen him leave in search of Garrick, just before the storm; no one had seen hide nor hair of him since then.

The last person to have seen him was Garrick.

He was ready to burst into tears, but trying desperately not to. Where was Lionel? Had he tripped in the mud and been knocked unconscious? Was he all right? What if he were dead! Garrick was terrified for his brother—and terrified of his father, who seemed to be blaming him for Lionel's sudden disappearance.

Garrick slid off his horse and ran past his father to the spot where he and Lionel had stood together just outside the keep on the cliff ledge.

"I was standing over there, on that ledge," Garrick managed, choked with fear and tears and anguish. Please, he was praying. Please let him be all right. "Lionel was, too. Then he climbed back over the wall. I didn't watch him leave."

His father rode over, looked down at the sea, and gave him a look probably intended to kill a hundred grown men—or reduce them to sniveling cowards. The earl wheeled his mount and rode over to the assembled men. "Fan out. We will cover every inch of ground between here and the manor. He can't be gone. We will find him shortly. He cannot have vanished into thin air."

But he had.

Because Lionel De Vere, the viscount of Caedmon Crag, heir to the earldom of Stanhope, was never seen again.

PART ONE

The Return

CHAPTER ONE

ASHBURNHAM, WEST SUSSEX, 1760

She stood outside in the shadows cast by the moon-embraced clouds, reluctant to go into the house. It was a pleasantly cool June night. A whisper-soft breeze caressed her bare arms and caused tendrils of silvery blond hair to escape the many braids coiled around her head and tickle her neck and cheeks. The gentle sounds of a harpsichord drifted outside from the terrace doors, left ajar, so that guests could wander the sweeping lawns with its rioting gardens. The house itself had been built just ten years ago by the current earl and was a solid stone structure with imposing Ionic columns, numerous balconies, and temple pediments front and back. Stone stairs led from the terrace where she stood to the unfashionably abundant gardens and the deer park. The melodious strains of the harpsichord suddenly, abruptly, shifted as the musician made a jarring error, and there was a moment of absolute silence.

In that moment, Olivia felt so much. Sensations she did not wish to feel. Fear, anguish, and desperation.

She closed her eyes as the musician played again, perfectly now, but without the flamboyance of one truly born to perform. All that day, awaiting the arrival of their guests, she had felt dread. As if, with the arrival of her husband and guests, some terrible event would come. Now her temples throbbed. Thus far, nothing had gone awry; there had been no disaster. Surely this time she was wrong, and her dread had been the result of her husband's return, nothing more.

How Olivia hated her cursed *gift*.

How she wished she had been born normal, like everyone else.

She knew she had to rejoin Arlen's guests. Her pulse pounding, she debated several excuses that would allow her to go upstairs, and not merely to retire. Were the candles still burning in Hannah's room? Just the day before yesterday, that foolish Irish maid had let them burn out and then had tried to argue with Olivia about the merits of leaving the child's room lit at night. Had Hannah's governess, Miss Childs, not been visiting her parents, the fiasco would not have occurred. Surely the candles remained lit tonight. Surely by now Hannah was soundly asleep and dreaming of happy things, like spotted ponies and sugar plums and the puppet show they had attended at the county fair last week.

Surely her eight-year-old daughter was not feeling what Olivia was feeling. Would she not have said something? Olivia immediately shut off that thought, pulling herself together, glad Arlen would return to London in a few days, glad that she and her daughter would once more be left to their own devices in the country—with their own secrets still safely held. Clad in a beautiful pastel floral and striped silk dress, her small waist accentuated by the huge bell skirt, one supported by wide panniers, diamonds and pearls glinting from her ears and throat, reluctantly given by her husband years ago, Olivia moved swiftly across the flagstone terrace, past a stone water fountain, and into the paneled-and-gilded salon where her husband's guests were gathered.

The harpsichordist continued to play, her small back to Olivia, her narrow shoulders set rigidly, telling Olivia that she hated playing for the assembly. As Olivia glided into the room, her sister-in-law, renowned as one of England's great beauties, lifted a slashing black eyebrow at her. Elizabeth's small, perfect nose was tilted just slightly in the air. Her look was clear. She knew Olivia was not at ease in this company—or any company—and she was filled with disdain.

When Elizabeth Wentworth was at Ashburnham, Olivia's duties as hostess were usurped. Olivia did not care about that, just the manner in which it was done.

As Elizabeth's cool blue eyes locked with Olivia's pale gray ones, Olivia wondered, as she had repeatedly for the past nine years, what had she done to make Arlen's sister dislike her so? Olivia had once attempted to be friendly, but now she avoided her like the plague, a task easily enough done, because Elizabeth hated the country as much as Olivia hated town.

The harpsichordist, Susan Layton, had finished the song. Olivia sat down next to her husband, taking a small, gold-caned chair. The company broke into a round of applause. Susan faced them, a pale, blond girl of no more than seventeen, a smile pasted on her face. Olivia applauded loudly. "Bravo," she called, so the shy young lady could hear. Silently she thought, How courageous you are.

Susan sent her a grateful glance, rising, giving the company a small curtsy. Her cheeks were red.

"Doesn't she play well?" Sir John Layton, a bejowled man with a huge frame that even his velvet coat could not contain, beamed at his daughter. His powdered wig was askew, his puffy cheeks flushed. He was a brewer, knighted a dozen years ago for some service to the Crown. He had made such a fortune that he could have bought the earldom of Ashburn several times over—or so Arlen had said.

Olivia liked him very much, in spite of his antecedents and the fact that his periwig was always slipping. He had quite the proverbial heart of gold. Arlen, she knew, merely pretended to be his friend. She had yet to glean what purpose Layton served the man she had married.

"Extremely well," Elizabeth said smoothly with a look of boredom that belied her words.

Susan's mother, Lady Layton, was a tiny, attractive, birdlike woman, and she smiled her thanks quite nervously—she had yet to say a thing since arriving at the estate. Henry Wentworth, the marquis of Houghton, sat beside her. He

was half as tall as Sir John and twice as wide, and was
soundly asleep. His stocking-clad ankles were hugely swollen with gout. His feet overwhelmed his buckled shoes.
Elizabeth snapped her japanned fan loudly, and the marquis
awoke with a start. "Do you not wish to hear me play, my
lord?" she said as she stood up.

Arlen suddenly gripped Olivia's wrist. "Where have you
been?" he whispered, his dark eyes boring, his face close
to hers.

He was hurting her, but Olivia did not try to pull her
hand away. "I needed air."

He kept his voice low as the company around them continued to discuss Susan Layton's abilities as a harpsichordist and Elizabeth took her turn, sitting gracefully, and with
supreme confidence, in front of the instrument.

"You always need air when I am entertaining," he said,
his eyes flashing. "I protest, madam, for I am only in the
country two months a year!"

Olivia forced herself to smile at her husband. Two
months, she supposed silently, was far better than three.
"My headaches are far worse than ever, my lord," she said
demurely.

The earl of Ashburn eyed her. He was a slender, dark-
haired fellow with features as perfect as his sister's, who
had just taken up the current fashion of wearing his own
hair, rolled, powdered and tied back, sans peruke. Olivia
knew that the ladies in London oohed and aahed over her
husband. She also knew that he kept an actress from Vauxhall as his mistress. She had even heard that his mistress
was with child. Not that she, Olivia, cared. She wished he
would never come to the country. She prayed his mistress
would give him a son. She dreamed of being left alone in
the country, just her and Hannah and their wonderful staff.

Arlen Grey, the earl of Ashburn, stared coldly. "And
what dreams do you now have? What delusions? What
nightmares?"

Olivia swallowed. "None, my lord," she lied. "That—
malady—is past."

He eyed her with utter disgust, and perhaps with real

loathing. It had not always been that way. Olivia had been married at the age of sixteen, and looking back upon the memory, one that was not happy, she could hardly believe she had ever been so naive, innocent, or trusting. How quickly all that had changed. And any fond feelings Arlen might have had for her had vanished the moment he had realized just how different she was—before their daughter was born. Now Olivia knew that he knew she'd lied.

Finally Arlen adjusted his lace cuffs, which frothed out from under his turquoise coat sleeves. His sapphire signet ring caught the light from the crystal chandeliers overhead. "I ask very little of you, madam," he said. "See to it that your dreams remain just that."

Olivia nodded, clasping her hands tightly together, wanting to escape upstairs now more than ever, yet knowing she could not. Was Hannah all right? And what would Arlen do if he knew about her current "dream"? For he referred to her oddly accurate intuition and premonitions as dreams. Olivia found herself watching Susan, who spoke quietly with her mother. She was obviously unhappy. Miserably so.

The desperation, the fear, was coming from her. Olivia was certain of it. She had been certain of it from the moment they had been introduced earlier that day. How she wished to help her. But what could be so terribly wrong?

Susan suddenly looked up at Olivia, as if feeling her eyes upon her. Olivia gave her an encouraging smile. She knew she must befriend the young girl in order to prevent a catastrophe. She did not know how she knew it. But she did. It was always that way. The unwanted knowledge—truths that were never complete.

Arlen broke into her thoughts. "Elizabeth is about to play," he said, and he settled back in his seat. "My sister is one of the finest musicians I know, and her voice is unsurpassable," he said proudly to everyone present.

"Hear, hear," the marquis agreed. "My wife is, in general, quite unsurpassable."

Elizabeth accepted this praise as her due, not even a spot

of pink upon her alabaster cheeks as she gracefully inclined her head.

"Yes, we have heard all about Lady Houghton's talents," Sir John said expansively. "Please, my lady, do play for us." His pretty words were spoiled by a sudden belch.

Olivia smiled at him.

And Elizabeth smiled benignly at the crowd, then began to play. In fact, she was more than adept at the harpsichord. Note after note rippled sweetly across the room. "Ah, yes, lovely," Sir John said with a sigh. But the way he was regarding Elizabeth, Olivia was quite certain he referred not to the music, but to the musician herself. The marquis, she noted, was drifting off once again.

Then Olivia heard it. The child's scream. She jumped out of her delicate Hepplewhite chair.

Elizabeth's back was to her and she continued to play. But the entire company stared at Olivia as if she had lost her mind. And Olivia realized that she had been the only one to hear Hannah scream—that the scream was only in her mind.

She knew that the candles had burned out.

Fury—and the need to rush to her daughter—engulfed her.

"Is something amiss, Lady Ashburn?" Sir John asked with concern, also rising to his feet.

"Nothing is amiss," Arlen said unpleasantly, standing. He gripped Olivia's wrist. "Sit down." His tone was filled with warning.

Olivia did not obey. "Arlen. My lord. I must go upstairs."

"I told you to sit down."

Elizabeth stopped playing and turned. "Why, whatever is wrong, sister dear?"

"You will sit down," Arlen said flatly.

"The candles are out," Olivia returned. Then she stiffened, seeing the anger in his eyes—thinking he would strike her—forgetting they were not alone. For Arlen never spoke of his daughter publicly; in fact, few peers even knew of Hannah's existence.

"Is that what this is about?" Elizabeth stepped forward, her lavender skirts rustling. She actually came between them in spite of her wide skirts and laid a graceful hand on Arlen's arm. "Do you still coddle her?" She spoke only to Olivia, her tone low. "She still insists on sleeping with candles, for goodness' sake?" She was amused. "You must not allow a child to dictate terms, Olivia dear. How you spoil Hannah."

Arlen gave Elizabeth a warning look. "Continue playing, Elizabeth."

Elizabeth shrugged, but before she could turn, Olivia spoke. She rarely argued with Elizabeth, but this was very different. "And how many children do you have, Elizabeth?" She fought to control her anger.

Elizabeth's eyes widened. Her blue eyes darkened. "Well, when I consider the circumstances of your own child, I should think it is fortunate that I have none."

Olivia understood her meaning exactly and almost clawed the other woman's face. Hatred, an emotion foreign to her, swept her in a heated rush. "If Hannah is spoiled, it is no less than she deserves," she said, low and strained.

"Is there a child in the house?" Sir John queried. "I'm sorry, I could not help overhearing. A blessed thing, a child is. Good God, is it a secret that you and Lady Ashburn have a child, Arlen?"

Arlen looked at Sir John, remaining silent.

Olivia wet her lips, knowing that she would be the one to pay for this, when it was not her fault—or was it? "It is hardly a secret," she finally said uneasily.

"The child is a girl, then," Sir John asked, surprised.

"Yes." Arlen finally spoke.

Olivia glanced at her husband and then at Elizabeth, who hid a smile, turning her face away, fluttering her fan. "Our daughter has recently had her eighth birthday," she said.

"Eight years of age!" Sir John was bemused. "I hadn't a clue. How odd. But then, had you a son, I'm sure we would all have known." His amiable manner was gone. His pale eyes were speculative. The man had not made a fortune by being an idiot.

"It is not a secret, Sir John. But Hannah is hardly an interesting topic for discussion." Arlen was perspiring and flushed. He faced Olivia. "Go, then." But his angry eyes told her that this was hardly over—that he would punish her in some form or other in the morning for everything that had thus far transpired that night.

Olivia curtsied to the company, distressed. Arlen was ashamed of Hannah, and Olivia had never been able to get over it or to forgive him for it. She caught Elizabeth's eye. Her sister-in-law seemed pleased.

Temples pounding now, Olivia left the salon, rushing up the stairs, tripping in her haste. The nursery was on the third story—and Olivia also slept on that floor when Arlen was not home. She heard Hannah crying, soft little whimpers, as she approached the open doorway. The room was now blazingly alight with candles.

The Irish maid sat with the child in the four-poster bed, her freckles standing out on her starkly white skin. She leapt to her feet as Olivia raced inside the child's room. "Mum, I beg your pardon," Megan cried.

"Mama," Hannah also cried, simultaneously, her arms outstretched. Her eyes were wide, unseeing, the exact same shade of silvery gray as Olivia's. For Hannah was blind. She had been blind since birth.

Olivia rushed to her daughter, pulling her into her arms, cradling her against her chest. Livid, she faced the young maid, who was now standing nervously by the doorway.

"You allowed the candles to burn out," Olivia cried, thinking, Thank God Miss Childs will be back in another two days.

"A blind girl don't need candles," the girl began.

"Just leave us," Olivia said, holding her daughter tightly. She would not explain, for it was almost incomprehensible. Hannah was blind, but she was terrified of the dark, insisting upon candles when she slept. "It's over now, darling."

Hannah held on to her hard, no longer whimpering. "I'm sorry, Mama, I didn't mean to cause you trouble," she whispered. "I'm sorry I'm such a coward."

"You are not a coward! You are incredibly brave," Olivia whispered, aghast, smoothing her daughter's pitch-black hair. It was tied into a single, waist-length braid. "I know of no other child as brave, my darling." She squeezed her eyes shut. Tears burned behind her lids. Arlen's angry eyes filled her mind. She was a peaceful woman, but she almost hated him.

"Then why am I so afraid when I go to sleep?" Hannah asked, a plea in her tone.

"Many people sleep with a candle lit," Olivia said gently, thinking, But if you are afraid of the dark at night, doesn't that mean you are also afraid of the darkness you live with every single second of every single day? Inside her heart, she wept. She lived with her tears the way Hannah lived with her affliction of blindness. Olivia held her daughter close and rocked her.

"Mama, don't be sad," Hannah said suddenly. She pulled back, and had she been able to see, it would have been as if she wanted to meet her mother's gaze. But Olivia looked into her beautiful, silvery, sightless eyes without her daughter being able to share the regard. Still, they shared other things, far deeper than a glance.

"I am only a little sad," Olivia whispered, forcing a smile.

It was a moment before Hannah answered. "Father is furious."

"It's all right, and you have not gotten me into trouble, dear, not at all. I can manage the earl." Olivia inhaled, trembling. She and her daughter shared far more than a deep sensitivity to one another's feelings and thoughts. Hannah was cursed with the gift, too. Only she hardly understood it at the age of eight. "Your father will be leaving in two days. There is nothing to worry about. And when he is gone we shall picnic again at the lake, every day, and read books together, and pick berries and flowers. When he is gone, we shall once again be free."

Hannah was silent, her expression doubtful.

"What is it?"

"What if he finds out?"

Olivia tensed. "He must not find out, Hannah, not ever, and he will not, not as long as you are very careful. Promise me." Her tone caught. "Promise me you will be very, very careful."

Hannah nodded, lying back against the pillows. "I promise."

Olivia did not relax. She did not know what Arlen would do if he ever found out that his daughter was as different as his wife, that she, too, had been cursed with the gift of sight.

Weeping. Soft and filled with anguish.

Olivia jerked awake. Was she dreaming? No, she could still hear someone, a woman, crying. She sat up slowly. Her bedroom was cast in darkness, for she had not left a single taper burning. She knew it was impossible to hear crying from any of the guest rooms, all of which were at the far end of the corridor. Was the weeping in her mind? Or had she been dreaming?

But she could still, just barely, hear it. Olivia shoved the covers aside, filled with unease. There was desperation in the insistent, barely audible sound.

It was Susan. Olivia had not a doubt.

She lit a taper and slipped on her light lawn wrapper. The feeling she'd had all day, dread filled, that something terrible was going to happen, swept her again, stronger than before. She hesitated. And thought, She will die.

Olivia froze, aghast with the thought, now etched upon her mind. It was not a thought she wanted. But she never wanted the thoughts God so often gave her! Who will die? Surely not that young girl, Susan Layton?

Olivia padded barefoot to the door and opened it. Her pulse was pounding. Across the hall, her husband's paneled oak door was solidly closed. She knew he had already retired, and for that she was thankful, while now she could only hope that he was soundly asleep.

She strained to hear. The weeping continued, but it did not seem to come from any particular direction, and certainly not from the opposite, far end of the corridor where the Laytons had their rooms.

What she was hearing, she knew, was in her mind, even though it sounded real.

Olivia felt it again, the absolute certainty that death was lurking not far away. Panic tightened her limbs. Why hadn't Hannah said something? This was so strong, and her daughter was far more gifted—or cursed—than she herself was. Why hadn't Hannah mentioned these feelings?

Olivia again glanced at Arlen's closed door. If he caught her up and about, she would be in an even more difficult position on the morrow than she already was. But she had to find Susan. Olivia turned toward the end of the corridor, the weeping stronger now, and with it, the sheer, stunning desperation.

She will die.

Olivia inhaled, heard soft footsteps, whirled. Hannah raced blindly toward her, tears streaming down her cheeks. But she did not make a sound.

Olivia's first thought was that the candles had somehow gone out. Her concern for Susan vanished. She rushed forward, embracing her daughter, who clung. A moment later Olivia propelled them both into her bedchamber, closing the door behind them.

"Mama, we have to help her," Hannah cried in a whisper, gripping Olivia's hands. "She is going to die if we don't stop her." Hannah tried to pull Olivia back to the door. "I saw it. Mama, please!"

"Susan?"

Hannah nodded, her silvery eyes huge in her pale face. "The lake. She has gone to the lake."

And Olivia saw it all then, the frail, female body drifting in the shallows, the pale white muslin dress billowing out about her—and the body was facedown.

"Stay here," Olivia ordered, adrenaline surging.

"No!" Hannah cried. "Don't leave me!"

Olivia took one look at her daughter, realizing that the weeping had ceased. Did that mean Susan was already dead? There was no time, dear God. She took her daughter's hand and together they raced from the room, down the two flights of stairs, and through the house. The lake was almost a quarter of a mile from the house. How could they make it in time to avert this tragedy?

Yet there was nothing but silence now, surrounding them, cold, cold silence.

"Run," Olivia cried.

They ran. The path, often traveled, was smooth enough, especially as it had not rained in some time, but periodically stones and pebbles dug into their bare feet. Fortunately the sky was lit with stars and three-quarters of a moon, illuminating the way. They topped a rise, panting and out of breath. Below, Olivia saw the lake, blacker than the sky, glistening silently—and she saw a white shape.

A white figure, walking into the water, step by agonizing step.

"No!" Olivia screamed. She released Hannah's hand and, lifting her nightclothes to her knees, ran as hard as she had ever run in her life. Her ankle twisted and pain shot up her leg, but she did not stop. The very air burned in her lungs, which heaved and begged for more. Ahead of her, the lake lapped the sandy shore. Susan was chest deep in the shining black water. And then she disappeared.

Olivia screamed, barreling into the water after her. Her nightclothes, coupled with the weight of the water, made it seem as if she were moving in slow motion, as if in a dream. Olivia pushed on through. The water reached up to her chin, and she ducked under where Susan had disappeared. Olivia could not swim and hoped the water didn't get any deeper.

The water was pitch black. But immediately she touched the fabric of Susan's dress. Olivia moved forward, bumped into the solid mass of Susan's flesh, and put her arm around her. She pulled her furiously to the surface, dragging her limp burden all the way.

Olivia gulped in air desperately. Before she had regained her breath, she turned to look at Susan, whose head lolled on her shoulder. Her eyes were closed, her cheeks pale.

Then her lashes fluttered and her mouth opened in a gasp as she too sucked in the precious, life-giving oxygen.

Olivia continued to hold her as her feet touched solid ground. They stood chest deep now, with Susan coughing and choking beside her. Olivia pounded her on the back until the choking had subsided.

Susan met her gaze weakly, then her face changed, becoming twisted with emotion. "Let me go!" she screamed, struggling.

Olivia slapped her, hard, across the face.

Susan gasped and burst into tears, collapsing against Olivia. Olivia held her and stroked her, murmuring soothing sounds. She raised her eyes to search for Hannah, who stood ankle deep in the water, facing them, listening intently.

"We are all right," Olivia called.

Hannah nodded. "I know. I heard," she called back.

Olivia put her arm around Susan's waist as all the strength and energy she had suddenly drained away from her, leaving her feeling exhausted as never before, then led her to the shore. Once there, they collapsed on the sandy ground. Hannah rushed to them and hugged her mother, hard.

Susan wept.

Olivia kissed Hannah's cheek and turned. She gripped Susan by the shoulders, shaking her. "It is not so bad. What you tried to do was terrible! Miss Layton, I beg you, please, rethink yourself!"

Susan shook her head. "You should have let me die. I wanted to die. Oh, God, death is far better than my fate."

Olivia grimaced, pushing strands of thick wet hair out of Susan's eyes. "Dear, dear child, you have a long and happy life ahead of you, I am sure of it." But she wasn't. She was only consoling the young woman; she had not a clue if she spoke the truth or not.

"No. I have a horrid life ahead of me—and death would be better!" Susan burst into tears again. Her shoulders shook as she sobbed.

"She is afraid," Hannah whispered to Olivia, her head cocked toward Susan.

Olivia nodded, for the fear was as tangible as the anguish and, now, the resignation. "What is so terrible that you tried to take your own life?" Olivia asked kindly.

At first, Susan was so upset that she could only shake her head. Her tears still fell. Finally she looked up. "I have been betrothed." Her tone was bitter. "To a man no one wants, no one else will have, not in all of England. My father has sold me off, so that one day his grandchild will be an earl." She swiped at her eye with a small, balled-up fist.

"And that is a fate worse than death?" Olivia asked gently.

"It is if your betrothed is Garrick De Vere, the viscount of Caedmon Crag." Her eyes filled with anguish again. "And that is why I wished to die, my lady."

Olivia stared. And the dark, anguished image of a man, one whom she had never met before, filled her mind. It was so clear that it was startling—she could see his chiseled features, his straight nose and high cheekbones, the strong jaw, even the color of his golden eyes. Had she met this man before? she wondered, surprised by the shock of recognition she had just felt. Then she felt so much more— his pain, his sorrow, his grief. The intensity of his emotions was far more than shocking; it was disturbing. "Is that not Stanhope's son?" she asked slowly, with trepidation, quite certain now that they were not acquainted.

"So you have heard of him?" Susan said, lifting her head.

"What I have heard," Olivia said slowly, "is sheer rumor, and not much of it. I thought he had been banished to one of the sugar islands."

"He was exiled to Barbados ten years ago, but he is in London even as we speak." Susan smiled without mirth. "He has returned to marry me."

Olivia wet her lips, oddly ill. "Is that not a cause for celebration, my dear?" she asked.

"I am to marry a man who murdered his own brother. That is hardly cause to celebrate!" Susan's gaze was accusing.

Olivia could not find a suitable reply.

CHAPTER TWO

The moon was shining more brightly than before. Olivia held Hannah's hand as they trudged back to the house, Susan beside her. In spite of the fact that Susan had been saved from taking her own life, the young woman was despondent. She hung her head and every now and then wiped a stray tear from her cheeks.

But Olivia had far more to worry about now. The house loomed into view, a solid, imposing square structure. She had not given a single thought to leaving it, but now she was anxious about returning without being discovered. What would Arlen say if he saw the three of them just now, with both Olivia and Hannah in their nightclothes, soaking wet and barefoot? He would demand an explanation. Olivia's grip tightened upon Hannah's palm.

They paused before the steps leading to the terrace. "Susan, you go in ahead of us. Try not to wake anyone." Olivia managed a smile, and she hugged the girl. "I do not think we should share the circumstances of this night with your parents—or anyone else." She held her gaze meaningfully.

Susan shrugged. "If my reputation is blackened, then I shan't be marrying well, will I?"

"He is not bad." The words had come unthinkingly. They had surprised even Olivia.

"How do you know?" Susan asked. "I'm sorry. Clearly you are one of the kindest ladies on this earth. I imagine you defend everyone. Even a murderer.'' She rubbed her temples. "I won't make a sound. And . . .'' She hesitated. "Maybe we can take breakfast together in the morning? We are leaving tomorrow for London.'' Her mouth pursed, and again she seemed close to tears. "I must meet my fiancé.''

"I would love to have breakfast with you,'' Olivia said. "Try to keep your spirits up, my dear.'' She watched Susan walk away, her heavy, wet skirts slowing her down, until finally she disappeared into the house.

Hannah clung to her hand. "Maybe Father is awake,'' she said uneasily.

"Don't be silly,'' Olivia replied with forced cheerfulness. But she was looking upward at the higher floors. Had she just seen a flickering light? She prayed they would not be discovered tonight. What excuse could she give? Her pulse beat hard. How she wished Arlen would go back to town.

"Come,'' Olivia whispered, taking hold of Hannah's hand. They hurried up the stone steps, across the terrace, and through the doors, which Susan had left open for them. The salon was cast in shadows, and it was almost impossible to see, so Olivia let Hannah lead the way. She did so effortlessly, around the sofa, past two chairs, around a small side table. They stepped into the corridor.

Arlen raised his taper. Candlelight flickered across his grim visage.

Olivia froze.

He stared, taking in every inch of Olivia's disheveled, wet appearance and then raking his eyes over his daughter. "What is going on here?'' he demanded. His gaze returned to Olivia but slid downward from her face.

Hannah shrank against Olivia. Olivia wrapped a protective arm around her. The lie came easily. "Hannah was walking in her sleep. I went into her room to check on her and found her gone. She fell into the water fountain, Arlen. I am lucky she did not drown!'' Hannah could not swim.

Arlen continued to stare at her. Olivia's unease and fear grew. Suddenly she realized that her wet cotton nightclothes were sticking to every inch of her flesh. Olivia inhaled, realizing then how transparent her soaking garments had become. Her fear changed. Arlen had not touched her in years, but he was staring at her breasts.

He lifted his eyes and their gazes locked. "So you went in after her," he said flatly.

Olivia felt herself shaking. She wanted to cover herself up. She reminded herself that Arlen had no carnal interest in her; he never had, not after Hannah had been born. But in that moment she recalled all of his groping in the year before Hannah's birth, and her stomach turned with sickening force.

"You have matured, Olivia," he said suddenly. "You are no longer skin and bones."

"I would like to go upstairs and dress, if we are to continue this conversation," she said.

"No." He looked down at his daughter. Father and child resembled one another almost exactly. Hannah was strikingly beautiful, just as her father was so utterly handsome. But for Olivia, Arlen's good looks were spoiled by the heart that beat inside his body. "And how long has she been afflicted with this particular *malady?*" he asked coolly.

Warning bells screamed inside Olivia's brain. She held Hannah more tightly. "It is not a malady. Just a child walking in her sleep." Her tone was high and tense.

His gaze was piercing. "Really? But she is your daughter, Olivia." And this time, very insolently, he glanced at her breasts. Olivia already knew her nipples were erect and prominently displayed by her wet nightgown.

"She is also your daughter, Arlen, or have you forgotten that?" she returned curtly.

He slapped her. Not terribly hard, but across the face, and it hurt. "Do not speak to me in such a manner. Do you understand?"

Olivia held her cheek, aware of Hannah trembling against her side, and she nodded. She controlled her anger. She mustn't let Arlen see her temper. It wasn't the first time he had struck her for her sharp, unruly tongue, and she knew it would not be the last. But she was astute enough to assume that if she responded yet again, he would beat her severely. No verbal repartee was worth that. Especially as she could not change the man that he was.

"Hannah, come here," Arlen said.

Olivia tensed, as did her daughter.

"I said come here," Arlen ordered harshly.

Her pulse beat so fast now, so shallowly, that it was hard to breathe. "Arlen," Olivia began, frightened, not knowing what he would do, not knowing what to expect.

Arlen took Hannah's shoulder and pulled her away from Olivia. Tears filled Hannah's eyes. He towered over his daughter, holding the taper aloft. "How often do you walk in your sleep?" he demanded.

Hannah was paler than her natural alabaster coloring. She swallowed. "Just this once," she whispered.

"If you lie to me, you will be whipped," Arlen said.

More tears filled Hannah's eyes. "I'm not lying."

"Arlen," Olivia tried, frantically. She knew he would whip the child if he decided she lied. And then Olivia would kill him.

He ignored Olivia and nodded. "Good." He continued to stare at her, into her sightless gray eyes. "Tomorrow I will have a physician examine you. I will get to the bottom of this."

Olivia wet her lips. "Arlen, Hannah has no malady."

His head whipped toward her. "And should I trust you?" he almost shouted. "You, who came to this marriage knowing of your cursed oddness? Purposefully deceiving me and my family? Knowing that if you revealed yourself, no one would have you? Not in all of society?" His voice had become louder. He would wake the servants, perhaps even his guests.

Olivia knew when to retreat. "I was sorry then, I am as sorry now. I never meant to deceive you." She kept her gaze turned down. The lie was monumental—her parents had indeed intended to deceive the groom and his family, and they had succeeded. Olivia had participated in the deception, incapable of disobeying her father, the earl of Oldham. Yet as sheltered as she was, she had known that it

was wrong to be dishonest—had even sensed that the repercussions would be enormous. But neither her father nor
her mother had wanted to discuss the marriage. She had
not been given either the choice of a groom or the choice
of honesty. They had wanted only to marry her off before
the truth was revealed.

She was immune by now to the hurtful recollection; she
had not seen either of her parents since her wedding day.
They had not even come to see Hannah after her birth. Nor
had they sent a note. "I did not understand the oddness
myself." Her tone sounded harsh even to herself. But dissembling, even as an act of self-preservation, was not easy
for her.

"Well, it is too late, now, isn't it?" Arlen was sarcastic
and cutting. "And we are both paying for your curse." His
glance skewered Hannah.

Olivia held her tongue, furious. Hannah was a gift, not
a curse. How she hated her husband. She could not help
wishing, just for a moment, that he would die before her
time and set her and her daughter free.

Arlen took a step closer to her. "The next time we have
guests, she sleeps at the gamekeeper's lodge."

Olivia's eyes widened.

Arlen faced Hannah. "Go up to bed."

Hannah hesitated, her head cocked toward Olivia.

Olivia stepped forward. "I will see her upstairs. That is,"
she added quickly, "if you do not mind."

Arlen eyed her with obvious distaste. "I do mind."

Olivia stiffened.

Arlen pushed Hannah in the direction of the stairs. Hannah's face was set and rigid as she started up them.

"Good night, darling," Olivia called, sick at heart.
"Change into something dry."

"Yes, Mama, good night," Hannah said thickly.

Olivia's heart broke. Hannah would curl up in bed and
cry herself to sleep. She had to go to her. Then she tore
her gaze from her daughter's back to find Arlen watching
her.

His smile was cold. "Do you know," he said, "that I

have drunk so much wine that I am considering availing myself of your body?''

The breath got stuck in Olivia's throat. She could not move.

"You are very tempting tonight, Olivia," he said.

Olivia folded her arms over her breasts. "You do not want another child," she reminded him with real fear.

"No. I do not want another deformed child like Hannah. But there are ways to avoid that, as you must know."

Olivia hesitated. "Please."

His eyes widened. "You beg me?" Suddenly he laughed. "I had never thought to see the day. Don't worry. I am not that insane." His glance was ugly and he turned abruptly and followed in Hannah's wake.

When he was gone, Olivia's knees gave way, and she sank onto the bottom step. She laid her head on her arms, which were folded around her knees, and cried. For all that wasn't, and all that should be.

STANHOPE SQUARE, LONDON

It had been almost eleven years since he had wandered the halls of Stanhope-on-the-Square. As he stood on the threshold of the breakfast room, a paneled room painted yellow with gilded wainscoting and a frescoed ceiling, memories flooded him. His mother sipping coffee in her morning gown, his father with his face buried in a daily newspaper, he and Lionel exchanging jabs beneath the table, jokes beneath their breath, and begging to be excused.

Tension riddled his body.

"My lord? There is a breakfast buffet," a servant said from behind him, pulling him out of his reverie.

"Just coffee, thank you," Garrick said, closing his eyes. The red setter, which stood by his side, shoved its cool nose into his palm. God, for one moment, one incredibly intense moment, he had been a boy again, in this very house. And his brother had been alive.

Lionel had never been found. He had never been seen or heard of since that stormy afternoon when he had suddenly disappeared, as if vanishing into the air itself.

Garrick shoved aside his thoughts, angry with them, angry with himself—it was his fault, after all, that Lionel was dead—and he strode into the room, the hound at his heels. He poured himself a cup of coffee that immediately proved to be as watered down and as weak as it looked. Scowling, he set the delicate porcelain cup and saucer aside. Coming back had been a mistake.

But the earl had written him for the fourth time in five years, on this occasion informing of his chronic illness, a weakness of the limbs and heart. His physicians expected him to live only another year or two at most. This time, the earl had begged him to return to England. They had matters, he said, grave matters, to discuss. Garrick had not answered any of his previous letters, as they had hardly been polite or contained requests. And he had set sail five months ago from the island that had been his home for the past ten years.

Stanhope was expected in town at any moment. Garrick had arrived two days ago, and a messenger had been promptly dispatched to Surrey to inform him of his son's arrival.

"Come," Garrick said.

He strode out of the breakfast room and down the hall. Opening a door, he let the red setter out into the gardens, then followed at a more leisurely pace. The air was cool, clean, and fresh, and Garrick sniffed it with appreciation. He was used to blazing heat. His dog looked at him questioningly, not straying as of yet. Garrick smiled and jerked his head. "Go."

With one happy bark, the setter bounded off. Garrick settled on the edge of a low brick wall, surrounded by roses—his mother's touch, he knew. The garden had changed, he saw. Once it had been full of flowers, but now it was filled with clipped hedges and tall, swaying trees. A pond had been added to the grounds as well, with a small bridge. Clearly the fashion for landscaping had changed.

"Garrick!"

It was his mother, and he stood, turning. He had not seen her either in over ten years, and his pulse increased. The countess flew across the short terrace and into his arms.

"Oh, my dear," she said, pulling back. "Why did you stay away so long?"

She had aged, but well; she was still a strikingly beautiful woman. "Hello, Mother. It is so good to see you." Garrick meant it. He wished he could say more. He had never stopped loving her, and he knew that his long, self-imposed exile had hurt her. That had not been his intention.

Her glance really swept over him now. "You have become such a striking man, Garrick. You are so tall and so dark. But darling, you must powder your hair—it is the fashion for young men, you know, and you must get to the tailor."

He did smile. "We have no use for powder on the island, madam, but why the tailor? Am I so horribly out of date?"

"Well, in truth, no one wears such an overly long coat, and color is quite the rage," Eleanor De Vere said very seriously. "But do not fear. I will arrange for Mr. Loggins to attend you this afternoon."

She was eyeing his breeches and boots. Garrick supposed he should have dressed properly in stockings and shoes.

"I do think you could wear crimson, my dear, perhaps for a waistcoat? And gold would do very well for a new frock coat, don't you agree?" Suddenly she touched his cheek. "I am so happy you are home," she whispered, her eyes flooding with tears.

Garrick only half heard her. The earl stood by the terrace doors. He had not stepped outside, and he stared at Garrick with mesmerizing yet hard blue eyes—a gaze Garrick had never forgotten.

Emotion overwhelmed Garrick. He did not want to identify any of the turbulent feelings roiling within him, but it was impossible not to recall the utterly accusing look upon his father's face when Garrick had turned away from the ledge by the keep fourteen years ago and said, "I was standing here when I saw him last."

He recalled the rumors, every single one, that had begun within weeks of Lionel's disappearance.

If Lionel De Vere is not found, if he is dead, then he *becomes the Stanhope heir,* they had all whispered.

But he had not killed his brother. And he had never wanted to be the Stanhope heir. Garrick suddenly closed his eyes. But hadn't he, for one awful instant, on the day Lionel had disappeared, wished that he were Lionel? The guilt was sickening.

Grimly Garrick took his mother's arm. "Let's go in," he said softly. He whistled once, piercingly, as he strolled with his mother to where the earl stood. The setter appeared and fell into place at his side.

"I should have guessed." His mother smiled, reaching down to pat the silken head. "What a beautiful dog, dear."

"Hello, Garrick," Stanhope said firmly.

He was not smiling, and Garrick did not smile, either. "My lord." He bowed slightly. His father had been using a cane, which he leaned on, but other than that he looked remarkably well—for a man about to die in a year or two at the most.

The earl's gaze swept him from head to toe, undoubtedly noticing his hair was a natural color and his wool coat was threadbare. Then he eyed the dog. "We have much to discuss," he said, and turned away.

Garrick followed him, and after escorting his mother inside, he kissed her cheek. "May I drive you in the park later?" he asked.

Her blue eyes brightened. "I would like that." She smiled. And then, on an indrawn breath, she added, "I have missed you so. I am so pleased that you have returned home, my dear."

He did feel guilty. "I'm glad to be back, too." It was as much a lie as the truth. He turned and walked after the earl, following him into the library. His father took his seat behind his massive, leather inlaid desk. Garrick sat down in a facing chair. The setter dropped to the floor at his feet. The room was book lined and dark in spite of the crystal chandelier overhead.

"And your journey back was uneventful, I presume?" Stanhope asked with a lifted brow. It was distinctly gray, unlike the very white, powdered periwig he wore. This one was much shorter than the style he had favored a decade ago.

"Quite. You do not look exceedingly ill, Father," Garrick said bluntly.

The earl settled back in his chair. "I summoned you home two times. You disobeyed. The ploy worked, did it not?"

Garrick checked his temper with an effort. "It worked. But I have no intention of lingering here. I intend to return to Barbados in a fortnight."

The earl's eyes widened in astonishment. "But you have only just arrived! You have been gone ten years!"

"By your orders, sir," Garrick said coldly, recalling the day he had been banished from his home for his supposed forced seduction of a young noblewoman.

"You dallied, yet refused to do the right thing!" Stanhope shot back.

"I was hardly her first."

"She claimed otherwise."

"She lied. But then, you would believe her, a stranger, over your own son," Garrick said coolly.

"In truth, I knew she lied. But you were stubborn, defying my authority, and you needed a lesson," the earl said with anger. "And I did not insist that you stay away for all this time. We both know that you refused to return these past five years. I can see that you have not changed, either. You still think to defy me at every turn, do you not?"

Garrick hesitated. "Actually, I do not think of you at all, much less whether to defy you or not."

The earl thumped his cane on the floor and stood. "You are my heir. You have matters to dispose of here—where you belong. Have you no sense of duty?"

"Very little," Garrick said grimly, also standing. The setter came to his feet.

His father was red. "I was a fool to think I could change

you by sending you away. You will never become more like Lionel.''

The blow was unexpected. But Garrick felt it like a fist to his abdomen, and briefly he was stunned, breathless, at a loss for words.

The earl came around his desk, barely using his cane. ''I think of him first thing every time I wake up, and lastly, before sleep comes. Damn it. You are my heir, and I forbid you to return to that godforsaken land.''

Garrick spoke, slowly and softly. ''You can forbid me all that you want, Father, but I am a grown man now, and will do as I damn well please.''

''And if I dispose of that damned sugar plantation? What will you do then? Return to work like a common yeoman on someone else's land?''

''I will go to America and start my own estate.''

''With what funds?''

Garrick only smiled.

''What? Have you been embezzling from my plantation?'' the earl cried.

''That is a very serious accusation,'' Garrick said. ''But know this. Since I went to Sugar Hill, profits have increased ten times over in ten years. The plantation is making twenty-thousand pounds per annum, Father, no small sum. Because of me. And you see almost every penny of that profit.''

''Almost—but clearly not all.''

Garrick chose not to reply.

''Will you at least admit that you have a duty here?'' Stanhope's tone had changed. ''Good God, Garrick, you are my heir, and one day you will inherit one of England's largest, wealthiest estates. We truly do have many matters to discuss.''

Garrick hesitated, fought himself—and lost. ''I admit to having a duty here, and I hope my admission pleases you. But Father, you look as if you will live another ten years at least, so why dupe me into returning home? Do not tell me it is the grave matters we have to discuss. Do not tell me you have missed me, either.'' He stared. That last admission would never come.

The earl leaned on the edge of his desk. ''I do intend to live another ten years, or twice that, if I can. But Garrick, you are my only *child*.'' He stressed the last word.

''I am fully aware of that.'' Garrick tensed. He sensed what was coming.

''You need a wife. More important, you need an heir yourself.''

Garrick felt himself smile—without any mirth whatsoever. ''I have time.''

''I wish to see the De Vere line secured—as soon as possible.''

''I do not think that is possible.''

Stanhope lifted a brow. ''No? Most things in life are possible—with a bit of compromise.''

''And why should I yield?''

''Because, if you give me what I desire, perhaps I will give you what you desire,'' Stanhope said with a smile.

Garrick's pulse was racing. He did not respond.

His father said, ''I have already betrothed you, and it will be announced tomorrow in all of the newspapers.''

Garrick knew he flushed, with real anger. ''You have gone too far—too presumptuously!''

''Her father is one of the wealthiest men in England. Sir John was knighted thirteen years ago for a deed he performed for the king. I do believe he relieved a very close friend financially, in very indiscreet circumstances. In any case, although her family is hardly noble, finding a bride for you has not been an easy task. Old rumors seem to linger, Garrick.'' The earl stared, pausing, but Garrick was so angry at everything, including the last slur, that he refused to reply.

The earl smiled briefly and continued. ''What is even better, she is not merely young and pretty, she is meek, and you may do as you choose without having to explain yourself. You will be able to control her completely, Garrick. I thought that of the utmost importance in your case.''

"How dare you do this without consulting me first?" Garrick said, very low.

The setter growled.

Garrick glanced at him, pointed, said, "Down." The setter dropped to the floor, where he lay, tensely crouched. Garrick was shaking.

"There was little point in consulting you. I knew you would refuse to wed if I asked you to."

"First of all, I do not yet need a wife, and second, I despise meek women."

The earl's gray brows lifted. "Your views, as always, are unerringly odd. We do not live in a Chaucer tale, my boy. No one marries out of fondness or affection, and certainly not in the peerage. What *can* you be thinking of? If you fancy yourself with some hot-tempered spitfire, good God, the roof will come down around both your heads!" He walked forward and laid a hand on Garrick's shoulder, smiling. "I have lived a long time, Garrick. I know and understand people and life. Susan Layton is perfect for you. Take yourself some red-haired mistress. Miss Layton will not say a word."

"And that is your way, too, I presume," Garrick flashed, thinking of his mother, who never defied her husband.

Stanhope's eyes hardened. "My life is not at issue here. Truthfully, it was not easy to arrange a marriage for you—because of the rumors—and I suggest you consider that."

Garrick turned away, feeling ill. Society still condemned him for Lionel's disappearance and death—for in time, one and all had assumed that he was dead. Although Garrick blamed himself for not leaving the ruined keep with Lionel and knew with every fiber of his being that if he had done so, Lionel would still be alive, society was accusing him of murder. Of murdering his brother—his very best friend.

The setter, Treve, sensing his distress, whined.

"She is expecting you to call upon her—she returns to town today," the earl said, interrupting his thoughts.

Garrick grimaced.

"Garrick. You are not thinking this through. All I am

asking is for you to get a son on her, and then do as you choose.''

Garrick turned. "Are you suggesting that once the deed is done, I am free?"

"I am suggesting that you wed her immediately, father a child, and if it pleases you, leave Susan here with me and your mother while you return to Barbados. If the child, when it comes, is a boy, you have fulfilled your obligation to me. You need never concern yourself again," the earl said flatly.

It was another unexpected blow. The earl did not care if Garrick left and never returned—not as long as his grandson remained in London, raised a Stanhope. God, he should have known. The earl did despise him—and he always had. "What you are suggesting disgusts me," Garrick said harshly when he was capable of speech.

"It is the way of the world!" his father cried, hands in the air.

"If I marry her, then she will return to Barbados with me," he said furiously.

The earl said nothing. But there was the briefest hint of satisfaction in his eyes—as if he sensed his moment of triumph was at hand.

Garrick managed to rein in both his temper and his hurt. "I am not going to have any part in this," he said flatly.

"You must give me a grandson. Even you know that," the earl said as emphatically. He stood with his face close to Garrick's. "You owe me," he said.

Garrick felt all the color draining from his face.

"You owe me," the earl repeated. "Damn it. If it weren't for you, I'd have several grandchildren by now—because Lionel would still be alive!"

Chapter Three

ASHBURNHAM

When Arlen was in residence, Olivia took her breakfast in her rooms.

She was an unfashionably early riser—up shortly after the sun. But then, she preferred going to bed early, and could do so, as she was hardly a great hostess who entertained into the wee hours of the night. But Olivia awoke later than usual the morning after she had rescued Susan Layton from her attempted suicide. The sun outside her window, with its open draperies, was high and bright. For one moment she lay unmoving, aware of being exhausted. And total recollection of the previous night swept through her mind.

Tension filled her. Slowly she sat up, tossing the covers aside. And she thought of the way Arlen had looked at her body, she recalled Hannah's face, strained with fear, and she closed her eyes, remembering dragging a struggling Susan Layton from the lake. What an evening it had been. She hoped never to have another one like it.

Olivia stood up, walked to the washstand, and dared to regard herself in the looking glass over the mirror. There were wide, dark circles beneath her unusually pale gray eyes. Her own skin was ever so slightly sun kissed, as she and Hannah spent so much time out of doors. She stared at her even features. They were not particularly striking, except for her pale eyes and moonlight-colored hair. Last night a stranger had also consumed her thoughts, a man she had never met. Garrick De Vere was not her affair, or did Susan's attempted suicide make him her affair? Or was this strange preoccupation with a stranger merely due to the fact that Olivia was a rescuer of those in need? She could not help but feel, very strongly, that the lord of Caedmon Crag had been very unjustly condemned, and not just by Miss Layton. Of course, as she herself knew firsthand, life was rarely fair or just.

There was a knock on her door and Hannah poked her dark head into the room with a smile. "Mama? It is so late. Miss Childs is back." She smiled briefly. "She said I should not disturb you, but are you ill?" Her tone was anxious.

Olivia smiled and went to embrace her daughter. "I merely overslept, my dear."

Hannah was relieved. "The Laytons are to leave this afternoon. Susan is downstairs. Mama, she is so frightened. I am so sorry for her." Hannah's brow was furrowed now, making her appear much older than her eight years.

"Dear," Olivia said carefully, feeling both her and her daughter being drawn inexorably into Susan Layton's life, "sometimes we must let what will be alone. Perhaps all will be well with Miss Layton and De Vere in the end." But she could not smile reassuringly. It would be such a terrible match, Miss Layton and Garrick De Vere, a disaster for everyone involved.

A disaster.

Olivia inhaled, aware of the sudden, nearly overwhelming urge to interfere and break off an engagement that should be none of her concern.

"Mama, it will be terrible if they wed," Hannah said, breaking into Olivia's thoughts.

Olivia stared at her young, concerned daughter, oddly breathless. Hannah's concern so clearly matched her own. "Darling," she whispered, touching her. She did not want this for her daughter. How could she?

"Mama? What is it?" Hannah whispered anxiously.

But Olivia hardly heard her, and she was no longer thinking of Miss Layton and De Vere. Instead she saw herself as a child, thin and blond, just a bit younger than Hannah now was. And she was strolling among fruit-laden apple trees, while her governess, a dour old maid whom she could not bear, sat on a plaid blanket with a book. The sky was perfectly blue and unblemished by clouds, the sun warm upon Olivia's back. Her cashmere shawl had slipped to the ground.

Screams. From nowhere, suddenly, without warning, they came. Horrible, unending, anguished screams. Olivia clapped her hands to her ears.

And blood. There was so much blood. White twisted sheets, soaked with blood.

Olivia cried out, stunned by the pain, the fear, the blood—death. She whirled, trying to locate the source of the screams, the bed. Miss Farrell continued to read, her spectacles slipping down her long nose. Olivia could not understand. Hadn't she heard the terrifying screams? Hadn't she seen all of that dark red gushing blood?

"Miss Farrell," Olivia whispered, and it crossed her stunned mind that the governess was oblivious of what was happening. But how could that be?

Stunned, confused, still glancing wildly around, Olivia realized that the dying woman was her older sister, Marianne.

Marianne, who was a bride of less than a year, and who was heavily with child.

Olivia started to run.

Miss Farrell jerked, dropping her tome. "Lady Olivia!" she cried, a reprimand. "Just where are you off to, young lady?"

Her sister was dying. Her beautiful older sister, who had gotten so fat with her pregnancy, and who remained doe-eyed over her dashing young husband. Beautiful, kind, laughing Marianne, Olivia's only friend in the world, in spite of their ten-year age difference.

Olivia raced through the orchard, seized with panic, blinded by pain, by fear, and by the imminence of death.

"Mama!" Hannah was tugging hard on her hand. "Mama! Oh, stop! You are scaring me!"

Olivia was torn violently from the past—a pain-filled past she had no wish ever to relive. Trembling, weak of limb, she sank into a chair. Marianne had been fine when Olivia had reached the Oldham residence. But precisely two weeks after that day, she had gone into labor, hemorrhaging and losing both the child and her own life. Although Olivia had not been allowed to see her sister until the very end, that one final glimpse had been enough. Marianne's death had been exactly as Olivia had foreseen it.

"Mama? What is wrong?"

Tears filled Olivia's eyes and she reached out to pull her daughter close. "I was remembering the first time I realized I had the ability to see the future," she whispered unsteadily. "I was just about your age."

"Your sister," Hannah said, her face creased with worry and sadness. "You told me about her."

Olivia nodded, moistening her lips, wishing she could forget the past—or at least Marianne's untimely, tragic death. She stroked Hannah's hair. "I was so confused," she told her softly. "I did not understand what I had seen, and when I tried to talk about what would happen, no one would listen to me." She could not smile. And after, when there were other instances where her premonitions proved true, she had been shunned. By Miss Farrell, who had left her employment; by her own parents; by the servants at Oldham Way.

Hannah was nodding gravely. "We must help poor Miss Layton, Mama," she said. "She needs us."

Olivia stared. "We must not interfere in the Laytons' lives," she finally said, wishing that the foreboding she had had was a mere figment of her imagination, knowing it was not.

Hannah merely gazed at her sightlessly, not replying.

"Can you help me dress, my dear?" Olivia asked. She felt very ill now, and it had nothing to do with what had transpired in her own life eighteen years ago. But it had everything to do with her own dear daughter and poor Miss

Layton and the stranger whom she had never met, the man whom Susan Layton was affianced to.

An hour later, clad in a white silk gown sprigged with green and yellow, Olivia went downstairs. Hannah remained upstairs with Miss Childs. Olivia found the company in the dining room. Arlen, Sir John Layton, and the marquis were playing whist. Elizabeth was reading a novel. Lady Layton was busy with embroidery, while Susan sat staring dully out a window at the park outside. Olivia was filled with compassion for the young woman. "I think I shall take my morning stroll through the park. Miss Layton, would you care to join me?"

Susan turned. "Oh, may I?" she asked with transparent eagerness.

"Of course," Olivia said, smiling.

When they were well outside, Olivia glanced at the girl. "Are you feeling any better today, my dear?"

Susan promptly burst into tears, shaking her head.

"Oh, dear . . ." Olivia patted her back while handing her a handkerchief. "Do you wish to talk about what is bothering you?" she asked sympathetically.

"This is horrid! As soon as I return to town Lord Caedmon will call on me and there will be an engagement party," Susan cried. "He will give me a ring, and our betrothal will be official." She halted, facing Olivia. "Lady Ashburn, I have become so fond of you. Please, won't you come to town with me?"

Olivia was startled. And even as a protest formed on her lips, he was there, in her mind, staring at her. A man who could so easily destroy this innocent creature. A man who might destroy them both.

Olivia's instant refusal died unspoken. She was appalled with her last thought, wished she had never had it. Was this, then, the disaster? Would it involve Susan's downfall—and her own?

"Please come to town with us," Susan said more softly, breaking into Olivia's thoughts. "We are already friends, are we not? I have no friends, Lady Ashburn, not really." She flushed. "The ladies of the ton are not very kind to a brewer's daughter, in spite of the fact that my father was knighted when I was so young that I cannot even recall another life.''

Olivia's pulse was pounding. Something was pulling at her, telling her that she must go to town with Susan Layton, that she *must* go. She closed her eyes, aware now that she was perspiring. She had enough problems, she did not need any more. She need not involve herself with Susan Layton—it would be dangerous. She had no doubt.

''My lady? You are pale. I have upset you. I have been far too forward. I am sorry,'' Susan cried.

Olivia shook her head and heard herself say, ''I am not overly fond of London, my dear. But I am fond of you, and perhaps it is time for me to return to town, for a short while, at least.'' She had not intended to agree, and she was stunned by her own words.

Susan clapped her hands. ''Let us return to the house and tell everyone. You will leave with us this afternoon?'' she asked eagerly, smiling now, dragging Olivia toward the stone manor.

They reentered the salon. Before Olivia could speak, Susan said, ''Mother, Father, I have asked the countess to come to London with us and she has agreed! I am so pleased! Why, she can attend the betrothal party, can she not? Perhaps she might even wish to stay with us!''

Olivia looked at Arlen, who was standing, his expression rigid. ''This is quite odd,'' he said, staring at her as if she had two heads. ''My wife is a country mouse. She despises town.''

''Miss Layton invited me and I would like to go,'' Olivia said carefully. Arlen did not want her in town and she was aware of it. But her course seemed clear—even if it was a course she knew she should not follow.

''I think it is a capital idea.'' Sir John stood. ''And you must stay with us—that is, if Ashburn doesn't mind.'' He beamed.

''I think my wife needs some time to think about this,'' Arlen said firmly.

Olivia looked around the company—all of the Laytons

were smiling, while Elizabeth regarded her with open amusement. Olivia could not believe her own audacity—it was as if some unseen force were compelling her—as if someone else were speaking for her. "My lord," she addressed Arlen, "I really do not need to consider this invitation. I am content to adjourn to town and avail myself of the Laytons' hospitality for a mere fortnight."

Arlen's smile was false. He shrugged. "It is a splendid invitation, is it not? But you never leave your daughter, madam. This shall be a first." His gaze was piercing.

Olivia froze, glanced at the Laytons. She could not go if it meant leaving Hannah behind. She had never been separated from her daughter for even a single day since her birth. It was an impossibility. "I did not think to leave Hannah behind, my lord," she began softly, her pulse racing.

"Nonsense! The child is content in the country, she would hate town. Besides"—Arlen smiled, eyes cold—"you must not impose upon the Laytons."

"But Hannah is a lovely child," Susan interrupted enthusiastically. "Surely she can join us, can she not, Father?"

Sir John shrugged. "I have no objection. When did you meet the child, my dear?"

Susan blanched. Before she could form a single word, Olivia stepped forward, smiling far too widely. "Hannah was sleepwalking last night. Susan was taking some air before bed. It is really quite simple."

"Oh, I would love to have a child about the house again!" Lady Layton cried happily.

Elizabeth took one look at Arlen's face and walked over to Lady Layton. "She is a burden, you know. Perhaps it might be better for everyone to leave her behind. She needs special care." She smiled at Olivia and said, "The poor little thing is blind."

A gasp sounded. It had come from Lady Layton, who was now fluttering her fan to hide her surprise. Sir John had done better; his eyes had merely gone wide, and now they were narrow and assessing as he stared at both Olivia and Arlen.

Olivia saw red, but she fought for control. "Actually, Hannah needs no special care at all. She is hardly an invalid. She sees with her ears and hands, Lady Layton—and often she sees far more than someone like you or myself." Olivia was shaking. She had to grip both hands to hide their trembling. From the corner of her eyes she saw just how angry Arlen was. He was flushed the color of ripe, red apples.

Then Lady Layton stepped forward and laid her small hand on Olivia's arm. "My dear, your daughter sounds wonderful, and I am delighted that she will join us."

"We are both delighted," Sir John said, also stepping forward. His smile was genuine. "But we do plan to leave within a few hours. Should you not have your servants begin packing?"

Her temples throbbing, Olivia nodded, grateful for the Laytons' kindness. She avoided Arlen's gaze, which was filled with a cold and brutal promise—one of retribution. She knew better than to even think of defying Arlen openly. What had possessed her?

Perhaps, when this tempest had died down, she would try to have a reasonable conversation with him . . . despite the fact that they had ceased having any kind of reasonable exchange nine long years ago.

"Yes, I will go and supervise my maids." Olivia managed to smile and left the room, her strides as brisk as she could gracefully make them.

It was raining. It had begun the night before and continued unabated all that day. The rain ran down the windowpanes in thick, solid sheets. Outside, the day was gray, dismal, and cold. Inside the salon, a fire blazed beneath the carved wooden mantel of the hearth. Lady Layton had pleaded a headache and retired to her rooms shortly after dinner. Sir John was at his club. Hannah was finishing her last lesson of the day, and Olivia and Susan sat alone in the parlor, Susan working a piece of embroidery, Olivia silently reading Shakespeare's sonnets. They had arrived in London three days ago.

Susan suddenly set her embroidery aside. "I do not understand. He is in town. But he has not called. The betrothal was announced in all the newspapers, and he has not even bothered to make my acquaintance. I do not understand!"

Olivia laid her book down. She did not understand, either. "He has not been home in many years," she said, finding herself automatically defending the subject of their conversation—a subject that still, somehow, managed to occupy a good portion of her waking hours—and some of her restless nights as well. "I am sure he has had many affairs to see to."

"I am glad," Susan said vehemently, a slight sheen to her eyes. "As everyone knows, he is a horrid man, and I am glad to postpone for as long as possible finally meeting him in the flesh!" She shivered.

Olivia leaned forward. "Susan, perhaps it would be best if you started thinking more kindly of the man you will one day wed? Perhaps he is not all that they say?" She had made up her mind that she would not interfere in this disastrous match. She had become genuinely fond of Susan in just a few days, and the fact was, for Susan, a brewer's daughter, it was a magnificent union. One day Susan would be the countess of Stanhope.

"Olivia, I have tried, truly I have, but everyone says he murdered his older brother. My God!"

Olivia stiffened. "That is a horrid rumor, one I do not for a moment believe."

But Susan continued as if she had not even heard. "He was, they say, the last person to see his brother, and of course, with his older brother gone, he became the heir. Who else would have done away with Lionel De Vere? And last night at Almack's I overheard two ladies saying that he has become a savage, truly, for he walks around sans wig, sans powder, a good deal of the time in hacking clothes, and then they said it was no surprise, because his father has begged him to return for many years—but he prefers the sugar islands—because he is a savage! Then I heard Lady Camdon saying he had seduced a fine young woman just before his banishment—in 1750, she said, it was a *huge* scandal—and that it was his refusal to marry her when it was his duty to do so that caused his own father to send him to the West Indies in the first place.'' Susan shuddered. ''It just gets worse and worse!''

Olivia had also heard the gossip since arriving at the Laytons'. ''I find it intolerable to condemn a man without actual proof of his guilt.'' She was angry.

''Olivia, you are just too kind,'' Susan said, eyes dampening. ''But do they not say that if there is smoke, there is a fire?''

Olivia sighed. ''Yes, that is an old adage. Susan, many years have passed since all these supposed crimes were committed. Perhaps he has sincerely changed, repenting his ways, if he has been responsible for some of the deeds.'' But she knew he was not a murderer. Perhaps a seducer of innocence, perhaps a savage, but not a murderer. Of this she had not a doubt.

Susan did smile. ''You are the kindest person I have ever met. Let me only say I hope you are right!''

Olivia smiled in return, turned, and reached for her handsomely bound volume of sonnets on the Chippendale end table. And there he was. She froze, her gaze on the window. He was stepping down from a huge lacquer coach, a coat of arms emblazoned in blue and silver on the door, liveried footmen swinging it smartly shut behind him. Olivia did not have to identify the coach or the arms to know that it was he. In spite of the rain, he was tall, muscular, and dark, and she knew, she absolutely knew, this was Garrick De Vere, the viscount of Caedmon Crag.

Susan cried out, apparently having seen their caller as well, her embroidery slipping to the floor. ''Oh dear Lord! Oh dear Lord, it is he!''

Olivia could not speak. Her own pulse pounded now with erratic force as she watched him hurrying up the block, the cape he wore swinging about him. His calves, she saw, were very muscular, and she did not think he wore padding, because his thighs, visible as the cape flapped open, were every bit as solid, hard, and defined. Olivia wet her lips. Her reaction to his sudden appearance was inexplicable. She had no reason to be so unnerved.

And she had not incorrectly imagined his appearance. It was exactly as she had thought it would be.

"I need salts," Susan cried in a whisper. "I am going to faint."

Olivia felt rather light-headed and in need of air herself, but now was not the time to give in to female vapors—which she had never before suffered from. She stood, bent, retrieved Susan's embroidery, and handed it to her. "You will do no such thing. Start sewing."

Susan, starkly white, blinked at her, tears appearing in her eyes, and she nodded. Studiously she began to sew.

"Susan, at all costs, do not cry," Olivia said. Susan nodded again as Olivia quickly returned to her chair, picking up the book. She opened it, saw it was upside-down, and corrected the error. She did not see a single word on the page as she strained her ears for the sound of his approach.

Footsteps finally became evident, growing louder still. Olivia stared at the blurred words on the page, her pulse more wild now than before. She felt her cheeks burning.

"Ladies, Lord Garrick De Vere, the viscount of Caedmon Crag," a footman intoned from the doorway.

Olivia looked up, as did Susan. Garrick De Vere stood on the threshold, as tall and powerfully built as he had first appeared through the windows. He stared across the room, not at Susan, but at Olivia. She slowly rose, setting the sonnets aside, aware of trembling. Somehow, their gazes had locked. And his was as golden as she had imagined.

Olivia curtsied, peripherally aware that Susan was doing the same. De Vere bowed.

Silence reigned in the room. Olivia became aware of it—worse, she realized she was staring openly at him—and that he was doing the same to her. She fought for control of her rioting senses. What was wrong with her? He was only a man, even if he was many inches over six feet tall and striking in his appearance. Had he not been wearing a dark green frock coat, a silver waistcoat, a fine silk shirt with lace cuffs and cravat, pale wool breeches, and paler stockings, she would have sworn he was a savage colonial, and that assessment had less to do with his unpowdered hair than the feral, frank way he moved and continued to stare at her.

Olivia stepped forward. "My lord, we are so pleased to finally make your acquaintance."

Amusement glimmered in his eyes as he came into the room. "Indeed." He made no effort to continue the conversation.

Olivia took a breath. "We have eagerly awaited this moment, have we not?" She turned to look at Susan, whose eyes were wide, bright spots of pink marring her cheeks. Susan managed to nod.

He folded his arms, eyeing Olivia.

Olivia's temper rose—could he not at least comment upon the weather? "In truth, we expected you several days ago."

His bow was slight. "I apologize for my tardiness." He paused. Olivia thought he would lapse into silence again, but he said, "Had I known what awaited me here, I might not have been so tardy."

Olivia shifted, because he continued to stare at her, not at Susan. Had he mistaken her for his fiancée? "My lord," she said, uneasy now, "might we offer you some refreshments?"

He shrugged. "If you wish. What are you reading?"

His question took her by surprise. "Shakespeare. I am fond of his sonnets. Do you like to read?"

"I read poorly," he said flatly. A hint of color appeared high up on his striking cheekbones.

She was surprised. She knew he was a man of great intelligence, could not imagine why he would read poorly, and saw that she had discomfited him, which was not her intention.

"But I should like it if you would, sometime, read to me," he said bluntly.

He thought she was Susan. Olivia was at once elated and

depressed. "My lord, perhaps Miss Layton might wish to read to you," she said a bit hoarsely.

He jerked, his eyes flying to Susan, who remained standing tensely and, it appeared, as yet incapable of speech. "I see I have made a vast mistake," he said, his eyes darkening. "Miss Layton." He bowed.

Susan, still speechless, curtsied ever so slightly. A tear seemed to shimmer upon her pale lashes.

His gaze moved to the embroidery she had left on her chair. "How pleasing," he said, his tone scathing.

Olivia flinched. She did not think him pleased at all. "Susan is also a very fine dancer. And she plays the harpsichord quite well." That was an exaggeration, but Olivia was not sure what else to say.

The viscount faced her rather coolly. "So you are her champion?"

Hotly Olivia said, "I am her friend."

His gaze held hers, softening. "How fortunate for Miss Layton."

Heat, red hot, streaked through Olivia's body. It was carnal. She was in shock.

He turned back to Susan. "And are you, also, fond of reading?" he asked.

Susan stared, appearing very desperate and quite mesmerized.

Olivia looked at her and prayed she would find her tongue.

"Miss Layton?" Garrick De Vere asked very imperiously.

"No," Susan whispered. "In truth, I do not like to read."

He nodded, as if her words came as no surprise. "What do you like to do? Other than embroider, dance, and play the harpsichord?"

Her blush heightened. "I . . ." She trailed off.

"Surely you have interests?" he queried.

"I enjoy the parks," she said, her small bosom heaving, "here in London."

His brows lifted. "Do you ride?"

She clutched her skirts. "Not well, sir. But I do enjoy a daily drive."

"I see." He remained unsmiling. "And what else occupies your time?"

Susan stared at him as helplessly as a bird about to be devoured by a cat.

"Well? Surely I must learn these things if I am to please my bride."

Olivia did not think he had any intention of ever trying to please Susan.

Susan swallowed. "I enjoy gardens."

"Gardens?"

"Vauxhall," she whispered.

"Then we shall go," he said, not kindly. In fact, he looked truly put out and annoyed.

"Yes," Susan whispered, her voice quavering. And Olivia crossed her fingers, praying she would not burst into tears. "As you wish, my . . . my lord."

"Are you about to cry?" he asked with sudden amazement.

Susan burst into tears, and with a sob, she raced from the room, tripping over her huge floral skirts.

Olivia was furious. Her blood burned as never before. Why had he tormented sweet Susan that way? So implacably? So ruthlessly?

He turned to Olivia. "She is exactly as I thought she would be," he said savagely. Then his searing gaze held Olivia's, and his tone changed. "And you, madam? Might I learn your name?"

Olivia fists were clenched. Even when she saw his gaze move quickly to her hands, she did not relax them, nor did she force a smile. "I am Olivia Grey, the countess of Ashburn," she said stiffly. "And you, sir, need a lesson in manners. How could you treat Miss Layton that way?!"

He stared, eyes wide, as if he had not heard her last sentences.

"My lord, sir, Miss Layton is a dear girl," Olivia began again, somewhat less heatedly.

"I am sure that she is," he said. "You are Lady Ashburn?" There was amazement in his tone.

"Is that cause for concern?" she asked, having no choice but to retreat from the topic of his badgering Susan. It was too intimate and unseemly a subject as it was.

He stared, his golden eyes intent. "So you are married to Arlen," he said quietly, as if to himself and not to her.

"You know my husband?" Olivia asked, surprise mingling with anxiety.

His smile was not particularly pleasant; in fact, Olivia found it menacing, although why, she could not say. "Let us just say that once, long ago, we knew one another," De Vere replied.

A frisson of dread swept over Olivia. What was happening here? His anger was obvious. Clearly he and Arlen were not friends; perhaps they were even adversaries of sorts. And he was betrothed to Susan, yet his presence was consuming her now in the flesh as it had, before this meeting, in her mind. And Olivia felt the presence of danger, there in the room with her. It was so strong, so overpowering, so sudden and unexpected, that her knees turned to jelly and she almost stumbled.

"Are you ill?" he asked suddenly, his gaze keen.

Briefly she could not speak, her gaze locking with his. What danger, and where? For whom—and when? The questions vied violently for her attention, but she was afraid by what she had felt and could not find any answers. Did it have something to do with Garrick De Vere's prior relationship to her husband? Or was it about him and Susan? Surely it had nothing to do with her!

"Lady Ashburn," he said sharply.

I am so overcome by this man that I am imagining things, Olivia told herself firmly. She forced a smile. "I am fine. Thank you." But she remained shaken.

He scowled and walked away from her, to stare out one of the salon windows into the pouring rain. Olivia studied his broad back. The rain drummed on the glass panes, loud and rhythmic. She did not think he padded his coats as some fops did—as Arlen did. Suddenly Olivia saw herself walking up behind him, placing her hands firmly on his back, pressing her body there, laying her cheek there—and she was appalled with her errant mind.

He turned abruptly—as if cognizant of her thoughts. This time their gazes collided wildly. Olivia had to look away. Thank God he had no gift, she thought desperately. How ashamed she would be if he could guess her thoughts.

"I would still like you to read to me," he said suddenly.

Olivia started. "Perhaps that would not be proper."

He smiled with amusement, eyes gleaming, and stalked forward. Oddly enough, Olivia's heart skipped and she backed up several steps, until a sofa blocked her way. He did not stop advancing until he stood inches in front of her—so close, in fact, that her skirts, held out by wide hoops, covered his legs from knee to toe.

"I am from an uncivilized island. I care little for propriety," he said.

She did swallow. "Well, that is fine for you, my lord, but I live on this particular island, where one does conform to a certain code of etiquette."

He smiled. "How prettily that was said." His eyes continued to gleam—settling on her mouth.

Her pulse was out of control. Was he going to kiss her? Her brain became so scrambled, she could hardly think. "You need not flatter me, my lord," she whispered.

"Why not, my lady? You are an exceedingly interesting woman."

Her gaze shot to his. "I am ordinary." She almost choked on the stupendous lie.

"You are far from ordinary," he said firmly. "You are the least ordinary woman I have ever met."

"Do you jest?" She was disbelieving.

"You know I do not." His smile had faded. "Truthfully, I did not return to England out of any real desire to do so. But now"—his gaze slid over her features, one by one—"I find myself exceedingly pleased to have done so."

Olivia was in shock. He was engaged to her friend, yet she was certain he was about to make some kind of illicit advance toward her. "You should be pleased," she said frantically, "for your bride is a lovely young woman."

"You," he said flatly, "are a lovely woman."

Olivia was finally rendered speechless. When was the last time anyone had called her lovely? She was quite certain that she had not been told that she was lovely since she was a young child—not since her gift had become apparent.

He stared at her for a long time.

"I am the Laytons' houseguest," she finally whispered. "I must plead a headache. I must retire." She curtsied quickly, inelegantly, about to fly past him. But he caught her wrist. And his huge, calloused hand did not merely dwarf her arm, it seared her, like the red-hot brand used on poachers, convicts, and thieves.

"You stay here? And not at Ashburn House? Is Arlen here with you?" he demanded.

She was not compelled to answer such intimate questions, but she said hoarsely, "Arlen stays at Ashburn House, my lord. Now, would you please release my arm?"

He ignored her, continuing to hold her firmly in place, shifting his weight so he leaned toward her. "I want to see you again," he declared. "When will that be?"

"You are mad! Insane! It is not possible," she cried.

"It is done all the time," He pressed forward. Olivia began to bend backward over the couch. "Or do you love, honor, and remain faithful to your husband, Lady Ashburn?"

She did not have to answer him, she told herself frantically. "Let me go. Please!"

"Are you afraid of me?" he said, backing up a step.

But Olivia did not breathe more easily, even if she could now stand upright. Dangerous, she thought. He is dangerous. "Yes," she whispered.

He released her. His expression had changed, ardent intention replaced by displeasure and disbelief. Too late, Olivia realized he had misunderstood—thought she was afraid of him for all the reasons society would have closed its doors to him had he not been Stanhope's heir. "My lord," she began.

"Do not bother to apologize," he said scathingly. His gaze raked her from head to toe. "I am sure our paths will cross again. Next time, I will try to restrain myself from overstepping all bounds." His smile was tight and angry.

And he was walking away from her, without even a parting bow. Olivia wanted to call him back, explain—worse, she almost ran after him, to halt him with physical force. But she did no such thing.

He was going to marry Susan. And she had never even contemplated an affair.

But her heart was hurting her now, the feeling sickening, pervasive. Olivia bit her lip, hard, so as not to call after him.

A moment later she went to the window and pressed her nose to the glass. Immediately it began to fog. She rubbed violently at the window and saw him pause in the downpour outside, about to step into the carriage, the liveried footman patiently holding the door open for him. Then he turned fully and stared not at the house, but directly at her, through the window and the rain.

Thunder rumbled in the distance. Olivia turned away.

CHAPTER FOUR

It was Lady Layton who summoned Olivia to her rooms.
Barely half an hour had passed since De Vere had left.
Olivia had remained in the salon, seriously at a loss. The
encounter—every detail of it, every spoken word—remained engraved upon her mind. She was very shaken. She
must, she knew, leave London immediately; coming to
town had been a mistake.

The door to Lady Layton's private sitting room was ajar.
Instantly Olivia understood why she had been summoned
upstairs. Susan was reclining upon the green velvet settee,
sobbing into a handkerchief. Her mother was at her side,
stroking her hair, looking extremely distraught.

Before Olivia could knock, Susan saw her and cried,
"Tell her! Tell Mother that I cannot marry such a miserable, mean man!"

Olivia was actually in agreement with Susan for once.
Having finally met Garrick De Vere she had no doubt that
it would be a terrible match, with devastating consequences
for the young girl. Of course, she could say no such thing.
Olivia forced a smile and entered the room. Lady Layton
stood, her relief obvious.

"Susan is easily given over to hysterics, but this time
she is truly distressed. What happened, Countess?" Lady
Layton asked, wringing her small hands.

"It was a difficult interview," Olivia said carefully.

"I cannot marry him!" Susan cried.

"It is all arranged," Lady Layton said with dismay. "Oh, Susan, he will one day be the earl of Stanhope. You will be a countess. One day, darling, your son will be an earl—and all of your children will be lords and ladies of great rank and consequence."

Susan collapsed into tears.

Olivia felt terribly sympathetic, and she went to her. "Susan, his manners were definitely lacking, but he is very handsome, is he not?" she tried.

Susan stared. "He is a savage! He looks like a . . . an . . . American Indian! His hair wasn't even powdered! I did not find him attractive at all."

"Oh, dear," Lady Layton said anxiously. "Do you think he might powder his hair for the betrothal party?"

Olivia did not think so. "I am sure he will," she said brightly. "Susan, I do not think he is a purposefully mean man. I think he has suffered greatly in his life, I think he is terribly unhappy." The words came from her unbidden. She had not reflected upon De Vere's true nature yet; she had been far too disturbed by their exchange and her overwhelming reaction to him. But now she was stunned by her own words, for the truth was so obvious. *How unhappy he was.*

"He doesn't like me, not at all," Susan said, sniffling. "And even if he is unhappy, that is hardly cause to make me so miserable." The tears fell again, and she dabbed at them with her linen handkerchief. By now her pale skin was blotchy, her nose strawberry red. Susan was not a woman who cried gracefully.

"His manners could be improved upon. He was hardly nice to me, either," Olivia said with caution. Dear God. The viscount of Caedmon Crag had made it clear that he wished to dally with her. At the mere thought, Olivia's heart lurched. What was happening? She had not thought herself to be a woman interested in matters of the flesh. Or was her reaction to a singularly attractive man a direct consequence of having been cloistered for such a long time?

She hid her hands in her skirts so no one might see that they were shaking.

"I think he was rather taken with you," Susan said, interrupting her thoughts.

Olivia paled.

"He could not take his eyes off you," Susan amended, "but then, you are so beautiful, I am sure that most men stare."

Olivia felt herself blush. "I am hardly beautiful."

Susan shifted and faced her mother. "Mother, please, tell Father I cannot marry that horrid man."

Lady Layton hesitated. "My dear, your father's mind is made up. And the contracts have been signed, the betrothal announced in all of the newspapers. Oh! I do not know what to do. If you did not marry the viscount, whom would you wed? It would not be such a spectacular match."

"But I want to be happy," Susan cried. "Mother, you are happy. Father loves you and you love him." Lady Layton flushed and started to speak, but Susan rushed on. "Oh, I know it is not fashionable to love one's spouse, but at least one must be friends, one must respect the person one is married to. Am I asking for too much? I only want a portion of what you and Father share."

Lady Layton sighed. "No, dear, you are hardly asking for the world, but maybe, if you give Lord Caedmon a chance, you might feel some friendship for him—and he might feel some fondness for you—and it would all turn out in time." She brightened.

Olivia almost choked. That scenario, she knew, was wishful thinking at its best. Yet what should she do now? She had promised herself she would not interfere, had even been trying to persuade Susan to accept the match. But the urge to interfere was overwhelming.

"May I come in?" Sir John asked from the threshold, smiling. "Or am I interrupting?"

One and all turned toward the robust knight. Olivia did smile. His huge wig, a few years out of date, was askew. His silver waistcoat was buttoned incorrectly, and one of his stockings was slipping. But his smile was as warm as his heart, and she was glad to see him.

"Please, John, do come in," Lady Layton said nervously.

His smile faded. "My dears, what is going on? Susan, you are distressed," Layton declared.

"Father, he finally called. That despicable man. It was the most horrid audience I have ever had," Susan said in a rush.

"What horrid man?" Layton asked benignly.

"Why, my fiancé," Susan cried. She held the handkerchief to her eyes again, sniffling quite loudly.

"Dear, I am afraid they did not get along very well," Lady Layton said. "But I am sure their relationship will improve."

"I despise him! And he despises me, things will not improve, I am quite sure. I cannot marry him!" Susan said loudly.

Layton was grim. "My dear, the contracts have been signed, the banns are being read, an announcement in the weekly *Times* has been published. I have garnered a magnificent match for you, and you should be thankful, instead of abed."

Susan's face crumpled. She wept.

Layton sighed and skewered Olivia with his usually friendly gaze. Now it was piercing. "Have you met His Lordship?" he asked.

Olivia was nervous. "Yes, my lord, I did."

"Is Susan exaggerating?"

Olivia hesitated as Susan stopped weeping to stare at her. "It was a difficult interview, my lord. The viscount has been abroad many years, and his manners are not what we are accustomed to. Susan was rather discomfited by his forthrightness."

Layton turned to his daughter. "Susan, I have pampered you your entire life, with real pleasure. But it is time for you to grow up. You are too easily distressed, my dear, you must become stronger. I have arranged a great match for you, and I expect you to be grateful."

Susan gazed at her father tearfully but did not speak.

"You have little choice in this matter," Layton continued seriously. "Daughters do not decide such matters in any case—why should you be an exception? I expect you to wed Lord Caedmon, and I expect you to be a dutiful wife. I expect you to come to admire him, if that is the best you can do, in time. I do not expect complaints. Most women would die to be in your place."

Olivia winced at his choice of words.

"I would rather die than marry him!" Susan said vehemently.

Layton's eyes widened. "I beg your pardon?" he said stiffly.

"I am sorry, Father," she said hastily, sniffling now. "But I will never admire him, never!"

Layton sighed. "I was warned that he was difficult and eccentric. But there are far worse things, let me assure you." He turned to his tiny wife. "Lady Layton, I expect you to coach your daughter in the affairs of the world. Explain to her how a marriage can be made a success, or how it can be made a failure. Above all, you shall inform her of her duties and role as a bride and wife. Susan is sweet and pretty. Garrick De Vere is a man. Perhaps eccentric, but he will not be averse to my daughter when all is said and done—if all is said and done correctly." Layton bowed, spun on his heels, and departed the room.

Olivia regarded Susan, who was dismayed but no longer in tears as she stared glumly after her father. Lady Layton came over to her. "Well, my dear, that is that. I do think we are going to have a long talk this afternoon."

"Father isn't going to change his mind, is he?" Susan asked.

"No," Lady Layton replied. "He usually knows what is best, my dear," she said gently.

Susan pouted. Then, "He will be an earl." She sighed.

"You should think about that, and all the other wonderful benefits of marrying the Stanhope heir," Lady Layton said quite cheerfully. "And just think, in another two days there will be that wonderful soirée to celebrate your betrothal. You have been waiting to wear that beautiful rose gown—and I have heard the ring he will give you is worth a fortune in itself. It is a family heirloom, you know.''

Susan did smile, just a bit. Then she said, ''If only he were not so big, not so dark, and just a bit more well mannered!''

''And that is what we shall discuss,'' Lady Layton said. ''How a woman like you brings a man like that to heel.'' She walked to the bell pull and rang it. ''It is going to be a long afternoon, so we shall need tea and cakes.''

Susan slid her slippered feet to the floor and smiled at Olivia. ''I suppose I should apologize for my behavior. It was terrible, was it not?''

''But I do understand,'' Olivia said gently, thinking that the Laytons were seriously deluded if they thought Susan could ever tame a man like De Vere. ''I am glad you are feeling better now.'' A sick feeling was welling up inside of her, one she recognized but wished she did not.

Susan hesitated. ''You weren't frightened by him, were you?'' Anxiety tinged her tone.

Olivia hesitated. De Vere had frightened her—but not in the way Susan meant. ''No, my dear. He did not.''

''It will be a wonderful party,'' Susan said, smiling again. ''And surely he will be less surly—and *surely* he will powder his hair.''

Olivia closed her eyes. The sickening feeling was far more intense. And there was no avoiding the voice in her mind. Nothing was going to go as planned, because of her, Olivia. Chills swept over her, and she begged to be excused.

How he hated these evenings.

At Sugar Hill it was different. With the setter sprawled at his feet, he would sit on the whitewashed verandah of the square, four-story plantation house, sipping rum as the sun turned into a flaming red ball, streaking the Caribbean sky with rainbow hues, lowering itself gently over the fertile green plains of his sugar cane fields. Beyond the last of the fields he could see a strip of pearly white beach and the placid, shimmering jade green waters of Sugar Hill cove.

"So. You finally called upon your fiancée," the earl said flatly. There was censure in his tone. The criticism could not have been clearer had he finished his thoughts by saying, "And it was about time."

Garrick kept his expression absolutely neutral as he turned to his father. He had not come home to argue with him, by God. Yet neither had he returned to be talked down to—he was no longer a child. He sat with the earl and countess at one end of the long rosewood dining table, waiting for supper to be served, the earl at its head in his silver periwig, rolled and tied back in a queue, and a dark crimson frock coat, an ice blue waistcoat, and an exquisitely ruffled white silk shirt. Garrick himself had indifferently donned the new clothing his mother's tailor had so quickly made up for him.

Huge silver candelabra graced the center of the table, making it hard for everyone to see one another. Garrick thought it preferable that his view of the earl was interfered with. Overhead, three large crystal chandeliers flickered with the candlelight of hundreds of white candles. He toyed with his crystal wineglass, finally taking a sip of fine French Bordeaux. "I did."

"And?" the earl demanded. "Have you come to your senses at last?"

"No, I have not come to my senses," Garrick said flatly.

The countess, clad in a brilliantly gold gown *à la française,* interjected quickly, "She is not only a pretty girl, she is very sweet, too, dear."

Garrick smiled without mirth. "I did not notice." He stared at his father. "Oh, yes, she was the plump brunette. I suppose she is passable enough."

The earl grimaced, the countess immediately reached for her wine and sipped it, and silence briefly reigned. "I will ignore that, as you wish only to provoke me. It certainly took you long enough to call upon her. I can only say I hope it was a pleasant call."

"Oh, it was quite pleasant—considering the fact that

Miss Layton is insipid, spineless, and a fool.''

Again Eleanor reached for her wine.

''I am sorry, Mother,'' Garrick said. ''But I refuse to pretend to be enamored of Father's choice.''

''She is a nice young lady,'' his mother whispered somewhat desperately.

The earl cut his wife off before she could continue. ''Have we not already discussed this? One does not choose one's bride for the attributes one prefers. As it is, most women, Garrick, in case you have not noticed, are as insipid as they are foolish. Just spend an entire evening at Almack's. Miss Layton will be the perfect wife—imminently pliable.''

Garrick glanced at his mother, but she was studying her plate, clutching her wineglass with one hand. ''Once again, we are in complete disagreement,'' he said harshly. ''And do you not think you should clarify your statement? For surely you do not include your wife in your judgments?''

''Garrick''—Eleanor finally glanced at him, her smile brief—''your father has not insulted me.''

And Garrick thought, but he should have.

''What does your mother have to do with this?'' Stanhope was annoyed. ''We are discussing your fiancée. As usual, you misunderstand me completely—but I think you do so on purpose. Layton has three sons, and Miss Layton shall undoubtedly birth you a healthy heir,'' the earl ended with real satisfaction. ''That is what is important, and little else.''

''A foolish woman like that, one whose first recourse is to resort to tears, will make me gray in a very few short years,'' Garrick growled.

Eleanor finished her glass of wine. It was promptly refilled by a servant.

''It was not easy finding you a bride. I did the best for you that I could, Garrick, considering that the entire ton thinks you responsible for Lionel's murder.'' Stanhope slammed his hand on the table.

Garrick was on his feet. ''Oh, so now it is murder? And

do you really think I give a damn what the peerage thinks about me?''

Stanhope was also on his feet. ''You have already proven that you do not give a damn about anything or anyone but yourself.'' He was practically shouting.

The countess gasped. ''Please! Please stop! Both of you!''

''Be quiet,'' the earl snapped, not even looking at her. He glared at Garrick. ''Your duties lay here, with me, yet you ran away years ago, for we both know the truth—I never meant to banish you! And to refuse to come home when you are my only son! And now you will fight me about this marriage? Have you no honor, Garrick? You are a fool, far more so than Miss Layton.''

Garrick was so angry that he was shaking. ''I have never been good enough for you, have I? Everything I said and did was always wrong. I have never won your approval, so why should anything change now? My only regret is that I did not leave England right after Lionel vanished, that I waited four more years. And as far as duty and honor go, Father, you are right. I have no honor. But then, this has never been a real home, so how can you blame me for not giving a damn about this earldom?''

The earl's face turned white.

''Garrick!'' the countess cried. ''I know you do not mean that.''

''Father believes he is infallible, and I cannot change how he thinks of me. Nor do I wish to try.'' Garrick flung his linen napkin on the table in absolute disgust. Yet there was hurt rising up inside of him, along with the anger, because a part of him had hoped that maybe things had changed—that maybe the earl had changed, becoming more reasonable in his old age. But nothing had changed. Nothing would ever change. He was a cunning, ruthless, powerful old man—and until he died, he would reign his kingdom like a tyrant.

''I am usually right,'' the earl said, recovering his ability to speak. He was furiously grim. ''And I am right about this. Your disloyalty to the family is shocking.''

"I have never ceased shocking you, now, have I?" Garrick said with real bitterness. He bowed to his mother. "I am afraid I have thoroughly lost my appetite." And with hard strides he left the room, aware of the tension-laden silence he was leaving behind.

At the table, the countess began to cry.

The earl threw down his fork, stood, and exited the room.

In the salon, Garrick opened the liquor cabinet and poured himself a glass of brandy. As he drank it, he felt some of the tension easing inside of him. How wonderful it was, he thought mockingly, to be home.

"Garrick," Eleanor said from behind him, her voice low and strained. "May I join you?"

He whirled, not having heard her approach, and saw her standing in the doorway, somewhat teary-eyed. "How can you live with him?" he asked. "How can you let him talk to you, and in front of you, the way he does?"

She entered the room, closing the two doors behind her. "He is my husband," she said simply. "Like yourself, I was not given any choice in the matter."

"And do you have regrets, Mother, about being denied the right to decide your own future?"

She sat on the sofa, arranging her full skirts about her. "It would be silly of me to entertain regrets after all these years. He is not a bad man, Garrick, surely you know that. Difficult, yes, very difficult, but ..." She hesitated. "He does love me, in his own way."

Garrick was so stunned to hear his mother speaking about love in reference to the earl that he could only stare.

"You do not think so," she said, low.

"I think," he said carefully, "that he considers you his family, as he does me. But I am quite sure he has no concept of what the emotion you are discussing is truly about. What interests Father is the earldom and its perpetuity, nothing else."

Eleanor bit her lip. "All peers are interested in perpetuity," she said.

"You defend him. You have always defended him. I

admire you, Mother, for your loyalty,'' Garrick said, salut-
ing her with his glass.

"He loves you, too!'' she cried.

Garrick made an inelegant, scoffing sound. "Please.
Would you like something to drink?'' he asked, even
though he was quite certain his mother was on the near side
of being foxed.

She nodded, looking up. "Susan is young,'' she said
gently. "Give her some time. Please try, Garrick, for all
our sakes. You must wed and have an heir.''

Garrick stiffened. He was being blackmailed into doing
his duty, and he supposed that said quite a bit about his
character—or lack of it. He thought of Lionel with the same
guilt as always, and then, grimly, he recalled his bride-to-
be. No amount of time would change Susan Layton into a
woman of fire and courage, a woman he might admire and
one day love. He shoved aside Olivia Grey's image with
real determination. She had been creeping into his thoughts,
against his will, ever since he had met her that afternoon.

"I will try for your sake, then, Mother,'' Garrick said
finally. He handed her the port. "Did you leave him alone
at the table?'' he asked. The idea gave him some satisfaction.

Eleanor shook her head. "He left before I did and has
already gone out.''

Garrick wondered who his current mistress was and said
nothing.

They sipped their drinks for a moment in silence. Then
Eleanor set down her glass. "If only there could be peace
between you and your father,'' she whispered.

Garrick stared at her. "We are never going to get along.
What he sees as black, I see as white.''

"I know,'' she whispered, staring into her glass. "I have
missed you so much, Garrick, all these years.'' She suddenly looked up, her gaze startling in its boldness. "You
are not happy, are you?''

He stiffened, and suddenly he was thinking about Sugar
Hill and Lionel. His brother was the reason he had gone
away, no longer able to stand the pain of not knowing

whether Lionel was dead or alive, whether he might one day come back. His father had also been part of the reason he had exiled himself to that tiny, peaceful sugar island—he had not wanted to become the Stanhope heir, and his father had made it clear to him, every day, that he was the one to blame for Lionel's disappearance—because he had been the last person to see him, to be with him, that rainy day in Cornwall when he had disappeared.

His pulse was pounding. "What is unhappiness?" Garrick finally said with a wry smile and a falsely casual shrug. "For that matter, what is happiness? We are all given our lot in life, are we not?"

To his absolute shock, his mother set her drink down and burst into tears.

He had not seen his mother cry in years, and this was so sudden, and so extreme, that for a moment he was paralyzed. Then he handed her his handkerchief and sat beside her, putting his arm around her. Garrick was distraught. He did not know what to do. "Mother? What is it?"

She shook her head, trying unsuccessfully not to cry. "I have missed you so. I thought about you all the time, missing you so much that it hurts. Yet I know you cannot stay here, and I know why." She covered her eyes and sobbed. "I do not blame you for running away from us, for choosing that little island over your home here. How right you are. This was never, is not, a real home."

Oh, God, he thought. He held her tighter as she sobbed against his shoulder. "You have always been a wonderful mother. I just cannot tolerate him. You were not the reason I left."

Her blue eyes, wet with tears, held his. She touched his hand and said, "I know. But it is more than that, isn't it?" She burst into tears again. "One day. One damned day in a lifetime, a single moment, and a family is destroyed. In one instant, a life is taken, and there is no happiness—not ever again."

Tears burned his own eyes, and he fought them. "Yes," he said harshly, once again standing on that ledge with Lionel, the two of them scared and alive. *What had hap-*

pened? How could someone walk away and vanish like that?

Gone forever. In one split second. If only he had left the keep with his brother. If only . . .

"Everything was my fault," his mother was saying harshly.

"Mother!" Garrick began in protest.

"No! All those years, I allowed him to praise Lionel, so loudly, and to discredit you as vehemently. Oh, God!"

He took her hands and held them. "Do not blame yourself for Father's behavior. No one can change him. No one allows him anything."

"Do you think I don't know what he did to you after Lionel disappeared? Do you think he did not do the very same thing to me? I saw him, time after time, look at you with utter accusation, utter blame. And he made it clear that he blamed me, too." She looked at him through eyes glazed with liquor and tears. "And I did nothing to defend you."

"There was nothing you could do," he said thickly. "Please, do not blame yourself."

"It is all my fault. You and your father . . . Lionel . . ." She did not continue, wringing her hands, choking back fresh sobs.

Garrick did not move. "Nothing was your fault. Let me see you up to your rooms," he said desperately.

"Your father, not a day goes by that he does not mention Lionel and you," she cried, as desperate as he.

Garrick stood, feeling his soul beginning to unravel. "Lionel is dead. We must bury him, Mother. The time has come!"

"How can I?" she cried. "How can I bury him when he is gone? Dead, certainly, but vanished without a trace, for all these years. Yet still he haunts us, you, your father, me, every day of our lives!"

He knelt before her, took her hands in his. "We must bury him now. There is no other choice, if we all wish to remain sane."

He had not wanted the evening to come to this.

To have old wounds torn open, fresh blood spilled.

"I have never forgiven myself," Eleanor cried. "You boys were out there on the heath because of your father. Why did I let you go? I should have insisted you stay inside in such inclement weather!" she cried. "But I could not speak up, oh no! As usual! I failed in my duty, I failed my sons."

And Garrick was overwhelmed by his mother's guilt and his own guilt and the past, which refused to die.

Chapter Five

She was shaking like a leaf. Garrick was disgusted.

The evening of his engagement party had finally come. Garrick and his fiancée stood at the head of the receiving line, her parents queued up after them, followed by the earl and the countess of Stanhope. The guests had begun arriving some time ago, and it would take a full hour, if not more, to receive all six hundred of them.

The evening, he knew, would be endless.

Susan continued to tremble, barely able to smile or murmur, "Good evening," and, "Thank you," to each of the guests. In that way, Garrick supposed, they made a perfect pair. He did not wish to smile, made no attempt to do so, and barely muttered the appropriate pleasantries to those passing by.

A man bowed to Susan and then to Garrick. His smile was wide and patently false as he wished them well. Garrick nodded, hardly hearing him. Two ladies next in line, resplendently dressed in taffeta evening gowns, were whispering rapidly behind raised silk fans, their gazes upon Garrick.

He strained to hear what they were saying, thought he heard, ". . . his brother . . . fourteen years ago . . . the earldom." He also thought they might have said, ". . . savage . . . that sugar island . . ." but he could not be sure. His cheeks burned.

It had been like this ever since the first guests had begun to arrive. Whispers and stares from afar, and then, when face-to-face, false smiles, false platitudes, false pleasantries and false congratulations.

He hated them all. He wished desperately to be anywhere but at the Laytons', the guest of honor, his mousy bride-to-be at his side.

Garrick glared at the smiling elderly woman who was saying, "And we have so looked forward to seeing you again, after all these years—" Her expression changed to one of severe shock, and she was so distressed by his expression that that she turned completely around, as if to escape him. Instead of continuing on to greet Sir John and Lady Layton, she crashed into the oncoming guests.

He did not care. They all despised him, and he despised them. He had known it would be this way when he finally went out into society. But in this case, he had not had a choice. His father had seen to that. And the earl expected him to have honor?

Then he felt her gaze and saw the countess of Ashburn regarding him as she moved toward him on the line. He stiffened, the sight of her an actual physical jolt. An instant later he realized he was staring, far too avidly. But she had lowered her eyes. A pink flush colored her cheeks.

He did not hear a single thing the next two guests said to him and Susan, had no idea even if he did reply.

"My lord," Olivia said with a curtsy. "Miss Layton." She straightened and glanced up, and their gazes locked.

"Lady Ashburn," he heard himself say. He was at a loss. "Thank you for coming."

She hesitated, her pale gray gaze searching. "I could not miss such an eagerly anticipated event."

He wondered if she had changed her mind. Would she, if pressed, consent to an affair? She was trembling, and in spite of the fear of him she had confessed to upon their single earlier meeting, he refused to believe that she thought him a murderer. He refused to believe that she could be fond of Arlen—that she would deny herself and remain faithful to him.

"Susan, you have never been lovelier," Olivia was saying, jerking him out of his thoughts. He glanced at his fiancée and felt nothing but disgust. Her eyes had filled with tears.

"Th-thank you," she sniffed. "M-my lady, maybe we can speak later, pri-privately?" There was desperation in her tone.

But Garrick was not surprised. She remained terrified of him. His jaw flexed. His bride-to-be was about to have a fit, and he was not going to coddle her.

"Of course, Susan," Olivia said, her tone warm and reassuring. She laid one gloved palm upon Susan's clasped hands and smiled at her. How obvious it was that she was attempting to give her courage and strength. Garrick thought it impossible.

"And you, I do hope, shall save me a single dance?" Garrick interrupted them.

Her pale eyes flew to his, filled with surprise. Her color heightened. He knew she could not refuse. To do so would cause raised eyebrows—and the Laytons were listening to their every word, as were the next guests in the receiving line.

"Of . . . course," she whispered, and tearing her gaze from his, she hurried away to greet Sir John and his wife.

He stared after her, not caring who should see, imagining her in his arms—but not upon the dance floor. He did not know why he wanted her so badly, but he was not interested in questioning himself. She felt it, too, he had no doubt, and in the end would submit to passion.

"My lord, we meet again, after so many years," a familiar voice drawled.

Garrick tore his gaze from Olivia in her silver gown—and faced her husband, Arlen Grey.

Grey bowed.

Garrick bowed. His insides had curdled with the sheer magnitude of his loathing for the man. And it had never been this strong before—in spite of their history of shared animosity. He glanced toward Olivia and saw her regarding them openly.

Garrick turned back to her husband and became aware of Arlen's sister standing beside him, smiling at him as she coolly fluttered a lacquered fan. Elizabeth, he saw, had not changed either in the eleven years that had passed since he had last seen her. She remained the too beautiful queen of ice and desire.

"Lord Ashburn, what a pleasure," he mocked. "I take it you have come to wish me well on the eve of my wedding?" They both knew Arlen's only wish was to speed him to his grave.

And Arlen smiled so widely, his face appeared in jeopardy of cracking. "Of course," he said as sarcastically. "Would I wish you anything else?" He suddenly reached for Elizabeth. "You do recall my beautiful and unforgettable sister? Now the marchioness of Houghton?"

"Madam." Garrick bowed over her hand, which she had extended, but he refused to lift it. He would prefer to burn in hell, without question. "Somehow, I did not think to find you here tonight, celebrating my betrothal."

Elizabeth smiled, but her eyes were ice. And she laughed coolly. "As if I would miss this event, dear Caedmon. Why, I have already chosen your wedding present."

"Such haste," he remonstrated wryly. "And where is your husband? Surely he dotes upon you and attends you constantly?"

"My darling Lord Caedmon, how correct you are. The marquis is my heart's very desire, as I am his. He will arrive, I imagine, at any moment."

"I am surprised he does not accompany you and your brother," Garrick said, staring with an unpleasant smile, a hidden meaning he knew she understood behind his words. Her decolletage exposed most of her small alabaster breasts. It was obvious to him that she had not changed at all in the past decade.

"Wentworth allows me all of my outside interests," Elizabeth said, fluttering her fan and her lashes at the same time. She laughed again.

"I am sure that he does," Garrick said, quite certain what those outside interests were.

Grey took Elizabeth's arm firmly. "You shall meet the marquis in no time at all." He was glaring. "Come, Elizabeth."

But Elizabeth did not move, her fan now moving with smoldering sensuality. Her eyes lifted and held his. "It has been a very long time, my lord, has it not?"

"I do not recall," he lied.

The languid look left her eyes, which instantly hardened. "It has been eleven years since we last saw one another, precisely," she almost snapped.

"Frankly," he said, aware that many eyes were now trained upon them, including Olivia's, "I had completely forgotten." He suddenly wondered if Olivia had heard all the rumors. He turned to look at her, but she was ignoring him now, engaged in conversation with a lady he did not recognize.

Elizabeth was smiling again. She faced Susan, her fan moving ever so slightly and very sensually. "My dear Miss Layton," she said, eyes gleaming. "How lucky you are. My congratulations and good wishes." Her smile widened. "To think that His Lordship returned from that savage little sugar island after all these years—in order to marry you. How ecstatic you must be, Miss Layton!" She laughed. "How flattered! How awed! How enamored!"

Susan's face crumpled. Garrick took one look at her and thought, If she cries now, in front of these two, not to mention six hundred guests, I am walking out on them all, my debts be damned.

And almost miraculously, Olivia appeared on Susan's other side. "Susan is extremely fatigued from all of the excitement. I do think she must retire for a few moments," she said gracefully.

"Olivia!" Elizabeth gasped with mockery. "You are still here? By now, I thought you would have fled home to the country. What a surprise. What could be keeping you in town?"

Garrick knew he was staring; every time they were in the same room he could not tear his gaze away, and something protective welled up in him, a feeling he had never in his life expected to have, not for anyone or anything, not since Lionel's death. He wanted to step between the marchioness and Olivia, but before he could do so, Olivia had turned to face her.

"What is keeping me in town is a very pleasant visit with the Laytons," she said quietly.

"So the country madam is now fond of city life?" Elizabeth was mocking.

Olivia did not bother to answer. "Come, dear," she said softly to Susan. "My lord?" she queried.

He applauded Olivia for ignoring her sister-in-law, not at all surprised that Elizabeth should dislike Olivia so obviously. He did find it interesting, though, that she did not look at her husband, not even once. Arlen, he saw, regarded Olivia with cool disdain and vast impatience.

"I do not mind," he returned, acutely aware of her proximity. "In fact"—he smiled, unaware that it was his first real smile of the day—"I insist."

And she smiled back at him, then took Susan by the hand and led her away.

She did not want to feel compassion. Not for Garrick De Vere. She did not want to feel anything for him at all; she wanted, desperately, to think of him as she would any casual acquaintance or, better still, a stranger. But the gossip was horrendous. Olivia heard the whispers about his shadowy past in every salon. No one had come to the Laytons tonight to congratulate him upon his good fortune. They had come to get a good look at him, to see if he had truly become a West Indies savage, and to decide if he had really murdered his brother in order to gain both a title and a fortune.

Another two hours had passed. Susan had returned to the receiving line after a brief bout of tears in the privacy of an upstairs bedchamber, where Olivia had comforted her and insisted, strongly, that De Vere was not a beast. But Susan was discomfited and stubbornly determined to believe the worst. "People are talking about his having murdered his brother, I have heard them whispering while

waiting on the queue, over and over again," she had
wailed. "No one has forgotten anything. Now I am involved in a scandal that should have died years ago!"

Olivia sighed, standing alone by one wall in the vast
ballroom, where many couples were dancing; hundreds of
other guests congregated on the perimeter of the room,
chatting and laughing as they sipped champagne and ratafia.
Earlier she had seen stunning buffets laid out in the dining
room, where other guests lingered and mingled, and the
game room and library were crowded, too. Olivia had chosen to remain in the ballroom, however, a distinct wall-
flower, because she wanted to keep an eye upon Susan.

But it was no longer necessary. Susan stood across the
way with her parents, chatting with half a dozen guests.
She was actually smiling and enjoying herself. But the reason for her improved mood was clear. De Vere stood some
feet apart from them, clearly keeping himself at a distance,
his hands in the pockets of his breeches, obviously bored
and disinterested in the fête and his fiancée. Against her
wishes, Olivia's heart went out to him. How alone he
seemed. How alone and how lonely.

She realized reluctantly that he and she had more in common than not. Too well, she knew what the stares and whispers were like. The pointed fingers, the nasty comments,
the snickers and being called names.

She did not want to remember her own childhood, just
as she did not want to see through the facade of boredom
and disinterest De Vere assumed. He was hurt. As she had
been hurt.

He had suddenly turned his back on the Laytons. Olivia
shrank against the wall, not wanting him to see her. As
there were probably three or four hundred guests in the
ballroom, she did not think hiding from his view an impossible task, even in the silver gown she wore. But, to her
amazement, before he turned to leave the room, he gave
her a direct glance. He had known precisely where she was
all this time. Had he been aware of her watching him, too?

He left, striding up the short set of steps leading into the
hallway. Olivia's heart beat hard.

Do not follow him, she told herself. Do not get any more involved than you already are!

But there was no denying that he was a compelling man. She had never been acquainted until now with a man even remotely like him. She did not know why he fascinated her, why even now she wished to go after him and speak with him. She reminded herself that he was marrying Susan, her new, sweet, young friend.

She must return to the sanctuary of Ashburnham. Arlen would probably be thrilled to have her leave town.

Her mind was made up. It was the only sane thing to do. She felt a distinct sense of relief—she would leave the city tomorrow. She also felt a distinct sense of loss, which was absurd.

Olivia closed her eyes, hoping to regain her wits and composure. When she opened them she saw a vaguely familiar older couple not far from where she stood, and she froze.

Her heart beat hard, wildly.

She clutched the folds of her gown, telling herself that it was not the earl and the countess of Oldham whom she now stared at—that the couple were not her father and mother. It had been nine years. She could be mistaking them. Olivia was trembling.

But he was tall and thin as he had always been, clad now in an embroidered velvet frock coat and sateen breeches, and she had always been short and stout and was now, nine years later, quite plump. Dear God, it was the earl and his wife, and they had yet to see her. The earl was conversing with some younger macaroni, her mother listening with a barely veiled look of boredom. Her heart continued to drum. She was paralyzed.

Then she lifted her skirts and moved purposefully forward, steeling herself for she knew not what. The countess saw her first. Her eyes widened, her rouged mouth opened and formed an O. Then the earl turned, saw her, and stared. He had paled, and both bushy gray brows were raised.

Olivia pasted a smile on her face and curtsied. "Father. Mother. What a pleasant surprise."

Her parents regarded her as if she were an absolute stranger. An endless moment passed. Clearly they were so stunned by her presence that all words of greeting failed them. Olivia said, far too swiftly, "It is I, Olivia."

"Well," the earl said, strained. He coughed. "How do. I thought you kept yourself in the country." And he drained his champagne.

Olivia looked from his dark eyes, which were avoiding hers, to her mother's equally dark but impenetrable gaze and felt all of the ancient hurt again—she was reduced, in that loveless moment, to being a child of six or seven years old. "Usually I do," she said huskily, "but I am a friend of the Laytons'."

"How odd," the countess said. "Sir John hardly has a reputable friend in the ton, but then, he was a brewer, was he not?" She sniffed disdainfully. "We, of course, have come only because of Stanhope." She stared. "But then, you were always an odd one, befriending beggars and strays, wandering about with your solitary ways, were you not?"

Olivia opened her fan and used it to cool her feverish cheeks. "Yes, Mother, I was always odd." She knew what her mother truly referred to was her gift of sight.

"We have seen Arlen, you know. But then, we see him about from time to time, as he is usually in town," she continued. "He never mentions you or the girl."

Her fan moved more swiftly, but the cool air caressing her face did not help. "The girl," she said somewhat woodenly. "Your granddaughter. Her name is Hannah."

"Oh, really?" The countess of Oldham shrugged. "I suppose you should bring her to Oldham House sometime for a visit."

"Yes," Olivia said, "I will." Her smile felt like it would crack at any moment. Her words were a lie. The pounding of her heart had become deafening in her own ears.

"Well," the earl said, and he coughed. He continued to avoid looking at her, his eyes darting about. "We must mingle, you know. Many friends here and such." He nodded curtly and turned to go, his wife with him.

Tears filled Olivia's eyes, and she hated herself for being such a fool. "She is like me, you know," she said to their backs, far too loudly.

They froze.

"Odd," she said. "She is odd like me."

The countess shot her a wide-eyed, hateful look over her shoulder, and the next thing Olivia knew, they were both hurrying away, as fast as their legs would carry them, into the crowd. It swallowed them up.

Olivia closed her fan and used two fingertips to brush her eyes, regretting now that she had approached her parents, and even more regretting that last foolish outburst. But she was undone. Once again, her parents had managed to fling daggers into her heart. She turned, knowing she must have fresh air or succumb to the vapors.

A hand caught her by the arm, halting her in her tracks. "But we have yet to chat, Olivia," a familiar, too silky voice said.

Olivia faced Elizabeth. "You startled me," she said, hoping she was not flushed and teary-eyed.

"Indeed I did. You were engrossed." Elizabeth's smile was pleasant, her gaze fixed on Olivia. "Was that not the earl of Oldham and his wife?"

Olivia knew her color increased. "Yes." Speech eluded her.

"Hmm. How long has it been since you have seen them?" Elizabeth mused.

Olivia regarded her, knowing that Elizabeth knew her parents had practically disowned her upon the eve of her wedding. "It has been some time," she finally said. She turned to leave, but Elizabeth fell into step with her, fluttering her fan.

"So what do you think of the illustrious couple we are honoring this night?" Her tone was amused.

"I hardly know what you expect me to say." Olivia paused beside a pillar, using her own fan to shield her expression from her sister-in-law.

Elizabeth shrugged far too gracefully. "Miss Layton is a bore. How long will she amuse a man like Caedmon?"

"I have no idea," Olivia said far too stiffly. "And marriages are hardly made for the sake of entertainment."

"Really?" Elizabeth's slashing black brows lifted. "A marriage can be very entertaining, you know. Oh, I beg your pardon. You would not know—being as you seclude yourself in the country."

Olivia did not know what Elizabeth wanted, but she sensed a deadly barb was to come. "I must excuse myself, I am overly fatigued," she said.

"Perhaps ogling Caedmon is tiresome work." Elizabeth laughed, halting Olivia in her tracks.

Olivia faced her, dread cresting within her. "I fail to find any humor in your statement," she said, feeling ill. She had been ogling De Vere. And the last person she wished to notice her insane attraction for the man was the marchioness of Houghton.

Elizabeth laughed and laid a delicate palm on Olivia's arm. "There's no need to deny it. Most women find him quite fascinating. I would imagine more so now than ever. I mean, after all, how many men are there in England with his tainted past, his dark looks, and his future fortune and title?"

Olivia was very uncomfortable. "I was not staring at Caedmon," she said.

"I think it is his past which most intrigues the ladies, don't you?" Elizabeth continued as if she had not heard. "I had met his brother, you know. We were all children at the time. He was blond and charming, very handsome, very kind. As different from Garrick De Vere as is possible."

"I doubt he murdered his brother," Olivia said with a flash of anger. "In fact, I am sure there is no truth at all to the rumors!"

Elizabeth stared. "My, how you defend him. Do you know him well?"

"I know him not at all."

"But you are acquainted with him. Clearly."

Olivia fumbled for composure. What was Elizabeth's meaning? "I am Susan's friend. I am the Laytons' houseguest. I met him when he called. You seem to be the one fascinated by him.''

"Me? I do not think so, my dear. My fascination with Caedmon ended many years ago—eleven, to be exact.''

Olivia wanted to know exactly what that meant and waited for Elizabeth to continue, finding it difficult to breathe.

Elizabeth gave her a coy smile. "He is a great lover, you know.''

Olivia stared, the dread welling, recalling the exchange she had witnessed earlier but not overheard, an exchange where both Elizabeth and De Vere had in turn evinced undisguised hostility toward one another. She wanted to tell Elizabeth that she did not care. She told herself to turn and leave immediately and not listen to another word. But she said instead, "What do you mean?''

"Well''—Elizabeth moistened her lips, raised her face, and leaned close to Olivia—"I mean exactly what I said. He is a lover *extraordinaire*.''

Jealousy, pure and simple, overwhelmed Olivia. But she told herself that Elizabeth was relaying pure gossip, nothing more. She tried to smile, knew it was sickly, and gave it up. "I am not interested in speculation and rumor, Elizabeth.''

Elizabeth laughed. The sound was loud, but as beautiful as the woman herself. "Who said anything about speculation or rumor? I speak the truth. Why, did you not know? My dear sister, he was my very first *affaire de coeur*.''

Olivia stared in sheer despair, wanting to clap her hands over her ears, knowing what was to come.

Elizabeth leaned closer. "We were lovers,'' she said succinctly. *"Lovers.''*

And she smiled.

CHAPTER SIX

Olivia did not move. But it was not shock that immobilized her, for she had known, hadn't she? Ever since witnessing their hostile exchange earlier that evening. A man and a woman could not hate one another so without having been intimate first. It was a sickening dismay that incapacitated her.

Elizabeth was one of the reigning beauties of the realm. She, Olivia, was truly a country mouse in comparison. De Vere's flirtation with her must have been just that, a simple, careless, meaningless flirtation.

Olivia could see them so clearly entwined in a heated, passionate embrace.

"My, Olivia, whatever is wrong? You have turned so pale. No, actually, you have turned green," Elizabeth said with utterly smug satisfaction.

She was going to be sick. Olivia felt her stomach lurching and turned to flee for the nearest privy. But Elizabeth seized her wrist, detaining her. "He was mad about me, but Arlen would not allow the match, for he was as strange then as he is now."

Olivia blinked at her, controlling her roiling insides with a great effort of will. "Really," she managed.

But Elizabeth was not through. "He ran away to that sugar island to mend his broken heart." She patted Olivia's back. "Chin up, my dear. You are not the first to pine for a man like that. It is quite common, you know, for a wall-flower like yourself to want such a rogue. Caedmon, of course, would never look twice at a woman like you.''

Olivia managed to say breathlessly, ''You are very wrong, I hardly care about him.'' And the enormity of the lie was stupendously obvious to her.

''I wonder what Arlen would think if he knew how in-fatuated you are?'' Elizabeth queried.

Arlen. Cold, cruel, and unpredictable—Olivia began to comprehend the immensity of her dilemma. ''Elizabeth,'' she began, a gasp.

''Don't worry, dear. I would never say a word. Besides, we'both know that if Caedmon knew the truth about you, he would not deign even to dance with you.''

The truth. She was going to be ill. If he knew the truth, he would be repulsed, as Arlen was, as her parents were, as everyone was. . . . Elizabeth continued to smile at her, knowing the truth herself, because there were no secrets between her and her brother.

Olivia tore herself from Elizabeth's grasp and turned away, aware of how rude she was being but unable now even to excuse herself. Blindly she stumbled toward the closest doorway. Elizabeth was going to reveal her dark secret to De Vere. And in that moment Olivia knew she could not bear to have him learn the truth about her.

''Dearest Olivia,'' Elizabeth called after her, laughter tingeing her tone, ''surely you are not in love with him?!''

In the hallway outside the ballroom Olivia spied the open terrace doors. It was hard to breathe: Elizabeth's taunt ech-oed in her mind; the truth echoed in her mind. She needed air, desperately. To her right were gaming rooms filled with gentlemen, to her left a huge salon and the buffets, already crowded with guests. Couples and groups filled the hall-way, but no one paid any attention to Olivia, for few of the guests knew her, as she remained so often secluded in the country. Olivia lifted her skirts and dashed outside.

Numerous guests ambled in the night air, sharing quiet conversation. Olivia raced to a quiet corner, gripped the stone balustrade, and leaned over it, panting hard. The truth.

The truth was that she was ugly and odd, that De Vere was toying with her, and that when Elizabeth told him about her gift, he would scorn her as Arlen had.

The pain was there again, welling up inside of her, choking her. She was sixteen, had been married exactly two months, and she lay naked in her canopied bed beneath the crimson coverings. She was not alone. Arlen crossed her bedroom, donning a dressing gown. Olivia averted her eyes so she would not see his body, relieved that their lovemaking was over. She throbbed, not pleasantly. Her body ached, and she was sore. His passion had been endless. She knew from experience that it would be days before she healed. She had fought to hide her tears when he had been inside of her.

He faced her, belting the silk gown. "Are you all right?"

She forced a smile, for she was well aware of her duty. "Yes," she lied. "I am fine."

He continued to regard her. "I am astute. I know you do not enjoy my attentions. The sooner you take my seed, the sooner we can dispense with these evenings."

Olivia felt hope. She sat up, clutching the covers to her neck. "Arlen," she whispered, flushing now with happiness and excitement, "I am with child."

His eyes widened. "What! And you have not told me?"

She felt her color increase. "I only just realized," she whispered.

But he paced forward, towering over her. "It is too soon for you to know," he exclaimed. "You have been my bride for exactly two months." His eyes darkened. "Unless you were already with child when you came to my bed—but I know a frightened virgin when I have one."

Olivia realized her mistake, and her happiness began to vanish. Through it, she had a flashing premonition that her marriage was about to change forever, but she ignored it. "Arlen. You do not understand."

"Perhaps you lie to spare yourself my attentions," he said coldly, in a tone she had heard often enough, but mostly with the servants.

She shook her head. "I just know," she said softly. "I

had a dream. We are to have a daughter—soon. By the year's end.'' And she felt the joy again, and so desperately wanted to share it with this stranger who was her husband. Then, perhaps, he would love her.

''A dream!'' he scoffed, turning away.

''No! You do not understand,'' Olivia had cried, and when he had faced her again, she had begun to explain how she could see the future, how she had been given this gift and had been aware of it since she was a child. Arlen had stared and stared, his eyes wide, with disgust at first, but then she had seen the fear and growing revulsion. Too late, she had realized the immensity of her mistake, a confession that should never have been. When her pregnancy was confirmed, and then later, when the child had been born, the cycle had become complete. The anger had turned to loathing, and there was revulsion, so much revulsion, and always, beneath the surface, there was fear.

''What else do you see!'' he would demand upon occasion, attempting to force her to use her sight for his own ends. But sometimes, when he yanked upon her hair and forced her head backward, brutalizing her so she would give him the answers he sought, she saw the fear and wondered what he was hiding.

The truth. The truth was that she was different from everyone else, and no amount of wishing would ever change it, and that the gift was, at times, a curse. And soon De Vere would know. Olivia had no doubt.

She lost the last of her control and retched over the stone balustrade, but her heaves were mostly dry. She clawed the pale gray stone, gulping air, until her stomach finally began to settle. Hannah had the gift, too. It was Olivia's greatest fear that not just Arlen but the entire world would learn of it one day, and she would suffer loneliness and scorn her entire life, as Olivia had.

It was her greatest fear that mother and daughter would share the same destiny.

Olivia closed her eyes, trembling, but not with cold. It was a pleasant summer night, she did not need a wrap, and the moon was a bright sliver in the sky, surrounded by thousands of winking stars. She must regain her composure. She straightened and glanced around, but no one was paying any attention, and for that she was relieved. There was a water fountain in the center of the terrace, and she went to it and used her handkerchief to clean her face and take a few sips of water. She was calmer, but a tension continued to afflict her.

She was grim. The evening had turned into a disaster for her personally, but she knew better than to let Elizabeth fling her barbs so accurately. She must never allow her defenses to be down again that way.

One thing was clear, though. Her interest in De Vere was obvious, and she must not cause any more tongues to wag.

She had Hannah to think about. Hannah to protect. Nothing else mattered, certainly not her fascination for a total stranger.

Olivia realized now that she stood alone by the fountain in the center of the terrace and that several gentlemen were eyeing her. She had no desire to return to the party inside the house or to be accosted by amorous suitors, so she walked swiftly down the brick steps to the lawn, leaving behind the terrace and house. A feeling of relief settled over her. There was no denying it. She found no charm in the social whirl; town held no allure for her.

Olivia strolled over to a small stagnant pond rimmed with glistening white stones and topped with floating water lilies. The pounding in her temples, which she had lived with all evening, had decreased. She settled herself on a small stone bench mostly concealed by high hedges, and carefully arranged her silver brocade skirts, despising the wide panniers she wore. She wondered if she could stay outside until the party was over.

It was an absurd thought. It was not even midnight. Supper had not been served yet, and a breakfast would later follow. An event like this would go until four in the morning, at least.

She actually entertained the thought of staying outside for the rest of the evening or else stealing into the house and joining Hannah upstairs in her bed.

A long, dark shadow fell across her, cast by the moon and the stars.

Olivia tensed, the hair on her nape and arms standing upright, while her heart plummeted with the speed of a boulder thrown off a cliff, knowing it was him even before he moved directly in front of her.

De Vere stared down at her.

Olivia stared up and rose slowly to her feet.

"You are missing the soirée," he said wryly.

She had to wet her lips in order to speak. "I am not inclined toward parties." Her pulse was racing wildly.

"How odd. Every woman I have ever met is inclined toward parties."

She hesitated. "I am different."

His gaze held hers. "Yes. You are very different . . . Olivia." There was not even a hint of mockery in his words.

She froze. His intimate form of address sent warning bells off inside her mind. "I must go," she cried.

But he stepped in front of her so she had nowhere to go. "Are you ill?" he asked.

Surely he had not been spying upon her earlier. "No. Not at all. I am merely . . . fatigued." It was hardly a lie.

He stared at her, searching her face, and for an instant Olivia was certain he had seen her retching over the stone railing. "Are you cold?" he asked, his tone suddenly gentle.

"No," she said, now wary. "My lord, it is an exceedingly pleasant night."

"That is too bad," he said, again wry, "or I might wrap my frock coat around you."

She did not move. The warnings again filled her mind. And for one instant the night became absolutely still around them—even the cicadas ceased their midnight song—and then, in the next instant, Olivia's heart was thundering in her ears, its beat deafening.

He smiled at her.

It was taut and rigid, and Olivia did not, could not, smile back. She knew she must leave the lawns.

"Why are you so kind to Miss Layton?"

The question took her by surprise, but then, everything about him was unpredictable. She hesitated. "I am a woman of compassion."

"That is obvious."

She stared up at him, wondering if she had heard admiration in his tone. "I must go in."

"You are afraid of me."

Her feet slowed. She had taken only two steps back toward the house. "And why would I be afraid of you, my lord?" she asked, trying to sound confident, thinking that she failed. Her tone was so utterly breathless in her own ears.

He stared. "Clearly you have heard all of the gossip. If you did not hear it years ago, you have heard it all tonight."

Her pulse continued to drum, thickly. "I do not attend gossips, my lord."

"I did not, in truth, think so. For I have reflected upon our last encounter, upon you." He let his words hang.

She could only gape. He had been thinking about her— as she had been thinking about him? "I truly must go. I must sit down for a while."

His teeth flashed, but briefly. "The bench is right here. No. You are afraid, Olivia, you are afraid of me, and it has nothing to do with ancient rumors. And we both know why, do we not?" he said softly—much too softly for comfort.

Olivia had not moved, in spite of her better intentions. She could not seem to walk away. Her gaze had found his mouth, which was full and intriguing.

"You are beautiful," he whispered.

No man had ever told her that she was beautiful before. His words uplifted her heart, against her better judgment. She searched his face, wishing he meant it, unsure if he did. It felt as if he did, but she could not help being reminded of Elizabeth then. Yet his tone had been thick with something she was not familiar with, something she knew intuitively to be desire. Her body had become taut. Abruptly Olivia walked away from him.

"Elizabeth is beautiful," she said, head down, her

cheeks unusually warm. "I am common." Her footsteps increased in pace.

He followed, falling into step beside her. "You are the least common woman I have ever met, and there is far more to beauty than what meets the eye. Except when one is fifteen years old." Again, he was wry. "Do not go," he said, his hip brushing her skirts. "Do not run away. Do not be afraid. Not of me."

She halted and turned, clasping her hands in a vain attempt to still their trembling. "Is this a coincidence?" she demanded, this time testing him.

But again, she did not have to complete her thoughts for him to understand her. "No. I followed you outside." Their gazes locked.

She had assumed as much. She swallowed, drier than before, and far too acutely aware of the man standing inches away from her. Moonlight illuminated his face, highlighting his striking cheekbones and straight nose. She found him devastatingly attractive, but any woman would.

"Why were you ill?" he asked abruptly.

"I . . . I was upset."

"Why?"

She had averted her eyes, but now she met his unwavering regard. The urge to confide in him was overwhelming, but she must not give in to it. "I do not like London, or parties like this."

"*Moi aussi,*" he said with a small smile. "And perhaps your husband also falls in that category?"

She wet her lips. "They will talk about us. This is not a good idea, for us to linger here in view of all those upon the terrace."

He stared grimly. "I am used to it. But of course, you wish no such thing upon yourself." Then he gripped her arm, his teeth startlingly bright in the darkness. "The bench is not in view of the terrace," he said quietly.

She inhaled as he guided her back to the stone bench, closing her eyes, torn and confused as never before. She wanted to tell him that she, too, was accustomed to whispers and stares, she wanted to reach out and touch him, comfort him. But she did not dare. She could imagine far too well the strength of his arm, the warmth of his skin, the feel of muscle, flesh, and bone. Oh, God. She did not just want to comfort him. She wanted his kiss. Could even imagine what his lips tasted like.

What was wrong with her! Arlen might loathe her, but he would never condone her having an affair, and if he threw her out of his house, he would separate her from Hannah. Not because he loved his daughter, but because he was cruel and perverse and would wish only to hurt and punish his wife.

"My lord, we must not do this," she said huskily.

Manicured hedges blocked their view of the terrace and house now as they stood by the bench. His hands settled on her shoulders, his grip firm and uncompromising. There was a steely look in his eyes. "We must not do what, Olivia?" His tone was raw silk.

"We must not be here, together, alone," she said, faltering. His stare was so intense, it was mesmerizing.

He began to smile. "I beg to disagree," he said very softly.

Before Olivia could reply, his lips were on her throat, nibbling the extremely sensitive skin there. She could not form a single word, as wet heat flooded over her.

There was laughter in his tone. "Olivia? What is it you wish to say?"

His wickedly skilled mouth was moving to her ear. Chills swept over every inch of her body as she opened her mouth to reply—and tell him to stop. But then his tongue slid into her ear.

All words failed her.

His tongue began a rhythmic penetration. Hard and strong, again and again. It was shocking. It could make her think of, and want, only one thing. There was no mistaking what he was doing, what he was suggesting. Her knees buckled.

"Olivia," he whispered, finally licking her lobe, "what is it?"

"We must," she finally began, but then he kissed her

cheek, *hard*. It was almost a bite, and the raw, suddenly unleashed power of it made her legs give way—she clung to his arms now to stand upright. And his arms were as hard as boulders, the muscles there as big.

He kissed her jaw the same way, with frightening intensity, almost but not quite hurting her, and then he laughed like the devil and slid his tongue over her lips, just briefly slipping the tip between them. And his mouth was on her ear again. "This is meant to be, Olivia," he said as he licked and sucked her ear. "You and I, together, this way."

She could not even whisper *no*. Her mind was dazed, her body racked with a feverish longing, which she now understood. She had hated Arlen's passion. But she wanted this man in her bed. She wanted his body on top of hers, his manhood inside of her, and she wanted it now.

Olivia did not recognize herself.

Soft whimpers seemed to be escaping her throat.

He thrust his tongue into her ear again and again and again. The way he would, she knew, thrust himself inside of her—soon. Olivia felt faint. Dizzy. Longing overcame her, she could not think. "God," she heard herself cry. "Oh, God!"

His arms were around her, crushing her. "God what?" he demanded.

"Please," she cried, looking up at him. And to her amazement, she nipped his jaw, the demand female and timeless.

He caught her face in his huge, powerful hands and seized her mouth with his. He did not hold back. His mouth opened hers, his tongue thrust inside, strong and hard, his teeth grated on her own. Their mouths ground, melded. Olivia found herself kissing him back frantically, found her striking at his tongue with her own.

"I want you," he said, and Olivia found herself on the bench as he continued to kiss her. "I want you, now," he rasped, and he bit her neck.

She realized she was tearing at his hair—his queue having long since come undone. She could not say yes. But neither could she say no, and Olivia nipped his jaw, again and again, insisting on what should never be. Then their mouths came together again, hot and hard, savagely.

He was on his knees, fumbling with her skirts. "I hate hoops," he said between kisses that began at her lips and ended at her silk-clad breasts.

"We shouldn't," Olivia panted, but he cut her off. His mouth took hers again in another thrusting kiss, while his palm slid up beneath her petticoat on her bare inner thighs. Olivia cried out. His fingers had halted just inches from her sex.

"Tell me you will deny us," he demanded, palming her hard.

The breath escaped her; she could not speak if her life depended on it. No one had ever touched her this way before, and she did not want him to stop—when she damn well knew the consequences. She moaned.

"Tell me," he said more gently, licking her neck, her collarbone, and finally, the flesh just above the low neckline of her gown. "You are wet, Olivia," he whispered, "and we both know why." He was stroking her now, uncovering every fold.

"Please," Olivia heard herself cry. "Oh, please, Garrick."

His fingers slid over her, between lush folds, and stroked up against the apex until Olivia was shaking uncontrollably, whimpering far too loudly, yet incapable of restraint—until she knew she would soon die. She gasped, panted, opened her eyes and saw the star-filled sky.

"Do you want me?" he said.

"Yes," she whispered, and it was close to a sob.

"I want you. I want you so badly I do not know how I can wait."

Olivia knew she could not wait, either. "De Vere," she cried.

"Die for me, Olivia," he commanded, his fingers rubbing now.

But Olivia really did not hear him. An intense pressure the likes of which she had never felt before was building inside of her, and she gasped, her entire body stiffening.

For one blazing instant she met his eyes. He was watching her, she realized, but she was on the edge of a precipice. And then it happened: she no longer saw De Vere, as an explosion racked her body. Olivia cried out.

The sound was smothered by his lips. When she floated ever so gently back to reality, the brilliant bursting stars fading from her mind, she realized that he held her in a grip of iron. She blinked, trembling, her thoughts becoming coherent again. But before she could truly comprehend what had just happened, he reclaimed her mouth. It was another endless and demanding kiss.

De Vere broke it off. He suddenly wrapped his arms around her tightly, burying his face between her neck and shoulder, his entire body taut. Olivia blinked, found herself gazing up at the stars, her breasts crushed against his chest. She had never been this relaxed in her entire life and was acutely aware of his tension. She could feel his thundering heartbeat against her breasts.

Her mind, unfortunately, had begun to function once more.

This should not have happened. Whatever was she thinking of? But that was just it: she had not been thinking. He had seduced her—and she had been more than willing! She must leave the pond, leave the gardens, leave him before they were seen together like this. Dear God. If Arlen ever learned what had happened this night, her entire life would be in jeopardy. In that single instant Olivia knew it with the certainty given her by her gift of sight—and she was terrified.

But as he held her, she found her hands in his long dark hair, and she felt something far greater than desire, something far more profound—and far more dangerous. She refused then to entertain any other emotions—she must not. But for one last moment she would savor his hard, trembling body as he held her, determined that it be for the very last time.

Desire. She had not known that it was like this.

Desire, but nothing more. For it must never be anything more.

Suddenly he set her aside, his gaze heated, his jaw flexed so hard it looked painful. "When?" he demanded. "When can we rendezvous?"

Olivia, no longer breathless but overcome now by sorrow, stood up. It was a moment before she could speak, and when she did, she was thinking about so many people—De Vere, his fiancée, Arlen, Elizabeth, and her own precious daughter. "We must not rendezvous."

He stood and caught her arm. "Do not play the ingenue with me." He was at once incredulous and angry. There was a warning in his tone. "We are both adults, Olivia. I know you are not fond of your husband. Surely you do not intend to deny us now. After this night." His eyes blazed.

She shook her head. "This is insane, this is a mistake."

"God damn it!" he shouted. Suddenly he towered over her. "I will not remain long in this country, Lady Ashburn, of that I can assure you. I suggest we take what little time the fates are giving us."

He was leaving? She was aghast—when she should be thrilled. "The fates?" Olivia struggled to think. "You are betrothed to my dear friend and I . . ." She stopped. And what? Oh, God. She had never met anyone like him before, had never been touched or held or kissed with such consuming passion, and she wanted him—dear God, she did—and if she dared to admit it, she had other, deeper feelings for him. It did not matter that she hardly knew him, for they were so alike, two lost, scorned, and deeply scarred souls. And Arlen had his affairs, as most married men and women did. But other wives did not have a blind daughter to protect.

"What, Olivia? What is it that you wish to say? What excuse do you wish to make? Or do you have a habit of teasing men? Perhaps it amuses you?" He was cool.

She gasped. "You know that is not true!"

"Then return to Ashburnham tomorrow. I will meet you there." He smiled slightly, his jaw flexed, the muscles twitching.

Olivia inhaled. His words—a command and a challenge—echoed inside her mind. She could not agree, of course she could not. Her instincts, her morals, her gift, told her that. But neither could she form a denial. No negative escaped her lips.

She was trapped.

He stared at her, his expression changing to one of impatience. "Your husband despises you. He keeps a mistress. You seclude yourself in the country, but you are young and beautiful and passionate. There is no dilemma here. Meet me at Ashburnham."

The tears gathered, burning her eyes. "I cannot."

H was disbelieving. "You will remain faithful to him? *Why?*"

"It is complicated," she whispered. How she wanted to tell him about Hannah. But then he would learn about her as well, and he must never know either secret.

"Really?" he mocked. "A man and a woman who desire one another is hardly complicated. In fact, it is as simple as life can be."

"How sordid you make this seem," Olivia whispered, hurt.

"How innocent you now seem," he returned. "Innocent and naive."

Olivia decided not to reply, but in that instant she realized that she was very inexperienced, in spite of having an eight-year-old daughter. She lifted her chin. "I would like to go inside," she said with dignity. "Before we are seen together like this."

He seized her arm, making it impossible for her to leave. "Then the next time we are in the same room, do not lead me astray with those damnable eyes of yours," he cried.

"I do not know what you speak of!" she cried back.

"Every time I walk into the room, you are staring with those silver eyes, and I can read your thoughts. I suggest you consider my proposition. You are not shackled by love, and I hardly marry for that emotion. We can amuse one another, my lady, trust me. I have no doubt." His eyes were frightening in their intensity.

Olivia was taken aback. "Will you release me?" she asked with a calm she did not feel. "I have offered you sympathy and friendship, nothing more. Whatever you think you have seen in my eyes, you are wrong," she said, a blatant lie.

Many emotions crossed his face in rapid succession, among them, Olivia thought, disbelief, renewed anger, and extreme disgust. "I have no need of your pity, Lady Ashburn, and even less need of your friendship." He laughed then. "You were hardly offering me friendship, my dear lady, a few moments ago."

She recalled the extent of her passionate behavior and knew she was turning crimson. "I have no time for amusements, not with you, my lord, or anyone else." She spun on her heel, reeling inwardly from his brutal attack.

He called after her, "That is not the impression I so recently received."

Olivia fled.

Nearly running the earl of Stanhope over in the process.

CHAPTER SEVEN

Garrick stiffened, watching Olivia disengage herself from his father. Gasping, "I am so sorry, my lord," she lifted her wide silver skirts and raced away, but not before he caught another glimpse of her especially pale visage, one strained with emotion. He fervently hoped her eyes did not glisten with tears, and he was already regretting his temper. He watched her fly back up the steps to the terrace, across it, and inside. With great difficulty, Garrick tore his gaze away from the wide-open doors where she had disappeared and met his father's heated regard.

The tension he had been afflicted with all evening increased. The last thing he needed now, after his encounter with Olivia, was a confrontation with Stanhope. He shoved his hands into the pockets of his pale blue coat and sauntered toward his father, determined not to let his own ravaged emotions show. Of course, Stanhope never missed a trick. "Do not tell me this is a coincidence," he drawled, knowing damn well that the earl's appearance outside was anything but that.

Stanhope offered him his snuff box. His expression was not pleasant. There was a light in his eyes Garrick did not like, one that made him even more wary.

"No, thank you," Garrick declined.

"Of course I did not leave the soirée to linger alone in

the dark. I have guests to attend.'' He closed the box after taking a pinch of snuff to one nostril.

Garrick grimaced, refusing to respond to the barely veiled barb that he was delinquent in loitering alone in the park.

''You may do what you wish, Garrick, but there is a time and place for everything, and a rendezvous with Lady Ashburn at your betrothal party is not appropriate.'' The earl was angry. His tone was hard but controlled.

''This was hardly a rendezvous,'' Garrick snapped. ''And I am tired, Father, of being spoken to as if I were a child. Ten long years have passed since I left England.''

''You hardly need remind me of your neglect! But perhaps you should not act like a child, eh, Garrick? You have responsibilities now, to me, to the earldom—to the union we have contracted to. Seducing the lady in question under Sir John's nose is intolerable.'' The earl adjusted his cuffs angrily. ''And do not take me for a fool.''

Garrick laughed. ''Intolerable for whom? It was quite tolerable for me.''

Stanhope ignored that. ''I saw the two of you. Clearly she does not want you, Garrick. Fortunately she is possessed of the common sense her gender so usually lacks. I heard her refuse to meet you. Why press where you are not wanted? Leave her alone. There are many willing women in this town. I can find you what you need if you wish me to.'' And he smiled, as if he and his son were bosom buddies.

Garrick was furious. He did not like being rejected in the first place, but having his father an eyewitness to the event was even worse. ''Do not think to procure for me,'' he flashed. ''And you do not have a clue as to what I need, my lord.''

''You are flesh and blood, a man, I know exactly what you need,'' the earl said with sarcasm. ''And if I saw you and the countess, so did any number of guests. I have no doubt that by the time this fête is over, Sir John will have learned all about your dalliance. Why is your judgment so lacking? Or do you want to annoy me—or even thwart me, now, at the eleventh hour?''

''Father, if I wished to thwart you in your determination to see me wed and bedded with an heir upon the way, I would be on a ship bound for the West Indies right now. You have blackmailed me—or did you forget?'' Garrick moved past his father, but the earl fell into step with him.

''I have not blackmailed you,'' Stanhope said with such utter indignation that it was clear he believed his own words.

Garrick decided to give it up. His father would think what he wished to think—what was convenient and served him the best.

Stanhope smiled as they crossed the lawns, taking Garrick's silence for compliance. ''Good, then that is settled. I trust that you will leave the countess alone, doing what is right and honorable by me and your mother.''

They had reached the terrace. Garrick lowered his voice with an effort, aware that they were being watched by many ladies and gentlemen. ''No,'' he said flatly. ''You cannot trust me to leave the countess alone, I will do exactly as I please.''

He spun on his heel and left.

Olivia continued to tremble as she dashed into the house. Her temples throbbed. She was confused, torn, and pain warred with anger. Garrick De Vere was difficult, he was persistent, and he had just been terribly forthright—and cruel. Was that the kind of man he was, in the end, when thwarted and denied? Vicious and cruel?

Her heart refused to believe it.

Olivia slowed her pace as she entered the dining room, to find guests at the various buffets. She was not hungry. How could she be? She was far too distressed. She would never become his mistress, in spite of the shocking desire he had aroused within her. She fanned herself, aware of her burning cheeks. He must think her a lightskirt, to have behaved in such a fashion . . . and those cries! Her heart thundered. She used her fan more determinedly. She must not think about it, or entertain such desire, not ever again. She must not even allow herself the tremendous compassion she felt for him; it was too dangerous, a connection she did not want, a connection that might lead her elsewhere. And as he had no interest in friendship, why, then that meant there was nothing for them at all.

Which was as it should be. An involvement with him would lead only to disaster. Olivia trusted her inner voice in this instance completely.

Then she recalled his stunning kiss. They were already involved.

And not only were they already involved, she had no doubt he was not about to give up his pursuit of her.

"Olivia! Where have you been?" Susan cried, hurrying over. She left behind two young, smiling fops, both of whom had been fawning over her.

Olivia glanced away, frantically seeking some modicum of composure before facing her young friend—Garrick De Vere's fiancée. Now guilt stabbed her, competing with the shame. She managed a weak smile. "I was taking some air." She must escape this party. She must escape town.

She must escape him.

Susan linked their arms. "A wonderful party, is it not? I am having a wonderful time!" She turned and waved at her two grinning, amiable admirers. "Isn't he handsome? That is Lord Bartholomew. He is the younger son of an earl and has just been commissioned in the army."

"Yes, the party is wonderful, and your young admirer is quite splendid," Olivia said, trying to forget Garrick De Vere, his commanding presence, his hurtful words, his stunning kiss—and her own shocking behavior.

"And *he* has disappeared," Susan said, whispering now. "Isn't that wonderful? I hope he has gone home and left his own guests!"

Olivia regarded her. "Dear, I am happy that you are enjoying your engagement fête," she said in a rush. "It has been a fabulous party. And I have so enjoyed being a guest here these past few days. Susan, I know you will think me awfully remiss, but I so miss the countryside."

Susan blinked—and then her face fell as comprehension set in.

"Dear, surely you would not mind if I returned home tomorrow? I do not feel well in the city, if you must know, and I think that Hannah is terribly homesick," Olivia continued desperately. She had to go home. There, surely she and Hannah could return to their previous peaceful existence, one free of complications. And he would not follow her to the country, expecting her to rendezvous.

That thought was too disturbing to contemplate.

But Susan was dismayed. "Hannah loves London, she told me so—this afternoon Miss Childs took her to a museum. Olivia, are you ill? You seem terribly distraught."

Hannah had gone to a wax museum with Miss Childs and had raved about the trip, Miss Childs having described the sights in intimate detail, while Hannah had explored the figures herself, with her sense of touch and smell. Olivia swallowed. "I am the one who is homesick, my dear, but I am embarrassed to confess as much."

Susan gripped her hands. "But you cannot leave me now! I do so enjoy your company, and there is so much to do to prepare for the wedding, I do not think I could manage without you," she wailed. "And what will I do when he comes calling the next time if you are not present? You know my mother, she never says a word in mixed company. She would be useless!"

"Has a date been set, then?" Olivia asked. Her temples were throbbing again, and she rubbed them tiredly, aware of dismay, another emotion she did not need or want.

"My mother has suggested September the fifteenth." Susan was no longer smiling. "I do not know why we have to rush so."

That was three months away. Olivia did not know what to do.

"You cannot leave me now," Susan said, her voice strong now, as she had taken Olivia's silence for compliance. She smiled. "You have become such a dear friend! And you can chaperone me when he comes to call." Her smile faltered. "Olivia, I cannot be alone with him. Surely you understand that?'' Her tone was desperate. "Dear God, I am trying not to think about it, but in truth, I am still sickened every time I think about actually marrying him.''

Olivia could not smile. Her eyes were wide, her pulse racing anew. Chaperone Susan and the viscount of Caedmon? This was too much to bear. "I fear I must retire,'' she cried. "The events of the evening have quite undone me.''

Susan nodded, her gaze worried, and kissed her cheek. "Do not worry. We shall have a lovely time this summer, you and I.'' And she whirled, hurrying back to her two young men.

Olivia watched her beaming at Lord Bartholomew, closed her eyes briefly, turned to leave—and came face-to-face with the earl of Stanhope.

He was smiling. "Good evening, Lady Ashburn. What a splendid affair.''

Olivia's heart dropped right to her feet with sickening intensity. How much had he seen? How much did he know? She snapped open her fan and used it to cool herself. "Good evening, my lord. Yes, it is a splendid event.''

"I have not had the pleasure of your conversation in many years,'' Stanhope said, his smile remaining in place. "You prefer the country, do you not, Lady Ashburn?''

"Yes, in fact, I do,'' Olivia replied. "You are probably better acquainted with my husband.'' Too late, she wished she had not brought Arlen up.

"Lord Ashburn and I hardly frequent the same circles,'' Stanhope returned evenly, but his gaze was unsettlingly direct. "I prefer to attend White's and Almack's; he prefers the beauty and excitement of the opera and the stage. In fact, I hear he is hardly ever in the country.'' He smiled.

Olivia backed up a step, stunned that Stanhope would make such a veiled reference to her husband's mistress—a beautiful stage actress. Had he been suggesting that Arlen avoided her, Olivia? She managed a rigid smile. "I am well aware that Arlen prefers life here in town to that in the country. For me, it is the countryside that is beautiful and exciting.''

"So then you shall be returning home?" he asked, raising one pale eyebrow.

Olivia stared, reassuring herself that he could not have heard De Vere insisting she return to Ashburnham. "I do not know," she finally said, wishing he would turn and go.

But he did not. "The bride-to-be is quite lovely, do you not agree?" Stanhope continued.

"Oh yes," Olivia managed, her every instinct warning her to flee this man. She felt as if she were being pushed backward into a corner, a trap. "Susan is so lovely."

"My son is a fortunate man," Stanhope said, no longer smiling, staring her directly in the eye.

For one moment, Olivia was still. *He knew.* He had seen it all. Then she began whipping her fan back and forth, feeling as if her smile were made of plaster and about to crack. "He is very fortunate," she said, her tone oddly high to her own ears, "and I do wish them well."

"I am certain you do, Lady Ashburn. Why, a kind, generous, and loyal woman like yourself could do no less than to genuinely bless the match. Of course, as the couple hardly knows one another, there will surely be a few rough patches in the courtship, but they are well suited, the contracts have been signed, the date set, and I am certain both bride and groom can withstand any minor altercations. Do you not agree?"

Olivia was riveted by his piercing blue gaze. Stanhope was warning her not to interfere—and making it clear that the nuptials would transpire no matter what actually happened. He was a very powerful man. There were few peers who outranked Arlen, and even fewer whom Arlen respected and feared—but Stanhope was one of them. "Yes," Olivia finally whispered.

The earl of Stanhope did smile. "I am quite certain I saw your husband in the other room. He was looking for you, you know."

Olivia's heart lurched. Of course, Arlen had not been seeking her. "I shall attend him immediately."

"Undoubtedly he did not think to search for you outside, on the lawns—by the hedges and the bench."

She did not move. She did not even breathe. Stanhope's threat was vividly clear. He knew, and now he held her passionate encounter with his son over her head. He would tell Arlen—if it suited him. And Arlen would punish her—doing God only knew what. "Undoubtedly," she whispered.

His smile widened, and finally he bowed. "It has been a pleasure conversing with you, Lady Ashburn."

Olivia could not reply.

Stanhope left. Olivia remained unmoving, frightened now. Suddenly she needed to be with her daughter—immediately. She would retire and just for a few moments slip into her daughter's bed and hold her. What if Arlen tried to separate her and Hannah? It had always been her greatest fear. Arlen was clever. He knew there was nothing worse he could do to her.

She turned and left the ballroom, hurrying down the hall, ignoring everyone. Then she saw Arlen standing on the threshold of the gaming room with three other gentlemen, and she stumbled, not wanting to approach him in order to go past him. He was smiling and animated, clearly well on the way to becoming disguised. But then he saw her and his expression changed. His smile vanished, his eyes turned cold.

Olivia paled. He was the last person she now wished to speak with. She stood unmoving several feet away, recalling Stanhope's threats. Recalling her own errant passion with another man.

But Arlen detached himself from the other two gentlemen and walked over to her. Without preamble he said, "Is this a new part of your character, my dear? Are you now disloyal and disobedient?"

She gasped. Every detail of her encounter with Garrick De Vere flashed through her mind—but surely Arlen did not know about it! *Unless he himself had seen them.* "I do not intend to disobey you, Arlen, not ever," she said, incapable of smiling.

"You have upset the bride," he said, his smile remaining in place. It did not slip. It was ugly.

She felt herself beginning to pant. Like a small hunted animal, she felt trapped, awaiting a bloody blow. Stanhope had told everyone—or other guests had seen them! "Arlen," she began, her bosom heaving.

"Sir John told me that you spoke with Susan and said you shall leave town. Has it not occurred to you to ask my permission first?"

She stared at him, comprehension slowly sinking in—and with it a huge relief. "Leave town?" she whispered. This was not about her dalliance upon the lawns. Olivia remained in some disbelief.

"I never said you could return home, my dear," Arlen said quite unpleasantly.

Olivia refocused with a great effort. Carefully she said, "I would never disobey you, Arlen. I thought you preferred it that I return home, but there was no time to broach the subject."

"Apparently Miss Layton cannot do without you," Arlen said, staring. "Sir John has been most laudatory about you, my dear. How he sings your praises. But he is quite worried about his own daughter, rightly judging her as having not one whit of sense, and he is afraid she will disgrace herself in these next few months before the wedding if left to her own devices." He watched her very closely now.

"What are you implying?" Olivia asked with real trepidation.

"You are to be his daughter's anchor in this stormy sea of her impending matrimony!" Arlen chuckled. "You are going nowhere, Olivia."

Olivia was stunned. "Surely you do not deny me the right to go home?"

"I do." He was smiling.

Olivia's heart fell. The full extent of her predicament was only just becoming obvious. "Arlen, I cannot."

"You can, and you shall."

"You are punishing me," she said, becoming angry, "for coming to town in the first place."

Arlen shrugged. "I do not care what you think. I only care how you conduct yourself."

Olivia stiffened. Was that another innuendo aimed at her last encounter with the viscount of Caedmon Crag? No. It was impossible. If he had heard about her and De Vere, they would not be discussing Susan Layton right now. "You know how loyal I am," she said stiffly, pierced with guilt and hating her own lie.

"Do I?" he said, his unpleasant smile remaining upon his handsome face.

Olivia could not respond. Her near adultery prevented her from taking up her own defense.

Arlen came closer, bent, and put his face so close to hers that his nose almost touched her cheek. His breath, when he spoke, was foul, reeking of gin and tobacco. And Olivia did not miss the exotic yet familiar perfume wafting from his clothes. "You asked for this, my dear. You asked to come to town, and now you are here—and here you shall remain." He smiled. "Now you too shall play the game. Keep Miss Layton in line. Walk her to the altar if need be."

Arlen gave her a condescending glance and walked briskly away, leaving Olivia shaken and dismayed and staring not at the wall, but at De Vere. She gasped, wondering how long he had been standing there, watching her argue with Arlen—watching Arlen mistreat and abuse her. Their gazes were locked. His was frankly penetrating. And Olivia had the oddest urge to go to him and seek his strength— as if he could help her.

But he was the cause of her misfortunes. Unable to bear up for even another moment, her mind whirling in confusion, Olivia lifted her skirts and hurried away, this time upstairs to the sanctuary of her own bedchamber.

"Ashburn."

Arlen paused. He had just entered the billiards room, and it was the earl of Stanhope seeking him out. He stiffened. Because of what had happened eleven years ago, Arlen harbored ill will toward Stanhope. They were not friends, would never be more than wary acquaintances. Arlen was alert. Why would Stanhope seek him out?

Bows were exchanged. "Congratulations, my lord, on a propitious alliance," Arlen said politely.

"Thank you," Stanhope said flatly. "We are all very pleased with the union."

Arlen felt like laughing but did not. Any idiot could take one look at Caedmon and see that the man detested his bride and the engagement, if not all of society in general. "My sister was just commenting the other day that it was about time your son came home and did his duty," Arlen said, a previous evening flashing through his mind. Actually Elizabeth had had quite a bit to say on the subject of Caedmon's return and engagement, but he was not about to reveal that conversation to Stanhope.

"The marchioness has always been one of the few women I admire for more than her beauty," Stanhope said smoothly. "How rare it is to find great beauty and vast intelligence."

Arlen knew that Elizabeth raised most men's brows, and he bristled, but inwardly. "My sister is undoubtedly a great rarity. Everyone admires her."

"And you most of all?" Stanhope said, smiling pleasantly.

But it was a blow, and Arlen felt it as such. He stiffened.

Stanhope continued to smile, saying, "I think it very admirable that you guard and protect your sister so well, Ashburn."

Arlen managed, "Thank you." He wet his lips. "I have been her entire family, as well as her guardian, since she was ten years old. I take my familial duties very seriously."

"Perhaps, Ashburn, you should guard and protect your wife as well."

Arlen was so disturbed by Stanhope's previous innuendos that he was now thrown entirely off guard. "Olivia?" Incredulity laced his tone.

Stanhope's smile faded, and he stepped closer, grim now. "My son is headstrong. And incapable, I think, of exercising the least bit of decorum. Perhaps it was a mistake, eleven years ago, for me to allow him to leave England."

Arlen stared. What the hell was coming?

"Truthfully, he has not changed. He is filled with disrespect, and he remains, I believe, a child who thinks to thwart me."

Arlen nodded carefully. "He does seem the same," he finally said. "Headstrong, and exceedingly eccentric."

"I wonder how many people saw him with the countess in the park a few minutes ago?"

Arlen was in shock. "Olivia? My wife was outside with Caedmon?" He did not believe it, not for a moment. Olivia was a meek country mouse. She had no nerve, no initiative, and ice ran in her veins instead of hot red blood. How well he knew.

"Sometimes, it is not the best idea to ignore one's wife for too long. I know women. They do not want our attentions on the one hand, but if we leave them be, they become bitter and angry and defiant." Now Stanhope smiled, nodding quite sagely. "A man, it seems, just cannot win, not where the female gender is involved."

Arlen's pulse pounded. Olivia was a mouse. A country mouse. If a man like Caedmon blinked at her, she would run away in terror. Of that he had no doubt. Or did he?

"My lord, did you yourself see my wife in the park with your son?"

Again a grim smile. "I did. Ashburn, I suggest you keep a close rein upon her. A very close rein. My damnable son was pursuing her. There is not a doubt upon my mind. I witnessed the entire event."

Arlen stared, speechless. When his mind came to, he just knew that Stanhope had not seen anything illicit. It was an impossibility. Olivia was not a woman of passion.

Before Arlen could find his tongue, Stanhope said, smiling, "Let them do as they will after the nuptials." And he bowed, then walked briskly away.

After the nuptials? Arlen gazed after him, beginning to shake, wondering what, exactly, Stanhope had seen. His shock had incapacitated him, when he should have demanded a precise account. He had the urge to go after Stanhope and ask him now just what he had seen, but his pride forestalled him. He felt his own cheeks beginning to burn.

And he had an image of Olivia in Caedmon's arms, an image that infuriated him.

CHAPTER EIGHT

Three months. Those two words drummed in Olivia's brain as she held Hannah's hand the following day and wandered through the crowd at St. Bartholomew's fair. Miss Childs strolled at their side. A huge, festive throng from all walks of life had gathered at the city fair, one of London's largest. They had only just arrived, but Olivia barely paid attention to the crowd, the performers, or the booths. Arlen would force her to endure the city until after the wedding, which was three months away—unless something drastic happened to change his mind.

"Mama, why are you squeezing my hand so tightly?" Hannah protested. But her head was cocked to the side. She was absorbing all of the sounds around her.

Olivia came to her senses, relaxing her grip and managing a smile, the latter for Miss Childs's benefit. "I am sorry, dear. I was lost in thought."

"I smell gingerbread," Hannah said as shouts suddenly rang out around them. "What is happening? Is it a fight? Are they boxing?"

"There is a wrestling match to our right," Olivia explained as they paused, not attempting to penetrate the ring of spectators screaming at two wrestlers, both young, brawny men stripped to their waists. In the crowd cheering and jeering the two young men were finely dressed gentlemen and equally splendidly attired ladies, farmers, dairy

maids and other country folk, merchants and their appren-
tices, domestic maids, and even a pair of friars in long dark
robes. A Scotsman was playing bagpipes not far from
where they stood, contributing impossibly to the excitement. A fiddler and his monkey were adding to the ca-
cophony as well; the swarthy musician played while the
monkey danced about on a long leash, to the delight of
several ragged, laughing children gathered around them.

"A tuppence to see the freak, a tuppence to see the
freak," another man was crying behind them.

Olivia and Hannah turned. A spindly-legged elderly man
stood outside of a painted booth that advertised the world's
ugliest man, less human than beast. The drawing on the
poster did indeed show the monstrous form of a hunchback
with twisted features, which immediately hurt Olivia. No
man should have to suffer so. Behind the old man, inside
the booth, the poor being could be seen seated upon a stool,
clad in rags, his head hanging down. For once, Olivia was
glad Hannah could not see.

"Mama, let's go see the monkey," Hannah said, tugging
on her hand in the direction of the small animal and his
owner.

Miss Childs, who had stepped away from them for one
moment, handed them all gingerbreads. "Thank you," Olivia said, taking a bite. But the spicy sweet flavor could not
help her shake off her unhappy thoughts. What if she spent
an entire summer chaperoning Susan and De Vere? The
thought terrified her.

But matters were becoming far worse. Olivia was starting
to feel real dismay whenever she thought about their wedding—a dismay she had no right to.

They moved toward the fiddler, undoubtedly a Gypsy.
Laughter and giggles surrounded him. Then the other children saw Hannah and their amusement faded as they stared
at her, realizing that she was blind. Olivia tensed, her grip
upon Hannah's palm tightening. "Eh," said one of the children with an unkind snicker. "Lookit the blindie!"

Olivia pulled Hannah to her side, but before she could

even speak, much less turn to go, the two other urchins were laughing and pointing at her daughter.

Hannah was no longer smiling. Tears filled her eyes.

Olivia felt for her daughter, reduced in that instant some twenty years to her own anguished childhood. "She's coming! She's coming! Hide!" the village children shrieked and screamed as Olivia wandered down the meadow path. The half dozen children raced away, leaving her standing alone in the meadow, absolutely bewildered, absolutely alone.

They hated her. They were too young to fear her yet.

And then a small stone landed on top of her head. Olivia flinched, glancing up through the branches of an oak, and saw one skinny boy scrambling down the trunk, laughing. Before he turned and ran, he stuck his tongue out at her. And then he was gone.

A tear slipped down her face.

"Eh, lookit the monkey! 'E's doin' a real dance, by gawd!"

The boy's shout jerked Olivia out of the past and she saw the monkey continuing to hop around, looking adorable in his little frock coat and top hat as the Gypsy played. The children had forgotten Hannah. The two scruffy boys and the ragged little girl giggled again, and beside Olivia, Hannah also laughed softly.

Olivia looked down at her beautiful daughter, treasuring her smile. The pain of the moment was gone. But it was moments like this last one that made Olivia prefer the country to anywhere else—the country and the safe, impenetrable confines of Ashburnham. "He is dancing," Olivia told Hannah. She cleared her throat. "And quite well, too. One skip one way, two another, and a perfect little bow."

"I know. What is he wearing?" Hannah asked eagerly.

"A red frock coat and a gray top hat," Olivia replied. "His leash and collar are gold."

"Is he brown?" Hannah asked. "Brown and furry and soft?"

"Yes."

The children squealed with laughter as the monkey did a somersault; Hannah laughed, too.

Olivia allowed herself to drift mentally as Miss Childs stepped into the breach, describing the monkey's antics for Hannah. She glanced around to decide where to take her daughter next, remarking the shooting match soon to take place and a puppet show already in progress. There were booths offering jewelry and plate, others offering scarves, ribbons, and lace. A peddler was hawking toys. On the far side of the square was the Priory, where inside, hundreds of merchants were exhibiting some of the finest cloth in England. But buying a beautiful piece of silk was not on Olivia's mind.

Since she had met him, he was almost all she thought about. And she did not want to be consumed this way. Why wouldn't De Vere leave her alone? And what was wrong with her?

"Mama, look!" Hanna cried happily.

Olivia realized that the monkey had come close to Hannah and was now regarding her with unblinking curiosity. Olivia did not move, watching as Hannah squatted, holding out her hand trustingly. Olivia, though, was tense, and she looked up. As if reading her thoughts, the Gypsy said, "He doesn't bite, madam."

Olivia hadn't thought so, and in any case, Hannah had a very special way with animals, some kind of unique, inexplicable bond. The monkey crept closer. Hannah murmured to it. Suddenly it leapt right into her arms, where it clung to her neck.

Hannah cradled it close, smiling. "He is soft!" she exclaimed.

Its master came over to them. "I've never in my life seen him do that."

Olivia hoped the monkey was not diseased. "Hannah, that is enough," she said quietly, wishing she did not have to interrupt.

"Mama . . . ," Hannah turned in protest.

Olivia said not a word, and Hannah put the monkey down reluctantly. It scooted over to its master, climbing quickly up the man to ride his shoulders. Olivia reached into her purse and handed him a guinea. His eyes widened and he bowed. "Thank you, my lady, thank you," he said.

"Shall we go to the puppet show?" Olivia asked, again taking her daughter's hand.

Hannah nodded somberly

But Olivia's feet failed to move. Standing watching the wrestlers was none other than Garrick De Vere.

His back was to them, but Olivia would know him—feel him—anywhere. She was aghast and she abruptly reversed direction. "Let's buy some cloth for a new dress for you, dear," she said, pulling Hannah back the other way. Suddenly aware that she was perspiring, Olivia opened and fluttered her fan.

"Ow," Hannah cried. "Mama, you're hurting me."

"Lady Ashburn, are you all right?" Miss Childs asked with concern.

Olivia imagined that her cheeks were red hot. But they must flee. "Come," she snapped, tugging on her daughter. But as she did so, she half turned to glance at him one more time.

And De Vere was staring at them. With all-too-penetrating eyes.

Her heart dropped like a weighted sack of bricks. And Olivia could not move.

His gaze holding hers, he started toward them, apparently in no rush. Unlike the other evening, he wore his hair unpowdered and pulled back. His dark blue frock coat, while cut from fine cloth, was not ostentatious, and neither was the dark gray waistcoat he wore beneath it or his softer gray breeches. Yet as unfashionably drab as he was, he was still the most striking man Olivia had ever beheld. Then she realized that a large red setter was at his side.

He paused in front of her and bowed. "Lady Ashburn." His gaze went to Hannah and Miss Childs . . . and back to Hannah again.

Her heart beat hard and fast. She knew she would never control her temper if he was condescending or disparaging toward her daughter. Olivia curtsied quickly and pulled Hannah closer. "My lord, good afternoon."

He tore his gaze from Hannah's face with her unseeing, unblinking eyes. "This is unexpected," he said.

She almost said, "Our meeting or my daughter?" Instead she smiled, the expression forced. "My daughter enjoys fairs, as do I. This is my daughter, Hannah. And her governess, Miss Childs."

De Vere bowed again. Hannah smiled at him and curtsied. "I also enjoy fairs," he said to Hannah. "It has been many years since I have been to one."

"Why?" Hannah asked.

His smile was rueful and brief. "I do not live in England. I live on a little island far away, in the Caribbean Sea."

"Why would you live there? Aren't you English? Your accent is English, and my mother called you 'my lord.' "

Olivia was trying not to gape. Hannah rarely spoke to adults, and never to strangers. Indeed, her world was restricted to Olivia, Lucy Childs, and some of the staff at Ashburnham. It was a small, isolated world, but one that suited them perfectly. For in their world there was no condescension, no fear, no harsh, overriding judgments.

But now she was conversing with De Vere as if they were old friends.

"I prefer Barbados to my native land, for many personal reasons," Garrick was saying very easily now.

"What an interesting name, Barbados," Hannah replied. She held out her hand. Garrick's setter, until now standing motionless by his right side, suddenly stepped forward and shoved its pointed nose into Hannah's palm. His brown eyes were warm and friendly.

"Treve, sit," Garrick said, a sharp command.

The setter sat.

"Oh, have I upset you? I love dogs," Hannah said quickly. "Is he beautiful? What color is he?"

De Vere suddenly faced Olivia, and she felt his eyes piercing right through her breastbone. "He is gentle, Lady Ashburn."

Olivia nodded. "I assumed as much. May my daughter pet him?"

Garrick nodded. His gaze remained on Olivia. But when he realized that Hannah had not moved, unable to see his nod, he started. "Please, Hannah." And he snapped his fingers and pointed at her. The setter stood and stepped forward, his expression alert, his tail wagging.

Hannah touched his wide forehead, then stroked behind his long, floppy ears, then bent and hugged him. "He is so big and so soft," she whispered.

"He is a setter, dear," Olivia said, her tone constricted. Why did she feel the urge to weep now? Why was this sight undoing her? "He is red, a fiery golden red. He is very beautiful," she ended in a whisper. And she looked up to find De Vere staring at her again.

He said, his gaze fixed upon her, "Treve is an Irish setter."

Hannah straightened, her hand still on the dog. "I wish that I had my own dog."

Now Olivia avoided Garrick's eyes. She was still perspiring, but the day was somewhat warm. Her pulse beat far too fast. "We have a cat, dear."

"Surely you have hounds at Ashburnham," Garrick said.

"But they belong to my father, and they are for sport, not for pets," Hannah said. "His sister doesn't like animals in the house, and that is that. I am lucky to have Thomas."

Garrick's jaw was flexed. "I see. Well, Hannah, you may borrow Treve whenever it suits you. He is a good companion, very neat, and very obedient. And he will not chase Thomas if you tell him not to."

"Really?" Hannah's eyes were shining. Her expression was ecstatic. "Really, my lord?"

"Yes. Until I return to Barbados, for then Treve comes with me." He smiled, his eyes soft.

Olivia hugged herself, his sense of humor not lost upon her in spite of her distress. This was not fair. He was wooing her child, and it seemed so right. But surely he was not kind like this—surely he sought only to influence her through Hannah. A heavier weight seemed to settle upon

Olivia's shoulders, because gift or no, she knew that De Vere was not by nature a cold or mean man.

"And when do you leave England, my lord?" Hannah asked with bold innocence, still fondling the dog.

Olivia tensed, and to cover her intense reaction to such a simple question, she bent and patted the setter, too.

"I have yet to decide," Garrick said. Olivia could feel his eyes on the top of her head. "Have you seen the puppets?" he asked.

"No." Hannah shook her head.

He slowly faced Olivia. "Lady Ashburn, may I escort you and your daughter and Miss Childs? Surely you do not wish to miss the next show."

Olivia straightened, finally meeting his intense regard. Many replies raced through her mind. They had to leave, they had another engagement, Hannah had her lessons. Arlen was waiting for them at Vauxhall. But all were false, and she would be caught by her daughter and Miss Childs in an obvious lie. She would probably be exposed by De Vere as well. She failed to smile. "If you insist."

The look he gave her was queer. "I do."

And the entourage set off, the two women, the child, the man, and his red dog.

The puppet show needed little explanation, not once it had begun. The puppets argued and fought, danced insanely and played tricks upon one another, causing Hannah to laugh merrily along with the rest of the crowd. Olivia, however, could not concentrate, for De Vere stood on her left side, his strong arm pressing against hers. Powerful and warm. She knew he was preoccupied, too. From the corner of her eye, she was aware that he kept looking at her instead of ahead at the small, colorful stage.

Suddenly his mouth was near her ear. "Let's walk. She will be fine here with Miss Childs."

It was as if numerous arrows sailed straight into Olivia's heart. She shook her head, not looking at him.

His hand closed on her elbow. "I wish to speak with you," he said, a whisper in her ear again.

She shivered. His breath had feathered her lobe, causing all kinds of unwanted sensations to rush along the many pathways of her body. How could a simple whisper make her think of last night's kiss . . . and more? Olivia glanced at him, about to tell him it was not a good idea. But their gazes locked, his oh-so-golden and commanding, and she nodded. Olivia knew her cheeks were flushed.

Garrick stepped over to Miss Childs, on Olivia's other side, Hannah between them. "We are going to inspect the clothes in the Priory. We will meet you back here in a half hour. Treve, stay." And he took Olivia's arm firmly and guided her through the standing audience back toward the center of the square.

Olivia did not look at him as he navigated their way through the crowd. Her heart drummed. She was afraid to know what he wished to discuss, yet she was compelled by far more than curiosity.

They paused without entering the Priory. "I am sorry I lost my temper last night," Garrick said abruptly, releasing her arm.

Olivia rubbed it, her gaze helplessly fixed upon his strong, striking face. "I am sorry, also," she said.

He winced. "Most women would simply accept the apology. But I should know better than to expect platitudes from you."

"Yes," Olivia said. "Is that all?"

His expression darkened. "No, that is not all." He paused, grim, looking now over her head.

Olivia waited.

Finally he met her gaze. "Can I drive you in the park sometime?"

She was speechless.

He glared. "I am not asking for a rendezvous."

"Is your fiancée invited as well?"

"No, she is not," he growled.

"Then I think I must refuse," she said, already filled with regret.

Suddenly he gripped her arms. "Olivia, why not do what

you wish to do? Or do you enjoy being victimized by your husband and society's mores?''

Olivia tried to step away from him. Dear God, if only he knew how accurate his words were! And she was afraid of him, more so than ever. ''Let me go. You do not understand.''

''No? You are not happy. That is obvious. I am trying to court you, damn it.''

As he still held her, Olivia thought he was about to shake her. ''Release me,'' she said, and added, her tone strained, ''Please.''

For one more heartbeat his fingers dug into her arms. Then he obeyed, stepping back slightly.

She crossed her arms tightly. ''You are trying to seduce me,'' she said. ''And I would have you know that I am hardly unhappy, not that that is your affair.''

His single raised eyebrow was mocking.

''I have a wonderful child and a wonderful life at Ashburnham. And if once in a blue moon I must come to town, why, that is hardly the end of the world.'' She knew her tone was too high—passersby were turning to look at them.

''My, how you do protest,'' he said, not kindly.

''Stop it.''

''If you are so happy in the country, then when do you plan to return?'' His tone was demanding.

Olivia stared, thinking frantically, unable to tell him the truth—that Arlen would punish her and make her remain in the city until the wedding. She was also recalling that he'd vowed to follow her to Ashburnham if she went. ''Susan needs me,'' she finally said, and that was part of the truth.

His laughter was scathing. ''Indeed she does! God!'' He threw both hands into the air, an uncharacteristic gesture, Olivia thought. ''Well, perhaps your character will, eventually, wear off upon her.'' He sounded bitter and angry.

''She is a kind, sweet girl,'' Olivia cried.

''I have no use for kind, sweet girls, as you put it,'' he ground out. ''Will you, or will you not, drive with me in the park?''

"No."

His eyes were frightening. "Will you join me for the theater and supper?" His tone was extremely low now.

Olivia shook her head as she fought to speak. "You cannot court me. You are not an eligible man."

"A day at Bath?" he demanded.

"No," she managed, a whisper.

He stared, clearly fighting a huge temper, clearly enraged.

"I cannot," she said.

He continued to stare. "And if I were not engaged?"

"I am married. I am not eligible," she said.

He was disgusted. It was written all over his face, mingling with his anger. And Olivia's heart went out to him in spite of his ceaseless pursuit. She touched his coat sleeve. "This is not meant to be," she whispered.

His gaze flew to, and collided with, hers. He did not speak.

She became light-headed immediately, in her mind's eye seeing them naked and entwined. And that voice, that damnable voice, said, *It is meant to be, and you know it all too well.*

Olivia was frozen.

"I disagree," he said finally. "This, surely, is meant to be. Otherwise I would not want you so badly."

Olivia inhaled, hard. "Stop," she began, trembling.

He cut her off. "I do not admire your integrity," he said. His gaze pierced right through her. "You see, I do not admire self-sacrifice."

De Vere insisted upon driving them home. Olivia's protest died, because Hannah was thrilled by his offer. Olivia hoped it was because of her instant attachment to his dog and not to the man himself. That would be, she thought, the very final straw.

They had taken a hansom to the fair anyway, because the two larger Layton vehicles had been in use and the smaller, open curricle would have been too crowded, but now, standing at the curb as his coach drove up, Olivia was sorry she had not suffered the slight inconvenience. And it was not merely because being in De Vere's presence was so difficult. For a part of her, foolishly, wished to prolong the afternoon. But she was sane enough to worry about being seen with him just the day after the Laytons' party. Tongues would surely wag another time. No one would believe it to be an innocent encounter. Especially because last night there had been little innocent about the brief moment of passion they had shared.

The Stanhope coach, a black lacquer affair, pulled up at the curb, four white horses in the traces. Her hand in Hannah's, De Vere and the setter on Hannah's other side, Olivia reminded herself they had not done anything wrong and her anxiety—and guilt—was misplaced. But was it? And were heads turning their way even now? She glanced around them as a footman rushed to open the carriage door. A pair of exquisitely dressed ladies were openly regarding her and the viscount of Caedmon Crag from the curb.

"Lady Ashburn?" Garrick drawled, having handed in both Hannah and Miss Childs. "Are you looking for someone?"

Olivia quickly turned to him. "Am I imagining it, or have we been remarked?"

His smile was wry. "I have been remarked, madam." He gestured at the bold coat of arms painted on the coach's doors in silver and blue. "I was remarked from the moment I arrived. The price one pays for returning from a long exile—or failing to wear a wig."

It was his second humorous remark of the day, and this time Olivia did smile. "Too often fashion fails its followers, my lord, and turns the wearer into a fool."

His brows lifted. "At last, a woman of common sense as well as intelligence and beauty."

She flushed, taking his offered hand. "Most men wear wigs, my lord, because they are bald. And I do think the women admire your hair."

He laughed, handing her into the carriage. His laughter, warm and rich and so very rare, wrapped itself around Olivia like a warm cocoon. De Vere followed her inside. The door was shut smartly by the liveried footman, while Garrick instructed the driver to take them to the Layton residence. He had settled himself beside her, facing Hannah and Miss Childs, and he leaned toward her. "Are you one of those women, my lady?" he asked too softly.

Would her schoolgirl blushes never cease? "You do not strike me as the kind of man to search out compliments."

He sank back against the velvet squabs, arms folded, eyes bright. "You are right. I withdraw the question," he said.

Olivia realized how attentive her daughter and the governess were to their exchange, and she promptly faced the window, gazing outside. She began to worry anew.

This was hardly a good idea. She could only console herself with the fact that Hannah was so happy, inseparable, it seemed, from the setter, and that the afternoon had not been prearranged. And the Laytons were not, thank God, at home.

The roads were congested, and the journey back to the Laytons' took a full half hour. In that time, Hannah asked De Vere numerous questions about his dog, including how it had been trained and where, one day, she might find an Irish setter for herself. That amazing conversation—and Olivia was amazed—veered once again onto the subject of Garrick De Vere's island home. Again, Hannah was stunningly inquisitive. Garrick finally began to regale her with the latest methods of planting sugar cane, a subject that would put most grown men, much less a child, to sleep. To Olivia's absolute bewilderment, Hannah was a rapt listener.

"What kinds of animals are there on the island, my lord? Are there monkeys and elephants?" Hannah asked when the viscount had finished describing the grueling labor involved in planting a field of sugar cane.

De Vere smiled, and it reached his eyes. "We do have monkeys, but I am afraid there are no elephants. But there are parrots, as well as many other kinds of beautiful, exotic birds. And our sea is filled with all manner of fish. Have you ever heard of a dolphin?"

Hannah shook her head as the carriage stopped in front of the Laytons' brick town house. "We are here," Olivia exclaimed, tearing her gaze from De Vere's relaxed, smiling face. She was fanning herself now. This day *had* been a disaster. She had learned far too much about the viscount; she was becoming far too involved. She was beginning to *like* him.

"Are you warm, Lady Ashburn?" Garrick drawled as the door was opened for them.

Olivia intended to reply. But before she could do so she saw, past the footman, Lady Layton appearing on the stoop in front of the house. She froze. And then her fan began a rapid-fire movement. What were they doing home?!

He shifted to follow her gaze. "Ah, the woman who shall soon be my mother-in-law." Sarcasm did enter his tone.

Olivia could hardly think. "Well," she said, her tone odd and high, "thank you for the afternoon. Hannah, Miss Childs, come."

"Mama, are you sick?" Hannah asked as Miss Childs climbed out first and then turned to help Hannah down.

"Of course not," Olivia said brightly. But her heart was sinking like a stone, for Lady Layton was coming down the steps and approaching the carriage. Her smile was false and plastered on her face. Everyone suspects, Olivia thought wildly. And then, but nothing has happened yet!

"Lady Ashburn, you are back early. How was the fair?" Lady Layton asked.

"Wonderful," Olivia said, stepping from the coach.

"Lord Caedmon, this is a dear surprise," Lady Layton said, her smile now genuine.

He stepped down from the carriage himself, as was only proper, and bowed over her hand. "Lady Layton. I, too, was at the fair. When I saw that Lady Ashburn and her daughter had no means of transportation, I offered to drive them home."

"That was so kind of you," Lady Layton exclaimed as Olivia froze. But Lady Layton must have been extremely distracted, for she did not appear to have heard Garrick's remark. "Please, do come in. Susan and I were about to have tea. We are thrilled that you are here."

"I am afraid I must decline your offer, madam, as I have several pending engagements. I shall try to call on Miss Layton in a day or two," he said, barely smiling.

Lady Layton's face fell, but then she quickly smiled. "Well, on the morrow, then, perhaps, my lord."

He bowed and climbed back into the carriage. Olivia stood self-consciously behind Lady Layton, holding Hannah's hand, trying to stare at the pavement as if it were truly mesmerizing. But nature forced her to look up, just in time to meet his suddenly inscrutable eyes. Or was amusement lurking there? He nodded at her, and the carriage rolled away.

Lady Layton turned.

Olivia knew that guilt was written all over her face.

Lady Layton said, strained, "Shall we have tea, Lady Ashburn?" And her tone was filled with tension and worry.

The reconstruction of the Houghton Place was finally over. Stone masons and bricklayers, carpenters and smiths, had been working feverishly for five years on the two new wings that Elizabeth had insisted upon shortly after her marriage to the marquis of Houghton, and only a month ago had they finished. Now the mansion took up most of the square upon which it was located. Six years ago Elizabeth had insisted that their neighbors vacate the adjoining premises in order that she might build the two new wings. Their neighbors, a baron and a well-to-do merchant, had resisted at first, but in the end the marchioness had prevailed through sheer force of will and a touch of social ostracism. As she had said, moving two families was mere child's play. After all, in order to construct her new country home in Kent, a Palladian villa that, she said, far surpassed the old Elizabethan home her husband had inherited, the entire village of Woodbridge had had to be relocated so as not to obstruct the new villa's views of the valley. Of course, the peasants had hardly objected to the move.

Arlen was glad the reconstruction in town was finished. He was a frequent guest at his sister's, and for years the noise of the hammers and saws had driven him crazy. Now, as he waited for Elizabeth to descend from her suite in the brand-new east wing, he looked around, admiring the huge, palatial proportions of the grand salon where he stood. The salon, and the entire wing, were magnificent enough to rival the duke of Marlborough's new home. That, of course, had been Elizabeth's intention. How highly Arlen thought of her judgment.

She swept into the room, shocking Arlen because she was clad in the same pale pink gown he had seen her in at a tea earlier in the day. Dismayed, he walked to her, immediately remarking that she was upset and angry. Her sapphire blue eyes were flashing, her mouth hard and tight. "Dear, we have planned a quiet supper, just the two of us," he said, his pulse racing swiftly now. "Or did you forget?"

She extended her hand, which he kissed. "I have not forgot, but I have no interest in dining out tonight. If you wish, we can dine here, as the marquis is in the country." She whirled and paced, face set.

Arlen followed her, relaxing a little. "Are you certain he will not return home?" he asked.

She faced him abruptly, arms akimbo. "Yes. You may do as you will. Arlen, I am upset!"

"I can see. Should I shut the doors?" he asked.

Elizabeth eyed him, not in a pleasant manner, almost as if he were hardly as clever as she. She rushed across the salon to close the two doors, then turned. "You don't know, do you?"

He wet his lips. "What are we discussing?"

"Your wife and Caedmon!"

He stiffened and then came forward. "I beg your pardon?" Stanhope's shocking claim of the night before returned forcefully to his mind. Yet Stanhope had not said that he had seen them do anything other than meet in the park.

Wouldn't he have said something if he had seen a torrid embrace? Arlen had not been able to ask. A proud man did not make such inquiries of another man. Besides, it was impossible. Olivia's character was so staid she should have been a nun.

"Did you not hear? That meek little mouse of yours was with Caedmon at St. Bartholomew's fair. I cannot believe it!" Elizabeth exclaimed.

Neither could Arlen. "They rendezvoused at the fair?"

Elizabeth eyed him. "Arlen, dear, I doubt it has gone that far, for your daughter and the governess were with them. He drove them all back to the Laytons', you know."

His pulse went wild. Hannah, at the fair? In the public eye? Hannah should remain cloistered! How dare Olivia saunter about publicly with her. Did she intend the whole world to know of their tragedy? "You were there?"

"No. But Lady Cynthia Steele saw them." Elizabeth's eyes darkened. "I saw the way she was looking at him at the Laytons' last night. Your little wife has discovered passion, my dear. She appeared ready to eat him right up."

Sometimes even Elizabeth went too far. "That was crude," he said coldly.

She waved at him dismissively. "Please. Cynthia said there is a great attraction between them, and if something has not yet transpired, it soon will. How dare he!" She whirled, pacing the length of the entire room, halting only in front of huge, oversize windows.

"I cannot believe this," Arlen said, aware now that he was shaking. "For Stanhope saw the two of them outside in the park last night, at the Laytons'."

"Believe it," Elizabeth said. "For I have heard that bit of gossip myself. Apparently Caedmon thinks to cuckold you again."

Arlen faced her, his pulse wild. "The bastard. I will kill him," he suddenly said. "I will kill them."

Elizabeth laughed. "Well, I do not think you need go that far, dear," she said, gliding forward. She slid her arms around him, her eyes bright. "Enough of mousy Olivia and her paramour. He is not coming home for several hours,'' she whispered, and they both knew she referred not to Garrick De Vere, but to her husband.

Arlen hesitated, but only briefly. He wrapped her in his embrace.

CHAPTER NINE

The note came well before noon. It was from Arlen, and he demanded that she return to Ashburnham immediately. A coach, he wrote, awaited her convenience. He expected her to depart with Hannah that morning. There were urgent matters, he ended, awaiting her attention at home.

Olivia was already dressed. She had taken Hannah for an early morning walk in the quiet neighborhood, mist still heavy upon the leafy treetops. Now she stared at the note, filled with trepidation and dread. This was what she wanted, to return home, to flee London. Why was she dismayed? And she could not help but conclude that it was yesterday's fiasco at the fair that had suddenly caused Arlen to change his mind and send her back to the country.

She was afraid.

She left her bedchamber, relieved that Arlen had not instructed her personally. Some of her fear abated. If he was suspicious of her feelings for Garrick De Vere, if he suspected anything, then he would have confronted her himself. It seemed likely that he did not know anything, but then why was he sending her home? Was he merely toying with her in his usual perverse manner?

Olivia worried now, recalling the earl of Stanhope's barely disguised threats. She was beginning to feel that it was only a matter of time before Arlen learned of her longing for another man—before the situation she had somehow become entrapped in exploded in her face.

And her heart must not ache now. Olivia reminded herself that she was eager to be home, very eager; and once there, she would soon forget that Garrick De Vere even existed. It was a promise she made to herself.

And once there, all temptation would be removed from her life. Her existence once again would be calm, routine, and trouble free. There would be peace.

Hannah was in the midst of a French lesson, but Miss Childs immediately stopped the verbal examination, turning to Olivia with a pleasant smile. "My lady?"

"We are returning to Ashburnham immediately," Olivia said, her tone falsely cheerful. "We must begin packing at once."

Miss Childs was surprised. "Very well," she said, standing.

"Mama!" Hannah cried sharply, an indignant protest. "Why? Why do we have to leave now? We had so much fun yesterday! I like London," she said passionately.

Olivia walked to her and stroked her hair. "Your father has ordered it, my dear, and that is that."

Hannah was silent, her expression dismayed.

"I am sorry. But perhaps it is for the best," she said softly.

"Will I ever see Lord Caedmon and Treve again?" Hannah asked with bitter sorrow.

Olivia was stricken. And she could not lie, because Hannah could practically read her thoughts. "I do not know. Probably not," she said hesitantly.

Hannah's face turned down, as if she were gazing at her hands. She kicked her slippered feet against the legs of her chair.

"I'm sorry," Olivia said again. She turned to Miss Childs. "When can we depart?"

"In a matter of hours, if the household maids will help us," Lucy answered, already opening the armoire.

Olivia nodded and left the room, slowly going downstairs. As she had thought, the Laytons were in the dining room, Sir John with his head buried in a journal, Lady Layton munching toasted bread, Susan with her embroidery. Susan looked up with a pleased smile.

"Good morning," Olivia said, hesitating on the threshold.

Sir John stood, laying down his paper. "Do come in," he said, his gaze steady upon her.

Olivia entered but did not sit. "Sir John, Lady Layton, my husband has instructed me to return home, where urgent matters await my attention. I am so sorry to have to leave in such haste, but apparently I must do so within a few hours. And I have so enjoyed your hospitality," she said earnestly.

Susan was on her feet. "Oh no!" she wailed.

Sir John gave his daughter a reproving look but came forward and put his arm around Olivia in a fatherly fashion. "My dear, I understand. In fact, Arlen spoke with me last evening upon this matter, so the news is no surprise to myself or Lady Layton."

Olivia was surprised. "I see." She studied him and could not read his thoughts, but clearly he was not unhappy that she was leaving. She hoped she did not flush. Did he, too, guess at the attraction that had so blatantly arisen between herself and De Vere? Had he not, just days ago, insisted she attend Susan all the way to the altar if need be? "Thank you for being so kind about such a precipitous departure," Olivia added.

"I imagine it is for the best," Sir John said.

Lady Layton came forward to clasp Olivia's hands. "We will see you at the wedding on September fifteenth, won't we, my dear?"

Lady Layton's relief was all too apparent. Clearly she wished Olivia to be gone. Olivia managed a smile, feeling awful for having carried on with De Vere, even for the briefest of moments. "Yes. I would never miss the event." She glanced at Susan, in that moment imagining her and Garrick De Vere standing at the altar in a magnificent cathedral, exchanging the vows that would join them together for a lifetime. That vision was so disturbing that Olivia immediately forced it aside. She did not know if her imagination was at work or her peculiar gift.

Susan came forward, teary-eyed. "I will help you pack," she said forlornly.

They left the dining room. As they walked upstairs, Susan was strangely silent. In Olivia's room, a housemaid was already filling her huge trunk with gowns, chemises, corsets, and petticoats. Miss Childs was ever efficient.

"I wish you could stay," Susan said.

"I know you do. But we shall still be friends. Always." Olivia smiled.

Susan stared at her. "I heard them talking last night, you know."

Olivia tensed. "Who, dear?"

"My parents. They think you are fond of him."

Her heart did stop before resuming a slightly frantic beat. She swallowed. "They think I am fond of whom?"

"Lord Caedmon." Susan's blue gaze was steady, her expression dismal. "Are you?"

She wet her lips, trying to choose a careful, suitable reply. "I do not dislike him, Susan, and I find it appalling that society condemns him so shamelessly for ancient crimes he may have never committed."

"You do like him!" Susan cried.

"And I do like you, and your parents, and most of this world," Olivia said.

Susan sighed. "You are too kind. They think you have a *tendre* for him. And they do not blame you, but they are worried, and think it better for you to return home at once."

Olivia flushed. "I do not like him that way," she said. As she uttered the words, she was aware of how monumental her lie was. And Garrick De Vere mocked her inside of her mind.

"I do think he likes you as well," Susan said softly. "He is always staring at you."

Olivia smiled weakly. "Susan, I am sorry if, in some way, I have interfered in your relationship with your fiancé."

Susan grasped her arm. "You have not interfered! I wish

he were marrying you! I do! My feelings have not changed." She shuddered. "I think he is a savage and a boor. I do not like him one single bit!"

Olivia regarded her with despair. And she said, "You must change your heart, Susan, in these next three months. Or your marriage will be a disaster."

Susan stared.

While Olivia knew that it was going to be a disaster anyway.

They had been traveling since noon, and within two or three hours it would be dark. A light rain had begun but an hour ago, what was so fondly called an English mist. The Surrey countryside was green and verdant, the land gently rolling. Roses bloomed along the roadside hedges and at the country inns and old stone chapels they passed. They intended to spend the night at the Alcott Abbey in Haslemere, which bordered west Sussex. Had they left earlier, they would not have had to stop for the night at all.

Olivia sat stiffly, leaning forward in her front-facing seat, staring out the window at the road ahead. They had just driven past the village of Harwood, and they were three-quarters of the way home. It was crossing her mind that she wished for a carriage wheel to break.

How foolish she was.

Hannah plucked her sleeve. "What is it, Mama?" she asked.

Olivia stared at the abrupt fork in the rutted road, not many yards distant. "Stanhope Hall is but a few miles from here. Of course, everyone is in London." Her pulse drummed. She was thinking the unthinkable.

Miss Childs eyed her. "Have you ever been to the Hall, my lady? It is very grand. The central part was built in the days of Henry the Eighth, you know."

Olivia was trembling. This is madness, sheer madness, she thought, do not even *think* of doing what you seem inclined to do! She looked at Lucy Childs. "Have you been to Stanhope Hall?"

Miss Childs nodded. "During a former employment, the

entire family spent a fortnight there as the Stanhopes'
guests.'' She added, ''Of course, that was many years ago.
I was only twenty years old.''

The fork was looming before them. Olivia jerked, looking at Miss Childs, who was probably thirty-five or so.
Breathlessly she asked, ''That was before the eldest boy
vanished?''

Miss Childs nodded. ''Both boys were about, I do remember, because they were an inseparable pair—causing
quite the ruckus with their comings and goings and the
boyish pranks they pulled.''

Olivia could not smile. ''You must have been at the Hall
just before the vanishing?''

''I do believe it was less than a year before Lionel De
Vere disappeared.''

Olivia turned forward abruptly, staring now at the fork
in the road so hard and unblinkingly that the dirt road finally began to undulate.

''Should we stop there, Mama?'' Hannah asked with eagerness. ''Wouldn't it be nicer to spend the night there than
at the old, cold abbey? They will not turn us away, you
know. I am sure of it.''

Olivia looked at her. Why did she wish to go to Stanhope
Hall so badly? He would not be there. He was in London.
Of course, he had spent a large portion of his childhood
there. He and the missing Lionel De Vere. It was as if a
mystery awaited her at the Hall, one that might be unrav-
eled if only she dared to go. It was as if she had to go.

Olivia folded her arms tightly beneath her breasts. If she
went, she would become more deeply involved with him.
She knew that. She was already deeply involved. Somehow,
inexplicably, against her will. And she suddenly rapped on
the roof.

''Godfriend. Take the right. We shall spend the night at
Stanhope Hall,'' she called.

''Very well, my lady,'' the coachman replied, and a moment later the team of bay horses veered onto the new,
smaller track.

Olivia was rigid with tension and breathless. She leaned

forward in her seat, straining to see. Hannah and Miss Childs had been rather garrulous up until this point, but suddenly the coach became oddly silent as it jolted and swayed along the dirt road, passing in and out of the murky shadows cast by huge elm trees. The pastures on either side were enclosed. Yellow wildflowers glistened at the foot of the split rail posts. Black-and-white-spotted cows grazed placidly by the road, oblivious of the rain, while in the distance large stone farm buildings could be seen, probably belonging to tenant farmers. The sky was darkening, perhaps with a summer storm.

"It was probably a good idea to detour to Stanhope Hall," Olivia said, glancing at the threatening sky. It had been a rainy spring, and the roads had hardly been good to begin with. Then she thought of Arlen. He would be furious if he knew that they had stopped at Stanhope Hall. Her pulse rate increased. Why hadn't she thought of him sooner?

And it struck her then that staying the night at Stanhope Hall might very well be the kiss of death.

Olivia instantly shoved that notion aside.

"Lady Ashburn, the Hall," Lucy Childs said with uncharacteristic enthusiasm. Her brown eyes were bright.

Olivia had already spied the tall, pale stone palace with its many lower wings and rounded corner towers sprawling atop the crest of a hill, perhaps a quarter of a mile ahead of them. Their coach traveled through the gloomy barbican, which looked as if it predated the reign of Henry the Eighth, and paused in the courtyard, a large grassy area the size of many country fairs. Here the dirt track had given way to pale, gleaming stone. The grounds remained immaculately manicured. Huge clipped hedges bordered the courtyard and filled the island in its midst, while large, shady oaks and elms dotted the lawns. A footman opened the door and the trio descended.

Servants appeared instantly from the house. Olivia walked forward slowly toward the two massive stone lions that guarded the front steps, chills sweeping up and down her spine. Glancing around, she felt almost as if she were being watched—which was ridiculous. No one, neither man nor ghost, peered down at her from the many tall, oval windows facing the courtyard on this side of the house. There was not a sign of life in or near any of the outbuildings, either, just the staff who had appeared from within the house itself.

A tall, thin woman stepped forward. "I am the housekeeper, Mrs. Riley," she introduced herself.

Olivia summoned a smile and explained their predicament. "I am Lady Ashburn, Mrs. Riley, and I do hope we are not imposing. But I think it is about to rain and we are still several hours away from Ashburnham."

"Say no more." Mrs. Riley smiled. "Yes, it is a good thing you decided to detour in this rain." She glanced at the sky. A wind had begun to blow, pushing at them from the southeast. "We have plenty of room to accommodate you for the night. The Hall is empty, you know. Everyone is in town to celebrate the return of the Stanhope heir from Barbados and his betrothal to Miss Susan Layton."

Olivia continued to smile, but the strain made her mouth ache. "Thank you, Mrs. Riley. We shall be gone at first light."

"Pshaw," the tall, thin woman said. She turned and began snapping out commands; their trunks were taken down and they were escorted inside. The foyer was vast, the size of most London salons, the stone floors speckled, a huge crystal chandelier overhead. As she stood in the cool, dark hall with its old, engraved, and relieved wooden paneling, Olivia could almost envision Henry the Eighth striding through the room, a huge ermine-trimmed cape flowing about him. Then she saw the two boys.

One was fair, one dark. They were racing through the hall in their soiled frock coats and stained knee breeches. Then the image was gone.

Chills rushed over her. She looked at Hannah.

Her daughter was pale, but her cheeks were flushed. She turned toward her mother immediately.

"What is it?" Olivia asked in a whisper.

"This is a sad place," Hannah replied in the same hushed tone. "There is so much weeping."

More chills. Olivia strained to hear, desperately, as if whatever Hannah was in tune with might answer her own questions. But she heard nothing, and she was dismayed. She bent closer to her daughter. "Who is crying?"

Hannah hesitated. "I don't know her name. But her heart is broken. She is so sad, so alone."

Olivia felt the sadness, too, but still failed to hear the woman. Perhaps, though, it was a Stanhope ancestor long since dead. Perhaps the countess's grief remained, for the loss of her firstborn son. She wanted to ask Hannah if she felt the presence of Garrick's dead brother but did not want to suggest anything to her daughter that was not meant to be—or that might frighten her.

Mrs. Riley returned from shooing the staff toward the kitchens and the guest rooms. "I will send up tea and cakes, my ladies, and by the time you get to your rooms, they shall be warm and merry, as we have fires even now being stoked and lit." She smiled brightly at them. "What time would supper please you, Lady Ashburn?"

Olivia hesitated, shaking off the quiet sadness that seemed to wrap itself around her like a threadbare yet serviceable shawl. "Mrs. Riley, we wish to be no bother. What if you send us up a light meal in our rooms? Perhaps at eight o'clock?"

"If that is what you wish, my lady. Now, let me show you upstairs. The guest rooms are in this part of the house. I hope you do not mind." They followed the apparently cheerful housekeeper through the hall and up steep, winding stairs. "This is the original part of the house, you know, begun and completed during the reign of Henry the Eighth. I could never understand why His Lordship and Her Ladyship keep the guest rooms here and not in the newer wings. Of course, it has been renovated four times since it was first constructed, as you can see." She barely took a breath. "They rarely entertain in the country anymore. It has been years, in fact, since they did so. Both of them are very fond of town. It's quiet here, you know, most of the time. They only visit once a year, and only because the earl loves to shoot.''

They had reached the third landing and started up a narrow corridor. Several portraits of various Stanhopes hung on the walls. Their costumes were Elizabethan, vast ruffled collars framing the faces of the lords and the ladies. ''I can imagine that Lady Stanhope prefers town,'' Olivia said politely. Of course, she did not know the countess at all. But she had seen her upon one or two occasions in the past and, of course, the other night at the Laytons'. She was an elegant, beautiful woman, and Olivia did not think her the kind to enjoy the country. She did not want to remember that evening at the Laytons' now, but it was impossible to forget.

''This used to be such a cheery place,'' Mrs. Riley said, thrusting open a pair of doors. ''Your room, my lady, and your daughter's. Miss Childs, your room is across the hall.''

Olivia entered a dark room with linenfold paneling. It was filled with shadows. The bed was the same dark oak as the floor and walls, and the hearth, where a fire danced, was stone. Had it been a bright, sunny day, the room might not have been so somber. Olivia smiled at Mrs. Riley. ''What a lovely room.'' The draperies, she remarked, had been opened.

''When the sun comes out, you can see just how fine the woodwork is,'' Mrs. Riley said. ''If you need anything, Lady Ashburn, ring the bell and ask any maid.'' She smiled and turned, about to leave.

''Mrs. Riley,'' Olivia said, detaining her, ''how long have you been with the family?''

The housekeeper's regard was steady. ''Twenty-five years, my lady, and in spite of everything, I cannot say I've ever regretted my service to the Stanhopes.''

Twenty-five years, Olivia thought. Garrick De Vere was just about that age. She said, ''You must have known Lord Caedmon since he was a boy—since he was an infant, I imagine.''

She smiled. ''Actually, he was born right here in the

Hall, and I was with the countess at the time of the delivery."

Olivia hesitated. "Did he not have an older brother?"

Mrs. Riley's smile vanished. "Indeed he did. It was quite the tragedy. Young Lionel De Vere, who was the viscount of Caedmon Crag until his death, as you must know, was about a year and a half old when his brother was born. I knew him every bit as well as I did Garrick. He was such a nice, good boy. He disappeared when he was fourteen years old. To this day, no one knows what happened." She blinked rapidly now behind the lenses of her spectacles.

"I'm sorry. I did not mean to pry, or to distress you," Olivia said, touching the woman's wrist. "I did recently meet Lord Caedmon at his engagement party, and I suppose my curiosity got the better of me."

"No harm done," Mrs. Riley said with cheerfulness. "And it is a blessing that His Lordship has finally come home after all these years. Now, if you will excuse me?"

Smiling, Mrs. Riley left Olivia alone with her daughter and Miss Childs.

"What is wrong, Mama?" Hannah asked quietly. "Why did you ask so many questions?"

"Mere curiosity, my dear, as I said." Olivia was not about to tell Hannah the truth, even though she disliked dissembling to her daughter. "Come, dear, let's see your room. Or would you rather sleep with me tonight?"

Hannah beamed. "You know I would."

"Very well," Olivia said, thinking she was probably comforting herself and not her daughter.

As Hannah moved carefully around the room, using a walking stick to explore its furnishings and proportions, Olivia walked to the window, pulled aside the old, dark gold velvet draperies, and found herself staring out over a vast amount of rolling Surrey countryside. Just past the barbican she could see the valley they had so recently driven through, with its tiny village and surrounding fields. She wondered if the death of Garrick's brother had discouraged the Stanhopes from returning to the country. Of course it had.

Suddenly Hannah squealed.

Olivia turned quickly, but not with alarm, for the sound had been filled with delight. And she froze.

Hannah knelt on the floor, hugging the Irish setter. The red dog's tail was wagging rapidly. Treve licked Hannah's face.

Olivia forgot to breathe. Her mind remained stunned.

"Mama! Look! Lord Caedmon's dog is here!" Hannah cried, glancing up briefly before burying her face again in the dog's silky hair.

Olivia lifted her gaze to the doorway.

De Vere smiled at her as he leaned casually against the jamb. He dominated the threshold with his imposing presence, striking countenance, and big body. "Lady Ashburn," he drawled. There was a glint in his eye.

Olivia had felt all of the blood draining from her face; now it returned in a rush. Oh, dear God, was all she could think. *He was here.* "You . . ." Words escaped her.

He lifted a brow questioningly.

Olivia fought for calm and could not find it. She was trembling. "You must have left town this morning," she cried, an accusation.

He did smile. "Actually, I left shortly after noon."

She stared. "That is when we left."

His smile broadened. "I know." And he sauntered directly into her bedroom, pausing beside her daughter and his dog. "Hello, Hannah," he said.

CHAPTER TEN

Olivia was trembling, watching as Hannah straightened and beamed. Her temples throbbed, but her mind was beginning to function again. Clearly he had followed her from London. She was certain of it—his appearance at the Hall was no coincidence. Yet she could not accuse Garrick De Vere of pursuing them all the way to Surrey in front of her daughter. And the utter irony of her having chosen to spend the night at Stanhope Hall did not escape her.

"This is wonderful, my lord," Hannah said, stroking the setter, who was as happy to see her, his entire red-furred body wriggling with joy. "We did not expect you to be here."

"I hardly expected it myself," De Vere said dryly. Thunder rumbled outside, in the distance, and he glanced at the window. The light mist had become a steady downpour. "Will you and your mother do me the honor of dining with me?" he asked casually, turning toward Olivia.

But Olivia was not smiling, nor was she feeling very casual. "We are exhausted from the trip, impromptu as it was," she said tersely. She imagined that her eyes flashed. What was he doing? And how could Arlen *not* learn of this? "My husband only notified me—and quite unexpectedly—that I must return home early this morning. You can imagine how hasty our departure was. It was a great trial."

His gaze was steady upon her. "Yes. I imagine that it

was a trial—to have to leave in such haste."

She was angry, and she was frightened. "I am afraid we must dine in our rooms tonight," Olivia said coolly. "We intend to leave at first light."

Hannah made a sound of protest, which they both ignored.

He was staring. "And there is no means by which I might persuade you to change your mind?"

"Do you refer to the evening meal, my lord, or to our intended departure?" Olivia asked in a sugary tone of voice.

"I refer to both," he said as silkily. "My hospitality can be limitless."

She folded her arms, breathless, dismayed, the blood racing in her veins, or so it seemed. How could she survive the night at Stanhope Hall now—with him there, under the same roof, with intentions that were neither innocent nor honorable? If Arlen should ever learn of this, why, God only knew what he would do. Olivia glanced out the windows. Night would soon fall, but the sky was already dusky and near impenetrable, rain pounding on the windowpanes. It would soon be a cold, bleak, completely inhospitable night.

"Even should you attempt it," he said softly, "I would not allow it."

She whirled. "Allow what, my lord?"

"I would not allow you to depart in this inclement weather," he said flatly. He reached out and touched Hannah's hair. "I hope to see the two of you downstairs at eight," he said, smiling slightly—a smile that was also in his tone. "In any case, if your mother allows it, you may keep Treve with you tonight."

Hannah had been smiling back at him, and now she gasped. "Surely you do not mean—for the entire night?" she cried hopefully.

"I do." He did glance at Olivia with those golden, persistent, too knowing eyes.

Olivia's arms remained crossed beneath her breasts. "I do not object."

His brows lifted. "I thought you wished to battle with me over every possible subject."

She pursed her mouth, refusing to reply.

He laughed and walked out of the room, then paused. "Eight o'clock, Lady Ashburn." Leaving the door ajar, he strode down the hall.

Olivia ran to it and slammed it shut. She was panting. Impossible man! She had no intention of dining with him, none. And what would happen later—after Hannah was asleep? The real problem, she realized, was that she did not trust herself.

"Mama." Hannah came over to her, her expression worried, the setter remaining faithfully at her side. "I thought you liked him. Why are you so angry? And afraid?"

Olivia inhaled. Having a gifted daughter was no easy task. And dear God, she was afraid Hannah was right. Afraid of Arlen, and even more afraid of what would happen in the wee hours of the night. She closed her eyes, already envisioning herself in Garrick De Vere's embrace.

But would that be so terribly wrong? The thought crept unbidden into her mind. Very shaken, Olivia refused to entertain it.

She put her arm around Hannah. "Darling, there are some things I cannot share with you, and my feelings right now are very personal. If I could explain them, I would."

Had Hannah possessed the ability to see, she would have stared. "But you are scared, Mama, and it worries me."

"There is nothing for you to be afraid of," Olivia said as lightly as possible. It was a terrible falsehood. Even if she resisted De Vere and her own desire for him, there was Arlen to worry about. Arlen, and the entire future—as it involved everyone.

"He is a good man. You do not have to be afraid of him. He is only sad, Mama. He loved his brother very much."

Olivia sat on a tufted ottoman, pulling her daughter closer. "Is this what you felt from my conversation with Mrs. Riley?"

She shrugged. "No. I just know. The way I know other things."

Olivia nodded. She hesitated, knowing that she herself was far too distraught to feel Lionel's presence should he be lurking about, on the verge of asking her daughter what she herself felt. But foresight was a gift, one not to be used lightly. She remained silent.

"What is it, Mama?" Hannah asked.

Olivia shook her head. "Nothing, dear. I am very tired from this trip. Why don't we wash a bit and freshen up before our supper? Afterward I will read to you in bed." She hugged her. "It will be a very cozy evening, just the two of us in this old palace, with the wind and rain outside."

Hannah frowned. "We cannot join His Lordship for supper?"

"Absolutely not," Olivia said far too harshly.

Hannah was resigned. Then, "Mama, I don't mind sleeping in my own room, now that Treve is here." She grinned. "He can sleep with me in the bed."

"No!" Olivia cried.

Hannah started.

Olivia regrouped, her pulse racing. "Treve can sleep on the floor, where dogs belong, and you will sleep with me." She forced a smile. "As we have already planned, my dear." Hannah would be her coat of armor, denying Garrick De Vere the success of his ill-laid plans.

They were not joining him, as he should have known, damn that stubborn woman.

Garrick had no intention of dining alone in the huge, ill-lit dining hall, with only the various ghosts of his ancestors for company and shadows dancing on the walls. He rose abruptly from the table, facing an anxious Mrs. Riley. "I have lost my appetite," he said sourly, lifting a bottle of wine and a glass from the table.

"My lord, may I send a tray to your rooms?" the thin housekeeper asked.

But he was already stalking down the dimly lit corridor,

careless of Mrs. Riley's question, hardly even hearing it. Why did she have to resist him—and their attraction for one another? They could have passed an extremely enjoyable evening—a prelude to an even far more enjoyable encounter later, after Hannah was asleep.

Garrick thumped up the stairs. His rooms were in the west wing, while Olivia and her daughter and the governess were in the central section of the house. This was absurd. Why did he want her so damnably much? He told himself that he should avail himself of another woman, but instinctively knew that would change nothing. And why did she keep looking at him as if she could see through the walls he'd spent a lifetime erecting?

He reached his suite and marched inside, directly to the windows. It still rained. He had forgotten how wet and dreary and cold his native land was. God, the truth was, he had not missed this country at all. But now, oddly, his eagerness to return to Barbados seemed to have somehow dimmed.

It crossed his mind that, considering the long-standing rivalry he had with Ashburn, it was probably for the best that Olivia held to her morals. He would not put it past Grey to sever his head from his body in a duel if he ever learned Garrick had cuckolded him with his wife.

Disturbed, Garrick drained half a glass of wine and refilled it. He refused to dwell upon Olivia, but as a result, his thoughts veered to Lionel, which hardly helped his mood. There were so many memories here, far more so than in town. Damn it. Would a day ever go by where he did not feel the ache of loss, the bitterness of guilt?

Lionel, Olivia. His thoughts swung wildly from one to the other, back and forth, like a pendulum clock. He had a sudden premonition. Lionel had haunted him for the past fourteen years, ever since his death. What if Olivia now haunted him in the very same fashion? Consuming his thoughts against his will, day in and day out?

The idea was terrifying. Garrick cursed, grabbed a heavy wool mantle, and left his rooms. A few minutes later he was walking head down in the starless night, a man alone, drenched by the incessant rain.

It had taken Olivia a long time to fall asleep. She was exhausted, but she could not stop thinking about De Vere, and as she lay there seeking sleep but failing to find it, she debated the many possibilities that lay in store for them both. When, finally, she did turn over and reach for her daughter, just before sleep claimed her, her last thought was that she was on a path, one she had no choice but to take.

Olivia awoke.

She awoke instantly from a deep, dreamless slumber, knowing that something was terribly wrong. Dread, and fear, filled her heart with sickening intensity.

Then she glanced over at the other side of the bed, for Hannah. Candles remained lit, casting some flickering light over the room. And Olivia shot upright, crying out. Hannah was gone.

Her heart had positively stopped. Now she looked around wildly, holding one taper aloft, but the room was empty, the door wide open. The dog was gone as well.

Her heart renewed its beat with pounding force. She touched Hannah's pillow, then the bottom sheet where her body had lain. The pillow and sheet were cool.

Olivia leapt from the bed, dry mouthed, almost insane with fear. Was Hannah sleepwalking? The hall was vast. How would she find her? What if Hannah hurt herself or, worse, wandered outside in this weather?

Olivia rushed from the bedroom, running across the hall to Lucy Childs's room. As she rapped upon the door, she prayed that she would find Hannah inside. A moment later the bleary-eyed blonde opened the door, and Olivia told her what had happened. The sleepiness vanished from Miss Childs's eyes. "I will help you search," she said quickly.

"Hannah must be sleepwalking," Olivia said intensely. "There is no other explanation. And when she awakens, she will be lost and alone and frightened." Her voice was high.

Lucy touched her hand. "She has the dog with her."

Garrick. "I am going to awaken Lord Caedmon," Olivia cried, turning and racing down the dark hall. None of the wall sconces remained lit. It was eerie. But there was no time to dwell on that now.

Lucy followed her. "I will wake Mrs. Riley."

Olivia barely heard. Could not De Vere somehow summon the dog—who in turn would lead them to Hannah? She pounded down the stairs, outdistancing Lucy. She recalled that the family rooms were in the west wing. Within moments she was hurrying up those stairs in her bare feet. She imagined that the family's rooms were on the second story, as was usually the case.

Olivia banged on the first closed door. "My lord! Lord Caedmon!" she cried. There was no response. "Garrick!" She pounded again and pulled open the door. A dark, cold room, filled with wavering shadows, greeted her, clearly not in use.

"Olivia?"

She whirled, to find Garrick standing wide-eyed in the hall outside of an open door in nothing but a pair of breeches that were not even buttoned. But she had no time to absorb either the sight of his muscular body or the obvious implication that he slept, apparently, in the raw. She ran to him. "Hannah is sleepwalking! I awoke to find her gone! We have to find her!"

He gripped her arms. "Olivia. Calm yourself. No harm will come to Hannah." His tone was commanding and firm.

She met his gaze and felt tears filling her eyes. His strength and reassurances were so dearly welcome.

He continued to hold her, but his grip eased. "We will find her. But it may take some time, the house is very large."

Olivia nodded, her pulse finally ceasing its wild rioting. Then she became aware of the musky scent of his bare chest—and just how bare he was. In fact, his chest was extremely hard and broad and dusted with dark hair. His arms, flexed as he held her, bulged with muscle. Her gaze slipped. His torso was beautifully sculpted; she could just see his ribs and the soft indentation below them. Then she glanced at his navel—and the dark hair swirling below, where his breeches had been left suggestively open.

Olivia flushed and looked away.

He released her immediately, turning and buttoning the flap. The glance he threw over his shoulder at her was dark and powerful. Olivia's heart drummed yet again. She watched him walk to his room and shrug on a shirt, which he buttoned as he returned to the hallway. Then he gave her a pointed glance.

Olivia realized she wore only a thin cotton nightgown, for it had not even occurred to her to throw on her wrapper. "I don't care," she said defensively, folding her bare arms across her chest. The nightgown was sleeveless. She was quite bare beneath it.

"Let's find your daughter," he said tersely. "Is Treve with her?"

Olivia nodded as they returned to the stairway. "Miss Childs is waking the staff."

"Good. We shall begin our search from where she was last seen. I imagine she is in the central wing, not far from your bedchamber." He allowed Olivia to precede him down the stairs. "Does she sleepwalk often?"

Olivia hesitated. "Recently she has begun to do so, and it worries me." She recalled Arlen's reaction to the one time she'd told him—falsely—that Hannah had been sleepwalking: the night Susan had tried to kill herself. In truth, Hannah had started walking in her sleep about a month ago. Olivia could not guess why.

"You should worry less," De Vere said as they entered the center wing. "Hannah is blind, and far more at ease in the dark than you or I."

Olivia did not hesitate. "She is afraid of the dark. At night she insists on sleeping with candles blazing in her room."

He stumbled, facing her.

Olivia met his gaze, which was wide and filled with concern, and nodded.

"Was she born blind?" he asked, taking her arm, his hand strong and warm and large on her bare skin. He guided her down a corridor. They could hear the staff speaking in hushed tones in the great hall.

"Yes."

He did not reply as they entered the hall. Two dozen servants stood there in their nightclothes, holding tapers. De Vere quickly divided them into pairs, ordering each to a section of the house. "You and I will take this wing," he said as the staff began to disperse. "And we will begin on the second floor where you have your rooms."

But Miss Childs had yet to leave the hall with the maid she had been assigned to, and she approached Garrick and Olivia. "My lady," she said, her tone low, "can you not *feel* anything?"

Olivia froze. She did not dare look at De Vere, praying he would not understand the question. And now her suspicions were confirmed—Lucy knew the truth. "I have been too frightened even to try," she said, as hushed. "We will speak later," she said, hoping Lucy understood that she did not wish to discuss this subject now.

Miss Childs hesitated, shot Garrick De Vere a glance, and left with the housemaid. Refusing to look at him, Olivia started for the stairs, calling Hannah's name. Garrick was silent as he followed behind her, but she could feel his gaze, unwavering, upon her back. A moment later he let out a piercing whistle. Olivia tensed but heard neither the little girl nor the dog respond.

They returned to the second floor and began going through the rooms one at a time, Olivia calling Hannah's name, Garrick whistling for the dog. No child cried out in response; the dog did not bark or howl. In her bedchamber, her spirits low, Olivia retrieved and donned her wrapper, avoiding his gaze again. Finally she looked up at him. "Clearly this floor is deserted. It is so quiet, we could hear a pin dropping."

"I agree," Garrick said, his golden regard slipping over her firmly belted robe.

"Would not your dog hear that whistle even on another floor?" Olivia asked as they went toward the stairs.

"He would. And he would come—if he could."

Olivia stumbled on the steps. She was ahead of Garrick, and he caught her from behind. She pushed his hands away from her body. "What does that mean?" she demanded, facing him on the narrow staircase. He had crowded her against the wall.

"Treve wouldn't leave Hannah alone unless it were safe to do so." He took her elbow.

"You're frightening me," Olivia said.

"There are no ghosts here. This is merely an old house with far too many rooms and hallways. Hannah is fine. But if she is frightened, my dog will stay by her side. Let's skip the next floor. They are probably not there, for Treve would have barked."

"What is on the fourth story?" Olivia asked as they again ascended the steps.

"The nursery, servants' rooms, and an attic." His tone was sober.

Olivia was pierced with the image of the two boys again.

"I used to play in that attic when I was a child," he said wryly. They had paused on the landing. De Vere let out a determined whistle. And they heard it, faint or muffled—a series of barks.

He gave her a swift, hard look and began striding up the hall, Olivia running to keep up with him. "Where are they?" she cried.

"That," he said grimly, "was from the attic."

The attic. Of all the places for Hannah to go. Why would she venture up into the attic—unless she had not been walking in her sleep, unless something, or someone, had compelled her?

At the end of the corridor Garrick pushed open a narrow door, and Olivia saw very steep, extremely narrow stairs that were cast in utter blackness. Her pulse beat hard. His single taper cast the barest glow in the cramped space. "You wait here," he ordered.

Olivia did not even reply; she merely followed him up the stairs. At the top of the stairwell was another door, this one half as tall as De Vere, and slightly ajar. He pushed it open. And the setter was there, wagging his tail, his entire body swaying with eagerness, brown eyes alert.

"Good boy," De Vere said. "She is here, Olivia."

Olivia pressed against him, straining to see over his shoulder, desperate to find her daughter safe and sound. The attic was as dark as the stairwell, but Hannah was sitting on the floor, her back against the wall, near an open window. Her white nightclothes stood out starkly in the darkness. She was not moving. "Hannah!" Olivia cried.

Hannah did not answer.

Olivia pushed past Garrick and crept through the small doorway. Once inside, she could stand upright. She rushed to her daughter. And the moment she dropped to her knees beside her, Olivia's heart sank. Hannah was sitting tensely near the attic's single window. Rain beat on the sill and poured inside. Half of Hannah's nightclothes were soaking wet. She was concentrating.

"Darling, are you all right?" Olivia cried, pulling her into her arms. But as she did so, the wave of grief hit her, shocking her with its strength.

"I am fine, Mama," Hannah said calmly. But her expression was severe.

"Did you walk in your sleep?" Olivia asked, glancing around at the shadows surrounding them. But no one was there, she was certain of it; it was just her and Hannah and, of course, Garrick and the dog on the attic's threshold.

"No. I was not sleepwalking," Hannah said.

Olivia stared. It was as she had thought. What secrets—what tragedies—were hidden at the Hall? Olivia's temples throbbed. Hadn't she felt that in coming here, she would unravel a mystery? And that mystery had to concern Lionel De Vere. She was convinced of it.

Hannah bit her lip. "She woke me up, Mama. That woman. She was so sad. I had to find her."

Olivia's pulse raced. She did not dare glance at the doorway, aware that De Vere was watching them and listening to their every word. She knew that she had come to Stanhope Hall for a reason. Something—or someone—awaited her here—another truth to be revealed. She had assumed that Lionel De Vere was involved, but now she was not sure. "We will talk about this later," she whispered.

Hannah shook her head. "She isn't here. I couldn't find her. But she was here, Mama. She left the window open."

As Olivia took Hannah's arm and tugged her to her feet, she noticed that Hannah had been sitting on an old, misty Scottish plaid. How odd, she thought, for the De Veres had not a drop of Scottish blood in their veins. "It is late and you have given everyone a vast scare. You may not disappear again like that, Hannah," Olivia scolded gently.

Hannah was silent as they crossed the attic. Olivia finally dared to look at Garrick. He was staring at them both. "What is she talking about?" he asked bluntly.

"I have not a clue," Olivia said too lightly.

"A very sad lady. She comes here to hide and cry. I wanted to help her," Hannah said.

Garrick studied the child, set down the candle, then held out his arms. "Let me help you out of the attic, Hannah," he said quietly.

As if she could see, Hannah walked trustingly into his arms. Garrick lifted her through the doorway and set her down on the stairs. Olivia allowed him to help her step through, her palm in his, the contact disturbing her even more than she already was. The setter stood patiently on the stairs, waiting for them, watching them.

And Olivia's head whipped around and she stared at the dog.

"What is it?" Garrick asked sharply.

The setter was relaxed, his tail wagging slightly, ready to follow his master. Olivia inhaled, not answering—determined not to. Of course no long-dead soul was lingering in the attic, for the dog would be aware of it. Animals could see and sense these things far more easily than their human counterparts. The setter was at ease now, but had he been as complacent before she and De Vere had arrived in the attic?

"Olivia," Garrick said as sharply.

Olivia met his gaze and looked away. "It is late. I must put Hannah to bed."

Garrick lifted Hannah into his arms. "Please take the

CHAPTER ELEVEN

Olivia sat beside Hannah, who was now dressed in fresh, dry nightclothes and tucked carefully into the four-poster bed. She stroked her hair. The setter slept quietly on the floor just below the bed.

"You look very tired, dear," Olivia said, thinking that Hannah would be asleep within moments.

Hannah yawned, answer enough.

"Dear . . ." Olivia hesitated. "That sad woman. Do you have any idea who she is?"

Hannah yawned again. "She is very beautiful. I would know her if I met her."

Olivia's eyes widened. Did this mean that she was not dead? "Hannah, I had assumed we were speaking of a lost spirit."

"I don't know." Hannah rubbed her eyes. "Sometimes I think so, but then I feel that she is still with us, Mama."

"Was there anyone in the attic with you before Lord Caedmon and I arrived?"

Hannah's eyes were closing. "No. She had already left."

Olivia watched her beautiful daughter as her lids remained closed and her breathing grew deep and even. She tried to think clearly, no easy task after the events of the evening. Perhaps Hannah might identify the ghost as a Stanhope ancestor from one of the portraits in the hall. Perhaps that was what she had meant.

Flickering light fell over her.

Olivia started, in time to see De Vere walking casually into her bedroom, holding a candle in one hand. He remained barefoot, in his snug breeches and silk shirt, the latter still hanging about his hips. His dark hair fell to his shoulders in thick waves, still untied. Her heart thudded wildly against her chest and she was on her feet. "You cannot come in here!"

He had left the door partially open. His smile was brief. "Is she asleep?"

A quick glance showed Olivia that Hannah remained asleep and oblivious of them. "Yes, she is, and I ask that you leave right now."

He set the candle in its holder upon the heavy side table beside the bed. Olivia's eyes widened as he straightened, his body inches from hers. "What was it," he asked, "that Miss Childs meant when she asked if you could not *feel* anything?"

Olivia felt as if she had been struck in the face with icy water. "I do not even remember what you are speaking about," she said huskily, perspiring now.

"You are hiding something. But what?" he asked very softly, his golden eyes somehow mesmerizing, making it impossible for Olivia to look away.

And she did look at his mouth. Then she tore her gaze back to his eyes, only to realize that he was smiling slightly again—knowingly. As if he could read *her* thoughts. Which bordered on the improper. "We cannot be in this room together."

"What did Hannah see in the attic? Or should I say, what did she *feel?*"

Olivia inhaled.

His hands closed on her upper arms. "I am not your enemy, Olivia. I only wish to help. Do we have ghosts at the Hall after all?"

"I don't know." His touch was making it difficult to concentrate on his words. She was remembering his kiss in the Laytons' garden.

"Hannah can feel the presence of a ghost, can she not? Her blindness helps her in this."

Olivia shook her head. "It is all the wild imaginings of a young child used to playing alone."

"I don't think so. Nor do I think that Hannah was sleep-walking," he said flatly.

"You may think whatever you want," Olivia began, and then she stiffened. "What do you know about that attic?"

He looked at her.

"You played there as a boy," Olivia cried, an accusation. "With your brother."

"We did. And we were always soundly punished for disobeying my father," Garrick said dryly. "You see, the attic was supposed to be under lock and key. No one was allowed up there."

Olivia remembered watching the shadows in the attic while trying to feel a lingering presence. But she had not felt anything. On the other hand, she had been too emotionally upset to use her gift. Strong emotions always interfered with her abilities.

"Did you ever feel anything?" Olivia heard herself ask.

Garrick hesitated. "I don't know. Maybe. It was never a friendly place. It was always dark, even on the sunniest of days, dark and dreary and sad."

Olivia stared at him. He stared back.

Suddenly he smiled and reached out to touch her cheek. "Little boys have wild imaginings, too."

Olivia jerked away from his touch, breathless now. And her reaction had little to do with the attic upstairs or any anguished soul.

"What are you so afraid of?" he asked softly. "Are you hiding from me, Olivia?"

"I am only afraid of your boldness!" Olivia said.

"I know," he said suddenly. "I know what you are afraid of now."

Olivia met his gaze and was shocked at the intensity she saw there. She knew, and tensed, her body preparing to resist him.

"Don't," he whispered harshly. Then his hands eased

and slid slowly, suggestively, sensually, up and down her arms.

Olivia bit off a cry, one that was hardly a protest. Myriad sensations, heated and delicious chills, were flooding her. She forgot that her daughter was asleep in the bed behind her.

His large hands stroked back up her arms, increasing her body's heat, fingers splayed, pausing below her shoulders. His thumbs rested firmly against the sides of her breasts.

Olivia inhaled. Her nipples hardened immediately. And she was wearing only two fine layers of cotton. She saw his eyes move to the two erect points on her chest.

His brilliant gaze lifted, met hers. His hands slid over and cupped her breasts, which were full and womanly. Olivia's heart pounded far more swiftly than before—it was becoming difficult to breathe.

"What is wrong, Olivia?" he whispered roughly.

She could not answer—not when his hands molded her so skillfully. "Garrick," she finally breathed.

Abruptly he framed her face with his strong hands, making her acutely aware of his power and her fragility, and his mouth was on hers, hot and hard and demanding. Olivia did not pull away, knowing that she should. His tongue thrust inside of her, strong and rhythmically, repeatedly. A wet heat gathered on the insides of her thighs. I must not, she managed to think. But she was gripping his bulging arms—she was kissing him back frantically.

His mouth had forced hers open. Now his tongue swept along the seam of her parted lips. "What?" he whispered. "What is it, Olivia? Tell me."

"Garrick." She clung.

His hands moved from the sides of her face to her buttocks. Olivia gasped. He continued to kiss her, penetrating her deeply, but he gripped her buttocks, separating them, then slid his hands impossibly lower. Touching her through the two fine layers of cotton.

Olivia cried out. She could not stand it, this, him. She became light-headed, needing more. Her knees buckled. His wicked hands did not stop. From behind, he caressed her femininity through her nightclothes. Olivia had to cling to his shoulders now to remain standing upright. She thought she might soon die. She was shaking like a leaf.

Then he tore his mouth from hers, staring at her with such a smoldering gaze that Olivia backed up into the side table. After giving her another look, one male and promising and lacking any possibility of compromise, he turned, snapped his fingers, and pointed at the bed. Olivia's mind began to function as the setter jumped up and lay down on the mattress beside her sleeping daughter.

Hannah. What if she awoke?

To her dismay, she was so feverish with wanting him, she hardly cared.

"Stay," De Vere said harshly.

"She'll wake up," Olivia began weakly.

"And she will be very happy," he finished, gripping her elbow tightly. Olivia found herself being propelled from the room. Her feet lagged behind her body. She looked back over her shoulder. Hannah remained nestled in the bed beside the red setter, whose tail was thumping slowly.

He clamped an arm around her waist as they entered the unlit hall.

"Garrick," Olivia began. She was torn. Her body demanded a physical union with him. But her mind refused, demanding a protest, demanding resistance. For lurking in the shadows, on the periphery, was an image of her husband, an accusing expression on his face.

"No," he said, pushing open the door to an empty guest room. He nearly shoved Olivia inside, then closed and bolted it behind them. He set the taper on the mantel, regarding her.

And Olivia looked at him. His expression was ruthless, the outcome of this evening already decided in his mind. The sheer force of his will was overwhelming. But hadn't she known from the beginning that it would come to this?

If she did give in to her desire for him, would it be the end of the world? She had never wanted to be with a man before, especially not like this. As Garrick had said, most women in her position had lovers; it was routine and eminently acceptable. It was not considered dishonorable.

But he was affianced to Susan Layton, her new friend. And not only did she not believe in adultery, she was not like other women. There was Arlen to consider.

A night like this could very well be the end of her world.

"Now is not the time to think," he said in a hard voice, unbuttoning his shirt.

Olivia's mental rampaging died. She watched him open his shirt inch by inch. Her breathing became constricted, and she clutched the folds of her nightgown. His dark skin was stretched taut over hard muscles, and his movements slowly revealed his chest, his rib cage, his abdomen. Olivia was mesmerized. It was almost impossible to think now, especially as her loins remained shamelessly swollen and aching. He tossed the shirt aside. His nipples were erect. Then Olivia took one closer look at him and inhaled loudly.

His manhood was fully erect, a massive length pressing up and out against his breeches.

He stepped to her, reaching for her. Olivia thought he was going to touch her, embrace her, kiss her—or even say something. Instead he pushed the wrapper off her shoulders and to the floor. Olivia was clad now only in the thin, white sleeveless nightgown. Two narrow lace straps held it up.

He looked. He looked at her throat, her shoulders, her upper chest. Then he looked at the hard pink points of her breasts. "I want your hair down," he said thickly. His own chest was heaving as if he had run a long distance.

Olivia started. Removing the pins took time, and shamelessly, she no longer wanted to wait for what he offered her.

He reached up and began removing pins. Olivia felt fainter than before, her heart speeding. No man had ever done this for her before. Even his fingertips, grazing her hair and scalp, were intensifying the desire. "What are you thinking, Olivia?" he asked softly.

"You know," she whispered. She had been imagining them naked and entwined, in the bed that was behind them. She caught his hands, stilling them, her own hands trembling. "I'll do it," she finally said, her tone shocking in its huskiness. And it was a statement of final acquiescence.

"Tell me," he returned as Olivia finished the task of removing the pins, hardly more adept than he.

She refused to answer him. She threw the braid over her shoulder and began to unravel it. Her cheeks felt feverishly hot. She knew he stared. She felt his impatience. And as she fumbled with the braid he moved behind her, embracing her. She froze. His palms covered her breasts, and his manhood jutted urgently against her buttocks.

He kissed her neck, at the nape.

Olivia moaned.

"I want you," he said, sliding his hands down her belly, lower and lower still.

"Yes," she cried.

He palmed her, hard, then began caressing her gently. Olivia gripped his forearms, almost clawing him.

"Gentle," he murmured, his mouth still nibbling her neck. Then he crushed her hard, rocking his hips against her, and held her still, for a long moment.

Olivia felt him throbbing against her. "I cannot wait," she heard herself gasp.

Abruptly he turned her around so they faced one another. His eyes, seeking hers, were fire. And he slid the straps over her arms, pushing the gown below her breasts. He cupped one breast, and his mouth found the nipple. He began to suck.

Olivia's mind ceased final functioning at last. Her hands were in his thick hair as he nuzzled her and licked her, and then her palms were on his shoulders, his back. His skin was like silk. Silk stretched over rock. She imagined the sight of his manhood freed of his breeches and shivered, her nails skidding over his skin.

He was raining kisses down her torso, he was licking her navel. He was greedy with his hunger. His tongue was firm, strong. Olivia gripped his head, aware of having lost control of some vital part of herself. She should stop him, for surely he could not continue on this downward path. But she did not want to stop him. Every flick of his tongue was sending red-hot pleasure through her. And he was kneeling now.

His face was on a level with her heated loins. And he looked up. His golden eyes caught hers, gleaming.

Olivia felt something in her heart, an instantaneous jolting, as their gazes locked. She knew she must ignore it. That she must not identify it.

But she wet her lips. "I've never felt this way before."

"I know," he said, and then his tongue slid over her lower belly, just inches above the thick, curly hair guarding her pubis. Olivia was shaking. And he said, "Neither have I."

Olivia barely heard, because he was pulling the nightgown down now, exposing her sex and her thighs, finally letting it fall around her ankles. His knowing fingers stroked up against the lips of her sex, opening her. And then his tongue was there.

Olivia could not breathe. She could not stand it. "Oh, God," she heard herself cry, a sob. He was standing, embracing her, his mouth on her ear, his hard, long phallus thrusting against her still throbbing loins. His hands cupped and held her buttocks. "Come to the bed."

She allowed herself to be guided there in the darkness, not trusting herself to speak. As she sat down, she realized he was stepping out of his breeches. He was a magnificent sight. She did stare.

"When you look at me like that, you will undo me," he said, pushing her slowly onto her back, his hands gripping her wrists, one knee on either side of her thighs.

"You are a stunning man," she managed to whisper, aware of desire rising so swiftly again.

"Am I?" He bent and nipped her lips, then boldly moved one knee between her thighs, then a second one, pushing them far apart. Holding her gaze with his, he dipped from the pelvis and brushed the tip of his huge phallus against her loins. Olivia cried out.

When she tried to move, wanting to embrace him and pull him closer, she realized she could not. He continued to grip her hands, holding each one firmly over her head. He slid himself over her wet, swollen flesh several times, and then he paused. "Tell me that you want me, Olivia," he demanded.

She met his gaze. "Yes. I want you, Garrick De Vere."

Olivia saw his eyes turn opaque with lust. "I cannot wait," he cried, and pushed his huge length into her. Olivia gasped.

Eyes closed, he strained inside of her, hard, heated, tight. Olivia had never enjoyed intercourse before; now she was in shock. The pleasure, the heat, the hardness, was far more than right; it was the greatest moment of her life. She found and met his thrusting rhythm eagerly. The explosive pressure was building, that bridge to ecstasy. Olivia realized she was making soft, whimpering sounds, that she was panting his name. He had yet to release her hands, but she knew she was about to become one with comets and shooting stars, and she wanted to hold him. She moaned, thrashing beneath him helplessly. She was ready to beg.

"Now, now, please!" she heard herself cry.

His eyes flew open, he released her hands, and their gazes locked. Olivia flung her arms around him; he lifted her leg and wrapped it around his waist, driving into her. Qlivia felt the explosion then, bursting inside of her, a huge shower of fire and sparks.

Garrick cried out, surging deeply, wetly, inside her. A tremor seized his body, and then he collapsed on top of her, his arms going around her.

Olivia could not move. She doubted she had a muscle that might work. Then she realized that the fingers of her right hand were stroking over his left shoulder, and she smiled, eyes closed. *Nothing* had ever been this right.

It was there, inside her heart, a joyful, joyous emotion she must not harbor or identify. It was so strong, so powerful, it felt like a spring bubbling up and gushing inside of her. It felt as if it must soon erupt.

He slid to his side, facing her. His words made her eyes fly open. "I want to make love to you all night."

Olivia stared at him, searching his expression for an inkling of his feelings and his emotions. She thought she saw something flickering in his golden eyes, something deeper, more profound, than mere lust.

But he only said, wryly, reaching for her, "Do you object?" knowing full well that she did not. She had proven that already.

Then Hannah's image, and Arlen's, flashed through her mind. Not far behind were the Laytons' accusing faces. Olivia's ready response died unspoken.

With one palm, he cupped her face. "Do not think now," he said. But his brow was furrowed. And Olivia knew that he was thinking about the future, too.

Olivia was awoken by Garrick. She felt his fingertips first, stroking tendrils of hair away from her eyes and face. She smiled, eyes still closed, knowing full well whom she was with. She had not slept more than a few hours that night, which had begun late to begin with. She had slept lightly and was instantly fully awake.

Her heart felt as though it were singing.

He was leaning over her now, whispering in her ear, his breath warm and sensual—as warm and sensual as the man himself. "Olivia. I must go. As it is, the staff is surely up."

Olivia tensed, eyes wide, their gazes meeting. Garrick was already dressed. She sat up, shoving off the covers, last night fading as reality took over. Disaster, she thought, staring at him. This could become the disaster awaiting them all.

She nearly jumped off the bed, diving for her nightgown, which she shrugged on in great haste. "What time is it?" The heavy velvet draperies were drawn.

"The sun is rising. It is probably half-past five," he said evenly, his gaze sliding over her.

Olivia had been reaching for her wrapper, and now she whirled, clutching it to her, afraid. "Everyone will know," she said hoarsely. This was the hour when household servants rose and began to prepare for the day.

His reply was not what she wished to hear. "I imagine so."

Olivia's impulse was to strike out at him, but this was

not solely his fault—it was her fault, too—she had wanted him desperately, and somehow, in spite of the uncertain future, she could not regret last night. He had taught her passion. She had never dreamed that she was such a sensual woman. And what about the song in her heart? Perhaps she was, for the first time in her life, falling in love.

The thought was terrifying.

"Perhaps, if you hurry, you can return to your rooms without being seen," Olivia said quickly. "And I must prepare to depart as planned, right after breakfast." She was already belting her wrapper firmly.

"I agree," he said, staring. His gaze was extremely penetrating.

Olivia stared back. In spite of her rising hysteria, she had one extremely powerful and lucid thought. When would she see him again?

He said, "When can I see you again?"

She tensed. "I don't know. We must think. This isn't right."

He cut her off before she could ramble on. "This is very right," he said. "And you know it, too."

Olivia shook her head, terribly confused, turning away. She unbolted the door, but before she could open it, his hand slammed down on hers, forestalling her. "I can see you tonight at Ashburnham. I'll stay at an inn. You need merely come to me when the household is asleep."

Olivia was frozen, facing the door, her back to him. Her pulse raced, but not with the anticipation of an illicit rendezvous. Dread consumed her, and with it an appropriate companion—a sickly guilt. "Is this the future, then? I cuckold Arlen, and you, your fiancée?" Her tone sounded bitter even to her own ears.

"Damn them both, yes," he said, again a near shout in her ear. He turned her so that she faced him. His thighs pressed hers against the door. "I never intended for this to be one single night, and I have little doubt that you feel the same way."

"I do not know how I feel!" she cried, a half-truth.

He jerked, his expression twisted. Olivia wanted to explain, for clearly she had hurt him, but she did not dare. It would only deepen their involvement—which should have never happened in the first place. After a long moment passed, he said, "Return to London. It will be easier for us to rendezvous there." His jaw was flexed and ticking visibly.

She shook her head, near tears. "I cannot. Arlen will not allow it."

"He is your keeper?" he asked, incredulous.

She hesitated and said, "I cannot defy him without suffering the consequences."

"I'll kill him," Garrick said.

Lionel's image flashed through her mind, a laughing golden-haired boy. But what her mind was trying to conclude was insane. Garrick had not killed his brother, and his last words had been an impassioned and common enough form of speech.

He read her mind yet again. "God! I meant that if he hurts you, I would kill him—I hardly meant that I am a murderer!"

Very clearly Olivia heard a cock crow. Dismay and fear overcame her. She turned, pulling at the door. "I cannot think about anything now, other than returning to Ashburnham." Then she looked at him over her shoulder. "Do not follow me there, Garrick, not after what happened tonight. It is too dangerous. I . . ."

"You what?"

"I have a sense of doom," she said, choking on the last word.

"A sense? Or a feeling?" he demanded.

Olivia shook her head and pulled open the door. Somehow he was close to guessing the truth about her—and he had already guessed the truth about Hannah. Olivia was shaking. What was happening to them all? And how was this happening? Just a few days ago she and Hannah had been at Ashburnham, happy and alone.

The cock crowed again.

Olivia glanced into the hall and thanked God, for the corridor was empty and silent and cast in early morning shadows. Not a soul—or a servant—was about. She stepped into the hallway, her pulse rioting now. She had only a dozen steps or so to go in order to return to her own bedroom, where Hannah slept with the Irish setter. She started forward. It was possible that their liaison might not yet become public knowledge.

Garrick fell into step beside her. She did not dare look at him. If she did, she might weep or give in to his impossible demands.

Olivia reached for her door. As she did so, she heard a series of footfalls coming up the stairs. She turned, dismayed, her heart thumping.

Mrs. Riley appeared at the end of the corridor. If she was surprised to see Garrick and Olivia standing outside Olivia's bedroom door, Olivia in her nightclothes with her long blond hair flowing about her hips, Garrick still half dressed from the evening before, both of them barefoot, she gave no sign. She approached swiftly.

Olivia sank against the door, trembling. This was, she had no doubt, the beginning of the end of her life as she now knew it.

"My lady, my lord, good morning," Mrs. Riley said. Her tone was taut with uncharacteristic tension.

Olivia looked at her and saw the excited sparkle in her eyes. Garrick was saying, "Good morning, Mrs. Riley. Are you looking for the countess?"

"Actually, my lord, I was looking for you. When I realized you were not in your rooms, I assumed you were checking in on the little girl," the housekeeper said. It was a gracious explanation for finding Garrick where he had no right to be.

He smiled slightly. "You thought correctly."

She handed him a sealed envelope. "This just came," she said, excitement filling her tone.

He stared at the seal. Even Olivia recognized it as belonging to his father. She also thought that Mrs. Riley somehow knew the contents of that sealed missive.

"Thank you," Garrick said. He broke the seal and opened the single piece of parchment. Within seconds he had lost every single ounce of his coloring. And his eyes were nearly bulging. He was impossibly pale for a sun-tanned man.

"My lord?" Olivia asked. When he stared at the letter, not responding, she took his arm. "Lord Caedmon!"

Finally he looked at her, still in shock, not speaking.

"I will bring His Lordship a brandy," Mrs. Riley said, and she fled back down the stairs.

Garrick leaned against the wall, reading the letter another time. "Oh, my God," he said. "Oh, my God."

"What is it? What has happened? Why are you so white? Did someone die?"

He lifted his gaze to hers. "No. To the contrary."

"I do not understand!" Olivia shouted.

He shoved the parchment at her, leaning now against the wall, still absolutely stricken. And he said, "Is this a poor joke?"

"Is what a joke?" Olivia cried.

At last he met her gaze. His eyes were filled with confusion. "But this is my father's handwriting. Dear God. Olivia. Lionel is not dead. He has returned."

CHAPTER TWELVE

Garrick strode into the foyer of Stanhope-on-the-Square, his strides brisk. He had made the journey back from Surrey in record time, and it was early afternoon. Apparently the earl had been waiting for him, because he had only just entered the house when Stanhope appeared from the opposite end of the marble-floored foyer. His face was grim, his eyes anxious.

"Is this a jest?" Garrick demanded. But his father was hardly a fool. And the tone of the earl's brief message had been absolutely serious.

"Would I ever jest about such a matter?" Stanhope rushed forward. "Good God, he appeared here yesterday morning. Why in God's name did you go to the Hall?"

Garrick grimaced. "A whim." He tried not to think about Olivia now.

The earl was exasperated. He took Garrick's arm and they began walking down the corridor and into the library. "Garrick. It might be Lionel." He paused and closed his eyes. "It is he. Dear God."

Garrick faced him, incredulous. "Father, have you lost your mind? Lionel died fourteen years ago. Fourteen years ago, Father. Whoever has appeared here, claiming to be him, is an impostor." But Lionel had never been buried. He had vanished; his body had never been found. And Garrick was acutely aware of it.

The earl stared, clearly dismayed and torn. "Of course, that was my first reaction. But he has an explanation for these past years—and he knows so much about our family." The earl paced, then paused. "He looks like him. He is clearly about the same age."

How could his father be so gullible? The earl was brilliant, his mind razor-sharp, and he had the common sense so often denied the upper crust of society but found among the impoverished who lived on the streets. Garrick studied his father and realized that he was not quite as tall as he had once appeared, his shoulders were not as broad, and his face, once so handsome and commanding, was jowled and wrinkled. My God, he thought, still staring. He is an old man. He may still be powerful, but he is old. And he is believing what he wishes to believe.

The earl was human—and flawed—after all.

"Lionel was fourteen when he died. It is impossible to say how he might look now, at the age of twenty-eight," Garrick said.

"Did Lionel die?" The earl whirled from where he stood at a window. It was raining yet again outside, and the gardens were shrouded in a wet mist. "He vanished. Without a trace. Into thin air. Or so *you* claimed."

Garrick folded his arms. "And what does that mean?"

The earl stared. "You were the last person to see him. No one vanishes. If it was an abduction, as everyone decided then that it was, why was there no ransom note?"

"There was no ransom note because the abductors killed him accidentally." Garrick was suddenly angry. "We have been over all of this before, Father. This person claiming to be Lionel is an impostor. What possible explanation could he have for being gone for fourteen years? If Lionel were still alive, he would have returned years ago—fourteen years ago, to be exact."

The earl rubbed his temples. "I am not a fool. I have already had all of the same thoughts as you. But . . ." He paused. Garrick now realized his father's face was oddly ashen. "He not only looks like him, he is very convincing."

"What has he claimed? Did he lose his memory during the abduction? It was an abduction, was it not? Now, suddenly, fourteen years later, he remembers who he is and he has returned?" Garrick's tone was bitingly sarcastic. "How convenient!"

The earl's jaw flexed. "He wishes to see you. He is very anxious to see you. Why don't you let him tell you? And afterward I wish to speak with you."

"Very well," Garrick said. In spite of himself, in spite of his common sense and his absolute belief that this was an impostor, his pulse was racing and he was short of breath. But it could not be Lionel. Lionel was dead. Garrick had convinced himself of that long ago. "Where is he?"

"Upstairs. In his old room," the earl said.

Before Garrick could turn to go, the countess was rushing forward, arms outstretched. Garrick took one look at her strained countenance and tearful eyes, and he put his arm around her. "Are you all right?" he asked, suddenly furious. He would unmask this fraud immediately. For this kind of game was far too cruel to be tolerated any longer.

She dabbed at her eyes with her handkerchief, shaking her head, but whether it was a yes or a no, Garrick could not tell. Clearly his mother was distressed. "Garrick," she said hoarsely, "Lionel has come back."

He gripped her arms. "Mother, stop it! This man—whoever he is—is a fraud. He seeks only to claim the Stanhope title and fortune. Lionel vanished fourteen years ago, and he is dead. Otherwise he would have returned long ago."

The countess stared at him, dabbing at her eyes continually with the embroidered linen. "He has reappeared—as abruptly as he once disappeared," she said. She started to cry. "It is a miracle," she said.

Garrick was stricken. He did not know what to do. "Mother, please, go upstairs and rest. Father and I will handle this."

She nodded, but before she left she said, "Your father is as convinced as I."

When she was gone, Garrick faced the earl. "It is unfair

to encourage her—to raise her hopes. I beg you to exercise prudence at the least.''

"Your mother would not be fooled in this instance."

Garrick looked at him. "And why not?"

"She is his mother," the earl said simply. "How could a mother be fooled by her son?"

He paused outside the room Lionel had used when they were children growing up together. Since that time, Garrick knew the room had been closed, the furnishings covered, draperies drawn, maids entering only once per annum to dust. His heart drummed, with anger mostly, but with other as intense emotions he dared not identify. He knew he was hesitating.

Garrick knocked. The door had not been firmly closed, and it opened under the pressure of his fist. He was prepared for an impostor. He was not prepared for the sight of the man who sat up from where he reclined on the bed, and he felt his heart lurch to an immediate halt.

The fraud—Lionel—also stared, standing. "Garrick," he said hoarsely.

Garrick was speechless. *It was Lionel!* That was his first insane thought. For, despite the many years that had elapsed, this man looked exactly as Lionel should have by now, and he was clearly cast in the image of the earl and the countess themselves. It was not just the blond hair and blue eyes, two attributes found easily enough among the population at large. There was a cleft in his chin. His lower lip was full. His nose was perfectly straight. Garrick was in shock.

Lionel came forward, hesitantly but beginning to smile. "Garrick, you are staring as if you have seen a ghost," he said.

Garrick inhaled. "Perhaps I am looking at a ghost," he managed. He fought for composure. This was not Lionel. But how could there be such a resemblance? Or was he, like his parents, too eager to see the similarities? He tried to find dissimilarities. Was not this man's jaw fuller than Lionel's had been? Were his eyebrows not a shade darker?

And he was not as tall or as broad shouldered as Garrick. When they were boys, Lionel had been taller and bigger. This man was very slightly overweight now, when Lionel had been lean. ·

But these last traits all might have changed with age.

"I am no ghost," Lionel was saying, smiling now. "But I cannot blame you if that is what you think." He reached out as if to touch Garrick's shoulder.

Garrick stepped away from him, trembling, in disbelief, still amazed, and very angry now. "I do not think you are a ghost. I think you are, simply put, a fraud." But he continued to stare. "You cannot be my brother. If my brother was alive, he would have returned home many years ago." He was aware of the hurt and accusation in his own tone.

Lionel's face fell. His gaze remained on Garrick. "Have you grown to hate me in the ensuing years? I am no fraud, but I do not blame you for thinking as much. If I were in your position, that would be my thinking exactly."

"But you are not in my position," Garrick said coldly. "You are the one who has suddenly wandered into London, claiming to be my long-lost, and undoubtedly long-deceased, brother. Have you suffered from a fourteen-year mental lapse?" he demanded scathingly.

Lionel shoved his hands in the pockets of his breeches. He was clad casually, in breeches and stockings, a simple shirt, and as simple a waistcoat. "I have. But not the kind of mental lapse you are thinking of. Won't you at least listen to what I have to say? Once, years ago, I would have never had to make such a plea—not to you."

Garrick froze, hurled violently into the past of his childhood, when he would have followed Lionel anywhere, done anything he asked, believed anything he said. "I shall enjoy this," he said finally, his hands also in his pockets. They were shaking.

"I was not abducted," Lionel said bluntly, his blue gaze—exactly the same shade as Lionel's had once been—unwavering upon Garrick's face. "Which is why there was never a ransom note."

"I do not understand," Garrick said uneasily, his heart

skipping and some emotion, dread, perhaps, rising up within him.

"I ran away," Lionel said simply, his gaze searching.

Garrick's heart stopped completely before starting again. "You ran away."

Lionel nodded. "Do you think that living here, growing up the way we did, was any easier on me than it was on you? Oh, I know I was the favorite, and I could do no wrong. But I was hardly the favorite because of being myself. I was approved of because I always jumped to his tune, always did as he demanded, never doing what I wished to do, never doing what I wanted. It was, in truth, unbearable—and getting worse with every passing day."

I ran away. Lionel's explanation echoed in Garrick's mind even as he listened to him speaking now. He was stunned. Was it possible? Had Lionel felt the same horrendous pressure from the earl as he himself had as a boy? "Lionel was not a rebel. He never complained about his lot in life. He wanted to please Stanhope. I was the one always complaining. I was the one always condemned and criticized. Lionel would have never run away. He could do no wrong. He was happy."

"You are wrong. Because I am your brother, and I did run away. I was not happy. The older I got, the closer I came to my majority, the worse it became. I was dreading the future. I could not imagine spending the next twenty years or so dancing to Father's never-ending tune. I was tired, Garrick. Damn tired of being his lackey." Lionel's eyes were filled with anger.

Garrick stared before turning away, running a hand through his hair, which was unpowdered and tied back in a queue, as was his brother's. He was trembling. But damn it, this man was not Lionel. Or was he?

What if it were Lionel?

"Lionel would have told me of such a plan," Garrick said harshly. "He would not have run away without telling me first."

"I couldn't. You would have insisted upon coming with

me.'' Lionel stared. ''How can you doubt me, Garrick? How?''

Garrick found it difficult to breathe properly. Goddamn it, he was right. He would have insisted upon joining him. How could this man not be Lionel? He knew so much. ''How could you do this to our mother? She cried for months afterward,'' he said tersely, wanting to also say, How could you do this to me?

''It was a matter of survival. I planned it for six months. Had there been another way, I would have taken it. I went to India, by the way. I bought myself a commission in the cavalry under an assumed name.'' Lionel grinned.

It was so familiar that Garrick's heart was wrenched hard. Was this man his brother after all? His temples throbbed, making his head hurt—but that was nothing compared to the pain in his heart—endured for fourteen endless years. Memories were flooding Garrick now. Wonderful memories, of the two of them up to their ears in mischief and trouble.

As if Lionel could read his mind, he said softly, ''Do you remember that snowy Christmas at the Hall? We hid behind the shrubs, which were frozen, of course, and threw snowballs at that fat Baron Margery and his even fatter son when they disembarked from their coach. Father was furious. We hid in the stables all day.''

Garrick felt like fainting for the first time in his life. How could this man recall that if he were not Lionel? He could hardly think. Could Lionel have run away, hurting all those who loved him so? Lionel had always enjoyed himself and had never experienced many regrets over his behavior. As wonderful as he had been, his life had been free of guilt— he could do no wrong. Perhaps, just perhaps, he could have run away so selfishly, so irresponsibly. God knew, Garrick had wished to do so often enough as a boy.

He thought about the last time he had been with Lionel, trying hard to remember every detail of the day Lionel had disappeared. He could not recall Lionel behaving oddly, the way he might had he been on the verge of running away. Or could he? ''The coin,'' he suddenly said. ''The lucky

Spanish coin. You tried to give it to me the day you vanished.''

"Yes." Lionel was smiling.

Garrick stared at him.

Lionel said, "I wanted you to have it because I was leaving."

Garrick really didn't expect a grown man to be wearing an old Spanish coin on a chain around his neck, but his glance went directly to Lionel's stock. "Do you still wear it?" he heard himself say.

"I gave it to a young fellow years ago, but it did not prevent him from dying of an ague anyway."

Garrick tried to clear his mind. He was confused. "Tell me, what made you decide to come back?"

Lionel paced. Briefly his back was turned. "I have never stopped thinking about you, Garrick," he said. He faced him again. "And Mother. Do you think this was easy? I have missed you terribly. But I had no choice, because I just could not live with Father breathing down my neck for the next thirty or forty years. Then, recently, I had a brush with death. A Bengal tiger. Actually, it was more than a brush with death. I almost died from my wounds. And while I lay recuperating, all I could think about was my family, and that the time had finally come to return home." Suddenly Lionel's eyes were wet. He looked away.

Garrick was still shaken. His mind raced now but remained oddly blank. If there was a truth to be found, it was eluding him. Yet his heart was becoming oddly light, oddly exuberant. Insane organ that it was, it was daring to hope. Suddenly he thought of Olivia, which made his pulse race all over again. How he wished to confide in her now and share this astounding turn of events.

"So tell me," he said, knowing he did not sound casual at all, "about your first woman."

Lionel looked up, startled. Then he smiled—that awfully familiar grin. "Do I have to share everything?"

Garrick was not smiling. "Perhaps you do not know who your first was?"

Lionel stared. "I know. But you still doubt me, don't you?"

"I have no choice but to doubt you."

"It was Lady Marianne Compton. The redhead. At least, I think her first name was Marianne, it's hard to remember now. But she was about twenty, if I recall correctly, and she was newly wed. She and the viscount were guests at Stanhope Hall. She was more than willing. I was, I believe, thirteen."

Garrick wet his lips. "Her name was Madeleine. Madeleine Comden. And her husband was a baron, not a viscount."

"You have a better memory than I," Lionel said easily.

Garrick was trying frantically to think if a stranger might know of this or the incident with the snowballs. Lionel had bragged to just about everyone at the Hall about the loss of his virginity, hardly a gentlemanly thing to do, of course, but excusable given the circumstances—Madeleine had been gorgeous and his first. Even the earl had heard the gossip—and had reprimanded Lionel for his wagging tongue. Of course, he had then slapped his shoulder soundly, beaming with approval at such virility on behalf of his heir and firstborn son.

And that fat baron had been furious about being hit with half a dozen snowballs, some of which had struck his head and face. He had complained loudly about the delinquent Stanhope boys.

This man could be lying. He could be a fraud.

This man could also be telling the truth.

"Tell me more about the night you disappeared," Garrick said tersely. "Do you remember our conversation?"

"Frankly, I do not," Lionel said. "Good Lord, Garrick, that was fourteen years ago. I only remember we were at the haunted keep on the cliffs, and that it was raining, and that you would not take the coin."

Garrick reminded himself that most of England knew those facts, and he himself had brought up the subject of the coin, damn it. He swallowed, still oddly light-headed, still damnably hopeful. But he must not hope. He must not accept this man as his brother. Not yet. "What about your thirteenth birthday? Do you remember what Father gave you?"

Lionel smiled. "I do. The matchlock rifle."

Garrick remembered, too, because Lionel had been so pleased, and the earl had taken Lionel out immediately to test the gun—and Garrick had been left behind. *Jesus.*

"May I ask you a question?" Lionel asked.

Garrick nodded, cautious.

"Do you remember when we were boys, you were about six or seven, I think, it was at the Hall, and you and I went riding, eluded the groom, and then we got lost? We were only lost for a quarter of an hour or so, but you were scared, and frankly, so was I. We were both sent to bed without supper for that one." Lionel smiled.

"I do not remember," Garrick said stiffly. But at this point his mind seemed to have quit on him—he could hardly put a thought together.

Lionel's expression was somewhat smug. "One cannot remember even half of everything that is long since done, Garrick." He walked over to him for the first time. "It is really good to see you. I have missed you."

Garrick stared into his friendly blue eyes, unable to smile, remaining thoroughly shocked. But he had missed Lionel. He had missed him every single day of the past fourteen years. Elation was trying to penetrate the shock and the remnants of doubt; it was trying to creep over him. Did he dare believe in miracles? Did he dare believe in this one?

The man standing before him could be his brother. The story was incredible, but not impossible. And Lionel's disappearance had been as incredible.

"Can we not at least be friends, until you have had some time to sort out the fact of my return?" Lionel asked.

"I do not know," Garrick said. He turned to leave, then paused. Their gazes met. "If I find out that you are an impostor, you will pay a very serious price for all the damage you are inflicting on my family." Anger surged within him again. He thought of his mother, whom he had to protect. She had suffered enough in her lifetime. He even wished to spare his father the circumstance of a pretender. Then he thought of his own grief—and the joy, the insane joy, he would feel if this were truly Lionel.

"Garrick."

Garrick halted, facing the man calling himself Lionel. Facing the man who might very well be his long-lost brother.

"You have nothing to worry about," Lionel said.

CHAPTER THIRTEEN

Olivia was on her knees, a trowel in hand, a large straw hat on her head. It was tied beneath her chin with a pale blue ribbon. Hannah, similarly poised and clad, also was busy preparing the ground for the young potted roses they were planting. Mother and child were surrounded by nearly every color imaginable, for they were in the midst of what appeared to be a sublimely chaotic arrangement of blooming flowers, planted in no apparent order: begonias and geraniums, petunias and pansies, daffodils and tulips, sunflowers and daisies and roses.

Olivia welcomed the mindless task she had set herself. Gardening had never been a task before, it had always been a pure and simple pleasure. But pleasure eluded her now, furiously, and she had instructed herself to remain busy, spending the past three days since her return to Ashburnham housecleaning, sewing, and gardening. The manor had never been as dust free, both she and Hannah had new silk gowns, and they had planted an entire second vegetable garden. Now Olivia was determined to expand her flower garden, already overflowing with blooms.

She must not think about Garrick De Vere.

She must not think about what they had found at Stanhope Hall, what they had shared—and what they had no right to. She must not think about the future. De Vere was going to wed Susan Layton, as he should.

Olivia paused, closing her eyes, short of breath. The soil felt warm and rich beneath her bare hands, the sun too hot blazing down upon her back. She was light-headed. She was torn between exhilaration and despair. The appearance of Garrick's face, as he strained over her, the recollection of his devastating touch—worse, the feeling of him within her—overwhelmed her for the thousandth time since her return home. She was miserable. Nothing had ever felt so perfect, so right.

His expression, his absolute shock upon receiving the missive from the earl, was unforgettable.

She wiped her hands on a towel, but they remained filthy, and she dared not dab at her eyes with her fingertips. Oh, God. What had happened to her in such a short period of time? Was she in love, painfully so, with a man intended for someone else? If so, if this was love, then she was passionately involved, against her will. How *had* this happened?

She wondered if a man could make such ardent love to a woman without being hopelessly in love himself. She did not have a clue. But Arlen had never touched her or kissed her with such explosive intensity. She closed her eyes, sitting back on her thighs. Images, sensations, and feelings flooded Olivia with shocking intensity, with profound power. Before the other night, she had not suspected the depth of her passionate nature. Her heart yearned desperately for Garrick's love, but her body yearned for his touch—as desperately.

If only he had not followed her to the country.

But no amount of wishing would change anything.

"Mama?" Hannah interrupted her thoughts. She had risen to her feet and walked over to Olivia.

Olivia forced a smile to her face and cheer into her tone. "Yes, dear?" She stood. The muscles in her legs were finally returning to normal after that stunning night of lovemaking. How stiff she had been the next day.

"Please don't be so sad," Hannah said, reaching for Olivia's hand.

Olivia was stricken. She pulled Hannah close. What

could she say? She must not burden her own child with her dilemma, yet Hannah was no ordinary child, and Olivia was not even allowed the privacy of her own feelings and her own thoughts because of that. "Sometimes it happens that sad things come to pass," she said carefully. "But those sad things will also pass. I do believe there is a reason for everything, my dear. But Hannah, sometimes I wish you were not so aware of my thoughts."

"I'm sorry. But ever since we left Stanhope Hall, you have changed. You are worried and I am scared," she said bluntly. "It is Lord Caedmon, is it not?" she asked.

Oh, God. The last thing Olivia wished to do was frighten her already overwhelmed child. She must learn to control her rampaging emotions, yet she knew, deep down, that was going to be almost impossible. "Dear," she said carefully, aware of the lie, "Lord Caedmon is just a friend."

Hannah smiled. "I like him," she said.

Olivia's heart turned over. How right it could be—her and her daughter and Garrick De Vere. How scared she was. To be entertaining such absurd, impossible notions. And the worst part was that she did not trust herself.

She knew that she must not even consider the possibility of seeing him again, unless it was by chance and socially; still, dear God, she wished so much to be with him, one more time. She must fight herself now. Yet he was haunting her ceaselessly, which did not help. She carried him with her, in her mind, every second of every minute of every day. Was this love, then? An obsession of the heart and soul?

If so, Olivia did not want it.

Or was she lying to herself?

"Mama, the mail coach is coming," Hannah said.

Olivia turned. The road that led to the house wound through the surrounding fields, which were dotted here and there with grazing dairy cows. She could see a coach perhaps an eighth of a mile away, raising a small cloud of dust as it approached them. She did not question Hannah's perception. If Hannah said it was the mail, it was. Olivia did not know if it was her acute hearing, possibly coupled with vibrations in the ground, or her gift of sight that enabled her to identify the coach from this distance.

"Let's see if the postman is bringing us a letter, dear," Olivia said, taking Hannah's hand. They walked around the house to the front and waited in the circular, crushed-shell drive. As the coach turned into the drive, she saw that Hannah had been right: it was the mail.

The coach halted before them. The potbellied driver smiled at her and Hannah. "Good day, my lady, Miss Hannah. I have a letter for you from London," he said, jumping down to the ground.

Olivia knew De Vere would not send her a note, yet she was immediately so stricken with hope that she failed to reply adequately. "Good . . . day, Mister Smith. Thank you," she managed, taking the sealed envelope. Her heart fell. It was not sealed with the Stanhope wax crest. It was from the Laytons.

He climbed back up, but not before handing Hannah a sugar candy. "G'day, ladies," he said, whipping his horses forward.

A cloud of dust enveloped them as Olivia broke the wax seal, filled with dread now. She saw that it was from Susan, whom she suddenly had no wish to hear from.

"My dear Olivia," Susan began in a splendid, scripted handwriting,

"How I have missed the times we have spent together! And you are missing a lovely time in town, for there have been so many parties, and now that I am so successfully engaged, I have been invited to them all. Of course, it is a bit awkward. My fiancé has not escorted me to a single fête, and I am asked about that by everyone.

"I am confused. Apparently he did go to the country for a very short turn. But I do know he is back in town, and not only has he not escorted me anywhere, he has not called on me even once. Frankly, dear Olivia, I am relieved. Try as I might, I cannot find any fondness in my heart for Garrick De Vere.

"Have you heard the most astounding news? His brother, the one missing for fourteen years, has returned from the dead, or so this man claims! The ton is quite divided upon whether this man is Lionel De Vere or an absolute and very bold fraud. Olivia, I must tell you, he is quite the dashing bachelor about town! He is stunningly handsome, all the ladies are agog over him, and his manners are flawless. I, personally, believe him to be the long-lost Stanhope heir. No impostor could play the part so well, and he does resemble the earl, amazingly so! He has attended every fête I have been invited to, and we have shared a dance at every event. He is a splendid dancer, my dear friend. And his wit! He makes me laugh until my sides hurt. He is so charming!

"How could two brothers be so unlike? It is frightening. All the more so, and I know I should not be writing this, when I am engaged to the other one! As you can imagine, my parents are very distressed by Lionel De Vere's return. After all, I am supposed to be engaged to the Stanhope heir. On the other hand, the earl has not publicly announced Lionel to be his long-lost firstborn son. I suppose I must wait until that day comes. As it surely must. Again, I dare to confide in you, I pray that Lionel is the true Stanhope heir.

"Can you not return to town, my dearest lady? I would be so happy if you could. I am sure my parents would not mind. Having had some time to think about it, I do think they overreacted to Lord Caedmon's interest in you. After all, you are married yourself to a very fine man, and you are my dear friend. Do think about returning. I shall talk them around.

                   Your Loyal & Sincere Friend, Etc.
                   Susan Layton."

Olivia's hands were shaking by the time she finished the letter. Far too many emotions to count overwhelmed her, but first and foremost was the guilt that had haunted her since the other night. No matter that Susan had no affection for her intended; Garrick De Vere was her fiancé, Olivia was her friend, and together they had cuckolded the innocent girl. Olivia despised herself.

And what about this man who claimed to be Lionel De Vere? Was it possible that Garrick's older brother had returned from the missing after all these years?

Olivia had, from the first, assumed him to be an impostor, but now she thought about it. Rather, she tried to keep her thoughts at bay and let some feeling enter her body, a calm certainty that he was a fraud or that he was the long-lost firstborn. No such wave of certainty came.

"Shall we go inside?" she asked Hannah, dismayed.

"Are we going to go back to London?" Hannah asked with eagerness.

Olivia faltered on the front steps of the house. Arlen's image assailed her. He was the last person she wanted to see, because along with the guilt, she lived with a very real fear. What if Arlen eventually found out that she had spent a night at Stanhope Hall—and that Garrick De Vere had been there, too?

Olivia did not know what to think. Up until now, she had been a faithful wife. It had never occurred to her, not once in nine long years, to be otherwise. Arlen did not love her, he did not even want her. But Olivia knew him well enough to comprehend just how perverse he was. It would not matter that it was the popular fashion to have husbands and wives going their separate ways. It was tolerable for Arlen to have a mistress; he would never tolerate her having a lover. Olivia had no doubt.

He would punish her should he ever learn of her transgression—punish her and make her miserable. Her life had been difficult enough because of the burden of keeping secret Hannah's own gift while hiding her own premonitions. Now what? Olivia was afraid Arlen would take his anger out upon Hannah if he discovered her disloyalty. Arlen knew that Hannah was Olivia's single vulnerability.

They walked inside the house. In the foyer it was pleasantly cool. Olivia clutched the letter and envelope. Going back to London right now would be a mistake.

Maybe, if she stayed in the country, and De Vere married

Susan, she would forget about him. Maybe her feelings would disappear, evaporate. And the night they had shared would become a distant, nearly forgotten memory.

Olivia felt like crying.

But she did not. Foolish, yearning woman that she was, she could not help but think of another possibility. Maybe their engagement would be broken, if the man claiming to be Lionel De Vere were truly the Stanhope heir.

But even that would not change the fact that she herself was married.

"How did you talk me into this?" Garrick grumbled.

"I do believe half a dozen gins last night helped," Lionel said good-naturedly. He lifted a gloved hand and waved at a particularly pretty pair of ladies who were, at that moment, driving by them in an open rig on the riding path in the park.

They were riding two big bay hunters at the very fashionable hour of noon. The path was filled with colorfully clad mounted riders and horse-drawn vehicles filled with colorful, lavishly dressed ladies and gentlemen. Garrick was nursing a very sore head and throbbing temples, for he had somehow wound up in an exclusive gaming establishment the night before, where he had lost several hundred pounds at the card tables. Lionel had suggested the evening's outing. Garrick had been reluctant to attend but, as he was currently caught in the throes of a battle between his heart and his mind, had finally accepted the invitation in the hope that it might shed some light on whether this man was an impostor or not. But the only truth to be found had been that Garrick was a poor card player. In fact, he had not gambled in any shape or form in years. There were no clubs or gaming dens on Barbados. Lionel had won double what Garrick had lost.

The two pretty blond ladies giggled and simpered and fluttered their fans as Lionel doffed his hat toward them. He grinned at Garrick. "Easy prey, huh?"

Garrick eyed him, recalling in that moment that Lionel had always had a way with women. Whether a serving wench or a noblewoman, the female gender had been drawn to his easy charm and golden good looks as bears to a pot of honey.

"You have hardly changed," Lionel remarked, waving at another carriage, this one containing a brunette, a redhead, and a blonde. "You are as dour as ever."

Garrick ignored the trio of women, who were somewhat older and more sophisticated than the previous rig, as they sent Lionel some very suggestive and seductive glances. Lionel craned his neck to watch them depart once their landau had passed by. "Who was that brunette?" he exclaimed.

"In case you have forgotten, I have only just returned to town myself," Garrick said, thinking, He is so like Lionel. He must be Lionel. Or was he engaging in the same wishful thinking as his father and his mother—and believing what he wanted to believe?

"Why didn't you come with me to Madame Beaulieu's after the club?" Lionel asked.

Garrick avoided his regard. When they were children, there was little he could hide from his brother. He had no intention of telling him now that the single night spent with Olivia Grey, the countess of Ashburn, consumed and haunted him so that he could not contemplate passing an evening with a whore—or any other woman. In fact, during the past few days he had checked several very strong and unruly impulses to ride directly to Ashburnham and to hell with the consequences.

"It couldn't have anything to do with your recent stay in the country, now, could it?" Lionel said as they continued to walk their mounts down the shady path.

Instantly Garrick stiffened. "What does that mean?" But Lionel could not know. Mrs. Riley knew what had transpired that night, but before leaving the Hall, in spite of how shocked he was by the earl's missive, Garrick had taken a moment to speak with her. Although he had been indirect, he knew she had understood what he was insisting upon—absolute discretion. He trusted that their secret was safe.

"You apparently fled town without telling anyone. Father was very annoyed. You did not even leave notice of where you were off to. And you returned as precipitously. Mother mentioned that you have been out of sorts ever since." Lionel's tone was easy.

Garrick stared at him but saw no trace of a hidden meaning on his face. And he could not help it, but whenever this man called the earl "Father," he became rigid. Lionel smiled again before looking away, again to doff his tricorne hat at a particularly lovely passing lady.

Garrick relaxed, realizing he was overreacting because of a guilt he had no wish to feel. But he knew Arlen Grey well enough—or at least some time ago he had—and he did not think the man had changed. He was difficult, perverse, and at times cruel. He did not want Olivia placed in any jeopardy because of him.

"I am hardly a horny boy of thirteen anymore," Garrick said. "Easy women have failed to interest me for many years."

Lionel did eye him. "Well, I find a beautiful woman beautiful no matter her station in life. And Madame Beaulieu certainly has some extraordinary wenches."

"I'm glad you enjoyed yourself," Garrick said, feeling a distinct ache as he thought of Olivia, an ache not just in his loins, but in his chest. He had to see her again. But when?

"Ah, here comes Father," Lionel said, smiling as if pleased.

Stanhope approached astride a magnificent chestnut hunter. He pulled up facing his two sons, who had also automatically reined in their mounts. His hard gaze went from Lionel to Garrick and back again. "I was told the two of you were riding in the park," he said stiffly. "Lionel, did you forget that we had a date to sup at one at my club?"

Garrick stiffened with surprise. The earl was taking Lionel to his club—as if he were truly his son?

"Actually, I did not, and I was about to suggest that we return home so I could make my appointment with you, Father," Lionel said. "Why doesn't Garrick join us?"

"That is an excellent idea," Stanhope said, but his gaze was narrowed as it slid over Garrick again.

Garrick managed to recover from his surprise, but he remained perturbed. And Stanhope did not have to speak his thoughts aloud, Garrick knew precisely what they were. He himself looked like hell. He was aware that his eyes were bloodshot, his hair pulled back carelessly and, of course, unpowdered, and he had thrown on his clothes that morning quite haphazardly, choosing all somber colors. Lionel, on the other hand, was far more than handsome, he looked every bit a macaroni in his turquoise frock coat, darker blue waistcoat, silvery gray breeches, and white stockings. Garrick could sleep in the shirt he'd worn all day or wear the same clothes from hunting to supper, but not Lionel. He had been fastidious about his appearance. He had always looked superb—just as he did now.

"Come with us." Lionel laid his palm on Garrick's shoulder, causing Garrick to flinch ever so slightly. Their gazes met.

The earl stared, waiting.

Lionel's hand slipped away. "Well?"

Garrick turned toward his father, who was watching them closely. Too closely. "I do not wish to intrude."

"You are not intruding," the earl said quickly. "I would like you to join us. I would only ask that you powder your hair and change your clothes. I have many friends at my club who wish to meet you, Garrick."

Curtly Garrick nodded, inwardly surprised. Why did his father wish to introduce him around now, if he truly believed this man to be Lionel? It made little sense.

The earl also smiled, an expression that seemed curiously hard and, at the same time, satisfied. "Very well. I will meet the two of you back at the house." He wheeled his mount and cantered away.

They watched him go.

"I am surprised he wants me to come along," Garrick muttered. "Now that you are here."

Lionel shrugged. "He has not yet proclaimed me publicly to be his long-lost firstborn son."

Garrick studied him. "And is that what you expect him to do?"

Lionel stared back. "I am not lying about who I am; I am his firstborn son, yes, that is eventually what I expect."

Garrick made no reply, trying to see into his soul through his eyes. But it was impossible; his blue eyes were opaque. If this man were a fraud and a greedy fortune hunter, he was a superb actor.

"And will that bother you?" Lionel asked casually.

"Why would that bother me? I do not give a damn about the earldom, I never have. I prefer Barbados to this cold, wet land."

·Lionel seemed pleased, but he looked away so quickly that Garrick wasn't sure he hadn't imagined it.

"And if you eventually become convinced of my sincerity, then will we regain what we once had?" Lionel asked abruptly. "I know you still doubt me—just a bit."

"Even if you are truly my brother, I do not know if we could ever recapture what we once shared," Garrick said as bluntly. "There has been too much disappointment, and too much sorrow." He stared. "We buried you years ago, Lionel, and it was not easy. And there has not been a resurrection since Jesus Christ."

They entered the library. It was a large, high-ceilinged room, wood paneled and lined with books, with a huge blue-and-gold Persian rug and numerous chairs, sofas, and tables. Two massive crystal chandeliers hung from the gilded ceiling, which was painted a dusky blue. Garrick stood behind his father and Lionel. As they paused upon the threshold, heads turned their way. The quiet conversation in the library faded, until absolute silence reigned.

"Come this way," the earl said, smiling, and he led them to an arrangement containing an empty sofa and two club chairs, with the two dozen or so gentlemen in the room pretending to read their journals, dailies, and weeklies when in fact every single eye was surreptitiously cast their way, every ear intensely attuned to them. The earl sat upon the couch; Lionel chose to sit on the same sofa beside him. Garrick dropped into a facing chair, stiff with tension. He was sure that his face registered just how uncomfortable he was. He declined the pinch of snuff his father was offering them.

Immediately a gentleman in a huge peruke and an emerald green frock coat came up to them, bowing. "Stanhope, so good to see you," he said, smiling.

The earl stood. "Harding, how are you?" He turned toward Lionel. "You remember my sons, do you not?"

A brief moment of silence fell. Garrick knew that everyone was wondering, as he was, if the earl had just publicly stated that Lionel was the long-lost Stanhope heir.

Harding bowed then as Lionel rose to his feet. "My lord, this is a real pleasure." He was clearly trying not to gawk at Lionel.

"As it is for me," Lionel said, smiling broadly.

Garrick nodded at Harding. He was dismayed—and he was angry. It was far too soon to throw caution to the winds and accept this man as Lionel. And Stanhope knew it. What was his father doing?

"I am having a small supper party, Tuesday next," Harding was saying to Stanhope. "I have just penned the invitations. The baroness and I would be delighted if you and your sons could attend."

"I must check my calendar," the earl replied.

A pair of gentlemen now approached them. Bows were made all around. Again, Garrick watched the earl introducing Lionel to Lords Cantor and Talbot. He realized that the earl was careful not to use any titles—and he had not introduced Garrick by his title, either, which was extremely unusual. But then, if Lionel were genuine, *he* was now the viscount of Caedmon Crag.

"There is a match race next Sunday at Newmarket," Talbot said to the earl and Lionel. "I have taken three boxes. It should be a dashing good time. Perhaps you and your sons might like to join my party?"

"Father, that sounds like an event not to be missed," Lionel said with enthusiasm.

The earl smiled at him. "You were always fond of horse racing."

Lionel grinned. "A habit one cannot break."

"We shall be there, then," the earl told Lord Talbot.

Garrick stared at Lionel grimly. "Do you remember the time we raced our new hunters from the Hall to the village and back again?"

Lionel turned toward Garrick. His smile remained in place. "I'm not sure," he said easily enough.

"It was a summer day. Father had gone hunting with guests. We were under strict orders not to leave the grounds. But we eluded the groom. Do you not remember? I pretended to take a fall, and the poor chap left you with me while he went back to the Hall for help." Garrick attempted a smile. "You won. By a length."

Lionel now laughed, nodding. "I do remember, in fact. I believe it was one of the best instances of riding I have ever done."

Garrick stared. "How old were we?"

Lionel seemed to stiffen. The earl and the two gentlemen now regarded them, the latter pair quite interested, the earl sitting up so stiff and so straight, he could have been a statue. "What are you up to, Garrick?" Stanhope demanded.

"I cannot remember how old we were," Garrick said, standing slowly. He topped Lionel by a head. That fact satisfied him, oddly enough. "Can you?"

Lionel did smile. "You know, this is odd. I cannot remember either, but I would hazard to guess that it must have been a year or so before I ran away." The ton had, of course, needed an explanation for Lionel's disappearance and return, and the earl had confirmed Lionel's own story. By now it was common knowledge—and the cause of extreme tongue-wagging.

"An intelligent guess," Garrick now said. "After all, had I been less than twelve, I would not have been given my own hunter, now would I."

"Garrick, is there a point to this display?" the earl demanded, eyes flashing.

Garrick looked only at Lionel. "There was no race. There was no race to the village and back, and never did I pretend to fall from my horse and hurt myself so I could elude an attending groom."

Lionel no longer smiled. "We raced many times on horseback."

"But never all the way to the village and back."

Lionel stared, his expression somewhat pinched. Garrick was well aware that everyone was staring at them, not just the two gentlemen and the earl. "It sounded familiar," Lionel finally said. "I cannot remember every damn detail of our childhood, Garrick!" His smile was placating.

But Garrick did not smile in return. On the one hand, he did not like himself for setting this man up—because this man might be his brother, whom he still loved. But this man might also be a well-studied fraud.

The earl stepped between them, his face flushed. He faced Lionel, his expression rigid. "No one expects you to recall every single detail of your childhood, and certainly not I."

Lionel did relax.

The earl stared coldly at Garrick. "What do you think you are doing? Do you think this kind of public display is seemly?"

Garrick's jaw tightened. "Do you truly think, after all of these years, that I give a damn what your friends think?" he said, low.

"You are no more intelligent than a foolish child!" the earl snapped.

"Father, please." Lionel laid a restraining hand upon the earl. "You must forgive Garrick. Surely you can forgive him for harboring doubts if I can. Besides, he has a lot to lose if I am who I say I am. His anger and doubt are understandable. It is human. And he will come around in time." Lionel smiled. "Because I am telling the truth." How calm and clear his voice was. How confident.

Garrick jerked. He became aware of the whispers in the background. And he was certain he heard his name, Caedmon, juxtaposed with Lionel. Although Lionel had spoken casually, in one fell swoop he had made it clear to everyone in the room that Garrick's reason for attempting to discredit Lionel was his fear of losing the Stanhope inheritance. Had the blow been purposeful, or was he imagining something happening here?

"We will finish this discussion at home," the earl said so only Garrick could hear.

"Thank you, but no," Garrick replied coolly. "Believe it or not, Father, I am only trying to protect our family." Then he saw Arlen Grey detaching himself from a group of men seated across the room.

His heart lurched. Images of Olivia in the throes of passion flooded his mind, chasing away his cognizance of everything else; he forgot his father, Lionel, the other lords, and the current dispute. As he watched Arlen approaching, he was aware of how much he missed her. And he was aware of how much he wanted to protect her from her own husband.

He felt no guilt now. A deep and sheer dislike of her husband filled him as Arlen sauntered toward them.

"My lords," Arlen said with a smile. He bowed to the earl and Lionel and only faced Garrick cursorily. "This is a surprise and a pleasure. So how are you faring in London, De Vere?" he asked Lionel.

"Very well. Never better, in fact," Lionel said with a laugh. "And you? You remain in town? Did I not just hear that your beautiful wife has just returned to the country? Sussex, isn't it?"

Arlen's smile remained in place, but Garrick's pulse quickened. Arlen said, "My wife returned to Ashburnham four days ago. She prefers the country. I, of course, prefer town."

"So does my brother," Lionel said, not even glancing at Garrick. "Prefer the country, that is. He has also just returned to town. Three days ago, in fact."

Garrick stiffened, his mind grasping what was about to come—yet how did Lionel know? How could he know about what had transpired at the Hall three days ago?

"Oh, really?" Arlen stared, no longer smiling, his eyes almost black.

"I decided to visit the estate," Garrick said flatly.

"I see," Arlen said.

"Isn't Ashburnham rather close to Stanhope Hall?" Lionel asked.

Arlen stared at Lionel before regarding Garrick. "Yes. My home is but a few hours' drive from Stanhope Hall. How coincidental it is," he said. "My wife leaves for Sussex on the same day that you are in Surrey."

"Life is filled with the oddest coincidences," Garrick said dryly. "Far odder, in fact, than my happening to be at the Hall a few days ago."

A silence fell. Garrick knew what everyone was thinking. Thanks to Lionel.

Lionel broke the tension. "I am sure Garrick was not even aware that Lady Ashburn was in residence." He laughed.

Before Garrick could lie, Arlen spoke. His gaze did not waver. "Just as you happened to be at St. Bartholomew's," he said coolly.

"I enjoy the occasional fair." Garrick smiled, not pleasantly, and waited for him to ask if he had seen Olivia while in the country. He would, of course, deny it. But the facts were there, overly ripe and waiting to be discovered and devoured. For himself, he did not care. For Olivia, he despaired.

"And the countess also enjoys such mundane events." Arlen was flushed, and he turned to Lionel, inquiring stiffly as to whether he wished to join him for some gaming later that evening. As Lionel agreed, Garrick stepped over to the earl.

"I am leaving."

"Fine," the earl said, but his gaze was piercing. "Watch your step, Garrick."

Garrick turned away, surprised by the warning. He could feel Arlen's cold eyes upon his back.

"Garrick!"

He stiffened, and Lionel hurried after him, pausing

beside him. "Join us," Lionel said, smiling, as if the recent five minutes of dialogue, filled with innuendos and insinuations, had not just occurred. "Tonight after supper at the St. James. Perhaps you will have better luck tonight." He slapped his shoulder lightly.

"I do not think so," Garrick said, moving so Lionel's hand fell away. "I cannot win at the tables when I am up against you. You are a far shrewder player than I."

"Surely you are not harboring a grudge about last night?" Lionel exclaimed. Their gazes locked.

"I hardly care about a few hundred pounds lost last night," Garrick said evenly. But it was hard to control his temper. So very hard.

"You are angry," Lionel said with surprise. "But you are not angry about last night!"

"I am not angry about last night. I am not angry at all," Garrick lied coldly. He was not about to let Lionel know that his insinuations had infuriated him because they were accurate and, as such, very dangerous.

Lionel's easy expression vanished. "Perhaps we should stop playing games," he said.

Garrick had been about to turn away, but now he froze, fully alert. "And have we been playing games?"

"I think you are playing games," Lionel said. "Why don't you admit the truth?"

"What truth must I admit?"

"The truth is, you refuse to accept my return from the missing because you will lose everything—because my return means that you are no longer the Stanhope heir." Lionel's eyes were hard.

And their gazes clashed.

"That is why you are against me," Lionel said.

Garrick stared, taken aback. Then he turned and walked away.

CHAPTER FOURTEEN

Arlen strode into the foyer of Houghton Place as if he owned it. His temples throbbed with explosive force; he had just left Almack's. The marquis, he knew, was not at home. Earlier that day he had seen him in the company of several gentlemen at a popular dining establishment. The marquis had been well into his cups. When he did return home, he would nap heavily for several hours.

The butler was striding into the wide, high-ceilinged room. "My lord," he said, bowing.

"Is my sister at home?" Arlen snapped, aware that he was forgetting his manners but helpless to prevent it.

"The marchioness is not, but she is expected at any moment, for she has several guests coming to tea, my lord," the butler droned.

"I will await her in the library," Arlen said, already walking away. "The moment she arrives, tell her I am here and that it is most urgent!"

In the library, Arlen left both heavy rosewood doors open, knowing no one would dare walk in on him other than his sister. This house, in fact, was practically his own. Arlen felt very possessive about it, just as he was very possessive about Elizabeth. He was five years older than she, and their father had died when Elizabeth was ten, Arlen just fifteen. Their mother had already been buried for many years, and Arlen had not just taken over the reins of the earldom, in spite of a scheming elderly cousin. He had become his sister's guardian, finally arranging her marriage to the elderly, obese marquis of Houghton, a marriage that had satisfied him immensely. For Houghton doted on Elizabeth, yet was harmless.

Arlen poured himself a snifter of brandy, a drink he ordinarily eschewed until after supper. He had just downed half when Elizabeth appeared on the threshold.

For just one instant he took in her pale pink gown, her high bosom, her narrow waist, and her flawless beauty. Then he finished the drink.

"What could be so urgent that you insist upon seeing me in the middle of the afternoon?" she asked, coming forward. Her expression was haughty. "Arlen, I do not jump at your beck and call. Even as we speak, my guests are arriving. You cannot appear here as you will."

Arlen stared at her, then turned and stalked to a window that overlooked the street. He saw two coaches and a landau parked at the curb. One coach, a large, open phaeton, he did not recognize. But his senses were alert and he faced his sister. "Usually you are happy to see me, Elizabeth," he said slowly.

She folded her arms, eyeing him. The gesture pushed her small bosom into prominence. "What is on your mind?"

He was affronted and more wary than before. He stepped to her. "With whom are you having tea?" he asked.

Her expression did not change. "You are not my jailer, Arlen. Several friends. Why?"

He knew she was deceiving him now, and all of his suspicions about Garrick De Vere fell by the wayside. He grabbed her arm, and she cried out. "Whose phaeton is that?" he demanded.

"How dare you!" Elizabeth said furiously. She wrenched her arm free and faced him, her bosom heaving. "The phaeton belongs to Lord Kildare, if you must know."

Kildare. Arlen searched his memory, and suddenly the image of a young, handsome Scot came to mind. "Oh? Are you entertaining his wife?"

Elizabeth smiled coldly. "I am entertaining Kildare and

Ladies Hewitt and Faraday, if you must know.''

Arlen stared. Was she flirting with Kildare? Surely she was not sleeping with him. Or was she?

Her imperious brows lifted. ''Is there something you wish to ask me, Arlen?''

He rubbed his temples. ''Since when have you become so social with Kildare?''

She smiled slowly at him, then touched his cheek, a brief, sensual caress. Elizabeth kept her pale, polished nails long. ''Are you jealous, dear?'' she asked.

''Do I have a reason to be jealous?'' he returned.

She continued to smile.

He wanted to hit her. He wanted to shout. He did neither. There was a house full of servants about.

''I have guests waiting,'' Elizabeth reminded him.

Arlen jammed his shaking hands into the pockets of his breeches. ''I sent Olivia home four days ago. Elizabeth, I have just come from Almack's, and I have learned that three days ago Caedmon was at Stanhope Hall.''

Elizabeth's small smile faded. ''Well, well,'' she said, the sound not pretty. ''Now I understand your foul mood. And I do not blame you.''

''Is he cuckolding me? Or is it a coincidence?'' Arlen asked.

''Now is not the time to be stupid,'' Elizabeth said flatly. ''Stanhope Hall is only a few hours by coach from Ashburnham. There is no coincidence here. For God's sake, Arlen, the day before, he met her at St. Bartholomew's! The two of them are clearly having a liaison!''

Arlen found it difficult to breathe. He had never liked Caedmon, not from the time they had first met as children. But all that had changed eleven years ago, when a simple dislike had been turned into sheer hatred. He would never forget what the man had done to Elizabeth. He clenched his fists. This could not be happening again. It was a nightmare.

''Well? What are you going to do?'' Elizabeth demanded. She did not wait for him to reply. ''I suggest you go to the country and take control of your wife. While there, you might make a few inquiries among the staff and in the village. After all, undoubtedly they did not rendez-vous right in your own home. But if you wait a few hours before leaving, I will find out what I can here in town. I will make a point of it.'' She did smile.

He looked at her. Elizabeth belonged to a circle of ladies among whom gossip and information traveled far more swiftly than the daily news, for juicy tidbits revealed one day had already become well-known yesterday. She knew everyone, practically, in town, and she certainly knew everyone who was anyone, and no one could get to the root of a matter of gossip as swiftly as she. Within hours she would surely be able to tell him what it was he sought to know—unless Caedmon and his wife had been exceedingly clever.

''It was Lionel De Vere who told me that Caedmon was in Surrey the day my wife was sent home,'' Arlen said stiffly. ''If he knows something, then others must as well.'' He rubbed his temples. There was one bright spot in all of this. Caedmon might be on the verge of losing everything if the man claiming to be his brother were genuine.

''A good point,'' Elizabeth said cheerfully. ''When will you return to Ashburnham?''

He looked at her, thinking of Kildare, who was even now awaiting her in the pink salon, and he did not want to go. Was it his imagination, or was Elizabeth eager for him to leave London? Then he imagined Olivia in Caedmon's arms. ''I will leave first thing in the morning,'' he said.

Elizabeth smiled.

It was a daily ritual for Olivia to take a short walk after the breakfast she shared with her daughter. Hannah had her studies with Miss Childs, and Olivia would spend a half hour strolling briskly in the park, down the road, or even to the lake. In fact, the lake had been one of her favorite destinations. But no more, not since Susan's attempted suicide.

Olivia chose the winding dirt road that led to the small village of Ashburn. She was simply dressed in a striped blue-and-white gown, her hair was coiled in braids around her head, and because it was cool in the mornings, she wore a dark cashmere shawl. Birds were hopping in the trees above her head and the sun was shining, promising a warm, bright day, but Olivia's heart felt like lead.

She missed Garrick De Vere, was worried about eventually facing her husband again, and could find no bright promise in the future, not anymore. Until recently she had not even cared about the future. Her life had been placid and calm, except when Arlen infrequently came to the country. Her life, spent with her daughter, Miss Childs, and the staff, had been pleasant. There had been many ways in which to derive pleasure and joy from a single day. No more. Where had all the luster gone? Even the sun seemed a pale, dimmer shadow of what it had once been.

Is this hopeless? Olivia wondered, gazing unseeingly across the fields she walked by. Should she go back to town, just to see De Vere, her determination to avoid him be damned?

She paused, realizing a rider was cantering up the road. It was not an unusual sight, and she assumed it to be one of the tenant farmers. She was about to lift a hand in a friendly wave, but instead she squinted, because she did not recognize the horse approaching. It was a big, beautiful bay hunter, the kind of horse no farmer would ride. Not even Squire Horne would possess such a horse.

And the man riding it was large.

Olivia knew before she saw the dog loping alongside him. Little did she realize she was clinging to the split rail fence.

Garrick De Vere reined in the bay, staring down at her.

"Oh, my God," Olivia thought, then realized she had spoken aloud. Her heart now beat with amazing urgency.

"Hello, Olivia," he said, his golden eyes as penetrating and intense as she remembered.

Her mouth was dry. She could not speak.

He smiled and slid from the bay's back, walking over to her. "I hope you are pleased to see me," he said softly.

Her spine was pressing into the fence as she strained to

keep some distance between them. "What are you doing here?!" she cried. But she was glad to see him, so very glad.

"I think you know," he said, his gaze slipping to her lips.

She found herself looking at his mouth as well, wondering if he would kiss her on the public road, afraid they would be seen by a passing neighbor, yet wanting him to, for she was insanely remembering his taste and feel, God help her. She had no will. She wanted to be in his arms.

"I have missed you," he said abruptly.

Olivia tried to shake her head, but instead she heard herself say, roughly, "I have missed you, too, Garrick," knowing they should not be doing this.

His eyes blazed. Before she could react, he had both hands on her waist. Olivia thought he intended to pull her close and kiss her. Instead he lifted her up and set her on the horse. As she exclaimed in surprise, he leapt up behind her, put one strong arm around her, and galloped his bay back down the road, in the direction he had just come from, the setter running alongside them.

Olivia was dazed. She clung to the saddle, aware of his arm, which pressed her back firmly against his chest and torso, aware of the pounding of her heart, aware of how mindless she had become. She did not ask where he was taking her—she already guessed his intentions.

Up ahead there was a gate in the fence. Garrick reined the bay in, leaned over, and swung it open. He urged the bay through, then sidled his mount around so he could close the gate again. I must protest, Olivia thought. She did not. Images of the night they had shared at Stanhope Hall assailed her. She had missed him terribly.

He cantered his horse through the field, past more grazing cows, a few sheep interspersed among them. They passed through a grove of oak trees and were suddenly flying over a low stone wall. Garrick pulled the bay up, and the next thing Olivia knew, he had dismounted and he was pulling her down and into his arms.

"I have missed you so," he said again, his hands on her shoulders.

Olivia gazed into his eyes, searching their depths for a glimpse of his heart and his soul. Before his lips could touch hers, Olivia touched his mouth with two fingertips. "We should resist our passion," she whispered.

"I cannot," he said roughly. "You are my passion." And his mouth claimed hers.

All thoughts failed her. His hands, sliding over her back, were strong and insistent, and his body, pressing against hers, was hard and urgent. Worse, her own hands were exploring every inch of his back, his hips, his buttocks. Oh, God, it was so good to be reunited with him. She had not been sure when she would see him again—if ever.

Framing her face with his hands, he kissed her deeply, their tongues entwining. Olivia felt the explosive power of her love and was amazed anew. It fueled her need for him as nothing else could. How she wanted him. She wanted to be joined with him, to be a part of him, to be one. How she wanted to tell him that she loved him, but she did not dare.

His loins pressed against her, searing her with heat and promise. Olivia clung to him, crying out, her own urgency increasing. She buried her face between his neck and shoulder, panting harshly. His pulse thundered in her ears.

"I have done little but think about you," he said harshly, lifting his head. Their gazes met.

His eyes caused her heart to speed impossibly, her stomach to lurch; even her loins tightened in response. "I have been thinking about you, too," she said, throwing the last of too little caution to the wind. "You haunt me, Garrick."

He smiled, a real smile, one that lit up his eyes. "Good." Then he anchored her head with his hand in her coiled hair and kissed her, at once frantic and tender, rough and gentle. He pulled away from her. "Then that makes two of us."

Olivia smiled.

His expression was wry. "In truth, I did not expect to meet you on the road and waylay you like a highwayman."

"This is not right," Olivia said as they clasped hands,

hard. "But I am so happy to see you again."

He studied her.

Treve, who had been lying beneath a lonely tree, stood and walked over to her, wagging his tail. Olivia petted him, her mind racing, imagining that her feelings were written all over her face. "You should not have come. I received a letter from Susan the other day."

"I could not stay away." He took her hand again.

Olivia met his gaze. "I am married and you are intended to another—a sweet woman who is my friend. Recently I had decided never to see you again. It was the only possible decision to make."

He stared. His face had become odd, twisted yet expressionless. But she had seen the wound there in his eyes. It had not been her intention to hurt his feelings. He was far too sensitive. "Can we not even discuss this without an argument?"

He looked up. "Is there something to discuss? We are both adults. You have no relations with your husband, and I despise my fiancée. Yet you have decided that you no longer wish to see me. You have made yourself very clear." He stared.

Olivia's hand flew to her breast, as if that might prevent her frightened heart from racing. "I do not want to lose you, Garrick."

He jerked. "Then make up your mind," he cried. His jaw tense, he walked over to his grazing horse and took up the reins, Treve following him expectantly. "You should not be married to Arlen," he said.

She inhaled. "Don't."

"Don't what? State the obvious?" His eyes flashed.

"Arlen is my husband, Garrick," she said, almost revealing all her fears to him.

He stood in front of her. "Why don't you leave him?"

She froze, wanting to tell him everything—her hopes and dreams, her dark, dark fears. "I cannot."

He cursed.

"There is no solution, is there, to our dilemma?" she asked, her hand on her aching heart, thinking, I am going to lose him if this continues. He wants me to leave my husband, but Arlen will never let me go, and he will punish me through Hannah.

"I cannot think of one, other than to steal a few moments with you when we can do so," he said very grimly. "But moments like these are not enough."

Their gazes locked. Finally he held out his hand and she took it. They began to walk across the field, leading his horse, Treve trotting happily alongside them. "Did you see the man claiming to be your brother while in town?" she asked, still preoccupied with their discussion.

His tone became distinctly cool. "Oh, I saw him."

When he did not elaborate, Olivia glanced at his drawn face. She could feel his twisted, roiling emotions, grief, pain, guilt, hope, and last, anger. But she knew that she herself was the cause of many of his feelings. "Is he Lionel?"

Garrick hesitated. "He looks like him. He even behaves like him, or so it seems. And he knows a lot about the family, far too much, I think. It probably is he." He tore his gaze from Olivia and stared up at the sky, where fat, fluffy white clouds were passing by.

Olivia knew she could never clear her mind in order to use her gift to help Garrick now. She was too overwhelmed by him, too distraught, too frightened and confused. "You do not believe him."

He looked at her. "I don't know what to think."

"What happened in town to make you leave?" Olivia asked, gripping his arm. "Something happened. There is more than your having wanted my company."

He started slightly. "You are very astute. I had enough of Lionel, Stanhope, and the whispers and stares."

Olivia could no more stop herself from soothing him than she could stop herself from attending a bird with a broken wing. She slipped her palm to his forearm and rubbed it soothingly. "Are you staying at the Hall?" she asked gently.

"Yes. I decided to call upon you the moment I left London. I wanted to know, actually, how you were faring since

I had last seen you.'' His gaze locked with hers. "I am worried about you. Arlen worries me.''

Olivia tensed, trembling. "Arlen worries me as well,'' she heard herself say.

"Then leave him!'' he exploded. "Why do you stay with him?''

"He will never let me go,'' she cried in return. "There is Hannah to think of!''

"Hannah?'' he questioned. And Olivia knew he had not understood.

"How long will you be at the Hall?'' She rubbed her temples. "I need some time to think.''

"Indefinitely,'' he said. "And what do you need time to think about, Olivia?''

She looked up.

"Will you contemplate leaving him?'' he asked softly, taking a step toward her.

"No, yes, I don't know,'' she cried, unable to look away. "Having met you, known you, I am in a dilemma!''

"And I am not?'' he also cried. "I did not ask for this. I did not want to come home,'' he said. "I liked my life at Sugar Hill, and I did not ask to meet you, either, Olivia, nor did I ask for some damnable man to come forward claiming to be my brother—a man the whole world already accepts as Lionel—even, possibly, my father!''

"I know you did not ask for any of this,'' Olivia said with sympathy. "I have asked for very little in my life as well, Garrick. Until I met you, it was so simple, my path so clear. There was tranquillity.''

He stared for the longest time, in silence. Around them a cow lowed, a bird crowed, and the breeze whispered in the trees. "And now? Now how would you characterize your life?''

She could only share the truth—or some of it. "There is confusion. There is no peace. Confusion and fear and . . .'' She halted in midsentence.

"And?'' he prompted, his eyes very golden.

"There is excitement,'' she whispered. "There is joy.''

Tears filled her eyes, blurring her vision. "Being with you brings joy, Garrick."

His touch, brief and to her brow, was tender. "You make it sound like a confession," he said.

"It is a confession." Olivia realized that they had stopped in the center of the field and were facing one another. It was so natural, slipping into his strong arms.

"There is something you are not telling me," he said, his gaze tender now.

"Yes," she said, as if hypnotized.

"What is it?"

She trembled. "Arlen loathes Hannah."

His eyes widened. "How can that be?"

She shook her head. "He also loathes me. It is her blindness. He hates it, he is ashamed. . . . He blames me."

"He blames you for her blindness?" He was incredulous.

Olivia nodded, filled with fear, because they were but words away from the real truth—the secret of her wretched gift.

"Does he also blame you for failing to give him an heir?" Garrick asked.

She nodded. She knew what he wanted to ask. "But he does not touch me. He dislikes me far too much."

There was no mistaking the relief upon Garrick's face. "I am glad."

She looked away. "Not half as glad as I am."

He tilted up her chin, forcing her eyes to meet his. "You are afraid of him." It was not a question.

"I am so afraid. . . ." The words came pouring out, and she could not stop them. "I am afraid of what he would do to Hannah if I ever truly enraged him." She met his gaze. "If I left him, that would enrage him."

He stared. A long moment ensued. "You would not leave Hannah behind."

She knew she was breathing far too rapidly. "What can you be suggesting? He would hunt us down," Olivia said simply. "You are engaged to Miss Layton. We have shared one single night. Yet you ask me to run away, placing my daughter in grave danger, so I can be your mistress—''

"No! I would break off the engagement," he said fiercely.

"Garrick." She gripped his shoulders. "Even if you were free to marry me, I am married. Arlen will never divorce me, and he will never annul the marriage. He will never let me go, while in all likelihood, this man claiming to be your brother is a fraud. You have a duty to perform, and it requires marrying and begetting an heir, and you cannot possibly turn your back upon your family."

He stared.

"So you see," she said, in that moment overwhelmed with anguish, "this is a dilemma, is it not?"

He did not answer; his jaw was flexed, his eyes hard and dark.

"We are back to where we started," Olivia whispered painfully. "An affair, or nothing. I cannot risk an affair. Garrick, please, help me to be strong."

"You know I would do anything you asked, but I am weak, especially around you." He hesitated. "If I could, I would do the proper thing and ride away and never bother you again. Obviously that would be best for everyone, would it not?" His tone was bitter.

Olivia could not breathe. She was on the verge of losing him—should he do what was honorable now. She could not speak.

His smile was grim. "But I cannot ride away as if we had never met, or ever shared a moment's passion. Fool that I am." His regard was unwavering. "I am not returning to town, not yet."

"I do not know what to say, much less do," Olivia whispered. "I am so confused."

"As am I. I saw Arlen briefly yesterday at Almack's."

"What happened?" she asked, eyes wide. Dread overcame her. And when Garrick did not reply at once, Olivia knew with absolute certainty that the worst had happened or was about to. She grabbed his arm. "What happened?" she demanded.

His gaze was steady. "Lionel informed him that while

you were traveling home, I was at Stanhope Hall,'' Garrick said slowly.

Olivia felt all the color drain from her face. ''Oh, God.''

''Olivia, you must prepare yourself.'' Garrick held her tightly. ''If Lionel suspects the truth about us, then others do, too. In all likelihood, Arlen suspects something, thanks to my supposed brother. There is a good chance that Arlen will find out that you spent the night there—with me.''

Olivia did not even see his face, although it was inches from hers. She was paralyzed. ''He will come,'' she said, the wave of knowledge intense. ''He will come at any moment.''

CHAPTER FIFTEEN

Olivia paced in her bedroom, clad in the same gown she had worn earlier that day. She had run all the way home, refusing to let Garrick take her there. Her heart felt broken, her nerves felt shattered; she had a sense of impending doom, and she knew Arlen was on his way to Ashburnham, to accuse her of adultery. Oh, God.

And how had it happened that she and Garrick had parted from one another in anger and despair, instead of love? The future remained uncertain and fraught with danger. It felt hopeless.

There was a commotion outside. Olivia froze. Her windows were open, and she heard the sound of a carriage approaching. For one more moment she did not move, trying to rein in her panic and hysteria. And then she ran to the window.

She leaned forward, staring down at the Ashburn coach as it stopped in the drive in front of the house, directly below her. Liveried footmen leapt down from the back running boards and swung open the embossed door. As Arlen stepped out, Olivia shrank back behind the draperies, her heart in her throat, being very careful that he did not see her. Finding it hard to breathe, she waited for the rest of his entourage to appear. It took her a moment to realize that he had come alone.

That was not good. He never came to the country alone;

he always came with an entourage, one that usually included Elizabeth. Her senses screamed at her in warning yet again.

Briefly Olivia closed her eyes, her heart pounding with fear. And when she opened them, Arlen remained standing in the drive, clad in an emerald green frock coat and pale blue breeches, and he slowly lifted his head. Before Olivia could duck, his gaze went right to the window where she stood. Their glances met.

Oh, God. He knew. He knew everything, he even knew about that morning in the cow pasture!

Olivia was trembling. Quickly she walked to her dressing table and was made even more anxious at the sight of her frightened, guilty reflection in the mirror. She tried to rein in the panic and hysteria. No one knew about their meeting this morning, no one. Garrick had told her that he had left London suddenly, without telling a soul of his plans. As clever as Arlen was, he could not guess what had happened. He would not even know that Garrick was but a few miles away. She must keep her wits about her now. Otherwise she was in severe trouble indeed.

She must go downstairs and greet Arlen graciously, as if nothing were wrong.

Olivia crossed the room, determined now to dissemble, to lie. Her temples throbbed as she reached for the door and swung it open.

And came face-to-face with her husband.

"Arlen!" she exclaimed, her tone husky with her fear. She managed a smile. "I was not expecting you, but I saw you from the window and was just coming downstairs. Did you have a pleasant journey?"

Arlen stared at her with a cold, unpleasant expression. "Frankly, I did not."

Olivia's eyes locked with his, she felt his anger, and she recoiled. "I am sorry," she began breathlessly.

"Are you?" he asked, closing the door, which terrified her even more, and he stepped closer to her. He struck her.

It came without any warning, a smack across the face that sent her to the floor. But she did not cry out, because she had known he would hit her eventually. She crouched there, panting, trying to control the fear—an impossibility. He towered over her. She told herself that he could do anything she wished and that she would survive, she had to, because of Hannah.

"You stopped at Stanhope Hall. You spent the night there. It is all over London," he spat. Suddenly he was squatting beside her. His face was close to hers. "Caedmon was there that night. You are fucking him."

Olivia wet her lips. "No. I would never do that. I did stop there, but only because the weather was terrible—"

He did not let her finish. His fingers sank into the braided coils of her hair, cruelly, wrenching her head backward so she was staring up at the ceiling. He kept up the pressure, and Olivia fell onto her back. Otherwise her neck would have snapped.

"You are a liar as well as a whore. There is no such thing as a coincidence. You carry on with my mortal enemy. Damn you," he hissed in her face.

"No," Olivia tried to protest. "Why . . . why do you hate him so?"

"After what he did to my sister, how could you ask?" Arlen snarled.

Olivia's straining heart jumped erratically. "I . . . I don't understand!"

He pinned her to the floor. "He seduced her when she was fifteen, the bastard. And he refused to marry her. He ruined her, damn his soul for all eternity, and the whole world knew it—and knows it still."

Olivia could hardly breathe. His grip continued to pin her to the floor. Elizabeth had lied, and Olivia was glad, fiercely so. Tears fell from her eyes.

"Did he force you?" Arlen asked suddenly. "I could kill him. You know that I am a master swordsman. I could defend your honor and kill him."

"No," Olivia whispered. She comprehended that Arlen believed his own words, and if he was right, the last thing she wanted was a duel—for Garrick to be wounded or die. "No, Arlen, you must believe me. We only spent the night there, Hannah and I. She slept in my bed with me. We stopped because of the weather.''

Suddenly he threw his leg over her, causing her to stiffen. Terror replaced the fear, and with it came shock, because surely he was not intending to rape her. With one hand he lifted her dress and petticoats up to her waist, leaving her mostly naked and exposed.

''Don't!'' Olivia cried. ''Not this way!''

''Why the hell not? You are a whore, and I will treat you as such—and maybe if I take care of that itch between your legs, you won't think about rutting with Caedmon,'' he mouthed in her ear. And with one hand he palmed her sex.

Olivia wanted to weep, wanted to beg. Instead the tears began and fell silently, and no pleas came forth. She felt tremors racking her body, of fear and revulsion.

''Mama?''

At the sound of her daughter's voice, Olivia jerked, only to see Hannah standing in the open doorway, her face wrenched with confusion and fear. ''Everything is all right,'' Olivia began in a high falsetto.

''Mama! What is he doing to you?'' Hannah cried, coming forward, dressed for bed.

''Go back to your room!'' Olivia shrieked. ''Do as I say, now!''

Hannah froze.

Arlen rose slowly, releasing Olivia, who yanked down her gown. He turned toward Hannah, his eyes oddly bright. Olivia glimpsed his fixed expression before he faced their daughter, and she was stabbed anew with terror. ''Arlen,'' she whispered. In one instant, so many horrendous scenarios rushed through her mind that she was on the verge of retching.

But at that exact moment Miss Childs appeared, her face devoid of all color. She grabbed Hannah and whisked her away, firmly closing the door behind them.

Gasping for breath, Olivia said a prayer of thanks. But her relief was short-lived. Arlen turned toward her again. Olivia closed her eyes.

*   *   *

Garrick dismounted his bay, handing the reins to a groom, both perturbed and preoccupied as he strode up the front steps of the Hall and entered the house. It was midafternoon, another pleasant summer day, but his mood was hardly bright. He had tossed and turned for most of last night, for he had not been able to shake anything that had occurred yesterday morning from his mind—he could not shake Olivia from his mind. His desire to be with her had not dimmed. Could she really walk away from him, from them? But was there an alternative?

And what if Arlen Grey was on his way to Ashburnham? He had had an uneasy feeling ever since leaving her, and his unease had increased with the passage of time.

Last night it had been so very strong. And it was very strong now.

He was almost ready to ride back to Ashburnham, to make certain that all was well.

He paused in the foyer to shed his gloves and lay aside his riding crop, when footsteps sounded in the corridor directly ahead. Garrick tensed. All his worries and concerns vanished as a distinct feeling of expectation, tinged with warning, came over him.

Lionel walked into the hall. He smiled at Garrick.

Garrick stared back at him in shock.

"Hello, Garrick. You look surprised to see me. If you had stayed at Almack's a bit longer, or gone gaming with us that night, I would have told you that I was going to the country myself. Father suggested it a few days ago." Lionel continued to smile, but his glance moved appreciatively around the hall. "It has been a hell of a long time since I was here, you know. God, I have so many memories of this place."

Garrick recovered with difficulty. "You had already planned to come to the Hall?" His tone was heavy with sarcasm.

Lionel walked to him. "Yes, I had. It is not unusual, or odd. After all, I have remained in town until now. Father suggested I inspect the estate."

Garrick's jaw felt so tight, he wondered if he would break it. "Do not think to pull the wool over my eyes," he said. "You followed me here."

"That is ridiculous," Lionel said, his smile gone. "Absurd. Why would I follow you here?"

"I don't know—but I intend to find out," Garrick said.

"I came to inspect the estate," Lionel said again.

"Ah, yes. After all, you are the heir, and this will one day be yours." Garrick remained mocking, but he trembled with anger. It struck him that Lionel might wish to see for himself that Garrick was having a liaison with Olivia. But why? To cause trouble? Or to gain a trump card—one he might play later?

And had he not already caused enough trouble—at Almack's?

"Yes, one day the estate will be mine, and rightfully so," Lionel said, his confidence clear. "And you do not care. Or so you have said."

"I do not care, for I am returning to Barbados as soon as possible." If Lionel spoke the truth, and Stanhope had wished him to come inspect the estate, then the writing on the wall was clear. Garrick knew he should be pleased. He did not want any of this, and soon he would be free to leave this goddamn land, a place full of snobs and snits. Instead he was angry. Was this man his brother or a fraud? Could Lionel have changed so drastically over the years? There was another problem: Olivia and her daughter. Leaving them would not be easy. But if he left, her life might become placid and calm once again—Arlen might leave her in peace in the country. If he left, returning to Sugar Hill, one day, they both might forget these few passionate moments.

His heart rebelled against the dictates of common sense and reason. It ached.

"Does your bride know that you intend to live in Barbados?"

He went rigid. "That is hardly your concern, now, is it?"

Lionel sighed. "Garrick, I did not follow you here, nor

did I come here to fight with you." He held out his hand. "Can we not have a truce?"

Garrick stared at him in disbelief.

Lionel was smiling. "I am sorry about what I said at Almack's. I do not want to fight with you. You are my brother," he said. "No matter what you may think, no matter your doubts, you are my flesh and blood."

Garrick looked into his unflinching blue eyes and thought, It is as if he is speaking the truth. A chill swept him. "I do not give a damn about the earldom, I never have. And if you are who you say you are, then you know I speak the truth."

"People change. That is a fact of nature." Lionel's gaze was searching. "When I become the next earl of Stanhope, you will have nothing to worry about," he finally said. "I promise you that. You will never be left wanting." His hand remained extended. "Let's start over, Garrick. As friends."

Garrick stared at the offered hand, shaken and tempted to accept it. But somehow he could not. His suspicions held him back now.

"As boys we were best friends," Lionel said.

Garrick smiled tightly. "Neither one of us is a child anymore."

Lionel dropped his hand. His smile faded. "Very well," he said. "If that is the way you want it."

Garrick did not reply. He had no reply to make.

Lionel strode past him but paused at the front door. "I am afraid you shall have to dine alone tonight," he said suddenly.

"I think I can manage," Garrick said, relieved. The last person he wanted to spend the evening with was Lionel.

Lionel smiled, and it reached his eyes. "Arlen has invited me to dine with him and his wife tonight. I am off to Ashburnham."

Olivia dressed with great care for supper. Arlen had told her that they had a guest. She paused, seated in front of her dressing table, a wave of nausea overtaking her. She could not think of Arlen now without wanting to wretch.

He had not, in the end, raped her. He had been incapable of the act. But he had tried, and when he had failed, Olivia had seen the hatred in his eyes. She had thought he would hit her again or, worse, strangle her to death. Instead he had stormed from her room.

Olivia opened her eyes, glimpsed her expression in the mirror, and continued to tremble. No amount of rouge could put the color back in her face, and no powder was thick enough to cover the dark circles under her eyes or the garish bruise on the right side of her face.

She lifted one hand. The gown she had chosen was a pale lilac silk, and the cuff was ruffled. The ruffles hid the bruises on her wrists.

It could have been worse. She could have actually been raped—and then there would be the chance of conceiving another child. But such logic failed to comfort her. She had been grossly violated, and she was still ill. How could she endure her marriage now? She could never withstand such an assault again. She did not know what she would do if Arlen attempted to exercise his marital rights another time.

It occurred to her that she might procure a weapon for herself and keep it nearby. To defend herself.

Leave him. The words overcame her, echoing loudly in her mind, not for the first time. Yet Olivia knew Arlen would not let her leave him. He would hunt her and Hannah down. She had been up all night thinking about it. But she also knew that she and Hannah could not remain in the marriage, not after last night. Her heart lurched with sickening force. She did not know what to do, how to escape.

Mama! Hannah's frightened cry as she had stood in the doorway while Arlen held her down on the floor echoed through Olivia's mind. She trembled more violently, recalling the sight of her terrified daughter standing on the threshold of her bedchamber in her pristine white nightclothes. For the first time in her life, she thanked God that her daughter was blind, that she had not been able to see what Arlen had been doing.

Mama! What is he doing to you?

Olivia would protect Hannah at all costs, which meant she must sever her connection to Garrick De Vere. Her obsession for him had brought her to this predicament, and it had, in the end, done more than gravely disrupt her marriage. It had hurt her daughter. Her daughter had witnessed the dark underside of life, and Olivia was determined that she never have such an experience again.

Disaster would befall them all. This was a disaster, and the proof was neither her bruises, her fear, nor her daughter's fear, but the terrible pain in her heart. She had never imagined that loving someone could hurt this way.

There was a knock on her boudoir door, and Olivia smiled, her eyes moist with tears, knowing it was Hannah. "Come in, dear," she said softly, turning.

Hannah opened the door and came inside, smiling, holding a large piece of parchment in her hand. Olivia smiled back at her, and when Hannah reached her, she put her arm around her and hugged her. "What is this?" she asked, taking the drawing.

"I made this for you this afternoon. It's a rainbow," Hannah explained.

"It is beautiful," Olivia whispered, her voice choked. Of course, Hannah did not know what a rainbow looked like, and the drawing did not resemble any rainbow Olivia had ever seen. But the entire page was awash in brilliant colors. It was a startling, stunning tableau. "Why a rainbow, my dear?" she asked.

"Because rainbows are beautiful, and they bring happiness," Hannah explained.

"Yes, they are beautiful, and they do bring happiness," Olivia murmured, but she was thinking that they were also fleeting, ephemeral, an illusion. Was that what her love for Garrick was? An illusion?

No, it was not an illusion; it was solid and real. But like a rainbow, it would not last—for too many forces were aligned against it.

"I came to say good night. I know you have to go downstairs," Hannah said, kissing her cheek.

Olivia stroked her daughter's dark hair. "Yes, I do. Is our guest here?"

Hannah frowned. "He is."

"Is something wrong?" Olivia asked, instantly attuned to her daughter's distress.

Hannah shrugged. "I didn't meet him. But I can feel him, Mama. He is very strong. I don't like him."

Olivia absorbed that. Hannah had never made such a statement before without having first been in contact with the person. When Hannah did not like someone, there was usually a good reason for it. She had not liked one of the footmen at Ashburnham for several years, and he had turned out to be a thief, absconding with their silverware. A peddler trying to sell them knickknacks and housewares had also made Hannah unhappy, and they had later found out he beat his mute son.

But she was only eight years old. Olivia knew firsthand how, as one matured, logic, judgment, and emotions could interfere with the gift. So what was this? Their guest was downstairs. Why did Hannah have such feelings now, when she had yet to come face-to-face with the man?

Olivia kissed her forehead and stood. "Why don't you run on to your room. Tell Miss Childs I wish her to read you a nice story before bed. I will come in later to check on you, when I can."

They walked into the hall. "You don't have to," Hannah said, unsmiling, her wide, unseeing gray gaze hovering near but not quite on Olivia's face. "Don't make Father angry again."

Olivia tensed, almost choking on an indrawn breath. "I promise."

Hannah had paused at her door, which was ajar, but she did not go inside.

Olivia felt a sense of dread. "What is it?" As she did, she suddenly glimpsed, in her mind, a very handsome, slightly stocky, blond man, standing in conversation with Arlen, a glass of port in his hand.

"Did he hurt you?" Hannah asked.

Olivia jerked, wetting her lips. "Some men, sometimes,

lose their tempers and act in ways that they should not,'' she said very carefully. ''It is not gentlemanly, it is not honorable, it is not right.'' She spoke in a very low voice. ''He did hurt me, a little. Not a lot. I am fine today.''

''Your heart is hurt,'' Hannah said, choked.

Olivia gasped, her hand flying to her heart, which was indeed filled with anguish. But not because of what Arlen had done. It was because she was in a love with a man she could not ever have, whom she must, at all costs, stay away from now.

''We will discuss this another time,'' Olivia managed.

Hannah nodded. ''But Mama, I am scared.''

Olivia hugged her close. ''Don't be scared.''

''Let him help us,'' Hannah said.

Olivia froze. ''Who?'' she breathed.

''Lord Caedmon.''

Olivia trembled. She forced a smile, kissed the top of Hannah's head. ''I have to go downstairs. Good night.'' And she swung Hannah's door wide open.

Miss Childs, who had been sitting in a rocking chair by the window with a book, smiled and stood. ''Don't worry, my lady,'' she said. ''I will take good care of her.''

Olivia said good night again and closed the door. Then she leaned upon it, shaking, damp with perspiration. She would have to change the gown she had chosen with such care.

As Olivia paused on the threshold of the salon, she had a brief moment in which to study their guest and her husband before they noticed her. She took one look at the blond, blue-eyed gentleman as he laughed at something Arlen said, and tension stiffened her spine. This man was, she knew, the person claiming to be Stanhope's son.

She arranged her face into a smile, thoughts of Garrick flooding her, as she entered the room. She could not help looking almost wildly around, unable not to hope that Garrick had also come. But he was not present, naturally— Arlen had said they had but one guest. And after last night, dear God, she did not think he would invite Garrick to

Ashburnham. Being disappointed was absurd.

The two men turned to her. The man claiming to be Lionel De Vere instantly looked at the bruises on her face, which the powder only tempered and did not conceal. Immediately he moved his gaze away, bowing. She curtsied, relieved their initial meeting was over, the awkward and humiliating moment gone. As Arlen finished the introductions, she tried very hard to still her pounding heart and relax her tension-riddled body. She wanted to relax, to clear her mind, to immediately discern the truth about him, to decide if he were an impostor or not.

"This is such a pleasure," Lionel told her, his blue eyes warm, holding hers. How handsome and noble he appeared. And he was quite the epitome of fashion, clad in a gold frock coat, a green waistcoat, and dark blue breeches and pale stockings. His thick hair was powdered, his eyebrows were blond. "I have heard wonderful things about you, Lady Ashburn, and I have been looking forward to our meeting," he was saying warmly.

Olivia continued to smile. She could not get a clear sense of whether he was really Lionel De Vere or not. "Thank you," she said. "I am so pleased you could join us for supper," she said politely. But who, she wondered, had raved about her? He was, she decided, dissembling. He was not telling the truth.

She was quite certain of it.

"Shall we go in, then?" Arlen said, not having really looked at her once.

"Yes. I am sorry I was late," Olivia apologized, glad he was avoiding eye contact. She hoped he was ashamed. She knew he was not. He could not stand the sight of her, that was all.

"May I?" Lionel asked, holding out his arm.

Of course, his escorting her into supper was absolutely correct. Olivia gave him her arm. As he tucked it in his and they left the salon, a wave of intense feeling swept over her. Something was wrong. But what?

"And how do you like our home?" Olivia asked as they walked down the hall. Arlen followed them.

He smiled at her. "I like it very much. Ashburnham is beautiful, and your flowers are magnificent."

Olivia did smile, for her gardens were lovely.

"Almost"—he smiled—"as magnificent as the woman responsible for their creation."

Olivia cast her eyes down. "Really, there is no need to flatter me," she said, aware of how gross his exaggeration was. But she stole another glance at him, only to be confronted with his perfect profile as he spoke to Arlen, who was behind them. Like his brother, he was a very handsome man.

Then she realized what she had been thinking. She stiffened, perturbed, even dismayed. Did this spontaneous thought mean that he was, indeed, the long-missing heir?

"You have quite a treasure here, Ashburn, and I do not mean just the estate."

"Thank you. Yes, I am a very fortunate man," Arlen said.

Arlen was smiling, but he was a wonderful liar. "So how long will you be staying in the country?" Olivia politely asked their guest.

"I have not decided," Lionel said easily as they entered the dining room. He held out Olivia's chair and she sat down, arranging her skirts. As he moved away from her, his hands skimmed her shoulders. Olivia stiffened, not certain it had been a careless gesture or done on purpose.

Arlen remained standing, sitting only when Lionel himself did so. "It has been so long since I was at the Hall, and I have so many memories of growing up there, that I do think I shall linger a bit." He smiled at Olivia. "Besides, I am certain my brother could use my company. It would not do for him to be alone here in the country, I think."

She froze, recalling Garrick's warning. Lionel had somehow known about the night she had spent at Stanhope Hall and possibly about them. She did not think she imagined the innuendo—that Garrick would hardly be alone in any case because she, Olivia, were also there. She stole a glance at Arlen, expecting to find him surprised and angry after discovering that Garrick was but a few miles away. His expression was bland; somehow he had already known. Her heart sank.

"Yes, you grew up at the Hall, did you not?" She fought for composure.

Lionel smiled, sipping a glass of red wine just poured by a servant. "Garrick and I raised quite a bit of mischief growing up together as boys," he said with real warmth. "Our parents spent most of their time in town, whilst we remained at the Hall. But we did prefer it that way." He grinned.

Olivia studied him. He was very engaging. She could see why Susan Layton had been so charmed. And she was quite certain he had some very real memories of Stanhope Hall—which would lead her to conclude that he was Lionel De Vere. Yet he made her uneasy. There was something about him that bothered her, and Olivia strained to pinpoint what that something was.

He was speaking easily, with a smile. "I do remember one day Garrick and I stuffed our beds with pillows and stole out of the house after dark. We were very young, perhaps ten and twelve. We went all the way to the village and got soused on ale. Of course, we were found out." Lionel laughed. "Squire Merrill recognized us and dragged us home." He winced. "We did not feel well the next day, I do remember that. But a week later Father came and we truly suffered. Neither Garrick nor I could sit down for days."

Olivia managed a smile in return. He could so easily be the real Lionel. He was very convincing. But now she was aware of what was bothering her. It was a darkness. It was surrounding him. She could not sense if it was because he was being dishonest and lying about his identity or if it were something entirely different, a hurt, perhaps, or sheer unhappiness. But something dark was there, attached to him. Was it merely because his past was so tragic and blemished? He had disappeared for years. That alone would change anyone—that alone could make someone unrecognizable. And Lionel was hardly that.

"Do I have horns on my head? Or a gravy stain upon my cravat?" Lionel laughed.

"Olivia, you are staring," Arlen said with exasperation.

Olivia started, felt her cheeks heat anew, and began toying with the pickled herring that had just been served. "I am sorry," she murmured. But as she used her fork, the ruffled cuff on her wrist fell back, exposing the ugly bruise there. Immediately she laid down her fork, not touching her plate, dismayed, looking up. But their guest had turned to Arlen and was asking him if he felt like doing a bit of shooting in the morning.

She could barely relax. She had thought to hide the evidence of last night's attack by wearing this dress. Now all it would do was make it uncomfortable, if not impossible, to eat.

"That is a capital idea." Arlen smiled.

"Perhaps we should invite Garrick to join us," Lionel said.

Olivia was glad her mouth was not full, otherwise she would have choked. Unable to control herself, she glanced at Arlen. He was staring at her. Her heart beat wildly, uncontrollably.

"Another grand idea," Arlen said, his tone flat. "Let us invite him. We can send a servant to the Hall as we speak." And he smiled. "We shall soon have a full house, it seems. For the Laytons arrive tomorrow as well."

And finally, Olivia made a noise. Abruptly she reached for her wine and took a quick sip. It did not still her pounding heart.

"My dear, are you all right?" Arlen asked coolly.

Olivia nodded. A coherent reply failed her.

And Arlen smiled. "I am sure Caedmon will be thrilled to be reunited with his fiancée, don't you agree, Olivia?"

CHAPTER SIXTEEN

He still despised hunting. But Garrick had not even thought to refuse the invitation a servant had brought to him last evening from Ashburnham. He had arisen well before dawn to join the hunt.

"Shoot!" Arlen shouted as a bevy of grouse was flushed by the hounds from the field.

Garrick was slow to pull the trigger on his matchlock rifle, one that had not been used in years. By the time he fired, both Arlen and Lionel, standing shoulder to shoulder with him, had already fired twice and downed two birds each. Garrick squinted. The flapping, squeaking birds filled the pale blue, early morning sky. Their images were blurred. He tried to aim on one grouse. It seemed to reverse direction—flying backward. He fired and missed.

Lionel was taking his third, expert shot. As his mark fell to the ground with a thump, it was clear that he was an even better marksman than before. Arlen paused, having just reloaded. "So you still cannot shoot."

Garrick was watching his setter racing with the hounds, eagerly looking for downed prey. So tense that he could hardly move his shoulders, Garrick turned to face him and their gazes clashed and locked. The tension that reverberated between them was so strong, Garrick thought he could see the air thickening around them. He smiled. It was a cold, unpleasant smile. "I find blood sport far more than boring—I find it the extreme act of cowardice.''

Arlen stiffened. ''You call me a coward?''

A brief silence fell between them. The red setter appeared, a grouse in his mouth, tail wagging as he dropped it at Garrick's feet. Lionel lowered his rifle. ''We are out having a friendly hunt,'' he said, smiling. ''Garrick hardly called you a coward, Arlen.''

''I asked your brother.''

Garrick smiled again, as coldly. ''These birds have no chance. This is not even a sport. It is slaughter.'' Suddenly disgusted with himself for participating in the hunt merely because he wished to see Olivia, and equally disgusted by his jealousy over Lionel having spent last night at Ashburnham, he threw his rifle down.

''You quit because you cannot shoot to save your own life.'' Arlen laughed.

Garrick stalked away. But he heard Lionel say, ''He means no harm. He has always hated hunting. Let him go back to the house. I am sure the countess will be able to entertain him.''

Garrick's tension increased.

Garrick's steps slowed. He was approaching the house from the back, where a jumble of wildly arranged flowers in every single possible color formed a garden. His heart was drumming now, hard and loud, in his chest. Behind the garden was a slate-floored terrace. And Olivia was sitting there with her daughter at a table.

She had seen him, and she was staring.

He stepped onto the terrace, hesitating, watching as Olivia set her teacup down. He now saw the plates on the table she sat at and realized that she and her daughter were enjoying their breakfast outside, in spite of the early morning chill. It was unheard of—but the kind of thing he himself had done on too many occasions to count.

''Treve!'' Hannah cried, standing.

The setter wagged its tail rapidly, his entire body undulating, but he did not move from Garrick's side. Garrick realized he had stopped in his tracks and was staring at

Olivia as if he were a lovestruck fool. But perhaps he was. "Go," he told his dog, snapping his fingers and pointing at Hannah.

The setter bounded over to the little girl, who bent and hugged him hard. When she looked up toward Garrick, her sightless eyes were shining. "Good day, my lord," she said happily.

Olivia was also standing. "Good day, Hannah," Garrick said, trying hard now to remain in the present and not be swept away with memories of the past—memories of all the moments he had thus far spent with her, including the stolen, passion-filled ones. He wanted to be close to her— he wanted, at least, to touch her. Just once. "Lady Ashburn."

"My lord," she said throatily.

Having bowed, he finally walked over to her, and he froze. There was a dark discoloration on the right side of her face. *She had been hit.*

Olivia pressed her forefinger to her lips, her eyes finding his, hers filled with worry and a silent communication. When she spoke, her smile was forced. "How nice to see you again, my lord. Where is my husband and your brother?"

"They remain afield. It will be at least an hour before they are done with their sport," he managed, filled with icy rage and shaking because of it. Should he kill Arlen? Or should he merely beat him to within an inch of his life?

"Oh," she said, eyes wide, her tone odd and high. Again her smile was forced, and suddenly Garrick wondered if she were dismayed and distressed to see him. After all, he had no doubt that he was the reason she had been struck. Did she blame him for Arlen's brutality? And had this ever happened before?

"Hannah, why don't you take Treve around to the kitchens and find him some treats? Surely there is a nice mutton bone left over from last night," Olivia said.

"Oh, thank you, Mama!" Hannah cried. She paused. "My lord, may I? The kitchens are just around the side of the house. We had mutton last night. Does Treve like bones?''

Garrick could not smile. ''Of course. Treve, go with Hannah.''

But Hannah paused. ''My lord? Is something amiss?''

He focused. ''You are very astute, Hannah, for such a young girl. Or can you read my mind?''

Hannah's smile faded. Worried, she cocked her head toward her mother. ''I cannot read minds, my lord,'' she said tersely.

He stared, certain he had struck a nerve and was very close to the truth. But Olivia stepped swiftly between them. ''Go on, my dear. And tell the staff to bring Lord Caedmon breakfast. You are hungry, my lord?'' She faced him as Hannah and the setter ran off, disappearing around the side of the house. ''Don't ever do that again,'' she flared.

He did not answer. Instead he stared into her all-seeing gray eyes and then at the hideous mark on her face. ''I'll kill him.''

''No!'' she cried, coming forward and laying her hand on his arm. ''Do not make matters worse!''

Her touch was a brand. It branded him. Instantly his hands closed on her arms.

Olivia's eyes widened, and she looked frantically around them.

''I am putting you in jeopardy,'' he said, releasing her immediately. He, too, glanced around but did not see anyone in sight. ''I am sorry. What happened?''

She shook her head. ''Nothing. I fell.''

''Do not treat me like a fool,'' he erupted. Now he grabbed her wrist. She cried out.

Amazed, he released her, saw the pain in her eyes, and took her palm gently. ''Do not,'' she whispered, her eyes shining now with tears. But he ignored her, turning over her hand and pushing back the cuff. Her wrist was bruised and discolored, too.

His heart had never hurt him like this. And he had never hated anyone the way he hated Arlen. Immediately, before she could form a new protest, he inspected her other wrist.

She turned her head aside, blinking back tears. "What happened, Olivia?" he demanded. "Is this the first time? Or does he beat you as he wills?"

"Please, join me for breakfast," she said, blinking rapidly.

"You are crying."

"I am not crying." She moved away and reached for her chair.

"You are." He was aghast. He wanted to hold her, comfort her. Instead he moved her chair back for her and helped her to sit. Then he sat in the chair Hannah had vacated. "I caused this, didn't I?"

"Do you prefer coffee or tea?"

"Olivia!" His tone was sharp, and it carried. She blanched. He tried desperately to control his scattered wits and, worse, his frenzied emotions. "I must talk to you. There is no one about. Please."

"There is a house full of servants about." She hesitated. "This is not a good time."

He leaned forward. "When is a good time?"

"There is no good time," she whispered, avoiding his eyes. "Not for us."

He sat up, his pulse drumming. "You don't mean that."

She stared at the table, refusing to meet his eyes.

She could not mean it, yet he felt that his world was in jeopardy. "Olivia, I have to know."

She finally met his gaze. "Why? So you can assault him? And then where would that leave me and my daughter? He knows, Garrick. He knows I spent the night at Stanhope Hall, and he is convinced we are lovers."

"Oh, God." Garrick stared. He was sick. "You must run away. You must leave him."

She inhaled. "Why did you come? You did not have to accept the invitation."

He met her gaze. "You know why I came. I came to see you. I was worried about you." And he realized that he had been right to have felt so uneasy since last being with her.

She stood abruptly. "I am tired. I . . ." She hesitated, because their gazes remained locked.

"Don't go," he said, knowing she was fighting her desire to stay and have a few moments with him. "Olivia, we may not have another chance to speak privately. Please. Sit down."

Her gaze moved beyond him. "They are coming," she said. With a pale visage, she sank back into her chair, rearranging her expression into a smile that was false and stiff. Garrick shifted and looked behind him. Lionel and Arlen were almost at the garden, their rifles on their shoulders, the hounds milling about their legs. Both men carried a dozen dead birds, strung together on two lines.

"Garrick."

Her whisper was low and hoarse. He turned back to her like a shot.

She wet her lips. "I do wish to speak to you. God help me. I am just not sure when."

He nodded. "We will find a time."

"When are you leaving?"

"I will stay as long as my brother stays," he said.

She nodded, her shoulders squaring, as footsteps finally sounded on the slate behind him. She stood. "My lords," she said, continuing to smile. But her eyes were obviously filled with dismay and anxiety. Garrick also stood.

"I see you are entertaining our guest," Arlen said, dropping a dozen dead, bloody birds at her feet. "How kind of you."

Olivia stared at him, did not reply. One of the dead birds touched the hem of her pale dress, staining it. She stretched her smile. "My lord, have you enjoyed this beautiful morning?"

"Indeed I have." Lionel's exceedingly warm blue gaze held hers. It was a caress upon her face. Garrick stiffened suddenly, watching them.

Lionel bowed over her hand, taking it to his lips. "Lady Ashburn, you are a sight for my sore eyes. Now you have made the morning truly lovely."

Two spots of pink color appeared on Olivia's high cheekbones. "Thank you, my lord, but you do exaggerate," she said huskily, looking away.

Garrick could only stare at her in disbelief. He could not believe what was transpiring.

Lionel was speaking again. "Have you forgotten the promise you made last night? You offered to show me your greenhouse, and explain to me the vagaries of indoor planting."

Olivia nodded. "Yes, I did." She was clearly careful not to look in Garrick's direction.

"Perhaps we can do so after dinner? Would that be convenient?" Lionel grinned.

"Of course," Olivia fumbled, "as long as Arlen has not made other plans for you."

"As De Vere wishes," Arlen said, toeing the bundle of dead birds. "The Laytons will be here for dinner, we shall all be busy enough." He turned to stare at Garrick. "I am sure you must be thrilled to be reunited with your fiancée."

Garrick faced Arlen. "Hardly," he ground out. He sent Lionel a piercing regard, one filled with warning, but Lionel only smiled at him, as if he did not understand.

But Garrick knew he damn well did comprehend his meaning.

"I am so happy to see you," Susan cried, grasping Olivia's hands. The Laytons had arrived but moments ago. Olivia did not know where Garrick was; she had last seen him and the setter walking away from the house a short while ago, but Arlen and Lionel were in the salon with Sir John Layton and his wife, Lady Layton telling them how pleasant the journey had been.

Olivia was hardly relaxed. She hoped her smile was sunny and bright. "I am glad to see you, too," she lied. Under any other circumstances she would be, but not now, not today, with Garrick at the house as another guest. She felt herself flush with guilt just thinking about him. She had betrayed Susan dearly, and there was no way around the inescapable fact. "You look very well," she added.

It was the truth. Susan had never seemed prettier. Her

cheeks were pink, and there was a sparkle in her eyes. They stood in the foyer, the front door wide open behind them. Susan laughed. "As much as I love town, I do love Ashburnham," she explained. But her gaze was already wandering—toward the salon.

Olivia followed it. It was obvious that Susan was peeking at Lionel. "The men were hunting this morning," Olivia said.

"Oh, how nice." Susan tore her gaze away to smile happily at Olivia. Then her face fell. "Is he here, too?"

Olivia looked at the young girl, thinking that she was so foolish to dislike Garrick and favor his brother. She herself now regarded the foursome in the salon. Lionel was handsome and outstanding, and like the sun, he brightened the room. His presence was commanding. He did remind her of Stanhope. But something was wrong with him. She knew it, with the certainty that her gift of sight gave her. "Yes, he is here. I am sure he is eager to see you." She could not force her lips to curve upward. She felt no jealousy toward Susan, how could she? Susan was sweet and pleasant. But the situation remained intolerable. Why had they not stayed away from one another?

Arlen's furious image as he pinned her down the other night assailed her. And with the image, she envisioned Garrick's heated eyes and heard him say, *You must leave him.* If only it were so simple. If she took Hannah and ran away, she was placing her and her daughter at a grave risk. For if he found them, he would drag them home and make their life intolerable. Olivia knew it, because she had been married to him for nine achingly long years. Perhaps he would not just punish her through Hannah, perhaps he would actually hurt Hannah. She shuddered.

But how could she stay?

"I doubt my fiancé is eager to see me," Susan said. "He despises me, and the few times we have been in the same room, it is obvious." But now she smiled, and when she spoke, her tone was bubbly, like newly opened champagne. "The earl of Stanhope has been seen everywhere with his son. With Lionel, that is." She beamed. "At Almack's he introduced him around, and clearly, he's on the verge of publicly declaring him his long-lost and legitimate heir. As I am to wed the Stanhope heir, I am sure my father will soon be speaking to Stanhope about rectifying this coil. Isn't it wonderful?'' Susan quite cried.

"Do not get your hopes up," Olivia said gently.

"Why ever not? If I dwell upon marriage to Garrick, I shall surely go insane—or try to drown myself again."

"Susan!" Olivia grasped her arm, ready to shake her, but at that moment Lionel was pausing beside them. Olivia paled, searching his face to see if he had heard Susan's last incriminating remark, but his blue gaze was steady upon Susan, who was blushing prettily. His smile widening, he took her hand and bowed over it. "Dear Miss Layton. Soon you shall be my sister," he said. "How good it is to see you again."

Olivia was relieved. He had not heard. If anyone ever found out about Susan's attempt at suicide, the scandal would be horrendous—and should Susan not marry Garrick De Vere undoubtedly no one else ever would.

Now Susan's gaze was coy, flirting with his. "This is such a surprise," she said, wide-eyed. "I had no idea you were in the country."

He clearly knew she was besotted and clearly knew she lied. He laughed. "I hope this is a *pleasant* surprise, Miss Layton."

"Oh, very," she responded quickly, beaming.

Olivia sighed. Susan had no guile, and she did not think Lionel truly interested in her. Yet his eyes, fixed upon Susan, were now warm and admiring. They had been as warm and as admiring when directed at her, Olivia, yesterday and this morning. A glimmer of comprehension struck Olivia, and she narrowed her gaze upon him.

But as if he sensed her skepticism and her sudden inkling, he turned. "You two ladies make a lovely sight. An artist should paint the pair of you, perhaps outside, in the countess's splendid garden."

Susan blushed anew, while Olivia murmured, "That is very kind of you." She was coming to dislike Lionel, she realized. He was not sincere. But could he possibly be up to what she thought he was? Surely his interest in Susan and herself was not related to the fact that Susan was Garrick's fiancée and that she herself was involved with him as well?

"And where is my brother—Miss Layton's fiancé?" Lionel asked.

Susan grimaced. "He is out walking, according to the countess."

"Could he not even be present to greet you properly?" Lionel was exasperated. "Do forgive Garrick, Miss Layton. In spite of his behavior, which at times seems odd, he is a kind and caring person. It is just, I suspect, that having lived on that savage island for so many years, his penchant for eccentricity has been whetted, not dimmed." He smiled. "But I am sure that, in time, he shall establish new manners—with your devotion and aid."

Susan managed a weak smile. She did not reply.

"Have you been to the Hall yet?" Lionel asked.

Olivia stared at him, having no doubt now as to what was about to come. She was stiff with tension.

"No, I have not," Susan said, her eyes brightening with expectation.

"My brother." Lionel shook his head again, in mock exasperation this time. "Miss Layton, if my brother has failed to invite you for a grand tour, then let me do so. May I escort you over, say, tomorrow? Surely you wish to glimpse one of your future homes."

Olivia took Susan's arm before she could reply in the affirmative. "My lord, tomorrow I had planned a picnic for myself and Miss Layton and her mother." It was a fabrication. "Besides, surely Caedmon will wish to escort his betrothed to the Hall?" Her smile was strained.

Susan shook her arm free. "Can we not picnic another time?" she asked. She faced Lionel. "I would so love to see the Hall, especially if you showed me the house and grounds yourself."

Olivia had one coherent thought—Susan would be putty in this man's hands. He could seduce her at will, if he so chose. Then she was shocked at where her mind had led her. But had it been her mind or her gift?

Lionel had hesitated. "Perhaps I have been remiss," he said, glancing at Olivia as if *he* could read *her* thoughts. "But I was only thinking to make amends for my brother's lack of courtesy."

Before either Susan or Olivia could reply, Garrick stepped up to them, apparently having been standing just outside the open front door. "You are not remiss." He smiled, but his eyes remained cool. "Please, Lionel, escort Miss Layton to the Hall. I am sure she will be thrilled." His gaze swept over Lionel, moved to Olivia, and rested there. "I am sure she shall be in very good hands, Lady Ashburn."

Please don't, Olivia thought, gazing into his angry eyes. Please do not force an issue now.

Lionel smiled back at Garrick. Olivia could not decide if he were angry—his expression was completely, purposefully, masked. "Well, with your permission, I would love to do so. It shall be a charming afternoon, spent in charming company."

Garrick's jaw was set as he stared at his brother now. Lionel stared back, no longer smiling. Suddenly, briefly, the two men looked like two dogs about to converge on a single bone. When Garrick finally faced his fiancée, interrupting the brief moment, Olivia hoped she had not seen what she thought she had. She watched him bow, very cursorily, and she despaired. Susan was right. His ill will toward his intended was glaringly obvious—and that was not right. "Miss Layton," he said stiffly, "I hardly know how to greet you properly. I hope you have had a pleasant journey?"

Her expression anxious if not downright fearful, Susan curtsied. "My lord." Her tone was hardly audible. "It was—er—quite passable."

Garrick nodded curtly. "How fine," he said. Directing one hard look at Lionel, another piercing glance at Olivia, he spun on his heel and exited the house.

A silence reigned.

"Well," Lionel said lightly. "What shall it be? A picnic or a tour?"

Olivia took Susan's arm. "Go after him. He is your betrothed. Ask him if he will show you around the Hall.".

Susan stared. Her face crumpled. Tears filled her eyes. "I cannot. He scares me. He is hateful!"

Olivia turned, not even thinking, obeying her feet, which moved of their own will. Garrick was angry and upset, and rightly so. She had to go to him.

"Olivia. Come. You have not greeted Sir John and his wife properly," Arlen called harshly to her from the threshold of the salon.

And reality claimed her. Halfway to the door, Olivia faltered and froze. How much had Arlen heard and seen? She turned and obediently, her heart sinking, did as Arlen had asked.

CHAPTER SEVENTEEN

Garrick stood outside the greenhouse, his hands in the pockets of his breeches, staring through the partially opaque glass walls. His mood had never been more foul.

Inside, Olivia was walking among the various plants and blooms, with Lionel at her side. They were carrying on a conversation that Garrick could not hear. But every now and then Lionel would make a remark with his too engaging smile, and Olivia would smile in return.

Garrick knew beyond a doubt that Lionel wished to seduce Olivia away from him. Of course, he could not blame him or any other man for wanting her, but in this case he could not help but think that Lionel wanted her because he, Garrick, had had her first. Was he being overly sensitive and overly imaginative?

In the past, as boys, there had never been that kind of rivalry. In fact, Garrick clearly remembered his first passionate encounter with a serving wench in the village near Caedmon Crag. Lionel had also been intimate with the buxom young girl, but Garrick had been the first and Lionel had not cared.

Garrick continued to stare. Olivia was pointing at some stunning purple flowers Garrick could not identify, and Lionel was nodding with his incessant smile. Dinner had been as annoying. Lionel had managed to amuse the table with numerous anecdotes about his life in India. Everyone—except for Garrick—had been impressed with his narrow escape from the man-eating tiger. But he had included a story of his childhood—an adventure he had shared with Garrick at Caedmon Crag. During one of the first summers the boys had ever been there, they had come upon smugglers on the beach one rainy afternoon. Terrified and fascinated, they had watched the activities from behind huge boulders, fortunately not being discovered. They had spent the rest of the summer pretending that they were smugglers, playing in the caves the smugglers used.

How in hell did this man know about that? Unless he really was Lionel?

Garrick watched Lionel tuck Olivia's arm in his as they turned to leave the greenhouse. He was uneasy, and far more so than because the sight of them together disturbed him—which it did. If this man were his actual, long-lost, vanished brother, then he had changed. In a way, it was almost impossible to believe that he was a fraud, given his incredible knowledge of the family and the past. But Garrick disliked him. His feelings since meeting him had undergone numerous transformations, and he was left now with raw suspicion and a deep dislike.

Olivia's cheeks were damp and flushed when she and Lionel appeared on the gravel path outside the greenhouse. Garrick made no move to conceal himself, and she started when she saw him. Lionel smiled slightly, his eyes narrowed. "Well," his brother said easily enough. "Did you wish for a tour, too?"

Garrick strode forward. He had left his setter with Hannah in the house. "Actually, I think that is a wonderful idea." His unwavering gaze remained upon Lionel.

Lionel stared back, while Olivia removed her arm from his and looked from one man to the other. "I hope you were not feeling left out. I had assumed you would be walking on the grounds with your fiancée."

"I am leaving my fiancée in your very capable hands," Garrick said coolly.

Lionel's expression remained fixed—a slight, amused, condescending smile. "Miss Layton is charming. You should consider yourself lucky to be plighted to such a sweet and innocent girl.''

Garrick looked at him and had to laugh. "If you are so fond of her, why don't you marry her? After all, you are poised to inherit the earldom—why not inherit my bride as well?''

"Garrick.'' Lionel stepped forward and placed his hand on Garrick's arm. "I did not return to usurp anything from you.''

"No? Then why did you return?'' Garrick said harshly.

"I told you. I almost died. And I realized I had no choice but to become a part of this family again. Imagine if I had died!'' Lionel's tone rose. "I would have never seen you, or Mother or Father again.''

Garrick glanced at Olivia, who had said not a word. "We all assumed you died, many years ago. And we accepted it. Tell the entire world, if you must, that your near death is the reason for your sudden reappearance in our lives. But I, for one, do not believe it.''

Lionel stared, his eyes turning hard. Garrick stared back. And then Lionel shrugged and smiled at Olivia. "He has changed. The Garrick I grew up with loved me as much as I loved him. We shared everything, he and I. Everything.''

Garrick stiffened. His temples throbbed. Once again, Lionel spoke with unerring accuracy. Except, perhaps, for one fact. "You did not share your plan to disappear with me,'' he said.

Lionel glanced at Olivia. "I do not think we should discuss this publicly,'' he said. "And we have been over this once before.''

Garrick was oddly satisfied. For the first time since Lionel had returned from the missing and the dead, he had discomfited him. Now it was his turn to shrug.

Lionel bowed to Olivia. "Thank you, Lady Ashburn, for the tour. You have a unique way with flowers and shrubs, that is clear. I did enjoy myself.''

"You are welcome,'' Olivia said, glancing at Garrick.

"Now, of course, you can show Garrick your fine efforts,'' Lionel said. He nodded at Garrick and headed across the lawns, toward the house.

An awkward silence fell.

Garrick studied her. Could she like Lionel? It was clear to him that Susan had already fallen heavily for his obvious charms. But Olivia? Was she also entranced by his golden good looks, his sunny smile, and his manners and wit? Garrick could not stand the thought. ''You said you wished to speak to me,'' he said bluntly. ''If we go inside, we will have complete privacy.''

Olivia finally regarded him, trepidation in her eyes. ''If we go alone, inside, Arlen might think the worst.''

He saw red. ''This is intolerable! You remaining here, under his roof, after he has hurt you—when he does not even love his own daughter. And you have shackled me. I cannot stand to remain silent and inactive in this situation.''

''I am sorry if you are inconvenienced,'' Olivia said with some sarcasm. It was bitter.

She was the kindest person he had ever met, and her slight sarcasm wounded him. ''I know that this is all my fault,'' he began.

''No.'' She shook her head, her eyes suddenly clear and very silver, holding his. ''Our marriage has been horrendous from the start. Had we had even the slightest friendship, I do not think our . . . er . . . liaison would have happened.''

''How horrendous, Olivia?'' He had to know.

She stared. Finally she said, ''He disliked me from the first.'' Her color was high.

''Why?''

She shook her head and would not answer him.

He was grim. ''Even had you and Arlen been friends, what you and I have found is inescapable.''

Olivia hesitated. She was gazing behind him, and he turned to follow her regard. Lionel had paused some distance from them, a gold snuff box in his hands. If he was trying to overhear their conversation, he gave no sign of it. Garrick faced her, took her arm, and guided her toward the greenhouse. "I do not trust him. And sounds can carry in open spaces."

They stepped inside the plant-filled, glass-and-iron dome structure; Olivia's eyes found his, piercingly direct. Instantly Garrick became aware of how alone they were. He did not release her arm. Instead his thumb slid across the inside of her elbow in a small caress. It was impossible not to want her, and badly.

She looked at it, then up at him—into his eyes again.

"I have to touch you," he said.

"Don't," she said. And added, "Not here."

"Olivia. I miss you," he began, only too late realizing how selfish he was being.

She inhaled harshly. "Don't. Please do not make this worse. I don't know what to do. I am so confused. Arlen is watching me closely. And I cannot betray Susan," she finished. "That is the worst of it. I feel so guilty—but what we have shared has been so wonderful."

She was using the past tense. "Damn Susan! She wants Lionel, anyway." He was angry. "You know she despises me—she thinks I am a savage. As for Arlen, the sooner he returns to town the better!"

"If you did not act like a savage when with her, if you did not do your best to terrify her, she might think differently," Olivia flared.

His felt his jaw grinding down. "I cannot tolerate her presence for even a moment or two. Can you imagine the two of us bound together for all eternity in holy matrimony?" His laughter was at once bitter and incredulous.

Olivia stared. "No," she said softly. "I fear for the both of you if such a thing actually happens."

Garrick jerked, his gaze again flying to and locking with hers.

"Do you think," Olivia said carefully, "that your father will proclaim Lionel his firstborn and heir?"

Garrick hesitated. "I think so. He wants this man to be Lionel. Either that, or there is some ulterior motive to his behavior."

"What ulterior motive could there be? Even I am impressed with Lionel's recollections of the past.''

He stared, and it was a moment before he spoke. ''And just how impressed are you with him?''

Her eyes widened. ''You sound jealous!''

He was jealous, but he was not about to admit it. ''I am hardly jealous.''

''Oh, Garrick.'' Her tone was soft. ''You have nothing to be jealous of. Even if he really is your brother, I question his sincerity.''

His heart beat harder. ''But you do not question mine?'' he asked, as softly.

Her gray gaze held his. ''No. I do not.''

He smiled. ''Good.''

After a pause, Olivia said, ''Will Susan be plighted to Lionel instead of to you?''

''One cannot predict what the earl will do, he is so canny. But that would solve most of my problems,'' he added grimly. Suddenly he clasped her hands in his, refusing to let them go. ''Olivia, if that does happen, I am, at least, absolved of my responsibility to Stanhope.''

She stared, not saying a word.

''What if,'' he said slowly, ''I took you and Hannah away from here, far away?''

She was pale. ''You are not free to do that.''

''And you still fear Arlen,'' he finished for her.

Slowly she nodded.

''I will never let him hurt you again,'' he said roughly, never having meant anything more. In that moment, he was one single heartbeat away from pulling her into his arms, to hold her, reassure her—to feel her heart beating next to his.

Olivia looked up. He knew she knew what he was thinking, he knew she felt the impulse to seek his embrace, too.

Garrick's pulse drummed. He glanced around, only too well recalling spying on her just a few moments ago from outside, but saw no one. He took her by the shoulders and pulled her close. ''I need you, Olivia,'' he whispered, and he meant far more than just physically. He kissed her deeply, for an achingly long, bittersweet, desperate time.

When he released her, he was as out of breath as if he had just arrived at Ashburnham on foot. Tension assailed his entire body. It was torturous.

She stepped back, trembling visibly. "I cannot think clearly when I am around you. I must go back to the house!"

"Wait," he said, catching up to her as they stepped outside. "You wanted to tell me something. What is it?"

They paused on the gravel path. At that moment, a cloud covered the sun. A shadow fell over them.

Olivia wet her lips. "Garrick, you and your family should be careful."

All his previous desire vanished. "In reference to what? Or should," he asked slowly, "I say whom?"

She nodded, swallowing. "Something is not right. With Lionel."

He stared, his chest tight. He found it harder to breathe now than before. "Olivia . . . Hannah's abilities, to see things clearly—that others cannot see. Did she get that from you?"

"No!" Olivia cried. She was pale, her eyes frightened. "Hannah can only feel and sense things better than you and I because she is blind—and she has to rely on all of her senses, including her intuition, to make up for her blindness. That is all that it is, Garrick." Her gaze was imploring.

He nodded, touching her shoulder. "All right." He did not believe her. Hannah had a gift most often associated with Gypsies. He was certain of it. "Tell me what you mean."

"I am not sure. But something is wrong with him." She did not smile. "I am not a fortune-teller. I am not a witch. I do not have a crystal ball. I cannot read tea leaves. But my instinct tells me that something is odd here, odd and amiss."

"You think he is a fraud, a pretender—a liar," Garrick said flatly.

Olivia hesitated. "I do not know if he is a fraud or your missing brother. I have no . . . intuition . . . about that. But

I feel a darkness about him. Around him. If he is your brother, he has changed. Be careful. That is all I wanted to say."

If he is your brother, he has changed.

Her words echoed. They were very disturbing. Had Lionel changed? Was he, in truth, his missing brother? Had he become this truly unlikable person?

"Garrick?"

Olivia interrupted his thoughts. He looked into her eyes, which were searching his now, and he wanted to kiss her again, but tenderly, on the cheek or forehead. He could not, for the house was in plain sight behind them. He could not even lift his hand and touch her face, letting her know that her concern was welcome and that it moved him. So he smiled, from his heart. "Thank you for the warning, Olivia."

She finally smiled, too. "You're welcome."

His smile died. "But I did not need it. I do not trust him."

"That is probably best," Olivia said.

"Shall we go back to the house?" Garrick asked.

Olivia nodded, and they started down the white gravel path, careful not to touch or even bump into one another.

"My lady," Mrs. Riley cried, smiling widely. "It is so good to have you back!"

The countess of Stanhope managed a smile. "It has been a long time, has it not, Mrs. Riley?"

"Indeed it has," the tall housekeeper said. Passing by them were various servants with the earl's and the countess's trunks. Their coach was parked outside, the team of six being unhitched as the baggage was unloaded. The earl stood there, chatting with his stable master, who had come running out to greet him the moment they had turned into the drive.

"I do wish we had been informed of your arrival," Mrs. Riley said. "We had no idea, but your rooms are always kept in a state of readiness." She smiled.

"I did not know myself until last night that we were

coming to the Hall. His Lordship made the decision rather spontaneously," the countess said. Eleanor thought it was an understatement, and she was torn between anger and despair. She had not been informed about their departure until they had sat down to dine; thus she had been up half the night, directing the packing of her trunks. She was exhausted, but not merely from lack of sleep and the trip from town. Her fatigue was emotional.

Her husband, she knew, had returned to the Hall after all these years because Lionel was there. *If it really was Lionel.*

"Shall I set out a dinner for you?" Mrs. Riley asked. "Both of Their Lordships returned home rather late last night from Ashburnham, and made no plans for a midday meal. Both have gone out on horseback."

"Together?" Eleanor was curious, her heart thumping.

"I do not think so," Mrs. Riley said, her natural enthusiasm fading. Her direct gaze held the countess's. Eleanor saw a dozen questions in her eyes. Once, they had been somewhat intimate—as close as was possible for Eleanor to be to anyone, as she had no real confidantes in her life. She did not believe in airing one's dirty laundry, so to speak . . . especially as all the women whom she considered her friends spent most of their time gossiping behind one another's backs.

But she had not been to the Hall in ten long years. After Lionel had disappeared, they had come twice, during successive summers. But the memories had proved too painful for everyone, and once Garrick had been banished to Barbados, they had not come again. And they had never set foot at Caedmon Crag, where the vanishing had occurred. Neither Eleanor nor the earl ever would again.

"My lady?" Mrs. Riley cut into her thoughts.

Eleanor focused with some difficulty. Her concentration had become very bad of late. She was supposed to make a decision about dinner, but for the life of her, she could not decide—she did not care. The boys were out riding. Separately. An ache revealed itself in her breast. As children, they had been inseparable. Oh, God. If only it were Lionel.

Her glance settled on her husband as he stood outdoors,

now in the midst of an enthusiastic conversation with both the stable master and the gamekeeper. Stanhope was still a formidable specimen of a man. He was six feet tall, his shoulders remained broad, his legs strong and muscled, due, she thought, to his twice daily rides. Of course, he was stockier now than he had been a decade ago, but that weight gain was as natural as aging and dying.

Death. It weighed heavily upon her mind.

Stanhope was now crossing the lawns with both servants, on his way, she thought, to the stables. He had not bothered to tell her where he was going, or for how long, or if he wished to dine at any time in the near future. Despair and anger warred again within Eleanor. She turned and faced the housekeeper, but not before arranging her face into a pleasant mask.

"There will be no dinner. Prepare a menu for me for a lavish supper and I shall study it in my rooms. You may also send me a tray with some refreshments." She hesitated. "I will take sherry with my dinner."

Mrs. Riley nodded and rushed off.

Eleanor laid her hand, which was trembling, against her breast. Her husband had disappeared from view. The boys were out. She was alone.

But she was always alone, was she not?

She turned and walked through the hall, into the east wing, where the family's apartments were. Her steps were slow. As she climbed the stairs, her hand drifted upon the banister. She had thought that Garrick's return would fill the void in her life. She had been wrong. Nothing could fill the void in her life.

In her sitting room, she immediately went to the gilded lacquer sideboard. The cabinet beneath was locked. She could not remember where she had left the key, so she began a methodical search that led her into her bedchamber and dressing room. She did not spare a glance for the furnishings, heavily and brightly floral, which had once given her so much pleasure. She found the key on her dressing table, lying casually among glass bottles of perfumes, a silver brush and comb, and a plated hand mirror all arranged upon a beautiful silver tray. Holding it tightly, she raced back to the sitting room.

Squatting, she unlocked the cabinet and reached inside. But the bottle she withdrew had been opened and it was empty. Frowning, she found two more bottles in the same state. All three she quickly returned to their hiding place. When she finally stood, she held a full, unopened bottle of port in her hand with a cork opener. She quickly twisted the cork out, blew the dust off a glass, and poured herself a generous drink. When she had sipped half of it, the pain began to dim.

Should she not, she thought bleakly, know if Lionel were a pretender or not? Now her temples throbbed.

She finished the drink and put both the bottle and the evidence of her recent drinking, the empty glass, back into the cabinet, which she locked. The key she slipped down the front of her dress, into her corset. Then she left the room, moving quickly, her feet carrying her of their own volition back downstairs and into the central wing of the house. Her heart hammered uneasily, with fear.

Swiftly she climbed all the stairs, thinking, I do not even know if it is Lionel, God help me.

Tears now blurred her gaze as she reached the topmost landing. She did not stop. The corridor was absolutely silent as she traversed it, finally reaching the narrow doorway that led to the last short flight of stairs—and the attic.

Eleanor opened the door. She was nauseated. It was hard to think. She climbed the stairs. The door to the attic was ajar. Had it remained ajar like this for all these years? she wondered. She pressed it open and went inside.

Blinking, allowing her eyes to adjust to the shadows and darkness, she straightened to her full height, which was only an inch or two above five feet, and walked over to the window. Outside, the day remained sunny and bright, in glaring contrast with the dark attic. It was not the first time she had stood there, gazing out of the window, blindly.

Abruptly she pushed it open, knowing that if she jumped out, she would not be the first to have done so.

* * *

''Sir John, do come in,'' the earl of Stanhope said, smiling.

The robust knight entered the salon where Stanhope had been waiting to receive him. They were in the east wing of the house, and the room was large and bright, with new, modern, oversize windows looking out upon the grounds. Many blue-and-gold Oriental rugs covered the parquet floors, and the yellow papered walls were adorned with paintings in gold frames. Stanhope had been sitting at a beautiful mahogany desk with an inlaid leather top, and now he rose to his full height. Sir John, however, topped him by a hand.

The two men bowed. ''A drink?'' Stanhope asked. He had been expecting Sir John for some time.

''Why not.'' Sir John smiled. His wig was askew, as always.

Stanhope went to a beautiful japanned sideboard and poured two cognacs into snifters. He then handed one to Sir John and the two men settled on one of the several sofas in the room, this one a sunny golden damask affair. ''And how do you find your stay at Ashburnham?'' Stanhope asked.

''Entertaining, as always. It seems that my daughter has become quite attached to the countess.''

''I had hoped that by now she might become attached to my son,'' Stanhope said pleasantly.

Sir John continued to sip his cognac as if nothing were amiss, but he took the bait. ''Which son?''

''Her betrothed, of course.'' Stanhope smiled widely. ''Garrick may be eccentric, but many ladies find him quite attractive, I can assure you of that.''

''So I have seen,'' Sir John said, not easily. ''Apparently, my daughter finds him quite terrifying.''

''I shall speak to him about that.'' Stanhope scowled. ''His manners will improve, I promise you. Miss Layton will come to dote on him in time.''

''I suppose this brings me to the subject at hand.'' Sir John sat up straighter, setting his snifter on the low ebony side table. ''I no longer care that Caedmon's manners are somewhat brusque.''

Stanhope remained at ease, holding the snifter negligently in one hand. "Oh?" But he was alert. The duel of wits had begun in earnest.

"Let us not beat around the bush. You have been inseparable from Lionel since his return. He is living with you in your home. You have introduced him everywhere as your son. Am I correct in assuming that he is your long-lost firstborn?"

Stanhope finally set his glass down, on a separate table. "I have yet to make such a declaration formally."

"Will you?"

"I do not feel I have to advise you of that."

Sir John stood up—and so did Stanhope. "My daughter is affianced to the Stanhope heir. If this man is indeed Lionel De Vere, your firstborn and heir, then she is currently affianced to whom? Garrick or Lionel?"

"She is plighted to Garrick."

"So you deny Lionel's authenticity?"

"I do not." Stanhope stared, a slight, not particularly pleasant smile fixed upon his face.

Sir John did not smile at all. "Then clearly she is engaged to the wrong man."

"I brought my son to your attention as a candidate for your daughter's hand. You agreed. Garrick De Vere was accepted. I do not think she is engaged to the wrong man."

"But I engaged my daughter to the Stanhope heir, by damn!" Sir John finally exploded.

"Did you?" Stanhope was cool. "I am afraid you did not read the marriage contract thoroughly. There is no mention of the Stanhope heir there. Miss Layton was affianced to Garrick De Vere, the viscount of Caedmon Crag, and no other. There has been no mistake."

Sir John was red. It was a moment before he could speak. "You damn well know what my expectations were. The viscount of Caedmon Crag is the Stanhope heir! At the time of the contract, Lionel did not exist. Yet you will not allow the engagement to be broken—and re-formed betwixt Susan and Lionel?"

Stanhope palmed Sir John's shoulder, changing his tone. "Come, John. We should not argue over a marriage that is beneficial to us both. Garrick needs a woman like Susan, which is why I chose her, and you could not do better for her—that is an impossibility. Do not forget that you are marrying into one of the half dozen premier families in the land. This is a good union for our families; do not toss it lightly aside.''

Sir John shrugged him off and stared. He remained flushed. ''When I assumed Garrick to be your heir, I agreed to the union. We both know that no one else would affiance their daughter to him—given his sordid reputation. So I quite understand why you continue to insist upon this union—you shall find no other bride for your disreputable son. But Susan shall now lose a title. I cannot agree to this.''

Stanhope grabbed his arm before he could whirl and leave. ''For an intelligent man, you do not think clearly. You see, we are both in the same boat.'' His eyes were hard. ''No man of my station will allow a brewer's daughter to wed his heir, I can assure you of that.'' He smiled, hoping his meaning was clear. He knew everyone among the peerage, and no one would ever cross him—he would make sure Susan remained a spinster if Sir John broke off the engagement.

Sir John paled. Clearly he understood. Then he jerked his arm free from Stanhope. The earl watched him storm from the room.

Stanhope smiled. Sir John was no fool. He would not break the engagement, and Garrick would, by damn, come to heel.

As for Lionel, well, that was another subject entirely.

Chapter Eighteen

Five very long days had passed since he had last been at Ashburnham. It had been the longest five days of his life. He could no longer tolerate either his brother or his father; the pair seemed inseparable as they hunted and rode their way back and forth across the country. Worse, he knew he was expected to call on Susan Layton at Ashburnham. Stanhope had made himself clear on that particular matter, but his feelings for Olivia made that impossible. And he could not stand the thought of Arlen remaining in residence at Ashburnham with her.

He did not know how she was faring. He worried about her constantly. He had sent her a note three days ago, and he knew it had been delivered, but there had been no reply. Had Arlen discovered the brief missive? Had he put Olivia in more danger than she already was?

He would soon have the answer. Olivia and Arlen had already arrived at the Hall, as had the Laytons, for supper. His chest was tight. How could a man be both miserable and happy at the very same time? He was torn. He could no longer stand to be in her company with Arlen present. He did not trust himself to behave with discretion. But at least he would see her. He had to see her. The evening would be bittersweet. But it was better than nothing at all.

*　　*　　*

Garrick gave himself one final glance in the looking glass before going downstairs, hoping to appear composed. Everyone was present when he entered the salon. His eyes found Olivia instantly. She stood beside Susan Layton and her mother, looking far too pale and anxious. Even though Garrick had known that the Laytons were to be present, he grimaced. But more important, he wanted to spare Olivia any further distress, and it was obvious she was anxious about the evening. He would keep his distance from her, admire her from afar. She had purposely avoided looking at him, too.

He bowed to Lady Layton. "My lady, I am so pleased that we are having this evening together." As he straightened, he did not allow his gaze to wander to Olivia, but he was acutely conscious of her presence.

Lady Layton smiled, but not with her usual warmth. Something was amiss. "My lord, good evening." She was polite, but not very friendly.

Garrick dismissed it, now facing his fiancée. "Miss Layton." He bowed over her hand. He had little choice but to look her in the eye and force a pleasant smile to his lips. "I apologize for being neglectful of late. I am afraid I have been preoccupied these past few days."

Susan nodded, her expression obviously fearful, nor did she smile. She could not even manage "Good evening." She said nothing, avoiding his eyes.

Garrick turned to Olivia. And their gazes locked.

He felt the impact of her gaze, like a blow that went right through him. For one moment he could not speak, did not dare to try, certain that his voice would quaver with the depth of his emotions. "Lady Ashburn." He bowed and finally tore his gaze from hers.

She wet her lips. Two bright spots of pink marred her cheeks. "My lord." Her voice was thick.

Garrick took one glance across the room and saw that Arlen was staring at them, but so were Lionel, Sir John, and Stanhope. Arlen's gaze was blatantly hostile. He knew. Garrick had not a single doubt. His first faux pas of the evening already made, Garrick resolved not to let his passion for Olivia reveal itself again. He walked over to the men. "Am I late?" he asked.

"Hardly," Lionel said easily. "Mother is not yet down."

Arlen turned his back on Garrick, facing Stanhope. "It has been some time since I have been to the Hall, but I must say, you have kept up the grounds quite well. It was a beautiful drive."

Garrick received a scathing glance from his father before the earl replied. He nodded at Sir John, but the elderly knight seemed perturbed and distant. Lionel stepped closer, into the breach. "Have you been in hiding, Garrick? I have not seen you all day." He smiled.

Garrick went on alert. The truth was, his mood had been so foul that he had kept to himself all day long. He suspected a barb was on its way. "The weather warranted a quiet day of seclusion. I chose to read in my rooms. How was your day?" He stared, not giving a damn, already knowing that Lionel and Stanhope had spent the afternoon at cards. Their laughter had echoed in the halls.

"Quite the same. Father and I did play some whist, to help get by. Did you not arise very early this morning? Surely you have not been brooding since the crack of dawn?"

"And why ever would I brood?" Garrick said calmly, but inwardly he was alarmed. He had been up since dawn, and he had been brooding, but Lionel was no Gypsy fortune-teller. He could not know.

"I do not know. Perhaps you could tell me." Lionel's expression remained easy, but his gaze drifted in Olivia's direction. "Perhaps, my friend, you should be more careful of what you do and how you do it." He patted Garrick's back and walked away.

Garrick was rigid. He had the uncanny feeling that Lionel knew he had received a note from Olivia that morning. But that was impossible, was it not?

Could he have seen a servant from Ashburnham deliver it?

Lionel had walked over to the women, bowing to them all, his eyes too blue and too warm, especially, Garrick thought, when he turned them onto Olivia. Garrick watched them chatting, and in that moment, aware of the charm Lionel was purposely exerting, he despised him.

"I am so sorry that I am late," the countess of Stanhope said from the threshold of the room.

Garrick whirled, certain he detected a slur in her tone. She smiled at the assembly, striking in a pale blue gown with sapphires around her neck and dangling from her ears. She moved forward—and stumbled.

Garrick rushed to her, but not as quickly as Lionel, who had been closer to her. He stiffened as Lionel took her arm. "Are you all right, Mother?" Lionel asked with apparently genuine concern.

Garrick clenched his fists, but his gaze was upon his mother's face. She had been drinking.

"I am fine. I tripped upon the rug. Good evening, Lady Layton, Susan." The countess shrugged free of Lionel and moved forward with her customary grace. She held her head high and gave no outward sign that she was embarrassed by her near fall.

"We have been waiting for thirty minutes," Stanhope interrupted. "Must you be so inconvenient?"

Eleanor stiffened, her smile slipping. Before she could form a reply, Garrick reached her and took her arm. "You look lovely, Mother," he said. "I am so glad you took the extra time to make your toilette. It was worth the wait." He smiled.

Her eyes filled with tears. "Thank you, dear," she said huskily.

"May I escort you in tonight?" Garrick asked.

The countess nodded.

The moment broken, Garrick released her, and watched her join the ladies, who formed one animated group. Lionel was immersed in conversation with Sir John, while Stanhope conversed with Arlen. Garrick glanced once more at his mother, to make sure she was well enough, and then he walked away from everyone. Pausing at a large window, he stared out at the grounds. Dusk was falling. The sky had dimmed, and the sun formed an orange ball against the rolling horizon. Why was his mother drinking so heavily? He suspected Stanhope was the cause, but perhaps it was also Lionel. It made him so damn angry. The sooner this pretender was exposed, the sooner all their lives would return to normal—whatever that might mean.

He heard Arlen's voice among the mingled conversation, and he grew angrier. The only reason he was present in Surrey, much less at this supper affair, he realized with bitterness, was that he was incapable of removing himself from Olivia's vicinity. But that was going to change. It had to change. They could not continue this way. She must make a decision.

He felt her gaze upon his back, as if she knew, and he turned. Their gazes locked.

She detached herself from the ladies and slowly walked over to him. She moved with infinite grace. Her dignity, especially given the circumstances, was astounding. He was now motionless, his heart thundering in his ears.

She smiled, her gaze searching, but anxiety was also mirrored in her eyes.

"How are you?" he said softly.

"Fine."

He began to forget that they were not alone. The entire room ceased to exist. "No. I mean truthfully. He has not hurt you?"

"Nothing untoward has happened since the other night," she said, as low. "Thank you, Garrick."

He was immensely relieved. "I did not know about this evening until I received your message."

"I know." She must have seen the question in his eyes, because she added, "I suspected as much."

"Sometimes," he said, his gaze certainly as intense as his tone, "I think you know me far too well."

She wet her lips. "We are strangers, but sometimes I feel as if I know you completely, as if I have known you all of my life."

Her words made his heart sing. "Sometimes," he said slowly, "I feel exactly the same way."

She smiled.

He smiled. And he thought about the few times they had shared. He thought about the way she touched him, kissed him, twisted beneath him, the way she felt. He thought about the night they had frantically searched the Hall together for Hannah, she in her nightclothes, he barefoot and half-clad. He thought about the sound of her laughter, the searching scrutiny of her extraordinary eyes. When he came out of his reverie with an effort, he realized that Lionel was speaking to Miss Layton and that he had maneuvered her halfway across the room—clearly to eavesdrop upon him and Olivia.

Garrick looked across the salon and realized that while everyone was conversing, all eyes kept drifting to the countess of Ashburn and himself. He was angry. He despaired. Had he not promised to keep his distance from her tonight?

But he failed to walk away. What he wished to discuss with her was far too important. "Olivia, I am leaving for a while. There is something I must do. But if you wish, I will bring Treve over tomorrow—and leave him with Hannah until I return." His gaze searched hers.

Her eyes had widened. "Where are you going?"

"Are you alarmed? Do you fear Arlen?" he demanded. She swallowed. "No . . . I . . . I don't know." She glanced worriedly around.

"I have to go to Caedmon Crag," he said in a rush, aware that they were lingering far too long. "I don't know when I will return, but I will return. This situation"—he glanced at Lionel—"is intolerable." But he was also thinking about them.

She snapped open her fan. "You seek the truth." It was not a question.

He nodded, his gaze unwavering on hers. "I must go. I am compelled. But I do not like leaving you behind."

She flushed. The fan moved rapidly now. "There is no choice." She glanced over her shoulder at Arlen, and Garrick followed her gaze. Arlen continued to regard them even as he spoke to the earl. His gaze was ice.

Garrick glanced at Lionel. He appeared immersed in

whatever it was that Susan was babbling on about, but Garrick knew he was straining to overhear their conversation. "Olivia, while I am gone, you must make a choice."

She paled.

He did not let her speak. "It is not fair to either of us— and you know it, too. I await a decision from you when I return."

Her fan moved rapidly now, and two bright spots of pink colored her cheeks. "When do you leave? On the morrow?" she asked.

"Yes. If you need me, send word, and I will come instantly."

Her eyes grew moist. "I know." She hesitated. "I am afraid."

His heart was wrenched in two. "Then take Hannah and come with me."

She blanched. "That is not what I meant," she said when she could speak. "I am afraid for you."

He stared. "What do you see?"

"There is danger," she whispered. "Danger for you."

Again he glanced at Arlen, and then at Lionel. There was danger here, too. "The answer is there. I have to go." He was certain.

"Yes," she said. "The answer is there. You must go."

Arlen stared.

The men were smoking cigars and sipping cognac in the billiards room. The high ceiling was painted red, the walls were paneled in oak, and the huge billiards table held center stage in the middle of the room. Various card tables surrounded it. Stanhope had just racked up the billiard balls, and Sir John was chalking his cue. Garrick stood with his arms folded, as usual, having removed himself from everyone. Arlen continued to regard him. Sir John glanced at him and asked him if he wished to play. Garrick shrugged and replied, "Why not?" Arlen watched him choose a cue.

"What an enjoyable evening, eh, Ashburn?"

Arlen realized that Lionel was smiling at him. "Very," he lied. The evening had hardly been enjoyable. But he was damnably glad that he and Olivia had joined the Stanhopes for supper. He seethed inwardly but knew his face remained an implacable mask. Every time he had glanced at Olivia, he had found her peeking at Caedmon or Caedmon gazing at her. And whenever he had turned to Caedmon, it had been the same. The currents sizzling between the two of them were tangible. Not a single person at the Hall that night was unaware of the passion burning betwixt the two.

Now he was certain of it, too.

Arlen could not decide where to ship her off to. A convent in France, perhaps? Or to the remotest lodge he might find in Wales? Olivia had denied it, but he knew she was having a heated affair with the viscount of Caedmon Crag.

Garrick De Vere was cuckolding him again.

He desperately wished he were in town now, with Elizabeth. He had always been able to tell her everything. She was the wisest woman he knew, exceedingly clever, and her advice would undoubtedly be invaluable and worth following. She would know what to do.

Arlen's fists were clenched. He could not even comprehend why Caedmon found his wife alluring. She was pale and plain, and he knew firsthand that fucking a board would be more satisfactory. What man wanted to be with a witch who knew his every thought—or who might discover all his secrets? What man wanted to lie with a woman who had been cursed—and perhaps even spawned by the devil? Just thinking about her made him sweat. Sometimes, when she looked at him with her eerie gray eyes, he felt stripped naked, not to the bone, but to the soul. At those times, he felt on the brink of eternal judgment—as if hell beckoned from just around the corner.

He could not understand how, given her cursed oddness, Olivia had yet to discover his affair with Elizabeth. But they had been extremely careful once they had learned the truth about her.

Elizabeth. She had counseled him ill only that one time— when she had told him to stay with his new bride, advising him against annulling the marriage. She had pointed out that he needed an heir and they needed a pliable, meek, naive wife in his life, so no one might ever suspect the truth. Arlen had agreed with her at the time, still enraged at being so monumentally deceived by his bride and her family. And now it was too late for regrets. Olivia had not given him an heir, but a blind daughter whom he could not stand. Punishment, he knew, for her sins. Or was Hannah punishment for his sins? As always, it was a thought he refused to entertain.

Meanwhile he was stuck in the country, which he detested, in order to keep his wife in line, while Elizabeth flirted with that damnable Scotsman he had found her entertaining the other day. Arlen could not stand the thought of her and Kildare spending even an innocent moment together. Just as he could not stand the thought of Caedmon cuckolding him another time—making him a fool once again in the eyes of the ton.

"The meal was magnificent, but then, the countess always keeps the finest chefs on hand," Arlen heard himself say. He stiffened. Garrick had just laid down his pool stick and was saying, "I have changed my mind. Good evening." He nodded at everyone beside the pool table—that is, he did not gesture to either Arlen or Lionel—and he strode from the gaming room.

Arlen was flushed, and he knew it. Obviously Caedmon was off to rendezvous with his wife, right now, beneath everyone's very noses. Would he fuck her outside in the gardens? Of course he would! Arlen wondered if he could control the temper that was building inside him. He felt like a volcano, predisposed to explode.

"My brother has not changed at all in fourteen years," Lionel remarked, also having watched him leave the room. "He prefers solitude to even the best of company. No wonder he stayed for so long on that isolated sugar island."

Arlen almost remarked that he was hardly off to be solitary just then. "Your brother is a barbarian, and I am speaking openly because I know you think so, too." Lionel did not reply. "His manners have not changed. I hope it is suggested to him that he watch his step."

Lionel leaned closer. "Arlen." His voice was low and conspiratorial. "Garrick means no harm."

Arlen looked at him. "Then he should stay away from my wife."

Lionel stared. "I am sure they are just friends. The countess is a very respectable lady." He smiled. His tone had been uncertain and doubtful.

Arlen trembled anew. "Your brother has no friends. He has never had friends. Do not forget, I have known him almost as long as you. He is a recluse, incapable of friendship with anyone."

"Yes, he is an oddly reclusive fellow," Lionel said. "Well, in any case, I suspect he is off for a just-before-midnight walk with that hound of his."

And with Olivia. "Perhaps I shall take a midnight walk, too," Arlen said. He had to witness what he knew was about to unfold. He had to. He must catch them in the act.

And then what? Instantly, a duel came to mind. Garrick would die. He had never been a capable swordsman. Arlen smiled tightly.

Lionel seized his arm. "Before you go, I must ask you, do you have ghosts at Ashburnham?"

Arlen could hardly comprehend him, he was so intensely focused on imagining Olivia in Caedmon's arms and Caedmon dying in the arms of his second after a duel. He blinked. "What?"

"I did overhear the oddest conversation the other day at your home, between my brother and the countess."

Arlen momentarily forgot about rushing after Caedmon. "What odd conversation?"

"Apparently Hannah saw a ghost." Lionel chuckled a little.

Arlen did not smile. Hannah was blind. She could not see anything. Instead he said, "Hannah is a child."

Lionel's smile faded. "That is hardly what I overheard. Garrick was most inquisitive, and most insistent. He wanted to know if Hannah often saw ghosts and other things that most ordinary people could not see. I understand the child is blind."

A glimmering of something, a piece of knowledge, a truth, which Arlen could not yet identify, began to form. And it was filling him with dread. "Go on."

Lionel shook his head. He shrugged. "It was odd. The countess was quite upset—and very insistent that Hannah could 'see' nothing. Garrick wanted to know if Hannah's unique sensitivity, if you will, had something to do with her mother. The countess adamantly insisted that Hannah was only sensitive because she must rely heavily upon her senses other than sight in order to live in the world. The countess was quite upset. She said the strangest thing. 'I am no fortune-teller. I am not a witch. I cannot read tea leaves. I do not use a crystal ball.' I hardly understood this entire bizarre exchange. But surely a blind girl could not see a ghost!" Lionel laughed. "Except Garrick remained certain that she had."

Arlen was finding it difficult to breathe. Hannah, capable of seeing a ghost? Hannah, possessing some kind of "unique sensitivity," something to do with her mother? Olivia, adamant in her denials, frightened and upset? Caedmon, somehow having learned Olivia's secret? He was sweating heavily. No, it could not be.

"Of course, while I do believe in ghosts, I also believe a child is very creative," Lionel was saying easily. "She probably wanted attention and made up this episode of having seen a ghost."

Arlen did not see him. Was something going on here, something horrid, humiliating, something he should know about? Surely Hannah was not like her mother! Surely not! Surely he could not have been deceived these past eight years.

If she was, he would kill them both.

"Excuse me," he said stiffly. And he exited the room, his strides long and sharp.

Olivia could not attend the quiet chatter in the pink-and-gold salon where she sat with the other ladies. The first topic of conversation had been fashion, then it had been food—the countess of Stanhope being roundly lauded for her chef's preparations that evening—and now they were discussing Susan's wedding gown in great detail. In spite of the fact that Susan was hardly eager to wed Garrick De Vere, now she became animated as she described the gown's skirts, which were dripping with diamond-encrusted lace.

Olivia tried to control her restlessness and her mind. But try as she might, she could neither stop fidgeting nor breathe normally. The evening had been a disaster. She had been painfully aware of Garrick, and every time she glanced at him—and surely she had glanced at him a thousand times—she had caught him gazing at her with his incredible eyes. She had found herself wishing, desperately, for another intimate moment with him. He was right. They could not continue this way. It was not fair to either of them.

She had a choice to make. Dear, dear God. Take her daughter and run away with him, or end the relationship. The very air felt constricted in her lungs.

I await your decision upon my return. That flat statement echoed in her mind, and it was agonizing.

Olivia was at a loss. If only she had the courage to leave Arlen. If only she had faith in herself and in Garrick, if only she could believe that they could successfully elude Arlen and that, in time, he would let her and Hannah go. But she did not believe in any of those things, and could she spend the rest of her life as a man's mistress? For even if he shirked his duty to his family, she would never be free to become his wife.

Olivia blinked back a tear. Her heart was shouting yes.

She was so afraid. It was as if she stood upon a cliff. One step, and she would plunge off it—landing God only knew where.

I am leaving the Hall. I am off to Caedmon Crag.

His words returned to her abruptly, disturbing her mightily, another predicament for her to dread. She knew he must go to Caedmon Crag, but she was frightened of what awaited him there. Her senses shrieked at her in warning, even now.

"My dear Lady Ashburn," Lady Layton said in a kind voice, "did you not hear the countess?"

Olivia had been gazing blankly out one of the salon's large windows, into the dark, starless night. Now she started, immediately becoming aware of the absolute silence around her. Flushing, she realized that everyone was staring at her. All conversation had ceased. What must everyone be thinking? Did one and all guess that she pined for Garrick De Vere? Worse, were suspicions aroused that they were far more than acquaintances?

And then, from the corner of her eye, Olivia saw a man moving across the terrace, disappearing into the night. She froze.

"Lady Ashburn?"

Olivia blinked and regarded Lady Layton, hardly having heard her. There had been no mistaking who had just been outside. "I'm sorry," she said. "My mind was wandering. I do apologize." She could feel her color deepening.

"I only said how wonderful it is that there shall finally be a wedding in the family," the countess of Stanhope said. Her words were slurred. She was inebriated and still sipping her port quite steadily. She smiled brightly at Susan, her cheeks pink. "You shall be a wonderful daughter, dear."

Olivia watched her drink more port, feeling unaccountably sorry for her. She had never seen her so foxed before, but then, she had seen her only twice socially. But could she blame her? Stanhope was cruel and insufferable. And her sympathy was all the greater because she was Garrick's mother. How he must suffer when he saw her so anguished.

Susan now blushed, gazing fixedly at her hands, clasped in her lap. Lady Layton seemed hesitant now but was also clearly determined. "My lady," she began, finally looking the countess in the eye. Eleanor seemed startled out of her haze by Lady Layton's uncharacteristically firm tone. "We are somewhat confused. Susan was to wed the Stanhope heir. And suddenly Lionel De Vere has returned. We cannot make heads nor tails of this mess." She smiled quickly.

Eleanor blinked. "Oh. Lady Layton, I think I understand.

Well, Sir John must surely discuss this matter with my husband. It is out of my hands.''

Susan was now gazing at the countess with such hopefulness that Olivia felt sorry for her. She craned her neck and peered out the windows again, while Lady Layton said with real dejection, ''We had hoped for some support from you in this matter. You see, Susan and your son Garrick hardly suit. But there seems to be some genuine fondness between Lionel and my daughter. It would, in every way, be a far better match.''

Susan cried, ''I do so like His Lordship, my lady!''

There was no sign of Garrick outside. But Olivia knew he was there. As she stood up, the countess said, ''You must discuss this with the earl. It is a matter for the men to decide.'' She no longer seemed very happy. She drank quickly again.

Olivia summoned her courage, and said, ''If you will excuse me, I need a breath of air.'' Before anyone could comment, she swept across the salon and exited upon the terrace, which Garrick had crossed less than five minutes ago.

Outside, the air was cool and stunningly clean, as at Ashburnham. Olivia could not sniff it appreciatively, though, not when her heart was hammering so swiftly with both excitement and fear. She was being a fool to seek out Garrick now, with Arlen in the house, but she could not help herself. Lifting her pale silver skirts, she hurried across the terrace. Once on the lawns, she paused, straining to see. Then she thought she saw a shadow moving some distance ahead, in an open space between groves of large, looming trees. Olivia lifted her skirts again but took only one step forward when a hand seized her wrist, so painfully that she was whipped around.

''And where are you off to?'' Arlen demanded.

Olivia gasped.

He shook her. His grip remained brutal. ''As if I did not know! You are off to rendezvous with your lover, are you not? Answer me!'' he shouted.

Tears filled her eyes, tears of pain. "You are hurting me. Stop before you break my wrist."

He did not release her. He leaned forward; their faces touched. "Do you scream in pleasure when he fucks you, Olivia? Or do you lie there like a board, as you did with me?"

Olivia was horrified, terrified. Worse, she thought her wrist would soon snap in two. There was no possible response she could make, and when she remained mute, incapable of speech now, he increased the pressure on her arm. She cried out.

"Release her!" Garrick snapped.

Before Olivia could assimilate the fact that he was present, he had grabbed Arlen from behind and thrown him several feet in the air. Miraculously, Olivia did not collapse, although her knees buckled dangerously. She held her throbbing wrist, watching wide-eyed as Garrick pounced upon Arlen, who was sprawled facedown in the grass. He hauled him up to his feet by his collar and punched him directly in the face. Arlen fell backward onto the ground this time.

Olivia heard herself scream.

Garrick dove after Arlen, landing on top of him, pinning him down.

Olivia came to her senses. She rushed forward, recognizing that Garrick's fury was lethal—and uncontrollable. "Stop!" she shouted, grabbing him by the shoulders. "Stop, Garrick, please!"

Garrick looked up at her, his face unrecognizable. "Stay out of this!"

Arlen kicked him hard, in the loins.

Garrick collapsed, clutching himself. Suddenly Arlen was on his feet, sending another kick at Garrick, taking him in the chest. Olivia screamed again, because she saw the look in Arlen's eyes and knew he would kill Garrick if he could. As he started to kick again, this time clearly aiming for Garrick's head, Garrick released himself and wrapped both arms around Arlen's ankles. He went down in a heap, Garrick rolling on top of him.

"What's going on here?" Stanhope demanded.

"Stop them!" Olivia cried as Stanhope, Lionel, and Sir John came running across the lawns. Behind them, on the terrace, the ladies had come outside, straining to see what the ruckus was about.

Garrick had just hit Arlen again in the face, but Arlen had somehow managed to get both hands around Garrick's throat, and he was squeezing. Lionel reached the two first. "Good God," he said, reaching for Garrick, who was on top. "Garrick! Enough!"

"Garrick!" the earl shouted, also reaching for him. When both Stanhope and Lionel succeeded in dragging Garrick off Arlen, Sir John helped Arlen to his feet.

Olivia stood there, shaking uncontrollably now, covering her mouth with her hands. A tremendous amount of blood was dripping from Arlen's nose, and his left eye was swelling shut. Garrick, amazingly, hardly appeared the worse for wear. He stood with his legs braced apart, panting, his gaze still murderous. Lionel held one arm, Stanhope the other, as if he were a wild animal that would attack again if they did not.

"What is wrong with you?" Stanhope shouted at his son.

Olivia's daze evaporated. The ladies were all racing across the lawn. Oh, God. Everyone was going to think what Arlen thought—that she had been meeting Garrick—and it was the truth.

Garrick's jaw ground down, and he finally tore his gaze from Arlen. But it was not to look at or respond to his father. His intense, enraged eyes went to Olivia. "Are you all right?"

Olivia felt herself flush. The ladies had now joined them, the countess drunkenly confused, Susan and Lady Layton pale with shock. Olivia was afraid to answer him.

"Did he break your wrist?" Garrick snapped.

Olivia inhaled. Arlen said, shrugging off Sir John, "My wife is not your affair, Caedmon."

Garrick's golden eyes flew to Arlen. "Any woman is my concern if she is being abused by a man who is far superior to her physically."

Arlen stepped forward. He held a handkerchief to his bleeding nose. "You accuse me of abusing my wife?"

Olivia rushed to Arlen's side as a terrible silence fell over the group. "Arlen and I were only arguing," she managed, her voice sounding high and hysterical and on the verge of tears to her own ears. "It was hardly important. I am afraid you misunderstood." She did not dare look Garrick in the eye. "Arlen." She turned to her husband, whom she despised. "Let me put ice wrapped in linen on your eye." She still could not breathe. What would happen when they got home? Her limbs trembled uncontrollably. She must not think of that now. If she did, she would swoon, for the first time in her life.

"Lady Stanhope." The earl of Stanhope's cutting voice pierced through Olivia's terrified thoughts as he addressed his wife. "Do see to it that Lord Ashburn and his wife have a physician if they need one."

The countess looked at him as if his words were incomprehensible.

"That is," he said sarcastically, "if you can manage to find your way to the kitchens?"

She blinked, nodded, and turned away, weaving across the lawns.

"I'll go with her," Olivia cried. Not waiting for a response, not daring to, she turned to run after the countess. But before she did, she glimpsed them all, standing there in the night. The earl, disgusted with the turn of events; the Laytons, appropriately unhappy now that the shock was wearing off; Arlen, furious and filled with hate; Lionel, his expression strangely calm. And Garrick. His gaze was riveted upon her, frightening in its intensity, compelling in its concern, and demanding of her she knew not what.

Olivia ran after the countess.

It was the last place she wished to be—inside their coach with Arlen. She sat stiffly on the front-facing seat, hands clasped in her lap, as many inches as possible between her and her husband. The coach rocked forward as it departed Stanhope Hall. But Arlen had been adamant that they leave,

in spite of the late hour. Soon they would reach Ashburnham. Olivia was finding it difficult to breathe within the
tight confines of the carriage. Being alone with Arlen was
terrifying.

He had not yet said a word.

She was perspiring. She could feel his rage. It was em-
anating from him in waves. She dared not look at him. But
the explosion was inevitable, and she did not need her gift
to tell her that.

She could not go on like this for much longer.

He twisted to face her. "When," he said bluntly, "were
you going to tell me?" His tone pitched upward, high and
odd.

Olivia stole one swift glance at him. His nose was swollen, but hardly as ghastly as his left eye, which was closed
shut and discolored. She looked at her lap. "I do not know
what you are speaking of," she said huskily.

"No?" His fist came down on the leather seat, so hard
it sounded as though a gun had been fired. Olivia jumped.

"When," he shouted, his face now in hers, "were you
going to tell me the truth about your daughter?"

Olivia paled.

CHAPTER NINETEEN

Olivia knew she had to have misheard. "I beg your pardon?"

"I am very close to strangling you," Arlen ground out. "Hannah sees ghosts, does she not? And what else does she see?"

Oh God oh God oh God, was all Olivia could think. Breathing was no longer a function she was capable of. Neither was a coherent verbal reply.

"You have lied to me! She is a witch—just like you, her mother!" Arlen cried, vainly attempting to keep his voice low so that the footmen and driver would not hear them.

She swallowed. "No. I have no idea what you have heard, but I swear to you, Arlen, with my life, that Hannah is no more than a small, imaginative child who lacks any vision at all—she can neither see you nor me nor ghosts nor . . . anything else."

Arlen's chest heaved. "Caedmon knows about you, does he not? You told him."

"He knows nothing," she lied desperately.

He hit her. Across the face, on the same side as before. "Bitch! He knows about you, and our daughter is like you, and I should have gotten rid of the two of you years ago," he shouted, no longer trying to control his voice.

Olivia had crammed herself into the far corner of the seat as the coach swayed along the midnight-darkened road.

Her heart burst with fear. She must protect herself now—
so she could protect Hannah when they got home. If only
she could "see" whatever it was that Arlen was going to
do to them. But she could not. Her terror had thoroughly
incapacitated her gift. "Arlen, please, listen to me. There
has been no deception. Hannah is just an ordinary little
girl—and she is your daughter," Olivia pleaded, her face
burning from his blow. Vaguely she wondered if her jaw
were broken.

His face twisted as he faced her. "Is she my daughter?
Is she? I question that."

Olivia stared at him in shock.

"You are an adulteress, my dear, and we both know it.
If you could cuckold me now, who is to say that you did
not do so many years before? And that would explain my
having such a child—if the child were not mine!" he cried
triumphantly.

She was going to lose everything, including Hannah, if
he continued to convince himself that Hannah was not his
daughter. "Arlen!" Her tone bordered on a scream. "I was
with no one but you in those days. Hannah is your daughter!"

He grabbed her by the shoulders. *"In those days? So
now you confess to laying with Caedmon?"* His eyes were
black, glittering with near madness.

She nodded, crying now as he shook her ruthlessly, all
the while knowing that such a confession would ultimately
be her last mistake.

Satisfaction filled his eyes. "At least you admit that
Caedmon is your lover." He threw her away, against the
far side of the seat, where Olivia cowered in relief. She had
thought he would hit her again, if not beat her to death. As
it was, her upper arms throbbed from his cruel grip.

He turned his back to her. As the coach raced through
the dark, Olivia tried to control her trembling, her fear. She
must regain the power of her mind, she must think, she
must feel. Arlen was sitting as far from her as he could get,
planning God only knew what for her and Hannah. Tears
filled her eyes. Disaster. She felt it coming, it was immi-

nent. But hadn't her gift foretold it from the first moment she had met Garrick De Vere? Yet she could not blame him. She could only blame herself. She should have denied him, herself, she should have denied them both.

Olivia covered her mouth with one hand so she would not make a sound if a sob escaped her. She must think, she must plan. She and Hannah must escape before Arlen could decide how he was going to punish the both of them.

Cornwall.

Like a bolt of lightning, it struck her. Of course, she would take her daughter and flee there. She no longer had a choice. She would spend a few days hiding at Caedmon Crag, just enough time to plan some kind of future for her and Hannah, to decide where to flee to and how to get there undetected. While she plotted and planned, Garrick would protect her, keeping her and Hannah safe.

And it was not her gift that told her that; it was her heart.

The moment their coach stopped in front of the house, Arlen swung open the door, unaided by a footman, for he was too quick. As he leapt down and strode purposefully to the house, terror seized Olivia again. And she saw the future so clearly.

Hannah, clad in rags, surrounded by the oddest people, old, stooped women, young, greasy-haired hags, and gaunt, bony children, in a wooden room bare of any furniture. Something was very wrong, and not just with the place, but with everyone present—the women leered or wept, drooled or rolled their eyeballs, or even danced about, making monkeylike gestures and sounds. And Hannah sat as still as a statue in one corner, as if in a trance.

Olivia jumped out of the carriage, stumbling, one of the footmen steadying her by the elbow. She shrugged him off, the vision hardly receding, every instinct telling her she must not let the future unfold as she had seen it. She lifted her skirts and ran after Arlen, shouting for him to stop, to wait. "Please, Arlen!" she screamed.

But Arlen had disappeared into the house, and when Olivia skidded across the stone foyer, she saw him pounding up the stairs. Hannah was upstairs—hopefully sound asleep.

"Please," she screamed again, racing upstairs, tripping on her skirts, and landing briefly on her hands and knees. She hurled herself upward again. "Arlen! Stop! What is it that you think to do?"

But he did not stop, and by the time Olivia had reached the third-floor landing where the nursery was, she saw him thrusting open Hannah's bedroom door. Olivia was panting from her mad chase, but she sucked in more air and forced her legs to turn at an even faster pace. When she reached the threshold, she saw Hannah sitting up in bed, pressing her spine into the headboard, with Arlen leaning over her, his expression frightening, it was so filled with menace. From the expression on her daughter's face, which was taut and pale with fear, Olivia was certain she had been awake.

"Can you speak, or are you a mute, too?" Arlen spat at her. Hannah recoiled.

Olivia grabbed him unthinkingly from behind. "Leave her alone! She is only a child!" she cried.

Arlen whirled and threw her off, and Olivia landed hard on the wooden floor.

"Mama!" Hannah cried. "Mama! Are you all right?" Tears spilled down her cheeks.

"Forget your mother, damn it," Arlen gritted, grabbing her. "Now tell me the truth. You and your mother have deceived me, haven't you?"

Hannah did not answer, whimpering both in pain and in fear.

Olivia forced herself to sit upright. "Arlen, stop. Please, God, please."

He smiled coldly at his daughter. "You are a witch, like she is, aren't you? You can see ghosts. What else can you see, Hannah?"

Hannah's mouth was pursed as tears now fell from her sightless eyes. She shook her head wordlessly, trembling.

Olivia had lunged to her feet. Recognizing Arlen's expression, she leapt on him from behind before he could strike their child. Engulfed in rage, she tried to claw his face. He cried out, turned, and pushed her roughly away. This time Olivia hit the floor on her side, and pain shot through her hip. Hannah began to cry.

"Miss Childs!" Olivia cried, spotting the governess standing upon the threshold, her face white with shock and terror.

Then Olivia cried out, as Arlen grabbed her by her coiled braid. He dragged her to her feet.

"Mama! Mama! Don't go!" Hannah sobbed. "What is he doing?" she screamed.

Arlen was pushing her forward, across the room, to the threshold. "Miss Childs," he ordered calmly, "return to your room."

Miss Childs blanched, met Olivia's gaze, and turned to go.

"Please help me!" Olivia cried, knowing that Lucy Childs could not disobey Arlen.

"Help Hannah!"

Miss Childs hesitated, received a burning look from Arlen, and fled to her room.

"Mama!" Hannah screamed as Olivia was thrust inside her own bedroom. Arlen slammed the door in her face, and then she heard the lock turning. For one instant she stood by the door, stunned, barely comprehending what he had done. Then she realized her predicament. She was locked in her own bedchamber like a prisoner, and Arlen was insane with fury and alone with Hannah. Screaming, she began to pound on the door.

Pounding and pounding.

But no one came.

Hannah cowered in her bed, as far from her father as she could get, sobbing, the sounds jerky and interspersed with hiccups.

Arlen smiled at her and sat down. He could hear his wife banging again and again, ceaselessly, on her locked door. He ignored the sound, which now gave him immense satisfaction. "I am not going to hurt you. I only want to know the truth. I am your father, the lord and master of this house. So tell me, Hannah, about the ghost and everything else that you see.'' He smiled at her.

Hannah blinked at him through her tears. ''Why did you hurt my mother?'' she whimpered.

''Your mother lied to me. And if you lie to me, you shall be whipped.'' He was very calm, knowing now that he was in absolute control, that every mistake in his life was about to be rectified.

Hannah wept again.

''Have you seen a ghost?'' Arlen asked.

Hannah nodded, her face starkly white, gulping on a sob.

''What else can you see?''

Hannah hesitated.

Arlen reached out and took her face in one of his hands. ''Answer me,'' he said softly. If he squeezed, he thought, he might crush her jaw.

''She told me to never, ever tell,'' Hannah whimpered.

''And she will be punished for her lies. But surely you do not wish to be punished? Or should I beat the truth out of you?''

''I saw a ghost at Stanhope Hall,'' Hannah cried. ''A very unhappy lady. I wanted to help her! I knew . . .'' She stopped.

''You knew what?'' Arlen asked in his deadly soft tone.

''I knew you were coming tonight,'' Hannah said, tears spilling down her cheeks. ''I knew you were coming home to hurt me.''

Arlen stood. ''So you are cursed, too. Like your mother.''

''Please don't hurt her,'' Hannah whispered, wiping her runny nose with her hand. ''Please don't hurt us.''

He grimaced with disgust as he regarded her. ''You are not allowed to leave this room.'' He turned on his heel and strode out, shutting and locking the door behind him. He ignored his wife, who continued to bang on her locked door, screaming both his name and Hannah's. Would she continue this way all through the night? He did not care. He was leaving for London immediately, but not without giving the staff strict orders. And not without taking care of Miss Childs.

Elizabeth would know what to do.

Arlen went to Miss Childs's room and knocked sharply.

The door was opened instantly. Miss Childs stared at him out of wide eyes. She was now fully dressed.

He smiled at her, unpleasantly. "Pack your bags. You are dismissed. I expect you to be gone in the morning."

Olivia awoke. For one moment, before coherent thought returned, she did not understand why she lay on the hard, cold floor or why her body hurt her so, especially her face, hip, and hands. Then comprehension struck her with the force of a bolt of lightning. She pushed herself into a sitting position, wincing as she did so, for her hands were bloody and bruised from having pounded on the door for as long as she had. Oh, God. The house was absolutely silent. Where was Hannah? Was she all right? What had Arlen done to her?

She knew he had left last night. She had not been able to see the drive from her window, but she had heard him ordering the servants about in preparation to departing. Had he taken Hannah with him? She was sick at the thought.

And the vision she had had last night returned to her, more graphic and intense than before. Of her beautiful blind daughter sitting in some sparse room in a trance, surrounded by strange, mad people.

Olivia stood up, the pale gray light of dawn filtering into her room through the draperies she had never drawn. She teetered in her low-heeled slippers, at once severely exhausted and ready to run and do battle, if need be. She tested the door. It remained locked.

She wiped strands of hair out of her face—her braids had come undone long ago, and she did not care. Arlen might have left Ashburnham, but he had undoubtedly left instructions with the staff, and no one was going to free her from her room. She thought about Garrick, not for the first time, wishing with all her soul that he might come and rescue her and her daughter from the abysmal future. Had he, too, left, but for Cornwall?

Olivia walked to the windows and parted the draperies more fully. Outside, it was promising a beautiful day, for the morning lacked mist or rain. She lifted the window as high as it would go and put one leg across the windowsill.

The oak tree was some distance away, but she must not think of that now. She had no choice but to succeed in her escape. Olivia straddled the windowsill in her silver gown, fear rising rapidly inside of her. The closest branch of the tree that could support her weight seemed many feet away. Could she actually jump to it?

Olivia looked down. If she fell, she would die. And that wasn't going to help Hannah.

She needed Garrick De Vere. Desperately. She closed her eyes, not for the first time willing him to come. She no longer cared if he killed Arlen. Then she corrected herself, for she must care; if he did such a thing, the consequences would be severe. She did not want him imprisoned or, worse, hanged.

Olivia jerked, certain she was hallucinating, for she thought she had heard a soft rapping at her door. But no, she was not hearing things—someone was knocking. She sidled off the sill and ran across the room, seizing the knob. "Who is it?"

"My lady, it is I, Miss Childs," came a terse whisper.

"Lucy!" Olivia almost fainted with relief. "Hannah? Is she all right?"

"She has also been locked in her rooms. His Lordship has told everyone the two of you are to be left this way until he returns. He has not said when that will be," Lucy Childs whispered quickly.

"Did he hurt her?" Olivia cried. "Did he?" She had both hands on the door, which she leaned upon frantically.

"No. I have just spoken to her. But she is very frightened, my lady. And—I must leave. He has dismissed me. He ordered me gone by breakfast."

Olivia inhaled, clawing the door, furious with Arlen, hating him with all of the passion that roiled in her veins.

"Can you help us? Please, Lucy, I beg you. Unlock my door."

"He has taken all of the keys. I overheard the butler saying so."

"Does he mean for us to die of starvation and thirst?" Olivia asked blankly.

"I do not know what he is thinking, my lady. But I thought I should stop at the Hall on my way back to town and tell Lord Caedmon what has happened."

Olivia's heart jumped. "You are brilliant, Lucy, and I will never forget this, not ever! Please, go, and do hurry."

Olivia listened to Lucy's footsteps receding as she rushed away. She leaned against the door. Garrick would come. She was certain of it.

CHAPTER TWENTY

Garrick swung down from the carriage he himself had been driving, his setter leaping out with him. He was grim. His heart continued to thunder in his ears. From the moment he had spoken to Miss Childs, he had been filled with an iron determination. He stormed up the front steps of the Ashburn country home, intent upon rescuing Olivia and her daughter. Clearly Arlen was far more than dangerous; clearly he was insane.

He pounded upon the front door. It was opened instantly by a footman, whom he ignored. Garrick strode past him and into the foyer, the setter on his heels.

According to Miss Childs, the nursery was on the third story. And Olivia had her rooms there, across from her daughter's. He spied the stairs and ran to them. As he did so, the butler appeared. "My lord," he actually gasped.

Garrick did not stop, already halfway up the first flight of stairs.

The butler, ashen, raced after him. "My lord! I beg your pardon! May I be of some service?"

"Unless you have the courage to free Lady Ashburn and her daughter from the confines of their rooms, no," Garrick said, already on the second landing.

"My lord!" the butler cried, half a flight behind him.

Garrick took a brief look over his shoulder as he hit the third story running. Two footmen were also in hot pursuit.

But he focused his attention on the task at hand, seriously doubting the servants would waylay him. And her door was the third on the left. "Olivia!" he shouted.

There was a moment before she replied, a moment in which he felt her surprise—and her extreme relief. "Garrick! Thank God!" she cried from the other side of the door.

"Stand back," Garrick ordered, glancing at the butler and two footmen, who were now hesitantly approaching him with grave and shocked faces. "You three stand back as well," he ordered in his most commanding tone. "Treve, guard them."

The setter faced the staff, growling, his hackles rising.

They all froze. "My lord, this is intolerable. Lord Ashburn left me with the most explicit instructions," the butler began. His eyes were wide and riveted on the crouched, growling dog.

"Tell him the truth. I have broken into his home, and am now abducting both his wife and his child." With those final, calm words, Garrick stepped forward, kicking in the door.

The moment he saw Olivia he felt a vast relief, in spite of the anger that also flooded him. She still wore her silver dress, and it was torn and stained with blood; her face was discolored yet again, and her hands were red and swollen. Damn Arlen, he managed to think. She met his gaze briefly, already rushing forward, but not to embrace him. Yet the look she gave him said everything. Her gratitude, he thought, would be eternal.

"Hannah! Hannah!" She paused before her daughter's door, clinging to the knob, her ear against the wood. "Hannah!"

"Mama?" Hannah cried from the other side.

"Everything will be all right, darling. Lord Caedmon is here." Olivia swallowed.

Garrick trusted Treve completely to keep the servants at bay, and from the corner of his eye he saw that they were all appalled at the sight of Olivia's face and hands. Gently he took her by the shoulder and pulled her back. She leaned heavily upon him. "Hannah, it is I. Lord Caedmon. I shall kick your door down. Stand as far away from the door as you can."

"Yes, my lord," came the breathless, quavering reply.

"Are you off to the side?" Garrick asked. "The door will fly in, and it could hurt you if you are in the way."

"Yes, I am by the window," Hannah said.

"She is out of the way," Olivia said tersely.

Garrick kicked again, as hard as before. The door flew in off its hinges, wood splintering loudly. The sight he was greeted with undid him: the small, blind child, cringing in the corner of the room. But before he could rush to her, Olivia had raced past him, a silvery blur. She embraced her daughter, rocking her, crying now silently. It was by far one of the most unnerving sights of his life.

"Don't cry, Mama. I am all right," Hannah whispered, clinging to her mother.

"Pack her a small valise," Garrick ordered Olivia. He again glanced at the servants. "Willowby, is it not?" he addressed the butler.

Still ashen, the butler nodded. His face was shining with perspiration. "You may call off the dog, my lord. We will not interfere."

"Treve, come. Good boy," Garrick said. "Pack us up a lunch and dinner, for we depart in fifteen minutes."

Willowby did not hesitate. "Yes, my lord." He looked again at the countess, his mistress, and her daughter. "My lady, I had no idea. I am so sorry."

Olivia, still on her knees and holding her daughter, nodded, tears streaking her cheeks. "Just do as Lord Caedmon requests, Willowby, and all is forgotten."

They traveled hard all that day and well into the night, until the two chestnut mares Garrick was driving were exhausted and nearly lame. There was very little conversation as they made their way south to Cornwall. As it got darker out, it also got colder, the soft, lush green landscape becoming more hostile and more remote, with rock crags appearing along the coast, pastures becoming rock strewn, and gulls wheeling high above them.

Periodically he would glance back at the two occupants of his carriage. Olivia and Hannah huddled together beneath a cashmere throw, Treve with his head in Hannah's lap. From time to time Olivia would cry, but soundlessly, tears marring her pale cheeks. He was acutely aware of her anguish and her pain. He knew she did not cry over Arlen, but for herself and her daughter, in fear of the future and the unknown. Then they both fell asleep, and Garrick was free to think.

There was no going back. Olivia had run away with her daughter, and Arlen was a dangerous man. It was up to Garrick to protect her and Hannah and to provide for them both. And to do so properly meant that he must extricate himself from his betrothal immediately, even if Olivia were never freed by Arlen from the shackles of her own marriage.

There would be no reasoning with Arlen. The three of them must flee the country.

Garrick was grim, because his mind told him one thing, his heart another. How he wished to make a stand and fight for what was right! Unfortunately, he did not delude himself. He could not possibly best Arlen in a duel, which would be the honorable recourse. And Arlen's death under any other circumstance would not be a victory, even though it would be satisfying after all that he had done. The scandal would brand Olivia and her daughter forever, while he would hang for murder.

So they would run.

Knowing Olivia now as he did, he wondered if in time she would come to despise him for denying her a legitimate future, for living with her in sin, for taking her off to faraway, barbarian shores.

An inn appeared beneath a band of winking stars, the offshore breeze now gusty and filled with salt. The inn would do, he thought, halting the tired team in front of the somewhat ramshackle stables. A boy came running out to tend to the mares.

Garrick stepped from the carriage, handing the boy two guineas, turning only to find Hannah still soundly asleep but Olivia watching him out of wide silver eyes. He had not realized she was awake. He attempted a smile and failed.

"We can spend the night here," he said. "We will be at Caedmon Crag by midday tomorrow."

Olivia nodded, shifting and extricating herself from her daughter.

"Don't wake her," Garrick said before she could do so. He bent and lifted the child into his arms, waiting for Olivia to step from the carriage. More sea-cooled breezes swirled about them in a sea-laden mist. The few stars that had been visible earlier had suddenly disappeared. Strands of pale, moonlight-colored hair whipped around Olivia's oval face.

"What if he follows us here?" she asked.

"He returned to London," Garrick said, low. "It will be some time, I think, before he even learns of what has happened. I do not think Willowby will report this incident immediately. He will give us a bit of a head start." He was lying to spare her more worry and distress. Time, he knew, was of the essence. But he had come to Cornwall for a reason, one he was loath to give up.

Olivia nodded, her expression both grim and anxious. "But once he learns of this, he will chase us down. I know him. He will come to Cornwall, Garrick."

He met her eyes. "And we will be gone," he said simply.

"We?" Olivia whispered hoarsely. A tress of her hair caught on her mouth. She pushed it away.

"I will take you wherever it is that you wish to go," Garrick said, his heart drumming. "I cannot abandon you and Hannah now. I was thinking of America."

Olivia stared. "And will we run from him forever, you and I and Hannah?"

"Is there an alternative?" he retorted, far more harshly than he had intended.

Olivia suddenly shook her head, adamantly. "I do not know what to think. I am so confused. Yes, I have left

Arlen. But you cannot simply run away from your obliga-
tions. You have family here, Garrick. I could not forgive
myself if Lionel is proven a fraud, yet you do not honor
your betrothal—and your duty to your father. And what
about Susan?''

''I intend to unmask Lionel,'' Garrick said, ''which is
why I am here. He is a fraud, Olivia. And Susan will be
relieved if I disappear, in effect breaking our engagement.''
His tone was sharp. The problem was, he could not clearly
envision the future, in spite of his intentions. He was
afraid—afraid of Olivia's integrity.

''She will be hurt when she learns what happened tonight,'' Olivia said tiredly. ''There is no way she could not
be hurt, not by your behavior, but by mine. And Arlen will
undoubtedly have you charged with our abduction. Dear
God. There is no simple solution. I only want to be free.''
She turned away, her shoulders sagging with her fatigue
and with, he thought, despair.

He fell into step beside her. ''Free of me?''

She faltered. ''You know that was not my meaning,''
she said softly.

He derived little comfort from her words. Garrick followed her to the inn, acutely aware of his own dismay and
fears. Arlen seemed to be the least of their problems in that
moment. Should he ever be caught by the authorities, he
would defend himself. It was Olivia's attitude that worried
him. Her morality might ultimately destroy them. He had
just found her. He was not ready to walk away; he was
incapable of it. But if she insisted on following some damnable code of ethics? Then what would he do? What could
he do?

A small voice inside his head told him he must stand
and fight, as illogical and hopeless as it seemed, for a future
so bright it must not be denied.

''My lord,'' a maid said, opening the first of two adjoining
doors. Blond and buxom, she gave him a coy glance as she
stepped aside. ''This one's fer yer sister,'' she said, smiling
at him.

Garrick ignored her smile and her tone, which told him that she did not think Olivia his sister at all, and he carried Hannah inside and laid her gently in the middle of the big bed she would share with her mother. Olivia also came inside; the blond serving maid waited at the door.

"I can find my own room, thank you," Garrick told her.

She shrugged. "But I thought to show it to you personally, meself," she said huskily.

Garrick walked over to her and handed her a few coins. "Good night."

Disappointment flitted across her face, and she said, "Mebbe you'll change yer mind later, me lord. Just ask fer Maggie if you do." She left.

Garrick closed the door and turned. Olivia sat on the side of the bed beside her sleeping daughter, having removed her slippers. She was gazing up at him.

"Do your feet hurt?" he asked softly.

"Yes. Everything hurts. She is quite pretty," Olivia said.

Garrick studied her face. "Are you jealous?"

"Yes. Frankly, I am."

He froze at her words, then he walked to her and sat beside her, cupping her face in his large hands. "She might be pretty, but you are beautiful, and extraordinary," he whispered.

Before he could kiss her, she said, "You are right. I am not ordinary."

He pulled back a little. "Did you see the ghost, too?"

Tears shimmered in her eyes. "A Gypsy once told me it was a gift. But it is not a gift. It is a curse."

He slid his hands from her face, down her neck and to her shoulders. "Tell me," he said.

She shrugged, sniffed. "I don't want to know things. But sometimes, truths are revealed to me. Truths, and the future. I was about Hannah's age when I first came into my gift. I saw my sister's death."

"I am sorry," he said, reaching for her hand.

She smiled, but it was feeble. "I did not see the ghost Hannah saw at Stanhope Hall. But I felt an incredible sadness, Garrick. It was very powerful."

"I cannot think who might be lingering in the attic," Garrick said truthfully. He saw a tear trickle down her cheek and brushed it away with the pad of his thumb.

"I also knew that a disaster would befall us if you and I allowed our passion to rule us," Olivia said with evident agony.

"That is not fair," he began.

"No. Do not interrupt. The warning was very strong. And look at all that has happened because of our feelings for one another. Both of our worlds have been destroyed. My future, and my daughter's, is in jeopardy."

"So you would have denied us?" He was incredulous.

"No. But Arlen is not a reasonable man, surely by now you understand that. He has always hated my gift. And feared it."

"Why?" he interrupted her. "Why does he loathe you so?"

"In part, it is because my family and I deceived him. He is not a man to forgive and forget. He cherishes his grudges. He thinks I am cursed, and I believe, because he is so wicked himself, that he fears some kind of curse upon himself. He thinks Hannah is a curse." Her tone caught and she gazed down at her sleeping daughter, touching her small, fisted hand. "Hannah and I have kept her ability a secret. She is much stronger than I am, Garrick." Olivia shuddered. "I am frightened for her. Her ability to see and feel the truth and the future is far too strong for such a young child. What kind of life will she ever have? Will she suffer ostracism, as I have?"

"She will have a wonderful life, with you as her mother, and one day, a home of her own," Garrick responded, meaning it.

"But who would have her? My family despised me for my abilities, just as Arlen despises her. I grew up alone. They feared me, avoided me. I had no friends. The other children were so cruel—like my parents, they feared and shunned me, too. I have spent my entire life protecting Hannah from the outside world—from the scorn and criticism of others." Olivia shuddered again. "My parents have never written to me or visited me once they managed to marry me off. Is this not history repeating itself? What will Arlen do now? If he ever finds us, his animosity for Hannah will be even greater—of that I have no doubt." She looked down. "What can Hannah's future possibly be?"

"You could not have stayed. We will assure Hannah a bright future, you and I."

"Will we?" She met his gaze. "In America? So you will turn your back on your family? In America, will we live together, out of wedlock, in sin, pretending to be man and wife? And when we arrange a marriage for Hannah, that will not be discovered? I am assuming, you understand, that Arlen will not hunt us down like animals. I'm not sure what to do, Garrick! And if he accuses you of a crime? That frightens me, too! I only know that I must not let him find me or Hannah, yet now you are in danger, too."

Garrick swept her into his arms and held her, stroking her long blond hair, letting her weep in fear and confusion. "I will do my best to protect you both," he said. "We are going to have to manage one day at a time, Olivia," he whispered.

But she did not hear him. "If I could have, I would have stayed with Arlen," she cried against his chest. "And kept the truth about Hannah a secret. Her future, then, would have been assured."

"But it did not work out that way. Arlen found out about Hannah's gift, just as he found out about us. We cannot change the past, Olivia. And what about your happiness?"

She looked up. "My happiness? How can I think about myself right now? I am a mother. I must protect Hannah. And now I have involved you. Now I am afraid for you, too."

"Do not fear for me," he said. "And I mean it."

"So what will we do? We have no choice now but to keep on running away. And I cannot help but wonder if, you did not flee with us, Arlen might, in time, forget us and let us go."

He stared. It was a long moment before he could ask the question haunting him—the answer of which he dreaded.

"Is that what you want? For me to send you on alone and return to my family?"

"No. That is not what I want. But neither do I want this. Arlen will do something terrible—I am certain of it." She was blanching. Perspiration dotted her forehead.

He gripped her arms. "You have seen something!"

"No. No. I have not." She looked away from him, avoiding his eyes—lying.

He was certain she had seen a future that was terrifying. He inhaled, trying not to guess what it might be—afraid to know. "Olivia. I did not lie when I said I cannot abandon you and Hannah. I am not about to allow the two of you to flee alone to America, without my protection. Is that clear?" he asked softly, inhaling the fragrance of her.

"If you come with us, he will never cease trying to find us. That is what I truly think!" she cried.

He had the very same feeling. That feeling—that knowledge—made him sick. "Then one day, a time will come for him and me to settle this in a timeless fashion."

"Oh, God," she said, her eyes widening. Then, "Why won't you tell me about you and Arlen?"

He stiffened. "I will tell you when the time is right," he said.

"This has something to do with Elizabeth, does it not?" she asked, her tone bitterly high. "You were her lover, once?"

She had heard the rumors. "Yes, it does have something to do with Elizabeth," he said flatly, uncomfortable.

"She told me," she said, her gaze searching.

He was dismayed. "I can imagine what she might have said. But Elizabeth is an unscrupulous, self-serving woman. And she is a liar when it suits her to be one."

"Did you love her?" Olivia asked, her tone strained.

"No. I was a boy, Olivia, and she was very beautiful, and very seductive. I did not care about what was inside her head or her heart. I only cared about what she wanted from me. I hope I do not have to be more explicit."

Her face was grave. Her eyes remained searching. "I think I understand. And Elizabeth would have told Arlen what suited her most to tell—and he would never forgive you for being with his sister. Perhaps she fell in love with you—and that is why she hates you to this day.''

He stared. A pause ensued. ''Elizabeth loves only herself, and I am surprised you might think otherwise.''

''Yes, you are right, but maybe, in spite of her vanity, she did fall in love with you as much as is possible for a woman like her.''

''I had never considered that possibility before. Can we not let it rest? That was eleven years ago. I was fifteen years old.'' He pulled her close. ''It is so irrelevant—except for the fact that Arlen has hated me ever since.''

''And that is hardly irrelevant,'' she whispered. ''But I wanted to hear it from you. It has been bothering me.''

''I understand,'' he said softly, embracing her one more time. ''I hope you are not jealous of something so old and so tired—especially when you are so much more beautiful than she could ever be. You are the woman I want, Olivia. Has that not been clear?''

Her eyes filled with tears. ''I am so silly. Yes, Garrick, it is very clear. You have placed your life, and your future, in jeopardy for me and for Hannah. You have been very clear from the moment we met, in fact.''

Recalling that meeting, which had gone awry, he smiled and kissed her nose. She moved into his arms, clinging to him, her face pressed against his chest.

He stroked her back. Thoughts that had little to do with either Arlen, his sister, or their journey arose. ''We have gone round and round in circles. Come with me to my room,'' he whispered.

She tensed, gazing up at him.

He gripped her hand, hard, and brought it to his mouth, kissing it with all the passion he felt for her. He watched her eyes darken as he let her hand go. He hesitated only a moment before pulling her close, this time claiming her mouth with his. Love fused with desire. He had never wanted a woman this way before. It was stunning . . . it was terrifying. What if, tomorrow or the day after, she disappeared as suddenly from his life as she had appeared? As she seemed intent upon doing? Or if Arlen found her and dragged her away?

But now Olivia kissed him back with the same feverish longing he was consumed with, and maybe with the same fervent love—and the very same fear. When she broke away, glancing at Hannah, who continued to sleep, he said urgently, "Come to my room. Please."

She met his gaze. "I want to. But what if Hannah wakes up? Alone, in the dark, in this strange room?"

Garrick tried not to groan. "I want you. I need to be with you." He did not say, What if we never have this opportunity again? But in his mind, he was aware of a clock ticking, as much so as if there were a pendulum clock standing in the corner of the room.

"I need you, too," she said. "Terribly. Oh, what is happening to us?"

Garrick stood. Leaving her now was extremely difficult. "Perhaps we are falling in love," he said softly. Staring. She had never told him that she loved him, and he wanted to hear it now.

"Perhaps?" Her mouth was pursed. "I fell in love with you a long time ago, Garrick De Vere. Perhaps before I ever laid eyes upon you."

His heart sang a little and danced, and in spite of her odd statement, he thought he understood it. But he wanted to know exactly what she meant. "How is that possible?"

She hesitated. "I met Susan and her parents a few days before you called upon her in town. At Ashburnham, where they were visiting. As soon as she told me of her engagement, I saw you, Garrick, as clearly as if I had already known you. I saw you, and knew you—and knew you were innocent of all those who had been accusing you for years of murdering your brother."

His heart turned over, hard. "Is that usual, Olivia? To hear of someone you have never met and—"

"No," she cut him off. "It has never happened to me before." Her gaze locked with his.

"I am glad," he said harshly, and he pulled her hard against his chest and kissed her again.

When he released her, she smiled up at him, touching his cheek with her palm. "In spite of the warning, we were meant to meet, Garrick."

"Yes. We were. This was meant to be. And it is my intuition which has told me that—from the very first." He smiled, but then he grew grim. "Plan on leaving at first light, Olivia."

Her relaxed expression vanished, replaced by worry.

"Try not to worry," he said. "Let me do the worrying."

She nodded. But she was no longer smiling. And he knew she was thinking about Arlen now, and the oh-so-uncertain future, as was he.

CHAPTER TWENTY-ONE

It was late. The moon was nearly full but constantly obscured by huge, drifting clouds. From time to time a star would appear, only to be swept away by the windblown shadows. Below the road that led to Caedmon Crag, the surf crashed upon the rock-strewn coast, loud and resonant, deafening.

It was cold, far colder now than it had been at any previous point in their journey, and Olivia huddled under her mantle after making sure that Hannah, who slept soundly, was securely covered up. The ocean continued to roar somewhere below the road, but to the right she could see the endless band of the ocean, stretching away into eternity, glittering ebony in the night. She shivered, her gaze turning to Garrick's broad shoulders. They were set with tension. He had not spoken to her or turned to look back at her for hours.

She did not have to be gifted to know that returning to this place where his brother had disappeared fourteen years ago was difficult for him. It would be extremely difficult for anyone. But she was gifted, and she was also highly attuned to him by now, and she felt his misery, his confusion, his anger, and his fear. She could not understand that last emotion. What frightened him? The truth?

She imagined that if she were in Garrick's place, she would be hoping against hope that Lionel was genuine and not an impostor. On the other hand, she had witnessed the barely veiled and bitter rivalry between the two men, and the earl's favoritism. Of course, Garrick would be torn.

She herself had many reasons to be afraid now. It was only a matter of time before Arlen came hunting for them. She did not want to stay in Cornwall, or England, for that matter, for more than a few days. She could not even bear to contemplate what might happen if Arlen did find them, and she had long since banished that odd vision about Hannah into the farthest reaches of her mind. But what about Garrick? He had been firm—he would not abandon her and Hannah. Yet did she dare run away with him? That would fuel Arlen's fury and determination as nothing else would. The situation seemed so hopeless.

Her thoughts were interrupted by the looming shadows of a building just to the left of them. The windswept clouds were racing past, and it almost seemed as if the building wavered back and forth in the gloom. Careful not to disturb Hannah, Olivia leaned forward. ''Is that Caedmon Crag?'' she asked Garrick, her tone hushed.

He glanced back at her briefly. ''No.''

She waited, and when he did not reply immediately, she thought he would not; but after a long pause he said, ''That's the ruins of an old, eleventh-century keep. There are some caves below it in the cliffs, and smugglers have been using them for centuries.''

She felt the chills then, creeping upon her spine, her arms, the nape of her neck. She was aware of the setter, until now lying at her feet, suddenly sitting up. The dog whined, his ears pricked.

The surf continued to crash on the coast below them, the wind moaned. ''*Garrick.*'' Olivia stiffened, certain she had heard the sound of Garrick's name, a distant sigh upon the wind.

He turned briefly again. ''Did you say something?''

''No.'' As she spoke, myriad sensations took hold of her. The night had changed. It was no longer empty and benign. Olivia stiffened, automatically reaching out her hand. Something, or someone, was making itself known to her.

She could not identify what, or whom, it was.

Come closer, she pleaded inwardly.

"Do you feel anything?" Garrick's question cut into her thoughts.

"Yes," Olivia whispered, her pulse pounding. She did not want to talk to Garrick now. She wanted to empty her mind, her self, and feel whatever might be out there. But she said, "Something happened here. Is this where your brother . . . vanished?" She had almost said, Is this where your brother died?

He suddenly halted the carriage. "We were here together, at the keep. I stayed. Lionel left." Anger had entered his tone. "He was never seen again."

Olivia sat without moving. Garrick was also motionless. Both mares had dropped their heads and appeared to be dozing. Hannah remained soundly asleep. The setter whined again, low in his throat.

Garrick and Olivia looked at the dog, who seemed to be gazing out into the night.

"What is it, boy?" Garrick asked softly. The wind seemed to pick up. The shrubs around them shifted. Not far by, a pebble sounded, as if dropped upon the rocks.

And briefly, stunningly, she felt it all: the night around them was filled with surprise, incredulity, anger, and finally, fear. Very real fear.

Olivia was frozen, not daring to move or to breathe, even as the carriage was rocked by a sudden gust of wind. As if from a distance, she heard Garrick speak to her but could not decipher his words. And then it was gone. As suddenly as it had been there. Nothingness filled the void of the windy night. Sheer emptiness. Just the wind and the sea, the stars and the trees, and the empty shell of the keep.

Perspiring, Olivia glanced at her daughter to see if she had been disturbed by the encounter, expecting to find Hannah awake and as alert as she. But she remained soundly asleep, her small face relaxed, her breathing deep and easy. Olivia frowned.

Had it been Lionel? Was Lionel lurking about, for

some reason afraid to approach them too closely? Or, because it was so many years since his disappearance and
supposed death, if it was he, was he incapable of coming
any closer?

"What is it, Olivia?" Garrick was staring at her. "What
did you see?"

Olivia started. "Someone was here, Garrick, a moment
ago," she said quietly. She sat back in the carriage, waiting
now. He would try to come again. She was certain of it.

"I felt something, too," Garrick said harshly. "Was it
Lionel?"

Olivia met his gaze, which was angry. If it had been
Lionel, then Lionel was dead. "I don't know who it was,"
she said softly, wanting to touch and comfort him.

He hesitated and shook his head, at the same time lifting
the reins and urging the mares forward. "Perhaps we were
imagining things. The keep has always been said to be
haunted. This place has always felt odd . . . heavy."

Olivia would have said that it felt sad, dark, and oppressive. "I think you are right," she said to his back. "I think
the answer you seek is here. Or nearby."

He stiffened but did not reply, continuing to drive the
team on. A few minutes later, they were turning through
the barbican of Caedmon Crag.

The old, crumbling manor was pitch black inside the great
hall, until Garrick lit a torch. Immediately the stone walls,
hung with rusted maces and swords, blazed with light.
"There are no servants," Garrick said abruptly. "I'll go
fetch Hannah." His eyes held hers, intense and probing.

In that one second, Olivia's thoughts changed dramati-
cally. She could imagine why Caedmon Crag had been left
unattended for all these years, and now the knowledge that
no one was there except herself, her daughter, and Garrick
De Vere filled her with a breath-defying expectation. She
accepted the torch, watching Garrick leave the hall. The
front door banged against the wall where he had left it
open.

She glanced around at the cavernous hall, which was

starkly empty except for one long, scarred trestle table and its chairs, and an old, faded wall hanging depicting a hunting scene. Suddenly Olivia envisioned two young boys engaged in mock swordplay in front of the huge, man-size brick hearth. She smiled, watching as they chased one another into the hall, the one fair and golden, the other dark and bronzed. Feints parried thrusts. The boys grinned as they challenged one another. The countess appeared, scolding them both, but the boys only nodded and resumed their wild play. Then the earl, magnificently clothed as always, strode into the room, his expression stern. The vision ended abruptly, but his appearance had been much like a huge storm cloud settling over a sunny tropical island.

Olivia hugged herself. Had she recalled a moment from the past or merely imagined the past as it might have once been? She did not know. But she was struck by the bond of friendship and warmth between the two boys—the two brothers. She had seen no such evidence of that bond since Lionel De Vere had returned from the dead. But people changed.

Garrick entered the hall, Hannah stirring in his arms. With one booted foot, he closed the door. "We'll take the rooms right above the hall," he said, his golden gaze piercing through her another time.

Olivia nodded, leading the way because she held the torchlight, her heart beating double time. Her slippers echoed loudly on the narrow, twisting stone stairs. On the second landing, trying to keep her thoughts at bay, she pushed open the first door she came to and saw a dark room, the stone walls having been whitewashed long ago but now almost the same dark gray as the natural stone outside. A huge four-poster bed dominated the room. Age had weathered it nearly black. Garrick moved past her and laid Hannah down in its midst. He began searching for bedding through the huge, warped trunk at its foot. "Mama?" Hannah whispered sleepily. "Are we here?"

Olivia hurried to her. "We are. Go back to sleep, darling. It's still the middle of the night."

Garrick covered Hannah with a wool blanket. And somewhere not far from them, abruptly, something fell, sounding loudly on the stone floors, a deafening crash. And a shutter or a door banged a moment later, downstairs, the sound thunderous. Olivia jumped.

"A storm by the morning," Garrick commented, but small frown lines creased his forehead. Olivia nodded, sitting beside Hannah, reminding herself that she was not afraid of spirits, not even the most angry of lost souls. She did not ask Garrick about the source of the crash and the banging.

He took a wall sconce and lit it, using Olivia's torch. "I have to go and tend the team. I'll be back shortly." His gaze settled with brilliant intensity upon her face. "I'll take the room next door."

Olivia trembled. All previous thoughts of ghosts and spirits vanished, and she nodded, breathless, unable not to think now about being in his embrace, in his bed. She glanced at Hannah, but she was already asleep. Far more than the trip had taken its toll upon her.

"Treve, stay," Garrick ordered the setter. And he strode from the room.

He pounded down the stairs, aware of the woman he was leaving behind, but even more aware of his surroundings. What the hell had just crashed to the floor? It had sounded like something on the floor above him. The floor above— where he and Lionel had had their rooms as boys.

In the great hall he stared. The front door was widely ajar, and he had slammed it closed after entering with Hannah. As he crossed the room, he could not help but glance around at the shadows that lurked against every wall, in every corner. He saw nothing.

He was trembling, he was sweating. He did not remember the manor ever feeling so unfriendly before. But he had not been back to Caedmon Crag since the day Lionel had disappeared. Perhaps it was his own bleak, angry feelings that were infusing the manor with such a dark atmosphere. And the atmosphere was dark—it was not his imagination.

He stepped outside, this time closing the door solidly and checking to make sure it was closed. The wind howled. The surf roared on the rocks below the manor. There was no doubt about it. A storm was on its way, a very bad one. By dawn tomorrow, he expected the manor to be in the middle of a gale. But that was fine. If Arlen thought to chase them down, he would be delayed.

Garrick approached the tired team and quickly unhitched both mares from their traces. He worked by rote, for he could hardly see, and he cursed the wind, only to realize that it wasn't the wind that was interfering with his vision, it was his tears.

He stopped what he was doing, holding both mares by their bridles now, staring grimly out into the gust-filled night. His stomach was clenched tight. Was Lionel dead?

And he wanted to smash his fist into the face of the man now claiming to be his brother. If he had not appeared in their lives, there would be no need for this flight to Caedmon Crag right now, filled with an anguish and a pain he had thought long since laid to rest.

Garrick led the two mares across the stony courtyard to the run-down stables. He wiped tears from his face and led both mares into two roomy box stalls. He'd brought corn mash with him, and he filled both mangers with it. Damn it. The man who had so suddenly appeared in their lives was not Lionel, his long-lost brother. For if he were, Garrick would know it. Once, they had been so close. Even if he had changed, becoming grasping, manipulative, and unlikable, Garrick would know it. This man was a fraud. He had to be. And his brother was dead. There was no other possibility.

He was a pretender, and Garrick had to unmask him. If it was the last thing he did.

Garrick left the stables, head down, fighting the wind. His gut was tight. His heart beat too hard for comfort. The answer to Lionel's disappearance was here, at Caedmon Crag. He was certain of it.

Garrick pushed open the front door, entered the sanctuary

of the hall, and pulled the door closed again. This time he
bolted it. As he headed for the stairs, he glanced around
one more time. No ghost of his long-lost brother materialized from the shadows. But he had the unnerving feeling
that he was being watched. It was, of course, his imagination.

The door to her room was ajar, light spilling from the
crack. He pushed it open and his smile died. Hannah slept
alone in the bed, Treve slept on the floor at the bed's foot.
Olivia was not present.

"Garrick."

He whirled—and felt as if someone had struck him, hard,
knocking all the air from his lungs. Olivia stood behind
him, in the hall, resplendently naked. Her long platinum
hair was loose, streaming over her full breasts and large,
erect nipples, caressing her curved hips, where the curly
tendrils parted, exposing her sex and her soft, pale thighs.
He had no thoughts now, save one.

He moved. He left the bedroom, shutting the door, taking
her in his arms. He kissed her like a starving man, without
finesse or grace—it had been far too long for that. His
palms slid over her hair, then underneath the mass of it, on
her smooth, supple back. He cupped her buttocks and
pulled her up against his stiff loins.

She cried out and kissed him back. Running her tongue
over his lips, she slid her hands down the front of his shirt,
beneath his coat, and then lower. Garrick froze as her fingers slipped over the length of his manhood. He closed his
eyes, letting her touch him.

Then he pushed her against the wall. Garrick wasn't certain whether she was unbuttoning his breeches or if he
was—or if they were both fumbling there together. She
kissed and bit his neck. She whispered his name, her cries
soft and encouraging.

His manhood sprang hot and full against her hip. Garrick met her heated eyes for one moment before bending
to taste her nipples. Then her hand was on him, squeezing, moving, rubbing. He pinned her to the wall, gasping.

One of his thighs had separated hers, lifting her left leg high and hard.

"Help me," she whispered.

"Yes," he said, bending. "Yes." He thrust, taking Olivia up the wall. She wrapped her arms around his shoulders, holding on tightly, sobbing with pleasure. Garrick thrust again and again. She cried out wildly. His mouth took hers, cutting off her cries, tasting her while driving into her hard and harder still until she climaxed with his name on her lips, her fingers in his hair, her nails in his skin.

She lay limp in his arms, her back against the wall, her head buried against his shoulder, his hands beneath her buttocks. Having just reached his own climax, Garrick began now to relish the warmth and softness and vitality of her. He held her. He did not want to leave her, not yet—this was where he belonged; nothing had ever felt this right. It was so obvious in that moment. She could flee Arlen—but not without him. Never without him.

The hand was soft and cool, kind, and not unpleasant. It cupped Hannah's cheek.

She stirred, aware of the caress as sleep left her. She opened her eyes, for one brief moment confused, not knowing where she was. "Mama?"

Hannah sat up, realizing she was alone. She had dreamed about her face being touched, she thought, and now she recalled that she was at Lord Caedmon's home in Cornwall. They had arrived late last night.

Outside, the wind howled like a banshee and the very first few drops of rain began to come down. Drip. Drip. Drip. But Hannah heard the rain as clearly as if she could see it. Although her world was black, she knew that the morning was dark and gray. Something was banging repeatedly, loudly, downstairs, probably a shutter or a door. The wind moaned, and lightning flashed very close by. Hannah felt it, and it was followed by a deafening crack of thunder just overhead.

She shivered, but not because she was cold or afraid.

Then she felt the human touch again, fingers slipping over her elbow and her arm, a palm closing over her hand. Hannah stared sightlessly as her hand was tugged gently forward.

Who are you? she asked silently.

Come. Although she heard no words, the idea materialized instantly inside of her head. As did another thought. *I won't hurt you.*

But Hannah already knew that. She slid from the bed, still dressed in her clothes from the day before. The setter sat up, its tail thumping; outside, the wind groaned, as did some nearby part of the manor. Hannah moved her feet around and found her slippers, then bent to put them on. The setter licked her face.

Hannah smiled, hugging him. She felt him wagging his tail again.

This time the hand tapped her shoulder, with impatience. No message could have been clearer. With the dog at her side, her hand on its collar, Hannah left the room.

He squinted through the darkness, knowing it would soon be pouring, sitting astride a tired hack because that had been the fastest way to travel. Damn it, but he could hardly see. He peered harder through the dawn. As he did so, lightning flashed, too close for comfort, and thunder rolled and cracked and rolled again. He was stiff with tension, because he hated thunderstorms—he had feared them since he was a child.

He hated this place, too. He had always hated it—with good cause.

He stared ahead. He had always known that Garrick would return to Caedmon Crag. He had known that it would just be a matter of time before he did so, but what he hadn't known, or even guessed, was that he would return with Olivia and Hannah. He was more than grim, he was furiously angry. But the time had come to stop this madness. He must stop them all.

The rain began. The wind slashed the icy cold fingers of water against his face, the only part of his body exposed to the elements, as he wore a huge cape with a hood. He spurred his mount forward, not caring that the gelding snorted in protest, as the manor took shape before his tired eyes. How ramshackle, how run-down, it appeared after all these years. He had not been back since the vanishing. And then he pulled up abruptly, seeing Hannah and the dog at the exact same time, the strange duo hurrying out of the barbican. His pulse roared.

Suddenly the child and the dog froze, as if aware of him, too. Immediately he rode forward, but at a rapid trot. Hannah whirled, no doubt turning to flee. He spurred his horse into a canter, coming up instantly upon her and cutting her and the dog off. And it was only because of the dog that he did not grab her. The setter had moved in front of Hannah, its hackles raised, its teeth bared.

He smiled his most charming grin and removed the hood from his face. "Hello, Hannah. I am sorry to scare you. What are you doing out and about in this storm? Surely you are not lost? Where is your mother?"

She gazed toward him as if she could see, except clearly she could not. Her eyes were ugly to him in their blindness. "You frightened me," she said, low. Her face was flushed. He could see the fear in those sightless eyes.

"I did not mean to startle you," he said easily. "Let me give you a ride back to the house. You could catch your death out here in this storm, you know."

She shook her head stubbornly.

"Perhaps you should call Caedmon's dog off," he said.

Again she shook her head. Her entire posture was that of a tiny soldier ready to flee or do battle.

"What's wrong?" he asked in his gentlest tone. "Hannah, surely you are not afraid of *me?*" His smile remained wide and firmly in place. "Come. Let me take you back to the house, before your mother wakes up and finds you gone. She will be furious then with us both."

Hannah backed away from him, a single cautious step at a time.

The dog was snarling now, preventing him from acting as he wished. "Why are you outside in the middle of the rain?'' he finally demanded, losing his temper and his patience.

She stared at him as if she could not, or would not, answer. Then she cried, "Leave me alone!" And she whirled, running away as hard as she could, the dog at her side, down the narrow road, which was rapidly turning to mud.

He watched her awaken, smiling. Being with Olivia like this was bittersweet. They had so many problems to face and to solve, but even a single night like the last one was worth all of the travail. "Good morning," he whispered, stroking her bare arm.

Her eyes fluttered open and she smiled up at him. "Oh, what a pleasant way to awaken," she murmured.

"I can think of a better way." He pressed against her, in case she had any doubt as to his meaning. Just being with her, watching her, thinking about her, had made him hard. He slid his hand down her rib cage.

But she tensed. "Something is wrong. Oh, God." She sat up instantly, the covers dropping to her waist, revealing her magnificent breasts.

"What is it, Olivia? What have you felt? Perhaps it is the storm which is bothering you." Outside, the world was cast in a black downpour. One of the shutters, which was hanging lopsidedly against the window, kept banging against the house. Garrick had not slept well last night, and only partly because he lay in bed with such an extraordinary and desirable woman. The other reason had had to do with ghosts and vanishings and the truth about his brother, a truth he must unearth.

"It is not the storm," Olivia said, already out of bed. She stepped into her drawers and chemise, then threw a cashmere shawl about her shoulders. Barefoot, she rushed from the room. Reluctantly Garrick also slipped from the bed. Last night he had felt again as if the walls had eyes and were watching him. It had been an uncanny, eerie, yet not quite frightening situation. He had never felt that way before, either, and he did not feel that way now, in the light of this dismal morning. He was stepping into his breeches, thinking about the feeling of being watched, when he heard her cry out.

He rushed to Hannah's room, only to find Olivia staring at the empty bed. Half of the covers lay upon the floor.

Olivia whirled. Consternation masked her face. "I have not a doubt as to what happened." She ran past him, back into their bedroom, now throwing on her clothes. She made no attempt to don the many layers of her underthings.

Garrick moved behind her to do up the laces on the back of her dress. "Then enlighten me."

"Whoever was here last night—Lionel, perhaps—he contacted Hannah." She turned, her gaze locking with his.

Chills swept up and down his spine, his chest, even his goddamned legs. Had Lionel been watching him last night? "Why? Why Hannah? Why not you?"

"I am torn by your feelings, Garrick, and my love for you is interfering with my ability to see clearly, to feel clearly, to use my gift. But Hannah is very sensitive. Oh, God. She has been lured somewhere, but where?"

"Try to stay calm. We will find her." He kept his tone even, but as he donned his shirt, he was more than concerned. What if Olivia was right? Had a ghost, perhaps Lionel's, seduced the child into following it? Had this very same ghost watched him as he tried to sleep all of last night? Was he succumbing to madness himself, to even consider such a possibility? But he could not forget what had happened before, at Stanhope Hall. Hannah had felt someone in the attic—had she been summoned there?

"Christ," Garrick muttered.

"The only fact that relieves me at all," Olivia said swiftly, "is that I felt no malice or evil, neither here nor at the Hall. Still, Hannah is blind and defenseless." Her last words caught in her throat.

Buttoning up his shirt, he said, "Treve is with her. He will protect her with his life."

Tears shone in Olivia's eyes. "Oh, why didn't she come to me first?"

Garrick started to respond, but Olivia cried out, "Ssh!"

gripping his shoulder with such strength that he felt her nails. He froze.

And very clearly, he heard footsteps in the corridor outside of their room. Heavy footsteps. Booted footsteps. A man's footsteps.

At least this was no ghost. But Garrick thought he knew who it was, and expecting Arlen, he regretted not having either a pistol or dagger on hand. He lunged around the doorway—and for the second time, he froze.

Lionel smiled at him. "I pounded upon the front door, but no one answered, and I decided to come in." He stepped forward, that single stride taking him into a position where he could now see Olivia in her disheveled state in the bedchamber, with the mussed-up bed dominating the room. He bowed. "Good morning, Lady Ashburn. I hope I have not interrupted anything?"

Olivia flushed. "Good morning, my lord. This is a rather early hour for callers, do you not think?" Her smile was so stiff, it might have been made of wax.

"I do apologize, but when my brother left the Hall in such haste, and so unhappily, I felt it my duty to come to his aid." He appeared chagrined. "Had I known he had guests here, I would hardly have come. Again, I do apologize, but you can count upon my discretion." Now he smiled.

Garrick folded his arms, not convinced by Lionel's theatrics for even a moment. Nor did he believe in coincidences. He had come to Caedmon Crag to learn the truth about his brother—and this man had suddenly appeared there as well. He could guess why. If this man were an impostor, then he suspected what Garrick intended to do and wished to forestall him at all costs. "You are always welcome in my home, Lionel," he lied. Of course, if this man was who he said he was, then he had every right to be at the manor—for Caedmon Crag belonged to him.

Before Lionel could reply and thank him, Olivia stepped between the two men. "Lionel, have you seen Hannah? Either in the house or outside?" Her tone cracked with her worry and anxiety. "She is missing."

"Missing?!" He raised both blond brows as he faced her. "She is not in the house? We must find her. We must search until we find her!" And he smiled.

While Garrick stared.

CHAPTER TWENTY-TWO

A blast of wind blew in the stable door the moment Garrick pushed it partially open. He was soaking wet. The rain pounded down now far harder than before. He had left Olivia combing the manor for her daughter, while he and Lionel had split up, agreeing to look for Hannah outside, despite what Lionel had said. Logic had led him immediately to the stables. If he had been outside in this torrential downpour, he would seek the first dry, available shelter.

Inside, the stable was dark and damp, smelling of old, moldy straw and horses. Both mares whickered as he came in, their heads appearing over the edges of their box stalls. He left the stable door open, but the illumination that was afforded him was minimal. "Treve," he called, squinting through the gloom.

A bark sounded from one of the empty stalls. Almost simultaneously, the setter's broad brow appeared as he stood with both front paws on top of the stall door, his brown eyes warm and eager. Relieved, Garrick walked forward and peered down into the stall.

Hannah sat in the far corner, hugging her knees beneath her stained skirts to her chest. Her face was pale and showed the marks of dried tears. She was gazing sightlessly in his direction. Bits of hay clung to her gown and braided hair.

"Hannah, it is I, Lord Caedmon," he said softly. "I am

pleased to see you found a safe place to avoid the rain."

"Hello, my lord," she said, her tone so low it was almost inaudible.

He opened the stall door and stepped inside, absently patting the setter's head. Hannah's expression was strained. She seemed distraught. "Are you all right?" Garrick asked. "You gave your mother quite a fright, disappearing from your bed like that."

"I'm sorry," she said, laying her cheek against her knees.

Garrick sat beside her in the old, moldy hay. "You do not seem all right. Are you afraid of storms?"

She shook her head and bit her lip, her eyes shining with tears.

He put his arm around her. "What is wrong? Why didn't you return to the house when it started to rain?"

She turned her face toward him. "I was afraid."

"Afraid? Hannah, have you seen a ghost?" he asked quickly.

She nodded.

When she did not speak, he said kindly, "I did not know you were afraid of ghosts." But his heart was thundering now, almost deafening him, with the oddest kind of hope. Had Hannah seen Lionel?

"I am not afraid of ghosts," Hannah returned evenly. "And especially not of this one."

"I do not understand. Then why are you hiding?"

"I am afraid of your brother."

He started, stunned, confused. "I beg your pardon?"

"I don't like Lord De Vere," she whispered, turning her face away from him, her cheeks flushed.

His mind whirled. She had seen a ghost. She was not afraid of ghosts. But she was afraid of his brother. Yet Lionel was not the real Lionel, he was a fraud. Wasn't he? "Lionel is here," he said cautiously. He did not know what to think.

"I know."

He smiled slightly. "Is there anything you do not know?"

She grimaced. "I met him on his way in, my lord. It was nothing more than that."

Garrick stared. Then he cursed the man calling himself Lionel for lying to him and Olivia about not having seen Hannah. Why had he done such a thing? A small, blind child lost in the rain could become quite serious, especially in the cold Cornish climate. The answer seemed obvious— because Hannah could unmask him. Yet Lionel could not know that, and surely Garrick was overreacting—Lionel might be a title hunter, but that did not mean he wished a small child ill. But was he, or was he not, his brother?

Garrick patted Hannah's shoulder. "You were hiding from Lord Lionel? Why?"

She shook her head, as if refusing to answer. Then she blurted, "He doesn't like me. I don't like him. I am afraid of him. He isn't good."

Well, Garrick thought, we are in accord on one subject. He studied her face, so angelic, now downturned. He was gaining confirmation of his feelings about Lionel from an eight-year-old blind girl gifted with an ability to see and feel truths that others could not discern. That thought made him grim. And he was even grimmer thinking about the fact that Hannah had referred to him as his brother.

But he said slowly, "Hannah, why do you think Lionel isn't good? What do you know about him?"

She shrugged. "He doesn't like me—or you—or Mama. He has come here for a reason. It is not a good reason. But I do not know what that reason is."

Garrick squeezed her shoulder. "Thank you," he said. "Hannah, earlier you called Lionel my brother. Is he my brother?"

She blinked, staring sightlessly at him. For a long moment she did not speak. "Yes," she finally whispered.

He also stared, directly back at her, his heart sinking. "Could you be wrong?" he asked after a pause.

"I do not know," she whispered, shifting uncomfortably. Her tone had become high and strained. "He isn't what you think he is. My lord, can we go back to the house now?"

He realized that she was upset and was furious with himself for pushing a small child for answers she might not have—or even be able to cope with. But he did recall that Olivia had said Hannah did not make mistakes. Could his brother have changed so much? If Lionel were not a fraud, then he, Garrick, was at fault for despising him so much. The worst part was that a stubborn part of himself insisted that Lionel was an impostor. "Let's go back to the house and have breakfast," he said, standing and holding out his hand to her. "You do not have to worry about Lionel anymore."

She hesitated, then reached out, and he clasped her small, warm palm in his, pulling her to her feet. "Thank you, Lord Caedmon," she whispered. "I am hungry."

"You have nothing to thank me for," he said, leading her out of the stall, the setter dancing around them.

Suddenly Hannah pulled back, just as a familiar voice rang out, "So there you are. I see that you have found her." And Lionel, standing on the threshold of the stable, smiled at them both.

Garrick was positive his smile did not reach his blue eyes. Protectively he put his arm around the child. "Yes, I have found her," he said.

"Thank God you have found her," Olivia said, hugging Hannah hard. Hannah, Garrick, and Lionel had just entered the great hall, having come in out of the pounding rain.

"She was seeking refuge in the stables," Garrick said, acutely aware of Lionel standing beside them. He had had the sense to wear a huge, hooded cloak and was now shaking the water from it. "From the rain." He smiled at Olivia and her daughter.

Olivia, to her credit, did not demand to know why Hannah had left the house in the first place in such inclement weather. And if Lionel understood his innuendo, he gave no indication of it. He also smiled.

"Let's get you changed into dry clothes," Olivia said, smiling briefly at both men.

"I think I shall also change," Garrick said, as every inch

of him was dripping wet. "Lionel, I am afraid we have no staff here at the manor. But I did bring a supply of goods with me. Everything is in the kitchen. Care to start a fire and roast some meat?"

Lionel raised both brows. "I have a better idea. Why not hire a maid or two to tend us while we are here? I am hardly a servant, Garrick, to prepare us meals."

Garrick smiled, eyeing him and folding both arms. "I did not know you were planning on staying," he said.

"Well, I think I should, all things considered." Lionel smiled at him, too.

"And just what considerations are you speaking of?" Garrick inquired as Olivia led Hannah to the stone stairs.

"Well, unfortunately, if I found you here, I do believe Arlen will, too. I am your brother. I do not think I should abandon you now." Lionel's gaze shifted to Olivia and Hannah, both ascending the stairwell. His point was clear: trouble was on its way.

Olivia faltered, then turned to look back at them. Her gaze, filled with consternation, met Garrick's before she and Hannah disappeared quickly upstairs.

"How brotherly you have become," Garrick said, unable to keep the mockery from his tone.

Lionel shrugged. "I will go find us a serving wench," he said, and left the house.

Garrick moved to stare out a dirty stained-glass window after him. What was he up to? Garrick would not put it past him to go to the village in order to send a messenger to Arlen himself, alerting him to Olivia's whereabouts. Lionel led his mount from the stable. Garrick did not have to see any more. He cursed, turning away and hurrying up the stairs.

. Olivia appeared on the threshold of Hannah's room as he approached, closing the door behind her. As she did, Garrick glimpsed the fire she had stoked in the hearth and Hannah standing in front of it, brushing her long, wet black hair. The setter lay at her feet.

"What has happened?" she asked without preamble, her gaze filled with worry.

"I trust Lionel as much as I might a Gypsy horse peddler," Garrick said grimly.

"I agree with you," Olivia said.

"Hannah is afraid of him. She told me that he is Lionel," Garrick said bluntly. "She also told me she had seen a ghost. I do not know what to think."

Olivia studied him. "I just spoke with her. She is very distraught. Garrick, did I tell you that, as I grew up, my gift became less predictable? My mind and my feelings can interfere with my ability to see and understand the truth. Perhaps that is what is happening to Hannah now."

Garrick put his arm around her. "If he is my brother, then he has changed. Olivia, we were so very close once."

Olivia slipped her arms around him. "People do change, Garrick. Maybe Hannah is wrong. I can tell you this much. I do not like him, either, and more important, I do not trust him. Something is wrong." She frowned. "And that includes his appearing here the day after us. He followed us from Ashburnham."

"Yes. I am in complete agreement with you." Garrick released her to rub his temples. He did not add the obvious, that Lionel now knew definitively about their liaison. As such a witness, he poised a definite threat to them. "You know, at times he will say something that seems so incredibly genuine to me. He probably is Lionel, dear God."

Olivia shrugged. "Whoever he is, he has much to gain— your father's title and fortune and power. Truthfully, it would not be hard to learn all about you and your family. A servant—or several—could so easily be bribed."

Garrick agreed. Then he pulled her farther away from the door. "Olivia, we must make plans," he whispered. "Arlen may be in pursuit of us as we speak."

She paled. "This is happening too quickly. We haven't had any time to think!"

"You must leave the country."

She stared. "So you have decided, after all, to let Hannah and myself go?"

"No." His tone was hard. "But I want the two of you safely gone before Arlen arrives, and I will join you shortly.'' Suddenly he felt certain that Lionel had gone into the village to betray them all. Time was running out. Had a clock been staring him in the face, it could not have been more clear. ''I want you away from here, immediately.''

''You will stay to unmask Lionel's impostor,'' Olivia said tersely.

''Yes,'' he said, seized with an iron determination. ''You and Hannah will leave today. I will hire you a coach. I will finish this with Lionel, and meet you in Calais.''

Tears glimmered in Olivia's eyes. ''I am afraid. Terrified. What are we going to do, run away from Arlen for the rest of our lives? He will never leave us in peace, Garrick, I am certain of it.'' Suddenly she cried out, staggering backward, flinging a hand up to cover her eyes.

''What is it?'' he cried, alarmed, reaching for her and steadying her. ''Jesus! What have you seen?''

She turned terrified silver eyes upon him. ''Oh, God. This is the second time—it was so strong. Hannah in this place—this terrible place—a place filled with mad people!''

His skin crawled. His stomach turned over. He pulled her into his embrace. ''Do not even think of such a thing!'' he said in her ear, very firmly.

She stared at him, gripping his shoulders, her eyes wide. ''And what if Arlen finds us first? Hannah and I will hardly be unremarkable—a woman traveling alone with a blind child—'' Her voice broke. ''God. What if I never see you again?'' Fear filled her silver eyes, making them huge.

''Do not say such a thing!'' he shouted, furious that she would even have such a thought—or was it a premonition? He was sick with his own fear, for it had struck him that he might not be able to unmask Lionel without Hannah's or Olivia's help.

She seemed to understand his thoughts. ''Hannah saw a ghost today. She refused to speak about it. I do not know why. But someone wishes to contact us. How can we go? You need us here!'' Olivia cried.

''No. I will unearth the truth without your help,'' he said firmly.

Olivia held his eyes, hers fearful and filled with doubt, finally, hesitantly, nodding. Suddenly Hannah screamed, startling them both.

"Mama!" Hannah shouted from inside her bedroom. "*Mama!*" Her cry was filled with alarm and fear.

Garrick moved first, jerking open her door so hard that the handle almost came off in his hand, Olivia on his heels. Hannah stood beside the bureau, motionless, unblinking, perhaps not even breathing, her hairbrush on the floor where she had evidently dropped it. Treve was whining, shoving his cool nose in her clenched hand, as distressed as a dog could be.

Olivia rushed to her, her face devoid of color. "What is it, darling? What have you seen?" she asked, panic in her own tone.

Hannah came out of her odd, trancelike state. "He is here," she said huskily.

Garrick glanced wildly around, almost expecting to see his brother materializing from the corners of the room as a ghost.

"Who, darling?" Olivia asked, low. "Lionel? Lord Caedmon's dead brother?"

"No." Hannah wet her lips. "Father. Father is here. Outside." And she hugged her mother, beginning to tremble and cry.

Olivia turned wide eyes upon Garrick, who rushed to the window. There he froze.

Two vehicles were parked in front of the manor, and the largest town coach bore the Ashburn coat of arms. A moment later he watched Arlen alight from the coach, adjusting his crimson frock coat. The rain had tapered off to a mere drizzle.

Garrick whirled. "Stay here. Do not leave this room," he commanded. His heart beat with thunderous force.

"Oh, my God!" Olivia clutched Hannah against her skirts. "He has found us!"

"I will not let him in," Garrick said, rushing from the room. He slammed their door closed, but he was thinking about two things—he did not have a weapon, and neither did he have a staff to enforce his will. Arlen had come with an entire retinue, and for all Garrick knew, his entourage included the authorities. He, Garrick, was one man. He could hardly prevent Arlen from seizing his own wife and child.

He pounded down the stairs and through the hall, flinging open the front door. He froze at the sight of the tableau that greeted him.

Elizabeth stood beside Arlen, adjusting her gloves, as resplendently dressed in a brilliant yellow gown as if she were taking a promenade on Oxford Street, and as radiantly beautiful. Another well-dressed gentleman was with her, a slim man whom Garrick neither knew nor recognized. And Lionel was speaking with Arlen. *Lionel.*

For one brief moment, Garrick looked at the man who claimed to be his brother and wondered if Lionel would back him up in the ensuing confrontation. Then everyone saw him. All conversation ceased as four heads turned in his direction simultaneously.

Elizabeth actually smiled at him, as if smugly pleased.

But Arlen was not smiling. He strode forward, his face a bitter, restrained mask of fury, ripping off his gloves. And he flung one glove in Garrick's face.

"I will meet you at dawn, by the ruined keep," he spat, his eyes blazing. He nodded over his shoulder at the slim gentleman standing sternly behind him. "Lord Manion is my second."

Garrick shook himself out of his shock. He had expected Arlen to demand that he hand over his wife and child—he had not expected to be challenged to a duel. How he would love to kill Arlen. Garrick smiled. But even as he smiled with a very real pleasure induced by the thought of killing Olivia's abusive husband, he knew that in all likelihood he would be the one to die. Arlen was an expert swordsman, while he had not fenced in years. "At dawn, then," Garrick said coldly. He realized that he was beginning to sweat.

Lionel came to stand beside them. "Come, my friends, surely the two of you can settle your differences more civilly?"

Elizabeth sailed forward. "A duel is very civil, my lord." She smiled at them all. "Besides, do you not think the current scandal calls for a duel? It hardly calls for a bow, an apology, and the doffing of a cap."

Lionel shrugged.

"And who shall be your second, Lord Caedmon?" Elizabeth asked Garrick quite sweetly. Laughter tinged her tone.

Garrick met her gaze, well aware that she was enjoying herself—undoubtedly envisioning her brother running him through, as she had wanted Arlen to do for eleven long years. He did not answer, because Lionel said, "I shall second my brother."

"Christ." Garrick looked at Lionel, whom he trusted even less than he trusted Arlen.

"Do you have a choice?" Lionel asked, his blue gaze holding his.

"Perhaps you should ask him if he has the courage to actually meet me at dawn," Arlen said with a harsh laugh. He glanced up at the manor, above Garrick's head. Garrick turned in time to see Olivia's face disappearing from the window. He grimaced.

Arlen turned abruptly. "Come, Elizabeth. Manion." The trio returned to the town coach, a footman closing the door after they had all clambered in. Garrick did not move, nor did Lionel, as the coach rolled away, followed by the other vehicle, which, Garrick saw, contained two burly manservants. He suspected it was intended for use by Olivia and Hannah. The servants were probably to be her prison guards.

He felt ill.

Elizabeth smiled at them from the carriage window and wiggled her gloved fingers.

Restraining his temper, Garrick glanced at Lionel and saw him smile at her. He knew he was flushed. "God damn it," he said.

Lionel patted his arm. Garrick was too distraught to shove him off. His so-called brother said, "So tell me, when was the last time you fenced, and are you any better at it than when we were boys?''

Garrick, about to stomp into the house and pour himself a stiff drink, wheeled back around. ''I haven't fenced in at least ten years, and undoubtedly I am far worse with a rapier now than I was as a boy.''

Lionel nodded. ''I suppose some prayers are in order, then.''

He had had it. ''Your prayers I can do without.'' He stormed into the house.

Olivia leapt to her feet from the four-poster bed, where she sat with her arm around Hannah, tears in her eyes, her face a ghostly shade of white. ''I heard! Arlen fences with a master four times a week! You cannot do this!''

''Did you pack?'' he demanded. His head throbbed. He must face Arlen, of course. But was there a way to survive the encounter?

''Pack?'' Her tone was incredulous, as if he had just asked her to stand on the top of her head.

He was jolted out of his thoughts by her tone. ''I am driving you to Fowey myself.''

Olivia ran forward; Hannah remained on the bed, listening wide-eyed and intently to their every word. ''I am not going anywhere! He will kill you!''

''I can manage a rapier very well,'' Garrick lied.

''Oh, so you practiced such a sport on Barbados? Don't lie to me now, Garrick De Vere!'' Olivia shouted.

He caught her wrist. ''Olivia, calm yourself. You have Hannah to think of now.''

She crumpled against him as he held her wrist. ''If we leave, you must leave with us. I won't leave you here, for him to murder,'' she sobbed.

He shook her once. ''I am not a coward. If Arlen kills me, so be it.'' He did not know where this sudden sense of honor had come from. ''But I do intend to protect you from him, and that means you leave Cornwall this instant.''

She wrenched her arm free of his grip. ''*No!*'' It was a scream. ''I am not leaving. Not unless you come with us!''

He stared in disbelief. "Why can't you understand? I cannot run away with my tail between my legs, not now, not like this—not from him."

She blinked at him through her tears. "Now is not the time for sudden pride, damn it!"

"What the hell does that mean?" But he knew.

"It means you ran away ten years ago, and have been running ever since—but now you choose to stand and fight? And what will I do when you are buried in the cold, wet ground?"

He seized her hand as she turned away, whipping her back around. Her words hurt as much as any future thrust of Arlen's blade, but then, the truth could so easily be brutal. He could not dwell on it now. "Tell me what you see." His skin was crawling. "Do you see my death?"

"I don't see anything," she gasped. "I can't see anything now. I am in a state of terror. I love you so! I cannot bear to see you die—and all because of me."

He thought she spoke the truth about not having seen his death. He pulled her into his embrace, held her hard against his heart, which beat furiously. "Please try to understand. Please try to cooperate. I may die. But you can be free. You and Hannah. Let me take you to Fowey." He closed his eyes, aware of the timeless fact that her body, held like this against his, did far more than fit perfectly. It felt absolutely right. "But you will not wait for me in Calais. It is far too obvious."

"No," she whispered against his chest. "No, Garrick, I cannot leave you, not like this." She began to cry again.

He felt tears trickling down his own face, because he thought it likely that he would die at dawn tomorrow. He could not outduel Arlen. And he did not need Olivia to tell him what he had known from the start, that Arlen wanted to kill him. Arlen had wanted to kill him eleven years ago. Nothing had changed since then. If anything, the passions had only intensified.

"I love you, too," he whispered against her hair. "But if I die, I do not want you to remain a prisoner for the rest of your life. Let me free you, Olivia. Let me free you and Hannah.''

She continued to cry, shaking her head, murmuring that she could not go. He stroked her hair and her back, finally realizing that Hannah also cried but silently, on the bed. Immediately he brought Olivia there, reaching with one arm for the child. ''Hannah,'' he said, ''everything will be all right.'' He released Olivia to wipe his own eyes with his knuckles.

Olivia broke away from him to hug her daughter. ''Don't cry,'' she said urgently. ''Don't cry. Tell me what you see.''

Hannah nodded, wiping her eyes. ''Blood, Mama. So much blood.'' Her tone quavered and was terribly high.

''What else do you see?'' Olivia demanded, on her knees, gripping her daughter's hands.

Hannah faced her sightlessly, her expression strained and intense.

''Hannah! Please!''

When the blind child did not speak, Garrick said grimly, ''Maybe we do not want to know the future, Olivia.''

Olivia looked at him in panic, but he saw the sheer will in her eyes. ''Hannah!''

''Mama—'' Hannah burst into tears. ''I cannot see. Only blood. I am sorry. I am too afraid, just like you.'' She wept.

''Oh, God,'' Olivia whispered. ''What am I doing?'' She crushed her daughter to her breasts, rocking her. ''What have I done?''

But Garrick was asking himself the same question, turning away from them both.

Dawn. It was cold and wet and angry, a sharp wind gusting, a mist in the air. The keep was shrouded by fog, as were the two Ashburn vehicles. Garrick and Lionel drove the carriage that Garrick had brought to Cornwall with Olivia, and they sat on the front seat side by side. Garrick halted the mares, braking the vehicle. As he did so, he watched the door to the town coach opening, Arlen, Lord Manion, and Elizabeth stepping out. The ground was muddy, and even from this short distance he could hear it squishing beneath their feet.

He felt detached. He had not slept at all last night, furious with Olivia for refusing to leave, furious with himself for ever touching her in the first place and bringing this all down upon them, hating Arlen, wanting to kill him, knowing he would not. There had been fear, too; he was not ready to die. But now, in the cold light of dawn, he felt oddly detached. There was no fear. There was nothing but regrets.

"Here. Maybe this will help," Lionel said, handing him a silver flask.

Garrick shook his head.

"Garrick. Contrary to what you think, I do not want you to die," Lionel said, taking a long draught himself. "I was up all night. Damn it. You were rotten with a sword as a boy. I do not want you to die!"

Garrick turned to look at him, aware that Elizabeth, Manion, and Arlen were staring in their direction. Both Elizabeth and Arlen had dressed for the occasion, Arlen in a peacock green frock coat, Elizabeth in a stunning turquoise ensemble with matching hat and black veil. Did she mourn his passing already?

Garrick regarded Lionel. His eyes flashed with anger, and Garrick shivered, seized now with the certainty that Lionel was telling the truth. But that was impossible. "I expect you to dance upon my grave," he said flatly.

"I will do no such thing! I am your brother, God damn it!" Lionel's voice was raised.

"You are not my brother," Garrick retorted, unable to keep his own tone down. But he stared, feeling ill. Was he wrong? He could swear that Lionel's concern was genuine.

"I am your brother," Lionel said, softly now, his gaze holding Garrick's.

Garrick turned away, disturbed. He jumped out of the carriage and almost fell in the mud but he righted himself, shoving aside his confusion and thoughts about Lionel. He stared down at the sloppy ground. The mud might kill him, or it might work in his favor.

Lionel also leapt down, but he did not lose his balance. "I sent a messenger to Father last night. He should know what is happening."

"He will also dance on my grave," Garrick said grimly.

"No," Lionel said. "You are his son. In spite of his ways, he loves you."

Garrick flinched, meeting Lionel's gaze. Lionel finally smiled, very slightly, and touched his shoulder, the gesture encouraging.

Manion was approaching, holding two rapiers. "My lords," he said, bowing.

Garrick bowed curtly. He inspected both weapons and chose one. Manion turned with another bow to bring the remaining sword to Arlen.

That was when Garrick became aware that something was wrong. He paused, uneasy, uncertain of what was now happening. The hairs on his nape prickled and he turned, not quite sure what to expect. And rushing up the muddy road was Olivia, on foot, holding Hannah's hand, the pair fighting the wind in their long, hooded cloaks. The setter was with them.

Garrick cursed. He shifted in order to see Arlen staring down the road at his wife and child. Arlen's gaze wavered, and he nodded at Garrick. "Let's get this over with. I did not think you would show, Caedmon."

"You thought wrong," Garrick said grimly, trying to put Olivia out of his mind. To Lionel he muttered, "Keep her out of this."

"My lords, ready yourselves," Manion was saying.

But Garrick really didn't hear him. Olivia was shouting, trying to be heard over the wind. "Arlen, please! I beg you! Do not do this!"

Garrick met her frantic gaze, but only briefly, because she was beseeching her husband. "Arlen! I will come home—"

"Lady Ashburn," Arlen said coldly, cutting her off, "it is a little late for regret. I shall deal with you later. After I have disposed of your lover."

Lionel took Olivia's arm, clearly sustaining her weight

while preventing her from running forward. "Please, Lady Ashburn, your interference now will not help anyone. You are only a distraction. Especially for my brother."

Tears streaked Olivia's face as she slumped against Lionel. Garrick turned away. His gaze met Arlen's, and he felt the other man's sizzling hatred. It was more than tangible, it was a heated, seething energy coiling about them both. But his own hatred was equally fervent. This man would imprison Olivia and Hannah if he could, in more ways than one.

He could not die. He could not let Olivia and Hannah be returned to this man's possession.

"My lords, you may begin," Manion cried.

Arlen smiled, advancing, sword held in a classic position. Garrick readied himself.

Arlen struck, clearly intending to deliver a fatal blow with the first thrust. Garrick managed to deflect it, and their swords locked, ringing loudly in the early morning air. The two men disengaged. Arlen lunged again. Garrick managed to lock swords with him a second time, but suddenly Arlen's blade was beneath his, and he felt the point ripping through his clothing and his side. He stepped back, panting, a shocking pain lancing through him. He glanced down and saw a bright red blossom of blood appearing on his clothes, spreading rapidly.

Olivia screamed.

Garrick stared at himself. He had not expected a wound so soon.

"I like the smell of your blood, Caedmon," Arlen taunted him, driving forward with a series of thrusts.

Their blades rang. Garrick did not know how he responded, crossing swords again and again, because Arlen was fast and deft and knew exactly what he was doing. Garrick was being driven backward. He knew he continued to bleed; he was growing dizzy. Arlen kept slicing Garrick's blade with his own, advancing ceaselessly. Garrick knew he intended to drive the sword from his hand. Then he felt Arlen's blade slicing across the top of his knuckles.

And in spite of his intense determination not to drop his sword, the blade fell from his hand.

Arlen shouted, triumphant, surging forward to deliver a blow to Garrick's heart. Garrick's spine hit the wall of the keep. He could retreat no more.

"Touché." Arlen smiled, poised to thrust forward.

"Arlen, no!" Olivia shouted.

From the corner of his eye, Garrick saw Lionel wrestling with her, locking her in his arms to prevent her from running to them. Hannah cowered behind them. The setter was barking.

Arlen moved. Garrick faced him. He saw him lunge and waited for that one terrible instant when Arlen's blade would rip into his heart.

But it never came.

Time seemed to slow as Arlen stepped forward, thrust his sword toward Garrick's chest . . . and tripped. And then time resumed its normal pace. Arlen went sprawling face-down in the mud, but his blade remained firmly in his grasp.

Garrick realized he had stopped breathing. A deathly silence seemed to have fallen upon the heath.

Arlen looked up, murder in his eyes. He began to get up—when he cried out.

Again he slipped, onto his face, but this time his fingers opened and the sword slid through the mud, stopping a few inches away and just out of his reach.

"A deadlock!" Manion shouted, rushing forward.

Garrick had not realized that he was clutching his side with his bleeding hand, but now he became aware of his pain, and his immense relief. Dear God. He had not been run through, he was not dead. His knees buckled as he leaned against the rough wet stone of the keep, slowly sliding down it and to the ground. He was very light-headed.

"No—" Arlen spat mud, trying to rise. "Damn it, I was tripped, and someone stepped on my hand!"

Manion was helping him up. "My lord, there was no one here but you and Caedmon. You slipped, I'm afraid, and lost hold of your sword. According to a gentleman's rules, the duel is over.''

Treve was licking Garrick's face, whining. Garrick looked down. There was so much blood. He stared. His entire right side was soaked with it, and blood drenched his hand. He was not even sure that he had all of his fingers. Would he die after all?

''Garrick?''

He glanced up at Olivia. Tears streaming down her face, she rushed across the muddy heath, stumbling as she raced toward him.

If he was dying, he needed her now. He needed her desperately, had never needed anyone more. His love knew no bounds. He had to tell her good-bye.

Suddenly Arlen was there, intercepting her. His body barred her way.

''Let me go to him!'' she screamed, pushing at his chest with both hands.

He seized her wrists. ''Get in my coach, Olivia. We are going home.''

''I cannot. Let me go! Damn you!''

Arlen threw his arm around her. ''Get Hannah,'' he snapped to his sister.

Garrick's world was fading in and out of sight. Treve continued to whine. It kept growing darker, and he knew that he fought unconsciousness. No, he wanted to say. Get your filthy hands off her. But he did not have the ability to speak. Olivia, he tried. I love you.

''Garrick is hurt,'' Olivia panted, trying to break free of Arlen. ''Is he dying? Oh, God, if you have murdered him, I will never forgive you!'' she shouted.

Garrick somehow managed to open his exceedingly heavy lids, which felt as if they were weighted down with stones, in time to see Arlen dragging Olivia to the empty coach. He actually pushed her up and inside. Elizabeth handed up Hannah. The two burly male servants climbed in after them and the door was closed.

But Olivia clung to the door, her face in the window. ''Garrick!'' she screamed.

How lucid his mind was. He wanted to tell her that he was all right, lie that it was, in order to reassure her. He wanted to tell her that he would love her forever, but he knew now that he could not, and would not be able to. He was filled with an odd knowledge, too. Death was intent upon claiming him, but he would see her again. If only he could tell her that. He watched her coach roll away, its image blurred and distorted. He closed his eyes. The blackness was welcome.

A very final silence fell.

And then he opened his eyes. Staring, he continued to watch the coach departing, but it was very strange, because he was looking down now, on the coach, and even on the keep. In fact, he could see his bloody, inert body crumpled there at the foot of the ruins.

The silence felt eternal. But then it was broken. "Garrick?"

The voice came from very close by. It sounded as if it were in his left ear. There was blackness again, and he fought it. This time, when he opened his eyes, the coach and keep were gone. "You cannot die. It is not your time. You cannot go."

Garrick's eyes closed. His body felt weightless, he felt as if he were floating. And he was aware of his heart, pumping the blood now, hard, with vast difficulty, through his body and his veins.

"Go back," Lionel said.

Garrick blinked, fighting to see. His vision was blurred, filled with spots and shadows and darkness. And he was filled with surprise. "Lionel?" he whispered, thinking, This is a dream. Either that, or I am already dead.

His thirteen-year-old brother smiled at him.

And the blackness came again.

CHAPTER TWENTY-THREE

The pain was immense. There was never real oblivion, in spite of the unconsciousness he slid in and out of repeatedly. The pain always remained, hellfire.

Olivia. Hannah. He had to help them. Her cries filled his tortured mind.

"Garrick?"

The blackness was enfolding itself over him again, in dizzying, nauseating, throbbing waves. He did not want to fight it. There was less pain when he slept. It was as close to peace as he could get.

But there was a reason why he must not sleep. A reason. He struggled to remember it.

"Garrick." The voice was harder, less kind, and far more insistent now.

Lionel. Lionel was here, the man claiming to be his brother, a man who might be a pretender, a fraud, a thief. That was the reason he must not sleep, must not be vulnerable, must not die. Or was it? Garrick tried to ward off the blackness with a huge effort. He began to sweat. He wanted to vomit; his insides curdled and heaved. He knew he must focus, he must think. It was a matter of survival; lives were at stake.

Then Lionel's handsome face was swimming before his eyes, coming in and out of focus. His cheekbones and jaw

danced and wavered in and out of his vision. His blue eyes
lightened and darkened and lightened again.

"Can you hear me?" Lionel asked. "Thank God you are
alive!"

Garrick did not even try to answer. He did not think he
could speak, in any case. Olivia. Was she all right? Arlen
had her now. She was Arlen's prisoner, she and Hannah.
That was the reason he must awaken, must get up. Olivia
and Hannah needed him—they were in jeopardy.

And rage filled him, in spite of the pain, making it worse.

"Surely you are not trying to get up?" A hand pressed
on his right shoulder, the uninjured side of his body. It felt
hard, ungentle. "You must rest. I do believe you have been
at Death's door," Lionel said, his visage still blurry. He
smiled. Garrick felt his palm on his forehead for an instant.
In spite of the horrific pain that seared the entire left side
of his body, anger continued to consume him. Suddenly he
was aware of just how helpless he was. If Lionel were an
impostor, then he hardly wished him well.

"It is probably a miracle that you have lived. You lost
so much blood. I want you to know that I have done everything I could to save you." Lionel smiled. "I have sat here
with you all night, Garrick. I did send for a physician. I
imagine a good doctor should be here at any moment."

Garrick took one last look at the man calling himself
Lionel before closing his eyes, doubting his every word.
Even if he were Lionel, no love remained between them.
Had he sent for a physician? Or was he sitting at his bedside
wishing him dead?

He recalled the duel. Lionel had been his second, Lionel
had seemed genuinely concerned for his welfare. Arlen had
run him through. It was a miracle that he still lived. Or was
it? Had he seen the ghost of his real brother, still thirteen
years of age?

It had been so real. But he had been close to death, so
very close, for he had lost a tremendous amount of blood,
he had been dizzy and barely conscious, and perhaps he
had imagined the encounter. That is what a sane person
would think. Garrick felt tears burning the backs of his

closed eyelids. He did not know what to think.

Lionel was staring at him, unsmiling. But the moment he realized Garrick was returning his regard, he smiled back. "Here," he said, holding out a glass. "Drink this. The little I do know is that you need water and other fluids. This happens to be broth. I did hire a servant after all."

Garrick reached out, but not to take the glass. What if the broth were poisoned? He struck it from Lionel's hand. "Get out."

STANHOPE HALL

If he died, dear God, she would be free.

Susan stood with her father in the pebbled driveway as the huge black town coach halted in front of the house. She clasped her gloved hands tightly, finding it difficult to breathe. Her thoughts were terrible, truly sinful, deserving hell.

Lionel alighted first. Seeing him, Susan found it difficult to breathe and her urge to weep instantly passed. She had never seen anyone more spectacular, more devastating, more resplendent and noble. Clad in a dark green frock coat and pale blue breeches with white stockings, sans peruke, he glanced her way with a slight smile. She sniffed, using a hankie, forgetting her terrible thoughts, smiling back.

The earl and countess had also clambered out, followed by a darkly clad man carrying a physician's black satchel. Sir John gripped her elbow, and as Garrick De Vere was carried by servants from the coach to the house, she was led forward. "My lord, my lady," Sir John intoned gravely. "We came as soon as we heard. We wish to offer condolences."

The countess, almost as white as her injured son, burst into tears, and ran after the two servants who were carrying him inside. Susan stared after them, feeling terrible now. Garrick had been unconscious, his head lolling, his coloring gray. Clearly he had been severely wounded. Then she glanced up and found Lionel regarding her. Her pulse raced.

The earl bowed, his expression bleak, grim. "Thank you, Sir John. If you will excuse me?" And he strode after his wife, disappearing through the Hall's front doors.

Susan and her father were left alone with Lionel. The two men bowed. "We do appreciate your concern," Lionel said, and then he faced Susan with another bow. She was certain that his blue eyes, holding hers, held a special message in them, for her alone. She smiled back, her heart fluttering wildly.

"How is he?" Sir John asked pointedly.

"Dr. McCaulkin says he will live, a true miracle, for he lost much blood."

Sir John stared. "I am glad," he said gruffly. "You were there?"

Lionel nodded. "I arrived early the day before the duel. Arlen arrived perhaps an hour after I did."

Susan felt herself flushing. She knew the story; everyone did. Arlen had challenged Garrick De Vere to a duel. Apparently Ashburn had been convinced that Olivia was having a liaison with Garrick. Susan knew it was not true. Susan knew her good friend would not do that to her. She knew there was an explanation as to why Olivia and Hannah had been at Caedmon Crag.

"Well, let us go inside," her father said.

Susan found Lionel gazing at her, and his gaze was mesmerizing.

"Susan? Are you coming?" Sir John asked from the Hall's front steps, staring at them.

"In a moment, Papa," Susan said hesitantly. Sir John left, and Susan turned to Lionel, only to find his warm gaze sliding over her in a way that thrilled her.

"This is a wonderful surprise," he said softly.

"Papa insisted we come." She remembered why they had came, and her face fell. "Because he is my fiancé. Oh, my lord! I cannot marry him!" she wailed.

"Come," he said, his hand under her elbow, and they walked around the side of the house, then began strolling across the green lawns. Susan remained thrilled, forgetting about her extremely ill fiancé. When they were safely out of earshot of the house, standing now not far from the gazebo, shaded by a trio of oak trees, Lionel let her go. Susan was disappointed. He said, "Miss Layton. May I be so bold as to address you as Susan?"

Her heart leapt. She trembled. "That would be wonderful, my lord."

"Then you must call me Lionel," he said, his gaze searching her face. His expression was intent now, he no longer smiled.

"I should be pleased to do so . . . Lionel," she said as demurely as she could.

"I know this match between yourself and my brother is no love affair, but truly, Susan, he is not a bad or evil person," he said soothingly. "He has merely lived on that savage isle far too long."

This was not what Susan wanted to discuss. She was silent, dismayed, and at a loss.

"A woman like yourself will fix up his ill manners, supply the polish, so to speak, in no time at all—if that is what you are worried about."

Susan looked down at her hands, clasped in front of her now. She remained silent. "I do not think he will ever change," she whispered. "Besides . . ." She trailed off.

"Susan," he whispered, and his fingertips touched her chin. "Tell me what you are thinking."

It was like a jolt of lightning, streaking through her entire body. Susan looked up, incapable of breathing. Did she dare speak? She hesitated.

"Perhaps it is my brother's . . . er . . . dueling . . . which has so distressed you," Lionel said.

"No." She was afraid to speak her mind when her heart begged her to do so.

"Unfortunately he had no choice but to accept Ashburn's challenge."

"I do not care about that," she said seriously, unable to look away from him.

"You do not care that your fiancé was accused of carrying on with the countess of Ashburn?" Lionel was incredulous.

"I do not love Garrick De Vere. Actually, I should be happy if his heart lay elsewhere. But everyone is wrong about the countess. Lady Ashburn is my dear friend. She only feels compassion for Garrick, she has said so numerous times." Susan smiled.

But Lionel was not smiling, nor did he return her smile, he was very grave.

"Is something wrong, my . . . er . . . Lionel?" Susan whispered with some trepidation.

He touched her wrist briefly. "I am sorry. I did not realize you and the countess were so close." Anger sparked his eyes.

"I do not understand," Susan said slowly. "Is there something you are not telling me?"

"I am glad you do not believe the gossip," he finally said.

Now she was alarmed. "My lord—I mean, Lionel, surely you do not believe the rumors?"

He did not answer her, but his expression was filled with pity.

And Susan thought of the kindest woman she had ever met, the most genuine, the most sincere, the dear, dear countess, and something sickened and lurched inside of her. Had Olivia lied to her, time and again? But Olivia was the kindest, most sincere person she had ever met! It was not possible. "Do not tell me that you think Garrick and the countess were involved," she said thickly.

After a fatal pause he said, "My dear, sweet Susan, I saw them together. Clearly the countess feels far more for my brother than mere compassion."

Susan stared in shock. "No."

"I'm sorry to be the one to tell you."

Tears filled her eyes. "No," she said thickly. "I am glad it was you." But the hurting inside her was awful, and it had nothing to do with Garrick. How could Olivia lie to her? Why hadn't she told her the truth?

His eyes fixed on hers. "A beautiful woman like you could do better, I am afraid, than my brother. Suddenly I am angry, Susan, for you. I am angry at them both."

Briefly she forgot the pain of betrayal. She wet her lips. Wondering if she should truly blurt out what was on her mind. "I wish to do better," she said softly.

"Do you?" he whispered, suddenly taking her palm in his and squeezing it gently.

"The real reason I cannot marry him is ... he is your brother." There, she had said it, dear Lord.

He stared. It was a moment before he spoke, and he did not drop her hand. "Yes. He is my brother, and if you marry him, that will make you my sister."

She almost burst into tears. Instead she felt them interfering with her vision. She nodded.

"I am not happy about that, either," he said harshly.

The tears stopped, and Susan blinked. "Lionel," she whispered. Did he truly feel as she did? Were they forming an understanding?

Suddenly he lifted her hand and kissed it, firmly, through the delicate leather of her lambskin glove. Susan's knees buckled. Her body throbbed. He said, "Susan, would you meet me in the gazebo later? I think there is much we should discuss."

She could hardly believe her ears. Meet him in the gazebo ... of course she should. "Yes," she croaked.

"After supper. After everyone has retired for the night. I'll go first. I'll light a candle. When you see it, you'll know the way is clear, and you should come," Lionel said urgently and low.

Susan nodded, at once stunned and thrilled. It was so romantic, and it was like a dream coming true—this knight in shining armor was clearly in love with her, too. "Yes," she said, smiling. "Yes, Lionel."

Garrick realized that he was at Stanhope Hall. He stared up at the ceiling in his bedroom. Jesus. He felt good enough, he realized, to try to sit up. The pain had dimmed to an unpleasant, incessant ache. Thank God the worst was over.

"What are you doing?" his mother cried from the doorway.

Garrick hadn't realized how hard it would be to raise his

upper body and shift himself so he was sitting up in the big four-poster bed. He collapsed against the gold pillows, sweating. "Mother," he said.

She ran forward to embrace him. "I would have called servants," she choked, attempting not to cry.

"Please do not weep," he said. "I am much better. Christ. I vaguely remember now. Lionel. The doctor. And you. You came to Caedmon Crag." He knew how hard that must have been for her.

She sat beside him on the bed, gripping his right hand. His left arm was in a sling. His entire torso was bandaged as well. "Yes, we came to Caedmon Crag, your father and I."

He stared, realizing in that instant what that meant.

"Garrick, I have thanked God every day in the chapel that you did not die! Ashburn wanted to kill you—and he almost did, from what I have heard!"

"Olivia." He realized he had spoken aloud. His worry knew no bounds. Where was she? How was she? He had to find out. He realized that he was leaning forward, trying to move one leg off the bed. Pain racked his side—no longer dull or dim.

He clutched himself with his one good hand, panting and crying out grimly.

"What are you doing?" Eleanor cried again. "You cannot get up!" She was horrified. "Dr. McCaulkin said bed rest for a fortnight."

"Olivia! Is she all right?" he demanded.

"Garrick, you are not getting up, and I am sure she is fine," the countess said. "Why wouldn't she be? She is not the first woman . . ." She stopped.

"She is not the first woman to what?" Garrick asked, sinking back against the pillows, hardly comforted by his mother's words.

"She is not the first woman to be caught with her lover," Eleanor said boldly.

But other women did not have husbands like Ashburn, and was that censure he caught in his mother's tone? He was weak, and in pain again, too much so to stand up, much less ride to Ashburn Hall. Yet she was in jeopardy, he was certain, and if anything happened to her, he could not forgive himself. He was alive—and he must protect her. "Where is she? And where is her daughter?" He could not stand being helpless like this.

"I assume they are at Ashburnham," Eleanor said.

"Someone is feeling better, I see," a familiar voice said from the doorway.

Garrick stiffened and turned his head, to see Lionel leaning against the doorjamb in a royal blue velvet frock coat and gold breeches. Lionel came forward, smiling. "I am so glad," he said—as if he meant it.

Garrick stared, in that first moment of true coherence recalling everything—the duel, the morning before when Lionel had walked in upon him and Olivia, a witness to their affair, and all of his suspicions. He stared.

"Is this my greeting?" Lionel joked, kissing Eleanor's cheek. "Good morning. Mother. I must say, supper was superb last night."

Garrick wished he had not walked in, especially not while they were discussing Olivia. He was quite sure his feelings had been far too obvious.

"Thank you, dear," Eleanor said distractedly.

"You are ravishing this morning, too. I see a good night's sleep has done wonders for you, as it has done for my brother." Lionel was jovial.

Garrick continued to stare. "You are in a fine mood," he suddenly said. "I would think it to be the opposite."

Lionel's brow furrowed. "Now why should I be grim?"

"Because I am not ailing."

Lionel no longer smiled. "I am glad you are on the mend, Garrick. Have I not proven my sincerity? I was your second at the duel. I cared for you for almost an entire day when you lay close to death before the physician came. Good God, what else must I do?"

"As far as I am concerned, you have not proven yourself," Garrick said, fists clenched. He felt his cheeks heating with his anger.

"Dear, don't do this," Eleanor whispered, cupping his

cheek. "You are not well yet. Please, a temper will not help you to heal."

Lionel stared, eyes hard. "I cannot believe you, truthfully I cannot. But then, you always had a chip on your shoulder the size of a mountain, ever since we were boys. Am I not right, Mother?"

Eleanor blinked at him. "I do not want the two of you arguing now," she said, her bosom heaving with her distress.

"Why don't you leave?" Garrick gritted, but as always when Lionel suddenly made statements that rang eerily true, he was taken aback and suddenly doubting himself.

"Mother is right, we should not fight," Lionel said, his tone changing. "The countess is at Ashburnham."

Garrick froze.

Lionel smiled. "It is common knowledge."

Garrick desperately wanted to ask if Hannah was also there, but he could not. He could only stare.

Lionel said, "You know, I have a grand idea. Why don't I call on her in your stead? I am more than happy to convey a message for you, Garrick."

His temper rose red hot again, in that instant. His smile was more a wolfish baring of his teeth, and he knew it. "I don't need a message bearer," he said.

"Well, at the least, I can tell her you are well on the mend," Lionel said cheerfully. He paused at the door. "Being as she is as concerned for your welfare." He bowed and left.

Silence fell. Garrick stared after his jauntily departing form, thinking of him at Ashburnham, while he, Garrick, remained weak and helpless and confined to a bed at Stanhope Hall. *Damn it.*

"Garrick, please. Do not allow yourself to get so upset," his mother said softly.

He met her worried gaze. "I cannot help it. Olivia is in the hands of a cruel man, Mother."

"The countess is his *wife.*"

His jaw flexed. His temples throbbed. The ache was worse now in his side, just when it had begun to diminish.

Eleanor forced a brighter smile on her face. "What is important is that you are getting better, that you are alive."

That was important, but only so he could protect Olivia and find out the truth about Lionel. "My instincts tell me that he is an impostor."

"What?" Eleanor paled.

Garrick attempted to sit up straighter. When Eleanor reached behind him to fuss with his pillows, he restrained her. "Stop. Please. Listen to me."

Her chest rose and fell too rapidly. "Please, Garrick," she whispered.

He caught her hand with his left palm. "Mother. I am well aware of the fact that this man looks like you and Father, and that he knows so much about all of us. But what do you really think? How can you not know the truth?"

She stared. "What makes you so certain? What have you found out?"

He thought her words strange but dismissed them. "I want to know how you feel," Garrick said.

Her eyes widened; she dropped her hand and stepped back. "How I feel?" she asked tremulously.

"He is your son! That is, if he truly is Lionel. If anyone must sense the truth, it is you!" Garrick quite shouted.

Her face crumpled. "I don't know. Dear Lord, I do not know what to think!"

He watched her pace away, covering her face with her hands, and he was seized with an inkling. "What are you hiding?" he cried.

She shook her head. Tears formed in her eyes.

"Mother?" His heart pounded now, adding to his general misery. For he sensed now he knew not what—and was filled with dread.

"I don't know," Eleanor said, looking up. "I don't know," she repeated. She paused. "Lionel is not my son. I am not his mother," she said.

CHAPTER TWENTY-FOUR

I beg your pardon?'' Garrick said, certain that he had mis-heard.

Slowly Eleanor turned away from him. She stared out the bedroom windows at the misty morning landscape. ''Your father would kill me if he knew I was telling you this.''

He had not misheard. Worse, he thought his mother spoke literally. Garrick leaned forward, one fist clenched, holding the sheets. ''You are not Lionel's mother?'' he gasped.

The countess faced him, her face pale, her eyes tear filled, her expression dismal, glum. ''Lionel was six months old when I married your father, Garrick. But I raised him as if he were my own son.''

Garrick was speechless, in shock. It was a full moment before he could speak. ''This is preposterous. The whole world must know. Who is Lionel's real mother?''

''She was the twelfth countess of Stanhope, your father's first wife,'' Eleanor said.

He was stunned anew. ''I have grown up believing you to be Father's only wife! I did not know he was married before you! How could such a secret be kept? And why?''

She shook her head, a tear slipping down one cheek. ''When I arrived as a bride at Stanhope Hall, the entire staff was new. And the village had been moved. At the time I did not think much of it. So many families have moved the local village, or parts of it, when they decide to rebuild their homes. I assumed Carston had been moved for the very same reason, because it interfered with the views or some such nonsense. But . . ." She paused, her tone throaty.

Garrick wanted to get out of bed but remained in too much anguish now to do so. His temples throbbed in unison with his side. The pain in his head was splitting. "To keep his first marriage a secret, he got rid of the original staff here at the Hall, and he moved the village. I am stunned. I must assume he sent some knowledgeable villagers away— but why? Why would someone go to such lengths? Did not the entire aristocracy know of this marriage?"

"I don't know. I don't know why he acted as he did, but I do not think his peers ever knew he wed Meg Mac-Donald."

"Meg MacDonald?!"

His mother nodded. "She was a MacDonald. Her family were northern Scots. Highlanders. Perhaps your father was afraid of retribution. I do not know."

"She was a Scot! What retribution? Why would there be retribution?" Garrick asked sharply.

Eleanor finally looked him in the eye, her back now to the shrouded drive and lawns. "I am assuming they were against the marriage. After all, the Scottish people are as fond of us as we are of them."

"My father secretly married a Highland woman," Garrick muttered. "Why would he do such a thing? Did he marry for love?" But even as he spoke, he knew it could not be true.

"Do not even ask me how a Highland lass met your father. He never told me anything. I never dared to ask."

"So you know nothing."

She hesitated.

"Well?" he demanded.

"I know that Margaret MacDonald was very pregnant when they wed. In one of her final months. I gathered that much."

He had been forced to marry her, it was the obvious conclusion. But Garrick could not imagine his father, then the earl of Stanhope, being forced to marry anyone—unless it was with a saber held to his throat. No, he amended, unless there had been a dirk held to his throat. "How did she die?" he finally asked.

His mother hesitated.

"Mother?"

Eleanor finally met his gaze. "She killed herself," she said. "By throwing herself out of the attic window."

"My lord, I am very sorry to interrupt, but we must speak," Sir John Layton said, flushed.

The earl of Stanhope looked up and spied the big-boned knight standing in the doorway of his library, his wig slipping, one ruffled cuff dangling out of one crimson coat sleeve, the other somehow tucked inside. He snapped shut the ledgers he had been working upon. He had far graver matters on his mind now than estate accounts, by damn. "Please, do come in, Sir John." He stood up as Sir John bowed.

When the robust knight entered the room, Stanhope saw that his pallid blond daughter trailed behind him, her eyes and nose red from a recent fit of weeping. Her tears had splotched upon her pale blue-and-white sprigged gown. Immediately he sighed, growing grim. Now he knew the subject about to be raised, the forthcoming nuptials, and he had not changed his mind.

His heart lurched. Garrick had almost died. The fool. The idiot. To duel with Ashburn when he was no match for the man. But thank God there had been a miracle in this life of bitter, harsh realities. Thank God his son was alive.

"I am afraid I must be blunt," Sir John said.

"Do sit down," the earl responded.

"I prefer to stand."

"I think I shall shut the door," the earl began, moving from behind his desk.

"Do not bother," Sir John replied sharply, freezing Stanhope in his tracks.

Slowly Stanhope turned. "Is there a problem, John?" he asked in his friendliest tone.

Sir John turned and dragged Susan forward. Susan now sobbed into an embroidered handkerchief. Stanhope was annoyed. "My daughter," Sir John said, "has been seduced by your son."

He was taken aback, but he hid his surprise. "Then we shall have to move the date of the nuptials forward."

"No." The single word was thunderous. Sir John had become red in the face. He raised his hand, his forefinger extended, shaking it. His entire body was shaking. "Your eldest son. Lionel. He seduced my daughter, by damn, and I expect him to marry her!"

Stanhope recoiled, eyes wide. But a moment later he had recovered from his surprise. He should have known. Calmly he asked, "Do you truly expect me to believe this . . . this . . . plot of yours to disengage your daughter from Garrick so she might wed Lionel?"

"This is not a plot. The bastard took her last night. Susan came to me this morning." Sir John grabbed her arm and dragged her forward another step. "Did Lionel De Vere seduce you or not last evening?"

Her mouth opened and no words came out.

"Susan!" Sir John barked.

Susan collapsed into a chair, sobbing hysterically into her hands.

Stanhope folded his arms across his tan waistcoat and eyed her dispassionately. "Theatrics do not move me. Nor do hysterics."

Sir John stepped in front of him, his posture ominous. "My daughter was innocent until your son—your older son—got his hands on her last night in the gazebo. She does not lie, Stanhope."

Stanhope stared at Sir John, then walked to the door and waylaid a passing servant. "Find Lord Lionel and tell him his presence is sought immediately in the library," he said.

Susan gasped, looking up. "Oh no!" she cried.

"Oh, yes," Stanhope replied grimly.

The ticking of the huge pendulum clock in one corner

of the room could now be heard as Susan abruptly ceased her violent crying, as Sir John and the earl waited for Lionel. Suddenly he was strolling into the room, an easy smile upon his pleasing features. But he took one look at everyone and his smile faded. "Good morning. What is amiss here?" He added, "Is Miss Layton ill?"

Susan, who was staring at him with wide, starry, hopeful eyes, immediately burst into tears all over again. And Sir John cried out, striding forward, his intentions clearly violent. Stanhope stepped between him and his son.

"You will marry her," Sir John cried as Stanhope blocked his path.

"I will marry whom?" Lionel asked with consternation.

Susan gasped and hiccuped on her sobs.

"My daughter!" Sir John shouted.

"Calm yourself," the earl snapped, and he faced Lionel. "Miss Layton claims to have been seduced by you last night. Is it true?"

"No." Lionel's reply was flat and immediate.

Susan ceased weeping, staring at him in sheer, nearly comical disbelief.

He looked at her. "Dear Miss Layton. I hardly seduced you."

Susan's eyes remained wide and stunned, her shoulders shaking visibly, her small bosom heaving. She was incapable of speech, even when prompted by her father.

Stanhope and Sir John turned toward Lionel.

"I see there has been a misunderstanding," Lionel said easily enough. "I did meet Miss Layton last night in the gazebo. She has made her feelings for me very clear in the past two weeks since we first met. But I am afraid I rebuffed her advances, gentlemen. She is affianced to my brother, dear God. I am sorry, Miss Layton, to have to say this," he added in a kinder tone.

Susan was standing now, her mouth hanging open.

"He is an incredible liar!" Sir John exclaimed. "My daughter might have fallen in love with him, but she would never put herself forward indelicately, not ever!"

"I am afraid we have reached an impasse, Sir John,"

the earl said firmly. "As I said earlier, this plot of yours will not work."

Sir John stared at Stanhope, his face now turning purple.

"Papa," Susan whispered in alarm—her first spoken word during the interview.

He waved at her dismissively, staring coldly at Stanhope. "The engagement is off," he said. "I am breaking it now. And I shall tell the whole world of the perfidy of your family, by God! Susan, come."

Unable to take her eyes off Lionel, tears spilling from them, Susan obeyed, walking woodenly to her father.

Stanhope spoke to Sir John's back when he was at the door, stopping him in his tracks. "Do you really want to do battle with me and mine, my friend? Do you truly think to win? If so, you are making a grave mistake."

Sir John gave him an incredulous glance. "I love my daughter," he finally said. "And she has been wronged. Some things are worth fighting for, no matter the cost."

"I will destroy you, John," the earl said in a tone better used to discuss the day's races.

Sir John took Susan's arm and propelled her from the room. A silence fell. It was broken only by the slow, loud, tick-tock, tick-tock of the pendulum clock.

"You fool," Stanhope said.

Lionel raised both brows in a look of extreme innocence.

Stanhope marched past him and slammed closed the door. "Don't play the gentleman with me. I know you took her. Miss Layton would not have a clue as to how to make an advance upon a man, even if her life depended on it."

"Father," Lionel began, his tone no longer light or easy.

"Why?" the earl demanded. "Why did you do it? Granted, she was easy, but there are a hundred women you could have had, without repercussions."

Lionel finally shrugged. "She is pretty enough. I am sorry. My male desires got the better of me—and she has been making cow eyes at me ever since we met. Besides, haven't I done Garrick a favor?"

"I wanted that marriage, by damn!" the earl roared.

Wisely Lionel remained silent.

The earl paced. After a pause he stood still, hands in his hips. "And if Layton has her examined?"

"I will deny it. I will say it must have been Garrick."

The earl looked at him, shook his head, and finally laughed, softly. "We both know Garrick despises her and would not touch her before the nuptials. I am quite sure he is waiting for the engagement to be broken off." His expression darkened and he cursed.

Lionel grimaced. "I am sorry, Father. I know what I did was wrong. I got . . . carried away."

The earl walked to his desk, but as he did so, he gave him a sidelong look. "Did you? I do not think you a man of passion, Lionel, unlike your hotheaded brother. I do not think you could get carried away by anything or anyone, not ever."

Lionel stared. Finally he said, "The apple does not fall far from the tree, does it, Father?"

The earl laughed briefly, gruffly.

Suddenly Lionel hesitated, appearing uncertain. "Father, this may seem a bit premature, but as you are in need of an heir, why do you concentrate upon Garrick? I am not the rebel that he is."

The earl smiled at him. "I am thinking about you, Lionel. Have no fear. Your future is very much upon my mind—and I shall soon take care of it."

Lionel searched his gaze and smiled. "Then I look forward to learning what it is you intend for me."

"In fact," the earl said quite casually, "tomorrow I intend to make a public announcement."

Lionel started. "A public announcement?" He could not mask his hopeful expression.

"Yes. Tomorrow I shall proclaim you the viscount of Caedmon Crag—and my long-lost heir."

Arlen paced his apartments in his dressing gown and slippers. He paused to pull back the draperies, but it had begun to drizzle and the morning was hardly inviting. He dropped his hand, closing the dark blue hangings upon the endlessly boring scene. In a few hours he and Elizabeth would leave for London, thank God, for the country could drive a man insane. But he had yet to decide how to punish Olivia.

Damn her. The bitch.

There was a knock upon his door and he turned, calling out, "Enter." His heart turned over as Elizabeth entered his room.

She smiled at him, and in that moment, clad as she was in a dark pink silk morning gown, she was the most radiant, beautiful woman he had ever beheld—but he had thought that since she was twelve. "Good morning, dear," she said. She briskly crossed the room and pulled open the draperies.

Immediately he walked to the door, which she had closed, and opened it. "It is but half-past ten. Neither of us is an early riser. Do you think you should be in my rooms?"

She waved airily at him. "No one would dare disturb us, Arlen. Oh, do not be such a prig. Everyone here knows how fond of me you are. Do close the door so we can talk."

His smile was forced, but he did as she wished. "I am sure that no one knows just how fond of you I am, my dear."

She lifted one brow and laughed at him, as if she did not care what the entire staff—or the entire peerage—thought. But then, that was Elizabeth. So very sure of herself. "We are off to town today," he said.

"I know. But, in truth . . ." She hesitated. "I have not been feeling so well, and I was thinking of staying here in the country for a few days."

Immediately he crossed the room and took her hands in his. He remembered that she had been ill during that horrid, endless carriage ride to Caedmon Crag, and he also remembered that she had not felt well soon after leaving Cornwall, after the duel. "But you despise the country far more than I."

"I do. But I mean it. The air seems to have settled whatever malady I was afflicted with. I am not sure I am able to spend an entire day traveling to town just yet. You can go on without me, Arlen. I do not mind. I would just spend a day or two more here, resting, and then I will join you in town." She smiled at him.

"I could stay here with you," Arlen said hesitantly. But he was thinking of how damn bored he was, how he had been so happy at the prospect of leaving Ashburnham. On the other hand, he was most content wherever Elizabeth was.

"Dear." Elizabeth cupped his cheek. "Houghton remains in town for two more days—I received the missive yesterday. Remember?"

He did, but barely.

"After that, he's off to his box in Scotland with some cronies of his. And you shall have me all to yourself in town." The look she gave him was very coy, very direct, very, very fatal.

Arlen quickly summed up the situation and nodded. "Then I will go on ahead of you, my dear, and amuse myself with a few male friends until your return. But I expect you to rest so that we can enjoy ourselves when you do return—at the end of the week."

Elizabeth smiled and kissed his cheek. "Have no fear. What else is there to do in the country but eat and sleep?"

Arlen did laugh.

"So," she said. "Have you decided what to do with your faithless little wife?"

Arlen stiffened. "Do you have to remind me of her treachery?"

"Tsk, tsk. And with Garrick De Vere, no less." She seemed amused.

"I had him. I was tripped. I did not slip," Arlen cried, furious that he had not killed Caedmon.

"I saw the entire thing, as did Manion. No one tripped you, Arlen. But Caedmon must enjoy cuckolding you, hmm?"

He hated it when Elizabeth taunted him, knowing she did it on purpose. "Perhaps I will cuckold him," he snarled, "after he weds Miss Layton."

"I doubt he will ever marry her, and Arlen, dear, could

you really ever desire that child?'' One imperious black brow lifted.

Her meaning was clear. He cursed and paced.

''Well, I certainly can quite understand Olivia's attraction to Garrick De Vere.'' She did laugh.

He whirled. ''Why do you now throw the past in my face?'' he demanded. ''Do I need to be reminded of your treachery now? Do I?''

She was wounded. She recoiled. ''I was sixteen years old. He was one year younger, but very adept. He seduced me, Arlen. I hardly knew what was happening—and we have gone through all of this before!''

Suddenly he found himself standing before her—and he had to know. ''Did you like it? Did he make you scream in pleasure—and in pain?''

''How dare you,'' she said coolly.

In that instant he thought he might lose her. ''Elizabeth! I apologize!'' he cried.

But she was walking across the room, toward the door. ''I will call you when I have returned to town—whenever that may be,'' she said, her tone dripping ice.

He hurried after her, putting his body between her and the door so she could not leave. ''I must punish my wife,'' he said with some desperation.

''I have the perfect plan,'' Elizabeth said, no longer cold and withdrawn. She smiled. ''I thought about it in the middle of the night. Obviously you will send Hannah away— and that will solve your problem of having such an odious child. Lock her up. I know the perfect place.''

''And Olivia?''

She shrugged. ''Let her stay here. She does so enjoy the country.''

''Elizabeth, do you think she will stay put? She will not, not unless I keep her in chains, and that, I believe, is against the king's law.''

''Arlen, drug her. Have her water and wine and tea dosed with laudanum morning, noon, and night. Reduce her mind to nothingness. She will wander around this house a demented old woman, well before her time. And who will

know the truth? I'll leave my maid here to do the deed."
Elizabeth smiled at him.

"You are brilliant," Arlen said, awed. "This way I will
avoid any further scandal."

"Absolutely." Elizabeth was smug, then suddenly her
expression changed. She turned a distinct shade of green,
her eyes registering alarm.

"Elizabeth!" Arlen cried.

But she was running across the room, bending over, and
retching violently into the chamber pot.

As much as Arlen despised sickness of any kind, he
loved his sister, and he went to her and helped her stand
upright when she was done. He guided her to a chair—she
leaned heavily upon him—and handed her a glass of water
and watched her drink it. "My God," he said after a few
minutes had passed. "You are still ill." She had been as
violently nauseated during their journey to and from Caedmon Crag.

"I am not ill."

"What?"

"I am pregnant," Elizabeth said without remorse.

He stared. "No."

"It is a fact."

He continued to stare, a dozen scenarios racing through
his mind. "Surely Houghton . . ." But that was hopeless,
for the man was impotent, or so Elizabeth had claimed.

She turned and stared at him as if he were an idiot. "Do
not be stupid," she said.

In the five days since returning to Ashburnham, Olivia had
been wise enough to keep to her rooms—and out of her
husband's way. But every passing minute was an eternity
as she waited for her sentence of doom.

Garrick. His death would be the first sentence of doom.
Did he live? None of the servants would accommodate her
whispered plea to go to Stanhope Hall for news. Did he
remain at Caedmon Crag? Was he dead? Had there already
been a funeral? Oh, God!

She covered her face with her hands, telling herself she

must not cry, she must be strong, he could not be dead. But there had been so much blood. She was never going to forget the sight of him, lying crumpled at the base of the wall of the keep, blood covering his torso, his breeches, and pooling on the ground beside him, dear God. And all because of her.

And it was futile to think that right now they could be together with Hannah in France if he had run from Arlen instead of accepting his challenge.

She had to know. She had to know the truth. She had already debated either walking or riding to the Hall herself. For she would walk the entire distance if she could not steal one of her husband's horses. But she did not dare leave Hannah; she did not trust Arlen.

She had to protect Hannah and herself from her husband's wrath, which would surely come. It was only a matter of time.

But now five days had elapsed since the duel, and Olivia almost dared to hope for a reprieve. Maybe, this once, Arlen would let things be, let the scandal die a natural death, and not seek revenge upon herself and her child. Then she decided that he would not be vindictive only if Garrick were dead.

She wept.

And when the tears finally ceased, for the hundredth time, the image of Garrick's bloody body remained engraved upon her mind. There was no point in prayer. She had prayed herself senseless. She had prayed until her knees were sore, her back stiff, her lips numb. She had prayed for his life, and she could not pray anymore.

If only she were not a mature, adult woman. If only she believed in miracles and fairy tales. But she did not. She never had.

Olivia crossed the threshold of her room, wiping her wet eyes, to press her ear against her closed bedroom door. When she heard no sound from the corridor, she opened it carefully, peeking out. No one was about. She swiftly crossed the hall and let herself into Hannah's room. Hannah was on her bed, playing with two small handmade porcelain dolls. She lifted her head and smiled at her mother.

Olivia went and sat beside her, holding her tightly. "I love you so," she said impulsively.

"I know, Mama," Hannah said. "I love you, too."

"What did you have for breakfast?" she asked lightly. Her tone belied the sadness in her heart. Hannah knew everything a child should not know by now. And she had said she did not think Garrick De Vere to be dead. On the other hand, she had confessed that she was terrified by all that had happened, and she did not trust herself anymore to know the truth. Her little girl was growing up. And she was only eight years old.

Hannah's face fell. "Eggs, Mama. I do miss Miss Childs."

"I know, darling," Olivia said, stroking her hair. Suddenly the door opened and Arlen stood there, causing her to cry out. In the next instant she saw his face, the hatred in his eyes, the satisfaction, and she drew Hannah to her side, holding her there tightly. The time had come at last, the time to face Arlen's wrath.

"I would like to speak to you," Arlen said calmly enough. "In your room."

He was going to do something terrible. Slowly, her hand still on Hannah's shoulders, Olivia stood up.

"Mama, don't go," Hannah whispered, gripping her palm tightly. "I'm scared."

Olivia turned, looked at her terrified face, and was frozen.

Arlen grabbed her elbow from behind and yanked her away from her child. "Come," he said harshly.

"No," Olivia cried, struggling to stay with her daughter.

"Mama!" Hannah cried. "Mama, don't go!"

But Arlen was dragging Olivia through the doorway, and outside of it, she saw several servants, including Hannah's new governess, a horrid, dispassionate woman Arlen had himself hired.

Hannah. They were going to take Hannah.

"No!" Olivia screamed as Arlen shoved her into her room and closed the door behind them both.

"Shut up," he said.

She panted, facing him, fists clenched, ready to take her nails and attempt to blind him herself.

"Why so distraught, Olivia? I merely wish to speak with you."

"What are you going to do with Hannah?" Olivia demanded, unable to breathe adequately.

"Did I say I was going to do something to my own daughter?" Arlen was so calm, and now he walked over to the pitcher of water on her bureau and poured a glass. He walked back and handed it to her. "Perhaps this will help calm you."

Unthinkingly, Olivia accepted the glass. "I am not thirsty. You will not hurt her? You will not send her away?"

He stared unblinkingly at her. "No."

She stared back. He was impossible to read. She reminded herself of how vindictive he was. She did not speak.

"I am returning to town in an hour or so. I am leaving you here, my dear, to your simple country life."

Olivia was as stiff as a board. Now, however, ever so slightly, she relaxed. "You are returning to town? And leaving Hannah and me here?"

He smiled slightly. "Why are you surprised?"

A new thought occurred to her. "Is Garrick dead?!" she cried.

"No." He practically spat out the negation. "He is very much alive, and from what I gather, on the mend. Although"—now he smiled—"I have heard that Stanhope is about to announce to the world at large that Lionel is his heir."

Olivia hardly heard the last, did not care; she was too relieved as she turned away from Arlen, trembling in all her limbs, to sink down upon the settee at the foot of her bed. With a shaking hand she lifted the glass of water to her lips and was surprised to find that lemon peel had been added to it, changing its flavor. She took two quick sips. He was alive. Thank you, God, he was alive.

Then her mind snapped to. If he was alive, why was Arlen being so reasonable? Slowly she lifted her gaze to his. "I do not understand."

"No? What is it that you do not understand?"

"Why would you leave us here?" Olivia asked cautiously.

He came closer, staring. His eyes had never been so hostile. "Actually, Olivia, I am leaving you here . . . alone."

She inhaled, stiffening. She had known.

"Hannah is gone."

"No."

He smiled. "Go look for yourself," he said.

Seized by terror—by a horrifying terror the likes of which she had never known before—she rushed to the door and opened it. Hannah's door was wide open—and the bedroom inside was vacant. Olivia cried out.

She thought Arlen chuckled behind her.

It was happening, the worst possible nightmare of a woman's life.

She whirled. "What have you done with her? What have you done with my child?" she screamed.

He shrugged, clearly amused.

Olivia whirled and ran across her bedroom to the windows that gazed out upon the front lawns. She peered out, gripping the sill—and saw a carriage departing, already halfway down the drive. *"Hannah!"*

"You will stay here, never fear, my dear," Arlen said from behind her. "Alone in the country."

Olivia turned. "Where are you sending her?" she cried savagely.

"Bedlam," he said.

CHAPTER TWENTY-FIVE

S he knew that she must get up. The reason was pressing. But try as she might, she could not grasp just why she had to rise from her bed.

It seemed unnatural, it was an immense effort, but Olivia managed to slowly turn her head and open her eyes. How stiff and strange her neck felt. And her head throbbed. She squinted against the glare. Why did her eyes hurt? Sunlight poured through the cracks between her partially drawn draperies. She fought to find her thoughts. Did she have to rise because it was, at the least, midmorning?

It was so hard to think. It was so hard to concentrate. Focus eluded her. And she was so dry, so terribly dry, as if linen filled her mouth. Olivia pushed down hard on the bed. It seemed to take a terribly long time, but finally she did sit up. Slowly she turned and stared at the blue-and-white Wedgwood water pitcher.

She was dying of thirst. The taste in her mouth was so foul. Bitter and foul.

Get up.

She stiffened. The voice inside her head was firm and clear, adamant. She must get up. And it had little to do with the morning, did it not?

Her hand shaking visibly—and Olivia could not understand her tremors—she reached for the blue-and-white pitcher and managed to pour some water into a glass. Why was this simple procedure so difficult? she managed to wonder. Why was she so sleepy, so numb? Why was it so hard to think?

Hannah.

Olivia stiffened. And for one instant she knew, she just knew, that her daughter was in trouble and needed her desperately. In the next instant, as she sat there in bed in her nightclothes at an hour that was very close to noon, she completely forgot her thoughts. What had been so horrifying? So urgent and pressing? *Why couldn't she remember?*

Her bedroom door opened and a servant Olivia did not know marched in, smiling somewhat briskly, navy blue skirts swirling. "Good morning, Lady Ashburn. My, but you have slept away half the day . . . again." The woman was twice Olivia's age, as thin as a rail, her red hair twisted back severely in a bun.

Olivia watched the woman as if through a fog as she strode to her side and promptly placed a breakfast tray upon her lap. She stared down at the scrambled eggs and fried steak, items she had no appetite for or interest in. The maid was now drawing open the chintz curtains. She turned. "Eat your meal, my lady, and then we shall bathe you and get you dressed."

Something was wrong. Olivia stared at the maid as if she had spoken Chinese, a language of which she had no knowledge. She was not well. She could not move, could not think. She never ate steak and eggs.

"Who . . . are you?" Olivia did not recognize her own voice. It was thick and hoarse, as if dusty and unused. It was so hard to form the words and speak.

"I beg your pardon, my lady?" The maid came over and leaned down to lift up a forkful of eggs. "I cannot understand you when you mumble. Please. Eat."

Before Olivia could truly grasp what was happening, the eggs were in her mouth and she was automatically chewing and then swallowing them. The eggs were bitter, and had been salted far too much. Instinctively she turned her head

away before the maid could jam another forkful of eggs
into her mouth.

"You must eat," the maid said firmly—in a tone no
servant should ever use with her mistress.

Something was wrong. Why was she being fed? Who
was this woman? Where was she?

Hannah.

"My . . . daughter," Olivia whispered—and more food
was suddenly in her mouth.

Although it was difficult, Olivia reached up and pushed
away the woman's hand as she swallowed the horrid eggs
again. But in doing so, she once again forgot what she was
thinking about. Tears suddenly filled her eyes. What was
happening to her?! Had she lost her mind?

"That's a good lady," the maid crooned in approval.

"I . . . will . . . eat," Olivia said, every word difficult to
enunciate. "By myself."

The maid folded her arms and regarded her with skepticism.

Olivia fought for control of her mind. She was perspiring
now. "Why . . . am . . . I sick?"

The maid turned away. "I will come back in half an
hour, my lady, to help you bathe. Make sure you eat everything on your plate."

Olivia did not bother to reply, vastly relieved as the
woman strode out of her room, leaving the door ajar as she
did so.

She looked down at the tray on her lap. She was not
going to eat. She wasn't hungry, and something was wrong
with the food. And she never ate eggs and steak.

Meow.

Olivia started at the sound of the cat. The orange tabby
that Hannah was so fond of leapt onto the bed. She smiled,
and as she did so, it felt as if her lips were stretched taut.
Her smile faded. She needed to see her daughter.

Her heart lurched. A terrible dread filled her. Hannah.
Something was wrong.

Meow. The tabby rubbed its head against Olivia's ankle,
purring loudly.

What was wrong? Olivia felt more tears gathering in her eyes. She had just been on the verge of an important revelation—an awful, horrendous one—and it had slipped away, dear God. What was happening to her mind?

With shaking hands she gripped the tray, now recalling her distasteful maid who had tried to force her to eat. She pushed the tray off her thighs, onto the bed. She must get up. There was something she had to do, she was certain of it—she just did not know what it was.

The tabby had stopped purring and was staring at the food.

Olivia smiled slightly and pushed the tray at the cat. "Pray . . . indulge yourself," she said thickly. She watched as the tabby began nibbling delicately at the eggs. Then she lifted the covers, which seemed to weigh two stone, and pushed them off. Very carefully, very conscientiously, Olivia worked her legs over the side of the bed, to the floor, and she stood up.

She almost fell, but she stopped herself by gripping the poster by the carved headboard of the bed. She was ill. She was weak and numb, she could hardly move, and she did not understand—and she was afraid.

Olivia took a deep breath, released the poster, and began walking to her bureau, tottering like a toddler. Once there, she gripped the top with both hands, using it for balance, sucking in air. The short walk had been as difficult as running a few miles uphill. Then her gaze met its reflection in the mirror. Olivia gasped.

She hardly recognized the woman she stared at. She was pale and thin, her face seemed long and gaunt, and nearly black crescents were under her eyes. Her long blond hair was snarled and tangled, as if she had slept in her braids for weeks. Oh, God. The woman in the mirror was an old hag—but it was she. *What was happening!*

It was as if she were in the midst of a terrible and bizarre nightmare.

Hannah.

Olivia stiffened, staring at herself, thinking, I must go to my daughter. She clung desperately to that thought, afraid she would lose it at any moment. She turned, began walking and weaving across the room, pushing herself to move more quickly. The bedroom door, still ajar, was her goal. She fixed her eyes upon the polished mahogany wood and the gleaming brass handle, refusing to remove her gaze, grinding down her jaw, determined now as never before. The door. She must get to the door. Sweat gathered on her brow and trickled down between her breasts.

When she reached her goal, she collapsed against it, beginning to cry in frustration and helplessness. When the tears subsided, she straightened, confused. She could no longer remember what she had been so intent upon doing. Why was she standing at the door in her nightclothes?

Olivia turned, leaning her back against the door, feeling frail and helpless. Then she saw the cat.

Lying like a corpse upon her bed.

Dead.

Choking off a cry, Olivia hurried to the best of her ability across the room, back to her bed. It was an endless journey. She sank down on the bed, reaching for Hannah's tabby. To her relief, he wasn't dead; he was sleeping, but deeply.

Thank God.

She cradled him in her arms. He did not wake up.

Olivia froze.

Then she looked from the unconscious cat to the tray of half-eaten food.

"Ah, my lady, what a fine appetite you had this morning."

Still perspiring, trying desperately to dwell silently upon one word—poison—Olivia stared at the maid as she sat in her bed. The tray was by her hip, the plates empty. Her cup of tea had been poured out of the window, the unfinished steak and eggs were wrapped in a chemise under the bed, the same place she had put the unconscious cat. It had seemed to take hours to perform such simple tasks.

Poison. Someone was trying to poison her.

Olivia was filled with fear. As the maid helped her up and into the water closet, she kept silently repeating the single word "poison" to herself, until it was a refrain in her mind that she could not forget. It took an immense effort. She did not even try to think upon who would do such a horrendous thing. It was hard enough remembering that she must not eat or drink anything.

"You have a visitor, my lady. Do you think you are well enough to receive him?"

Olivia looked at the red-haired woman. "A visitor?" she mumbled.

"His Lordship said you could have visitors if you were so inclined, and he left me a list of acceptable callers. It is Lord Caedmon." The maid smiled as she drew Olivia's nightgown over her head and deposited it on the floor.

Her pulse raced. *Caedmon?* Olivia allowed the woman to begin bathing her with a sponge and tepid water. She was trying to remember who Lord Caedmon was. And a pair of blazing golden eyes burned their way right into her mind.

Garrick.

Her heart drummed now, filled with love, filled with fear. Her memory seemed to be returning to her, because in that instant she knew she loved the man with the golden eyes, and she knew everything. A fleeting image of him straining over her as he made love to her swept through her mind, followed by an image of him engaged in a duel with her husband. Then the images were gone.

"You do recall Lord Caedmon, do you not?" the maid said, settling a silk shift upon her. "He is the Stanhope heir."

Olivia wet her lips, aware that the bitter taste in her mouth had lessened. The Stanhope heir . . . Garrick De Vere . . . Hannah. Her mind was returning to her. She knew two things now. She loved Garrick, she loved her daughter.

Olivia winced as her corset was laced up far too tightly. "Please do not," she said. Then she recalled the cat.

She was being poisoned, but her memory seemed to be returning to her, bit by bit, and she must pretend to be dazed and drugged.

"I beg your pardon?" the maid asked sharply.

"Please," Olivia said in a heavy whisper—her tone a conscious effort. "Too . . . tight."

"I am sorry, my lady," the maid said, easing up on the laces. "So, shall you take tea with Lord Caedmon? I have told him you are quite tired, having been ill of late."

Yes, she wished to see Garrick. Desperately. She was being poisoned, and she needed help. She trembled, murmuring an affirmation.

And then, as a petticoat was dropped over her head, she saw the Ashburn carriage driving away from the house. The memory was terrifying.

Hannah.

But it was Lionel's eyes that widened when she paused on the threshold of the salon, steadying herself by keeping one hand upon the door. She stared, remembering him immediately. Where was Garrick? She glanced wildly around the salon, but it was empty.

"Lady Ashburn," Lionel said warmly, strolling forward to greet her with both hands outstretched, the surprise gone from his face.

"My . . . lord," Olivia said, keeping her tone low, as Lionel took both of her hands in his. The odious maid was behind her. Olivia had just, suddenly, recalled her name. It was Miss Livingstock, and she was employed by Elizabeth.

He bent over her hand and kissed it. "I am . . . confused," Olivia managed. "I thought . . . Miss Livingstock said that it was Lord Caedmon calling."

Lionel grinned. "But I am the viscount of Caedmon Crag, my dear lady. My father has finally rectified a monumental error—recognizing me as his eldest and heir."

Olivia could only stare. Her mind was having trouble grasping what Lionel had said. She could not understand, she only knew that something was terribly wrong.

"I am so sorry that you have been ill, but I am pleased you are recovered enough to see me," Lionel continued.

Olivia nodded. She was in the throes of a huge disappointment, and even that puzzled her; she was also acutely conscious of the treacherous Livingstock standing behind her. The comprehension struck her now that Livingstock was the one who had been poisoning her. No member of the Ashburn staff would ever do such a thing, Arlen's orders or not. Was Elizabeth behind this? Her heart lurched.

"Come, let us sit, as you do seem tired," Lionel said, tucking her arm under his.

Olivia remained weak, and still not thinking with utter clarity, she was grateful for his physical strength as he led her to a chair. She did lean fully on him, trying to concentrate. Garrick was not coming. The disappointment made her knees weak. She needed help. Yes, that was it. And it was so important. But now she failed to remember exactly why she needed aid. The thought that Elizabeth was trying to poison her—maybe even murder her—was overwhelming.

If only she were well. If only she were not so weak—and so terribly vulnerable.

The thought seized her that she must get rid of the maid. As Olivia sat, she turned her gaze upon Livingstock. "Do . . . leave us," she said with a feebleness that was only partially feigned.

"I do not think I should do so. His Lordship's orders were quite clear." The maid came to her and began fussing with the cushions behind Olivia's back. Then she faced Lionel. "I am afraid, my lord, that your call must be limited to ten minutes. His Lordship has been very specific, being so concerned about his wife's health."

"Very well," Lionel said agreeably.

Now Olivia was frozen. Someone was poisoning her. She must escape this place with Hannah, and she needed help—Lionel's help. Then she stiffened, her heart lurching so hard that it felt as if it had just turned completely, sickeningly, over.

Hannah was gone.

She recalled the carriage leaving again, and her heart raced so hard and fast that she felt faint. Hannah had been in that carriage! What was she to do? Where was her daughter? What had Arlen said? Oh, God! Now she must think!

"Lady Ashburn." Lionel's concerned tone interrupted Olivia's racing yet scattered thoughts. "You have gone white. What is amiss?"

Olivia looked at him, trying frantically now to signal him with her eyes, thinking she needed help, needed to escape, needed to find Hannah—and she must not allow her memory to elapse yet again. She must not!

"My lady?" Lionel asked with real concern.

"Just . . . I am weak . . . I cannot . . . recall why," Olivia lied.

Livingstock seemed satisfied, and she walked away, going to one of the double-tiered windows to stare out. She was perhaps twenty feet from them, a stone's short throw away.

And her back was half-turned from them. Olivia reached out with surprising speed and agility and gripped Lionel's hand. His eyes widened. She leaned forward and whispered, "Help. Please. Tell Garrick."

And then she dropped her hand. She had instinctively asked Lionel to send for Garrick. It was Garrick whom she needed, Garrick and no one else. But had Lionel understood? She glanced at the maid. The maid remained oblivious, for she still gazed out the window at Olivia's colorful, blossoming gardens.

Olivia turned her gaze quickly back to Lionel. To her surprise, he was regarding her intently. Was he perplexed? Had he understood? How could she make him understand before he had to leave?

"My brother is well," he said suddenly. "This morning he was up and about, hobbling and in some pain, but he will be himself in no time at all, or so everyone thinks."

The duel flashed before Olivia's eyes. She had forgotten it. Now she recalled that Garrick had been so terribly wounded that she had feared for his life. Her relief, once again, was vast. He was alive. And getting well. But she needed his help. Could he help her if he was still in recovery? Lionel had not understood her plea at all, apparently. Olivia was filled with dismay.

"Tell him . . . I send . . . my best . . . to call," she finally said. If Garrick called, he would know in an instant that something was terribly wrong.

Suddenly the maid was facing them and speaking to them quite loudly. "I am afraid that Lord Caedmon's brother is not on the approved list," she said firmly. "In fact, His Lordship was very definite about that, my lady."

Olivia's heart sank.

Suddenly the butler poked his head into the room. He smiled at Olivia. "My lady, I am so terribly pleased to see you up and about."

Would Willowby help her escape? Olivia wondered frantically. "Thank you."

"Miss Livingstock, you have a missive from London, from Lord Ashburn."

"Excuse me," Livingstock said, and she left the room, her strides brisk.

When Willowby asked if they needed refreshments, Olivia shook her head, wanting him to leave immediately. The moment she was alone with Lionel, she gripped his knee, to hell with all propriety. He started. She leaned forward, speaking low and urgently. "Hannah is in trouble. Arlen sent her . . . away." Horror again seized her. She could not recall where Hannah had been sent—yet knew she had been told, knew she must remember. "Please. Tell Garrick to come."

Lionel took her palm in his. "Surely you are exaggerating your case, my lady?" His fingers seemed to caress the skin on the top of her hand.

"No! Arlen has done something terrible," Olivia cried, tears filling her eyes. "Please."

He lifted her hand and kissed her bare skin, his warm, moist lips lingering there. Then he smiled at her. "Of course I will pass the message along," he said, his gaze holding hers.

Vaguely Olivia knew he was making an advance, but she did not care. She was relieved and exhausted and ready to collapse from the trauma she had thus far endured. "Thank you."

"My, my," Elizabeth said from the doorway. "What a charming scene."

And Lionel turned white, dropping Olivia's hand as if it were on fire, jumping to his feet.

Elizabeth strolled into the room. "I decided to remain in the country for a few days," she said, smiling at them both.

He did not have his own valet; he had always thought that no grown man should need help dressing himself, but he had never been injured like this before. His side ached constantly, and his torso remained stiff and sore. Clothing himself had been a long, frustrating, painful chore. But he was dressed, and he must see Olivia.

By now Garrick knew she was not just at Ashburnham, but that Arlen had returned to town. He was hardly relieved.

As he began walking slowly down the stairs, cursing his wound for the way it impeded his movements, making him walk like an old, infirm man, he saw Lionel below him, standing on the ground-floor landing. He smiled up at him. Garrick faltered, gripping the banister hard for balance. It flashed through his mind that he must mend and quickly. He was surrounded by enemies.

"How wonderful to see you up and about like this!" Lionel exclaimed.

Treve's hackles were raised. The fact that his dog sensed Lionel to be the enemy pleased Garrick. "Easy, boy," he muttered. Perspiring from the effort it took him to go down the stairs, Garrick did not answer. Nothing was going to stop him from getting in a carriage and driving over to see Olivia.

"You know," Lionel said conversationally as Garrick finally reached the ground floor, coming face-to-face with him, the setter at his side, "I was just telling Olivia how well you were recuperating, and that you would be fully recovered in no time at all."

His heart stopped. "When? When did you see her?"

"Yesterday at noon." Lionel continued to smile.

So many emotions assailed him that Garrick was taken

aback. Lionel had been with Olivia. He was angry, he was jealous, he was torn and eager for news. "What did she say? How is she? How is Hannah?"

Lionel lifted one brow, giving him a lofty look. "She and her daughter are very well. We strolled in her gardens and discussed the blooms."

Garrick was afraid his surprise, mingled with newfound dismay, showed. "Surely she asked about me? Did she give you a message for me?"

"I actually volunteered the information that you were healing rather nicely, but no, she did not ask about you or convey a message for me to give to you. Perhaps the lady has had second thoughts? After all that has transpired?" Lionel's smile remained bland, but there was amusement in his tone.

Garrick felt as if he had been kicked in the chest by a mule, and for a moment all speech failed him.

"Don't you think you should be more discreet, Garrick? I only tell you this brother to brother. Apparently the entire peerage knows about you and her living together openly at Caedmon Crag, as if you were man and wife."

He was stunned again, but for a different reason. "We were there precisely two nights."

Lionel shrugged. "I am not responsible for what people are saying and thinking," he said.

A surge of fury went through Garrick, because in that moment he felt Lionel was probably directly responsible for that bit of gossip. And his confidence about Olivia's feelings for him returned. Lionel was trying to shake him up—and had almost succeeded. "Why don't you worry about your own indiscretions," Garrick said tightly. "I can take care of myself."

Lionel's gaze slipped as he eyed him, his manner rather condescending. "Can you? You are not merely ill with that wound, you have little common sense and an infamous temper. Brother to brother, I tell you this."

Garrick knew his smile was a snarl. "You are not my brother."

"Do not tell me we are back to that tiresome dispute!

Have you not heard? Father has publicly announced me to be his heir.''

Lionel's airy words, uttered with smug satisfaction, struck Garrick hard, like a physical blow. It was his third well-aimed blow of the morning. He should not be stunned, dismayed, or surprised. He should be glad, God damn it, as this now gave him the freedom he had always sought. He could sail away and never come back.

With Olivia and her daughter.

"Let me tell you something," Garrick said, low and hard. He shoved his nose close to Lionel's. "You are not my brother, and I intend to prove it.''

"You are so wrong," Lionel said, at once smug and confident.

"No." Garrick stared, fists clenched. "If it is the last thing I do, I shall unmask you," he said. Then he gripped the sling protecting his left arm and ripped it off, throwing it down at Lionel's feet. "Underestimate me if you will," he said, "but that is your mistake.''

"Garrick.''

Garrick was outside in the drive, about to climb into an open carriage with a groom's help, the setter already eagerly ensconced there, when he heard his father's voice. The earl was descending the front steps of the Hall, approaching him with rapid strides. Garrick stiffened, preparing for he knew not what. But both his mother's and Lionel's shocking revelations flashed through his mind.

The earl paused beside him, not the least bit out of breath. "I just saw your brother and he told me that you are off to Ashburnham. Have you lost your wits?''

Garrick was already riddled with tension. "First, he is not my brother—I refuse to believe it. And no, I do believe I have all of my wits, Father.''

The earl's jaw flexed. "I am certain that he is Lionel. Do you think I have not given this a great deal of thought? Do you think I would make a public declaration if I had a single doubt?''

Garrick stepped closer to him. "Lionel could not have changed so much."

Their gazes had locked. Stanhope shook his head. "You are still the most stubborn and contentious person I know. You think to thwart me, as you did as a boy. For we both know you care not a whit about the earldom. He, at least, cares. He, at least, is eager to honor me and do his duty."

"If I am stubborn, then I must have come by the trait from you," Garrick said caustically. "And you are right. I do not give a damn about the earldom. I never have. So this is why you accept him? Because he shall be your lackey?"

The earl stared at him. "I have no doubt that he is whom he says he is. And you are allowing your emotions to interfere with your judgment, as always."

Garrick stared. He would be the first to admit that his extreme sensibilities could so easily interfere with his better judgment. But not in this case. In this case, his father was not right. "This man is a grasping, greedy, cunning fraud."

Stanhope sighed. "When do you intend to return to Barbados?"

Garrick stiffened. "Now that you have no use for me, you are eager to see me go."

"I did not say that."

Garrick studied him. "I will return to Barbados only after I have proven my case," he said harshly. "When will you call off my engagement to Miss Layton?"

"Actually, fool that he is, Sir John has broken off the engagement," Stanhope said.

Garrick smiled. "Good," he said. At least he was free of that mindless twit. In fact, at that moment he realized he was free to take Olivia and Hannah away. It was very tempting, especially as it was not in his best interest to unmask the impostor.

But he knew he could not rest until he had done so. And if he were wrong? The notion that this man might truly be Lionel was frightening. But if he was, if he had changed so drastically, so completely, at least justice would have been served and Garrick could walk away without being haunted by unanswered questions and lingering doubts.

"Does Lionel know the truth?" Garrick gazed right into his father's eyes. "That we do not share the same mother? Does he know that his real mother killed herself?"

The earl paled, his eyes widening.

As it was the very first time in his life that he had ever taken his father by surprise, Garrick felt quite satisfied. He waited with suddenly infinite patience.

"So she told you."

"Yes. Mother told me that your first wife threw herself out of the attic window, here at the Hall, killing herself when Lionel was only five months old. A month later, you married Mother. How unhappy Margaret MacDonald must have been." Garrick watched him. "It has been a family secret all of these years. Why?"

The earl had recovered, although his expression was grim. "She should have stayed in Scotland," he said heavily.

"So the marriage was arranged? Or were you forced to marry her because she was pregnant?"

"She was very beautiful, and I was young." The earl no longer looked at Garrick. "Meg was wild and high-spirited and determined to get back at a young Highlander who had jilted her. I served a purpose in her life, although I did not know it at the time. Leaving Scotland is what killed her, Garrick, for it broke her heart. She hated England, and she hated me, too, I believe. She chose to die. But it was ultimately for the best. We were not suited. I can see that now, in hindsight. She should have been a brief affair."

Garrick could hardly believe his father had been swept off his feet by a Highland lass, enough to marry her. Perhaps he did not know him as well as he thought. On the other hand, it had been so long ago, did it truly matter? "But why was it kept a secret?"

The earl stared. "The union, brief as it was, was a vast mistake. She made a fool of me. And she took her own life." He hesitated. "I refused to annul the marriage."

Only a very unhappy woman would kill herself, and Garrick found himself feeling sorry for a young woman long deceased whom he had never known. He decided that the earl, out of cold pride, could easily feel compelled to cover up such a sordid affair. And he thought he saw regret in his father's eyes. "Does Lionel know the truth?"

"Yes. I told him when he was eight years old. Now, are we finished with this subject?"

"Absolutely," Garrick said, his mind racing with new and sudden possibilities.

"You cannot go to Ashburnham," Stanhope said.

His thoughts rudely interrupted, Garrick faced his father. "Unfortunately, Father, I ceased taking orders from you a long time ago."

"Arlen Grey almost killed you. The entire affair—including the time you spent with the countess alone at Caedmon Crag—is being avidly discussed in every drawing room and coffeehouse in London, by damn. What do you think to accomplish now? Do you wish to further the scandal? Do you wish to die in another duel?" His father's tone was scathing.

Garrick was rigid. "I have no death wish—as if it would matter to you."

"Do not throw egg in Ashburn's face another time," the earl warned.

Garrick had to admit it, but his father was right. "I am merely worried about her," he finally said, a part of him knowing he should never expose his feelings for Olivia to his father this way. "I wish to know that she is well."

The earl stared at him and shook his head, his feelings clear: Garrick's attachment to the woman was hopeless. "Send a message and a messenger. Besides, Lionel was there, and he spent some time with her. She is fine, Garrick. You will worsen the situation if you call at Ashburnham. Trust me, please. In this single instance. I know what is best."

Garrick rubbed his temples. His instincts shouted at him to go, go, go, but his mind was competing for his attention. He did not want to enflame Arlen any more. He did not want to place Olivia in any more jeopardy. But he did have to reassure himself that she was all right.

He would send his mother. The idea was brilliant, for he trusted Eleanor completely.

As long as she stayed off the port.

"For this one single time," he said, "I will agree with you."

The earl stared at him in surprise. "Well, well," he said.

BEDLAM

The room seemed very small, but only because so many women and children were crowded into it. Hannah sat frozen with her back to the rough, dirty wall. The smells around her made her want to choke and gag. Horrible odors were assailing her—unwashed bodies, vomit, urine, excrement. She did not move. She was afraid to move. And she did not know where to go.

The sounds were terrifying.

Hannah hugged herself, tears spilling down her cheeks, her heart beating hard and fast, desperately wishing her mother would come and take her away from this terrible place. Not far from where she sat, rocking herself rigidly, a woman who was heavy with child wailed in grief and fear. Her ceaseless wailing was so scary. But everything was. An old woman sat beside Hannah, mumbling beneath her breath. She spoke in gibberish, but Hannah could understand her every thought; she was not crazy—she was cursing the woman who had taken her husband and children away from her, causing her to be placed in this awful place.

There was weeping and moaning. The sobs and groans surrounded Hannah, filled the room. There was shouting, yelling, fighting. And a young woman, half child, half adult, rocked herself silently. Her anguish was so overwhelming for Hannah, the waves huge, tangible; and from time to time Hannah would cry, too, with her and for her, for a moment forgetting herself. The woman was heavily pregnant and grieving the death of her husband and another child. Her master had sent her to Bedlam because she was too heartbroken to work.

Mama, Mama, Hannah begged. Where are you?

There was one other child present, a little girl; and she wept and hiccuped intermittently. Hannah did not have to be told to know that she was both deaf and mute, but not blind. Hannah wanted to be her friend. She desperately needed a friend. She was so alone and so scared. But she was immobilized by the women surrounding her, by her despair, by her fear, and she did not dare crawl to her.

Tears kept trickling down Hannah's cheeks. Mama, she thought, please come. Please please please come! *I want my mother! Pleeaase!*

The tears streamed now, endlessly. Hannah had never wanted her mother more. She had never been apart from her mother before. She missed her so much that it was a huge, physical, racking pain. Although she didn't like her father, although she was afraid of him, her life had been safe and secure until now. She had not known that a place like this existed. But recently, in the past month or so, she had been having dreams, horrible dreams, of losing her mother, of strange, ugly, smelly women, of being lost and afraid. The nightmares had woken her time and again, but she had not told her mother, knowing that the dreams came from her gift.

She was so afraid. Never in her life had she been afraid like this before. She needed her mother. Desperately. Now. Why didn't her mother come and rescue her?

Where was she?

"Mama," Hannah whispered aloud. "Please, Mama, I miss you so!"

"Eh, gel, come close, so strange yew are, always keepin' to yerself."

The instant Hannah realized she was being spoken to, she shrank farther against the wall, wanting to disappear inside herself. She had adopted this tiny corner days ago, refusing to move from it. Go away, she wanted to say. More tears fell. She was so afraid, she could not speak.

Foul breath overcame her as the older, husky woman leaned close. "Sich a pretty little gel yew are, so pretty, an' so sad." Suddenly the woman started laughing, hard, making cawing, crowlike sounds, unable to stop. Her laughter was insane.

And her odd, mad laughter ricocheted in the stone room, which contained nothing but the other women and numerous pallets upon the floor, becoming louder and louder.

Hannah huddled her knees against her chest, crying silently now, unable to stop.

Suddenly the woman straightened. Abruptly her laughter ceased. "Wot?" the woman mumbled, as if to herself. "Wot?" she repeated, as if in a trance. Then, muttering unintelligibly, she turned and shuffled away.

Hannah slumped against the wall and burst into tears, unable to stop sobbing.

Everything will be all right.

The thought came from nowhere, filling her mind. But it had nothing to do with her gift.

Hannah jerked as she felt a presence settling down beside her.

But it wasn't the presence of any of the women or children in this asylum. It wasn't truly tangible, yet it was so comforting, so warm and familiar, and so human, that a wave of reassurance swept over her.

Hannah no longer wept. A hand covered hers, offering safety and hope. Her pulse began to slow. Her fears began to disappear. And the thought was there, loud and clear, inside her head.

Everything will be all right.

Hannah was no longer alone.

CHAPTER TWENTY-SIX

Elizabeth stood in front of a full-length mirror. A very slight smile was on her exquisite face as she pulled at the laces at the back of her white corset.

The whalebone stays loosened, and she pulled the corset up and over her head, then let it slip to the floor. She stood now in a sheer, knee-length lavender chemise, a single petticoat atop that, a collar of diamonds, and nothing else.

Bending slowly, her breasts swinging against the chemise, her nipples very large and prominent, glancing repeatedly at herself in the mirror, she pushed and shoved the brocade petticoat down until it sat in a heap around her feet. Her legs were long, the color of ivory, and lush. And through the chemise, the shadow of pubic hair guarding her sex was visible.

Elizabeth touched her full breasts. She slid her spread fingers over her nipples until they were achingly erect. Her splayed hands slid lower, over her rib cage, and lower still, passing her hipbones. They paused just above the mound of rampant femininity. Elizabeth smiled at the reflection in the mirror and turned languidly around.

Her eyes were very bright.

"You are the most beautiful woman I have ever seen," he said thickly, coming forward. A huge arousal strained the tight wool of his breeches.

Elizabeth's laughter was husky and sensual, but her gaze was riveted on his manhood.

He pulled her forward, both hands on her buttocks, on top of the chemise.

"Oh, God," she said as he separated the two mounds of flesh.

Half smiling, very intent, he met her gaze and dropped to his knees. One arm was now a vise around her upper thighs as he shoved his face against her. With his thumb, he pushed back the fold of one lip. With his tongue, he wet her.

She gripped his head and cried out savagely, standing braced with her legs apart as he alternately flayed her with his tongue and laved her tenderly.

He went down on his back. His hand was in her hair, pulling as he might on a leash or a chain, and she came down on top of him, on both hands and knees. Their gazes met. She whimpered.

He laughed. "Who gives the orders now?" he said softly. With both hands, he tore off the silk chemise.

"You do. Please. Help me." She ducked her head, trying to reach his loins with her mouth. But he would not let her, gripping her by a hank of her hair again.

"Open my breeches," he said.

She reared up onto her knees, panting, the thick diamond collar glinting, her breasts swinging in his face. As she fumbled with the buttons she began to moan. He caught one nipple with his mouth and then tugged it with his teeth.

He sprang free. He used his hand ruthlessly, pushing her head down. Then he cried out gutturally as his hard, hot, thick length pushed up into her mouth.

He felt the back of her throat. And he did not let her stop.

Moments later she was beneath him, her legs wrapped around his waist, and he was driving into her as hard as he could. They cried out together, bucking like animals, in a pool of their own sweat.

Afterward, he held her. Almost tenderly.

But Elizabeth sat up, shrugging free. She gave him a

look, coy and sidelong, and stood up. Once again supremely aware of her power, in complete control, she crossed the room, starkly, superbly naked—except for the diamond collar. It had been a gift. He sat up to watch her every movement. Her body glistened like wet pearls, her nipples like faceted rubies.

She came out of her dressing room having donned a pair of silver slippers with delicate heels, dabbing perfume behind her ears, and she sat in a chair, facing him. He stared. Her long legs lolled widely apart.

"I am getting tired of Houghton," she said.

He stood. He approached. He knelt and buried his face between her thighs. She stiffened immediately as his tongue began another unerring course. As it slid around and over her clitoris, she forgot about her husband, almost, and allowed her body to give in to desire. Her head lolled back against the chair.

He suddenly lifted his head and looked at her. Her eyes were closed, her cheeks deeply flushed. Lionel said, "Good. I am getting tired of him, too."

She thought about Margaret MacDonald, standing at the attic window and gazing out at the lawns in front of the house. The tableau outside was very still; it could have been a Poussin landscape painting. There was not a cloud in the sky, and bright, late summer sunlight threatened to scorch the lawns—it was by far an unusual day, the hottest of the season. Inside the attic, the air was close and still; it was hot and stuffy. She trembled. Had it been on a day like this that Meg MacDonald had committed suicide?

Eleanor gripped the windowsill. She stared down at the ground, so far below her. She could almost see the young, beautiful Scottish girl's body there, crumpled, broken, bloody.

And she had been beautiful. A long time ago, in Richard's desk, Eleanor had found a small portrait. She had known instantly that the stunning young blond woman with the incredible blue eyes had been his first wife.

How sad her eyes had been.

She leaned forward. The ground was five stories below her, but it did not look that far away. She stared unblinkingly at it until the shrubs and grass began to blur and perspiration trickled down her cheeks. If Meg had not killed herself, Eleanor's life would be very different now. Richard would not have been her husband for all of these years—but then, Garrick would not have been her son, either. So many hurtful memories swept through her mind, most of them of Richard, condescending and cutting and cruel. For years she had told herself how fortunate she was to have married the earl of Stanhope, one of the most powerful and wealthy men in the realm. But she just could not lie to herself anymore. Damn him. For everything, but mostly for a lifetime of loneliness and pain, and especially for disinheriting Garrick now.

Her grip on the sill tightened. Dear, dear God. Was Lionel back, returned from the vanished? Or was he, as Garrick insisted, a pretender?

But Richard was by far the wisest man she knew! He would never make such a mistake!

She was sweating now. Profusely. Tears, she realized, were blurring her vision. And suddenly she released the sill—only to push the window open wide. She leaned out.

And she wondered if, one day, she would share the same fate as Meg.

Eleanor choked on a sob she did not want to release. Meg had been so brave, to take her own life to escape a future of misery and unhappiness. She knew with her next breath that she herself would never be so brave. She was a coward. The port wine was her refuge.

As she stared down at the ground, almost unseeingly, the vision formed, unbidden, and she saw a woman's body there, bloody and broken. But the woman wasn't Meg MacDonald. It was herself.

Abruptly Eleanor straightened, her heart racing with uncomfortable speed. What was she thinking of! Had she lost her mind? For one instant she had been so tempted to throw herself out the window and leave the grief and pain and guilt behind!

She touched her flushed cheeks with trembling hands. If only she could remember the past. If only the port, consumed for almost two decades now, had not dulled her mind.

"Mother!" Garrick exclaimed.

She whirled, to see her son standing in the doorway, a look of horror on his face.

Immediately Eleanor stepped away from the window, but as she did so, something touched her from behind. She stiffened and turned, but it was only one of the curtains, lifted by the breeze.

Garrick strode forward, his chest rising and falling with the effort such movement cost him. He gripped her elbow. "What are you doing?" he cried. "What in God's name are you doing up here?"

Tears filled her eyes. "I . . . it is not what you think," she whispered, a protest.

"No? And what is it I am thinking?" he demanded, still ashen beneath his usual swarthy coloring. He had not lessened his hold upon her arm.

"I . . . I came here to think."

"This is where Margaret MacDonald killed herself." Angrily Garrick released her and moved past her, slamming the window shut.

"It's too hot. I opened the window for air," Eleanor lied, trembling now.

He stared, then turned and cracked the window. "You have been crying. Mother, please. Surely you were not going to repeat the past."

She met his worried gaze, saw the concern in his eyes and the love, and reached out and touched his cheek. "No. I was not."

His gaze was searching, and after a pause he nodded. "I don't like you coming up here."

She wet her dry lips and said nothing. The attic had never been more stifling.

"Come downstairs with me. I have a favor to ask of you," Garrick said.

Eleanor nodded and followed him across the small space

of the attic. He held open the tiny door for her. But she paused.

"Did you hear that?" she whispered.

"I did not hear anything," Garrick said, giving her a strange look.

Still, Eleanor did not move. She had thought she had heard a slight creaking sound. But it had probably been her imagination or old wood settling. There had been many times over the past twenty years, though, when she had visited this attic, seeking the solitude to cry and think, that she had felt as if the walls in the attic were watching her. There had been other times when she had felt nothing at all except her loneliness and grief. Now, the hairs at her nape prickled. Eleanor turned and looked back.

The window was closed.

And outside, not a single branch on any tree moved, not a leaf or blade of grass. There was no breeze.

Her mind was no longer dull, but razor sharp. She had not eaten anything all day except for the two forkfuls of poisoned eggs, and she had gone into the kitchens herself for fresh, uncontaminated water. She was not weak. She trembled with rage and the need to escape and rescue her daughter. Hannah, she recalled, had been sent to Bedlam.

The thought terrified her and made her ill. Her vision of her small, blind daughter surrounded by witless women had returned to haunt her now. She had not a moment to waste. Yet she must be careful and clever. Leaving Ashburnham would be difficult enough—she intended to do so in the dead of the night. But how would she manage to free her daughter from the asylum? How?

She could hardly walk up to the front doors, identify herself, and demand Hannah's release. Olivia paced, her temples throbbing, her mouth still uncomfortably dry. That, she supposed, was a lingering symptom of having been poisoned for a number of days.

Would Lionel give Garrick her message? And why was Elizabeth still at Ashburnham? The moment she left the manor, Elizabeth would send a messenger to Arlen, if not chase after her herself. Olivia did not underestimate the other woman.

She needed Garrick desperately, she needed his help. And she could not think about his dilemma now—that he had been disinherited.

Olivia's bedroom windows were open. She heard the shells in the drive crunching as a vehicle rolled up it. She ran to the window, filled with sudden hope. She inhaled, gripping the sill, briefly mesmerized by the sight of the Stanhope coach. *Garrick had come.*

Then she watched in disbelief as the countess of Stanhope stepped from the coach and the door was being closed behind her by a footman. She had come alone.

Olivia was stunned. Then disappointment overwhelmed her, so much so that tears blurred her eyes as the countess approached the house. She blinked furiously, using the back of her hand to wipe her eyes, dismay changing to savage determination. She would get a message to the countess. She must.

Her vision cleared, and Olivia now noticed that Eleanor was unsteady on her feet. Her heart sank. Had she already been nipping the port? She prayed not.

"My dear countess . . ."

Olivia froze at the sound of Elizabeth's voice, somewhere below her. "How wonderful of you to call." Elizabeth stepped from the house and into view, standing on the edge of the walk just below Olivia's window. She extended her hands graciously, gripping both of Eleanor's palms. "This is such a surprise," she cooed.

"Oh, Lady Houghton, I had no idea you were in residence," Eleanor said, seeming flustered. "How nice to see you in the country for a change."

"I have not been feeling the best, so I decided to stay on for a few days," Elizabeth explained. "But then, you hardly have been known to frequent the countryside, either, Lady Stanhope."

"No. Usually I don't." Eleanor seemed to be at a loss. "But how nice. I shall have company with both you and Lady Ashburn here." She smiled.

Olivia, standing at her window, suddenly knew what was going to come. She stiffened.

"Actually, the countess is very ill, and has taken to her bed. She is not receiving callers. Perhaps you should come back later in the week if you wish to see her—if you are still in the country yourself."

The countess seemed befuddled. "She is not receiving callers? How ill is she?"

"I really don't know, as she hardly spoke to me when I tried to inquire after her health this morning. But come inside, let us sit and have tea." Elizabeth took the countess's arm and they disappeared from view as they walked up the front steps of the house.

Olivia turned, walked a few steps, and collapsed into a chair. More tears filled her eyes, and she thought of Hannah in the madhouse. She gripped the arms of the chair, her nails ripping the floral fabric, finding it difficult to breathe. She was not going to get a message to Garrick, and he was not coming.

He was not coming.

She had no one to rely on now but herself.

CHAPTER TWENTY-SEVEN

Olivia lay in bed in her nightclothes in the dark. She was not asleep. It was very early, not even nine o'clock. She had purposely left the draperies open, and outside, the night was bright, with both a full, beaming moon and a thousand glittering stars. She was drenched in perspiration and as stiff as a board.

There was a single brisk rap upon her door and Elizabeth stepped into her room, holding aloft a taper. Olivia had already shut her eyes, forcing her fists to unclench and her breathing to slow to a deep, even rhythm. She listened as Elizabeth approached the bed, her silk skirts swishing softly about her, and was aware of sudden candlelight falling across her face.

"Are you asleep, Olivia?" Elizabeth asked.

Olivia slowly opened her eyes. "Who . . . who . . . who?" She spoke with a thick slur.

Elizabeth stared down at her, unsmiling, her face hard and cold and cruel. "It is I. Elizabeth," she finally said.

Olivia pretended to struggle to keep her eyes open. "Who?" she whispered thickly, as if she were deeply drugged.

Elizabeth bent over her, staring closely at her face.

Immediately Olivia closed her eyes, afraid that Elizabeth would see through her charade and realize that she was completely lucid. It was the hardest thing she had ever done, but she did not move, breathing slowly, so slowly, in and out, in and out. She was scared, very much so. But the stakes were so very high—the stakes were Hannah's life.

Olivia had never been more certain of anything.

Elizabeth straightened, some of the candlelight falling less harshly now upon Olivia's closed lids. A moment later she left the room, shutting the door firmly behind her. Olivia was dismayed when she heard the key turning in the lock on the other side.

She sat up, trembling, her nightgown soaking wet with perspiration. She had hoped to make her escape by sneaking through the sleeping house, but obviously that was not possible now.

She slid from the bed. Beneath her nightgown she wore a chemise. Careful to be utterly silent, she stripped off the nightgown and walked into her dressing room. She dressed in the dark quickly, methodically, efficiently, all the while thinking about her daughter, her chest tight with fear. Then she recrossed her bedroom and pushed open the window. Her heart skipped. Her only means of escape was the oak tree, and now it seemed very far away from the house.

She had no choice.

No one was coming to rescue her; she had to rescue herself.

She hitched up her skirts, wishing she were a man clad in breeches, and slid one leg and then the other over the sill, until she was sitting on it, her feet dangling down against the side of the house. Glimpsing the ground three stories below made her dizzy, and she forced herself to concentrate on the tree. She must throw herself at it and catch the single branch that faced her. It was heavy and solid enough, but Olivia had only one chance to leap to it, and if she did not, she would probably break both legs and both arms in the subsequent fall—if not her very neck. Then Hannah would not be rescued, dear God.

She was panting. She closed her eyes and prayed for strength and calm. When she opened them, the tree seemed even farther away than before, and she made the mistake of looking down just once and briefly; it was enough. Fear curdled her insides.

Then she imagined Hannah in that cold, sterile place, surrounded by insane, dangerous women, and she gripped the windowsill, gritting her teeth, digging her feet against the house. She jumped.

But not high enough. She missed the branch but managed to grasp the trunk of the tree. Frantically she tried to dig her toes into the trunk of the tree, losing what little grip she had.

Olivia fell.

She cried out as she fell down the tree, the bark tearing her hands and cheek and skirts. And the next thing that she knew, she had landed hard on her back.

She felt the air leave her lungs in a terrifying rush.

Her body seemed to snap.

The night above her exploded with fiery stars.

Olivia blinked as pain shot through her from her head to her toes. She lay prone and waited until, gradually, the night sky steadied itself and her vision cleared. The moon continued to beam down at her. She inhaled, not daring to breathe, not daring to move, gazing up through the branches of the towering oak. She had fallen the entire distance she had wished to climb, dear God. She did not know how badly she was hurt, but most of her body seemed to be throbbing in pain.

Gingerly Olivia turned her head. Her neck was not broken. Her head continued to pound. Hesitantly she wriggled her fingers and her toes, flexed her hands. Both her arms seemed to be in working order, and her legs were not broken. Fearfully she explored her head. A huge bump was forming at the base of her skull, but there was no blood. Slowly, hesitantly, she sat up.

She had survived the fall. Relief began, mingling with the bodily pain.

She levered herself up and stood—and almost cried out as a raging pain shot up her ankle to her knee. Her knees buckling, she reached for the tree for support. Tears blinded her as she fought to remain upright.

She hoped that she had only sprained her ankle in the fall. It hurt so much, she was afraid it might be broken. But surely, if that were the case, she would not be able to put any weight upon it at all.

Gritting her teeth, Olivia hobbled away from the tree, then broke into a limping run. Every step cost her dearly, but she could not give up now. It was a hundred feet to the stables, and the night was bright, there were few trees between the barns and house for concealment. She ignored the blinding pain in her ankle. When she reached the side of the stable she collapsed against the smooth wood, panting heavily, sobbing soundlessly, glancing back fearfully at the house. It remained dark and unlit. The salon downstairs where Elizabeth would now be sitting was behind the front rooms. She relaxed slightly. Then the sound of conversation inside the barn made her freeze anew with fear.

She stiffened, swallowing her sobs, calming her breathing, refusing to heed the pain in her ankle. She strained to hear. Two grooms were inside the stable, apparently drinking gin and throwing dice! Olivia despaired. She could hardly walk, she had to steal a horse, but now what should she do?

She tried to think through the encroaching panic. She could either wait until the grooms finished their evening of gaming and drink or she could make a go of it on foot. Immediately she realized she could not wait—it was far too risky.

As Olivia turned away from the barn to begin the very long trek to the village, she was again faced with the house. Before her very eyes, she watched a light appear in her bedroom window. Stunned, incredulous, disbelieving, she froze.

Her room went dark again. But within instants lights had appeared in the downstairs windows of the front of the house. Her absence had been discovered.

Olivia whirled. Her heart constricted, her breath in her throat, she ran across the lawns, holding her skirts high. Air stuck in her lungs. She forced her legs to churn, stumbling repeatedly. Her sobs mingled with her harsh breathing. Fear and panic overcame her, turning her mind peculiarly blank. She reached the first meadow and slipped under the split rails, panting like a wild, hunted animal, inanely understanding now how ferrets and foxes must feel when hunted down and backed into a corner. Clinging to the fence for support, she glanced back at the house.

A dozen servants bearing candles and torches were swarming down the front steps.

Olivia cried out.

Even at this distance, she could make out Elizabeth in their midst, who was clad in a pale ice blue gown that seemed white in the dark of the night.

Frantically Olivia turned and began running toward the first line of trees on the far side of the meadow, afraid she had already been seen—waiting to hear shouts behind her, shouts of "Halt!" There were thick woods ahead. She tripped now on the uneven ground, on stones and ruts, many times, as her legs gave way, her muscles burned with fatigue. The air she desperately sucked in burned her lungs; she could not take in enough. Finally Olivia's legs hooked a pair of dead twisted branches and she fell.

Sobbing, she pushed herself onto her hands and knees, looking back. The servants had fanned out, some heading toward the stables, others hurrying down the long, winding drive. She launched herself upright through sheer force of will, biting down through her lip in order not to scream in pain, and ducked into the edge of the woods, melting against a slender birch. Her ankle hurt so badly that tears streamed down her face.

Oh, God, she thought, and it was a litany. Oh God oh God. Please help me—please do not let them find me! She could not be caught. She had to escape; her daughter's life was at stake.

Olivia closed her eyes, seeking strength. She must pull herself together, she must not give in to fear or pain or fatigue. She had to hide—and she had to make it to Stanhope Hall. When she thought she had gained some semblance of courage and strength, she opened her eyes, only to see a carriage coming swiftly down the drive. It contained Elizabeth.

Olivia crouched, gripping the birch, mesmerized with fear. The carriage was rapidly drawing abreast of her hiding place. Elizabeth and the servants who were in it with her held torches, and they were scanning the sides of the road.

Olivia crouched even lower as the barouche drew parallel to the stand of woods. Elizabeth was crying, "I want Arlen notified immediately. We must find her, Harold, tonight."

The torchlit carriage swept past, continuing down the drive, finally turning onto the main road, heading north, toward Sussex—toward Stanhope Hall. Olivia wiped more tears from her face.

They had not seen her.

And then she turned and began limping through the woods.

He rode very fast, wishing now that he had taken a carriage, because his body was protesting the hard ride, especially his sore left side. But he had been so disturbed by his mother's report that he had left without hesitation several hours ago. Olivia was ill, bedridden. Garrick did not think it likely. He thought it far more likely that that bastard Arlen had locked her up.

Rage filled him as he drove his hunter hard down the road under a night sky filled with stars. If Arlen had hurt either her or Hannah, he would kill him, and not in a gentlemanly way. He would put his hands around his throat and strangle him to death. To hell with duels. He was not about to give Arlen the advantage, not ever again.

He should have gone to Ashburnham earlier, himself. He was a fool to have been deterred by his father, who did not understand what it meant to love a woman. But it was too late now for regrets. He must only hope that it was not too late to prevent something terrible from happening.

Chills coursed through him as he rode. Something terrible had happened. The closer he got to Ashburnham, the more certain he was of it. He was as sick with fear as he was seized with determination, and fortunately he was not

far from the Ashburn country home. There had been no one
else on the road; generally the peerage did not travel at
night, for fear of highwaymen and robbers. He slowed his
hunter to a trot, squinting ahead. An approaching vehicle
was emerging from the darkness of the night.

Garrick reined the bay hunter to a walk, patting his
sweaty neck. Treve was panting loudly, walking now beside them, abreast of Garrick's stirrup. The vehicle was a
carriage, he realized, an expensive lacquer one that could
belong only to a nobleman. And he was but a mile or so
from Ashburnham, the only manor in the vicinity. Garrick
reined his mount to a halt, tension riddling his body.

The barouche rumbled toward him, finally coming
abreast. Garrick had been told that Arlen had departed for
the city; still, he expected to see him in the passenger seat.
But Elizabeth sat there with four armed servants. When she
recognized him, surprise showed upon her features. "Halt
the carriage," she commanded.

Her coachman instantly obeyed.

Garrick drove his mount closer.

"What an odd surprise!" Elizabeth exclaimed. "Good
evening, Lord Caedmon. Oh, dear! I mean Lord De Vere!"
She smiled.

He was not in the mood to spar, and he stared. "What
are you doing out at this time of night, Elizabeth? Surely
you are not returning to London at this hour?" All he could
think of was, Something has happened to Olivia.

"I am Lady Houghton to you, De Vere," she said coolly.

"I know exactly who you are. Where is Olivia?" he
demanded. "And do not tell me that she is ill." He rode
even closer to the open carriage.

"Olivia is ill and in bed," Elizabeth said briskly. "My,
are you in love with my brother's wife? Perhaps he should
challenge you to a duel all over again."

"Regretting that I am alive? I am sorry to have disappointed you." He was disgusted with her.

"I hardly care if you live or die," she snapped. "But in
the end, you will go back to that little island, will you not,

with your tail between your legs—while your brother inherits everything." She laughed.

His temper flared. "I did not come here to discuss the impostor with you, and I happen to be very fond of that little island."

"You would be. You have turned into a savage, Garrick. You are worse than a colonial—but you were always odd and strange!"

He snapped. "Could it be, dearest Elizabeth, that you are still fond of me? In your own unusual way?"

"I was never fond of you!" she cried.

"No?" he mocked. "So it was disgust which made you slip into my bed one night without a stitch of clothing on your back?"

She inhaled, turning pale. To her credit, she ignored the unblinking servants. "That is a lie!"

"I am only sorry I availed myself of what you so freely offered. And it has been abundantly clear to me for all of these ensuing years that you have never forgiven me for failing to grovel over you as Arlen and other men do." He made a sound of disgust. "Beauty, my dear, is only skin deep, and a black core taints even the most perfect, seemingly unblemished fruit."

Her eyes were wide, glittering. "And *you* are a spineless coward as well as a savage and a fool. You and that witch deserve one another, I think."

"You tread dangerously, Elizabeth," he said, his tone so soft it was barely audible.

She stared, and finally, the gesture filled with disdain, she shrugged. "Go to hell, De Vere."

Her curse hardly unsettled him. He glanced at the servants, all of whom were staring directly ahead, as if deaf and dumb and incapable of having heard a single word of their conversation. "Where is Olivia? Why are you out on the road?"

"Olivia is in her bed, where she should be at this hour, and what I am about is not your affair."

She had hardly finished her sentence before Garrick had spurred his mount forward.

"Where are you going?" Elizabeth cried in alarm.

He tossed over his shoulder, "To Ashburnham, of course."

Olivia did not think she could make it. She had not gone very far since escaping the house, and now she limped down the road, every part of her body exhausted and aching, her ankle seriously in pain. The dead branch she had found to use as a cane did little to help her. She needed a lift, and badly. But at this hour, the only horseman she might come upon would be a highwayman, dear God.

Hannah. She must think about her quest, because that fueled her as nothing else could.

Suddenly she heard hoofbeats approaching rapidly. For an instant Olivia froze, filled with fear, because she had not a doubt it was a highwayman coming toward her, as if her thoughts had summoned him up. The night—a living nightmare—could not get any worse. Then she moved. With an agility and speed she did not think herself capable of anymore, she ran off the road into the woods, were she threw herself into the brush. She lay there, panting, her face buried in twigs and leaves.

The hoofbeats grew louder.

Gasping for air, tears stinging her eyes, in severe pain, Olivia sat up, brushing dirt off her face. On her hands and knees, she crawled to the edge of the wild shrub she hid behind. Parting thorny branches, she peered at the road as the rider galloped past, his steed kicking up clumps of dirt and dust.

Relief filled her as he passed—she had once again just missed being discovered. God, it seemed, was on her side tonight.

About to collapse once again, she glimpsed the dog loping at the horse's side. The dog—*a red Irish setter.*

She saw the big man astride the big horse.

Olivia staggered upright as man and horse and dog galloped away, in the direction of her home.

She came to her senses. She stumbled back to the road—

he was fifty feet away now—sixty—seventy. "Garrick!" she screamed. *"Garrick!"*

Horse and rider thundered away. Tears blinded Olivia, and she was at once immobilized and disbelieving and utterly desperate. Suddenly she started to run after them, knowing she could never catch up—and that he could not possibly hear her. She staggered down the road. *"Garrick!"*

He continued to gallop away. It was hopeless.

"Garrick," she sobbed, her feet slowing. It was hopeless.

Suddenly the dog stopped, turned, and barked.

A moment later he had wheeled his horse around, so abruptly that it reared wildly.

For an instant she stood there, staring at the prancing horse and the cloaked rider. "Garrick!" Olivia screamed, waving her arms.

The dog barked again. Then he was galloping to her, he was out of the saddle, his horse still flying down the road, and he was running to her. And suddenly Olivia was in his arms. She clung, closing her eyes, finding safety at long last.

And she wept against his chest, in fear and fatigue, in despair and relief.

"Olivia . . . Oh, God, I have been so afraid," he cried against her hair, raining kisses on the top of her head, holding her in a viselike grip.

She choked on the huge sobs thrusting their way from deep inside her heart, her soul. "Hannah," she tried thickly.

He touched her face and gasped. Olivia met his shocked gaze. "What happened!" he cried.

Olivia imagined that her face was covered with dirt and blood. "They drugged me. But I realized what was happening and stopped eating. Because of the cat. I waited for you to come, Garrick. I gave Lionel a message—" She could not continue. She covered her face with her hands, thinking of Hannah, crying now. "Hannah."

"My God," he said, taking her hands and pulling them

from her face. "Your hands are raw. The blood . . . your dress . . . your face."

"I jumped out of the window—they had locked me in," Olivia cried.

He crushed her hard against his chest. Olivia gasped in pain, because in doing so he made her step forward, unthinkingly, onto her bad ankle.

"What is it?" he cried, steadying her with wide eyes.

"My ankle. It's terribly sprained, or maybe worse."

"We are going to a doctor." His gaze burned. "I am sick, thinking of what he has done to you."

"He put Hannah in Bedlam," Olivia cried. "There is no time for a doctor. We must rescue her." She seized his shirt. "Help me, Garrick. *Help me.* Help me get my daughter out of that horrible place, and help us escape Arlen!"

Briefly she watched Garrick close his eyes, his face a grim mask. Then he pulled her close again. "Olivia, we will rescue her. Do not worry," he said, his tone tender yet firm.

"How?" she implored. "How? Arlen put her there. They will hardly hand her over to us!"

He looked at her. "They will hand her over. I promise you that," he said.

Suddenly she believed. She believed in him completely, in his strength, his loyalty, his word. Olivia nodded, leaning now upon him for support. She was brutally aware of how exhausted she was—but there was no time for fatigue yet.

"We must hurry." Garrick was decisive. "Elizabeth is looking for you." He glanced back down the road.

"And she has sent a messenger to Arlen," Olivia said, following his gaze, afraid that they would see Elizabeth coming around the bend at any moment.

"We need two fresh mounts or a ride," Garrick responded. Suddenly he lifted her into the saddle and mounted behind her. He kept one arm around her waist, and Olivia spooned her body into his. "We shall find something in the village."

Olivia nodded, worried now that they were going to meet Elizabeth before they even made it to the village.

And he understood. "Do not worry anymore, you have been through enough," he said softly, and in spite of his tone, it was a command. "I will take care of everything. You shall soon be reunited with your daughter."

"I know," Olivia whispered. She shifted so she could look at him. "Garrick, I have needed you so. I love you so." And the power of her love filled her eyes with tears.

"I love you, too," he said. "More than you can know."

Chapter Twenty-eight

"My lady," the footman exclaimed. "My lady! We were not expecting you!"

Elizabeth swept past the flustered footman and marched into the foyer of Arlen's town house, her sodden skirts leaving a trail of water behind her. She was exceedingly tired, very dirty, rather wet, as it had been raining ever since she had entered London's outskirts, and not in the best of moods. Traveling all night was hardly a pleasant experience, much less in inclement weather. "Is he still abed?" she snapped as the butler appeared at the foyer's other end. His face paled considerably.

"I do believe so, my lady," the uneasy footman said, his cheeks red.

"Lady Houghton." The butler came to life, hastening forward. "Please, let me take your wrap and gloves. I shall have a hot breakfast made up while we rouse His Lordship. Surely you wish to refresh yourself?"

Elizabeth glared at him, removing two nearly black gloves, which had previously been white, slapping them against his chest, then nearly throwing her damp cashmere shawl at him. "I shall rouse him myself." She strode toward the stairs.

"My lady!" the butler cried, flying after her. "That is hardly decorous. Please, allow me!"

But Elizabeth had just glimpsed her grimy reflection in

the mirror and she faltered, crying out. Soot, dirt, and mud marred not just her exquisite pale gray gown, but her face as well. Her hair had turned itself into what appeared to be a rat's nest. "Damn Olivia," she said beneath her breath, hopelessly attempting to pat a few curls back into place. Then she was rushing up the stairs.

The butler raced up behind her. "Lady Houghton! I strongly advise you to go to the dining room and allow His Lordship some time to rise and dress."

Ignoring him, Elizabeth gripped the brass doorknob of Arlen's room and thrust it open without even knocking.

And she stood on the threshold, arms folded beneath her chest, staring at the two occupants in the large, canopied bed.

The red-haired woman woke up and screamed, clutching the covers to her chest.

Elizabeth sighed, retrieved a flimsy garment from the floor—one that, she noticed, was quite torn—and towered over the woman as Arlen stirred. "Get up," she ordered, tossing the garment to her.

Arlen suddenly opened his eyes, saw her, and sat bolt upright. "Elizabeth!" His eyes popped from his head. His face had never been as deathly white.

"Now get out," Elizabeth said coolly to the other woman, "before I have you hauled out like a sack of rubbish."

The redhead jumped from the bed, blue eyes wide, using the wisp of silk to cover her breasts and loins, and ran from the room, past the aghast butler.

"My lord, I beg your pardon," the butler nearly wept from the doorway.

Elizabeth turned. "You may leave us, Barnes," she said. "Now."

The butler looked at his master for confirmation, and when he saw none was forthcoming, he turned and fled. Elizabeth marched to the door and shut it, then faced her brother again.

Buck naked, he stepped from the bed, then pulled on a

robe and belted it. His hands were trembling. "I can explain. Elizabeth—"

"Do shut up," she said. "Do you think I care about your French actress?" She eyed him. "Olivia has escaped, and her lover is with her."

Arlen stared as if her words were incomprehensible.

"Arlen!" she shrieked. "I have spent half the night searching for her, and when I failed to find her, I have spent the rest of the night traveling here, posthaste! And De Vere was on the road to Ashburnham. It hardly takes a wizard to know that he was meeting her. What are you going to do now?" she demanded. "Clearly they are planning to run away together. You fool!"

He inhaled, turned away, and mopped his brow with a handkerchief.

"Arlen! We could both be in trouble for what we have done—or, rather, what we tried to do!" Elizabeth cried. "What if she goes to the authorities and claims we were trying to murder her?"

Arlen slowly faced her, his eyes were hard and bright, his face no longer pale. He smiled coldly. "Have no fear. I know exactly where they are going, my dear, and I shall meet them there."

And Elizabeth's eyes brightened. "Bedlam," she said.

Elizabeth's carriage turned into the drive in front of Houghton Place. Rain pounded down upon the rooftop, and the early morning was dark and gray. She had the shades up and was craning her neck to see out the window. She smiled, espying the magnificent coach already parked in the drive. He had received her message—he had come. Her impatience was so great that she could hardly refrain from opening the door herself when her own carriage finally came to a halt. Lifting her dirty, stained skirts, she hurried up the front steps of the manse and rushed into the foyer.

Servants appeared, swarming around her, taking her gloves and wrap, their expressions impassive. No one seemed surprised by her unusual and disheveled appearance or by the fact that she had returned home without sending advance notice. "Where is His Lordship?" Elizabeth demanded of a servant.

"He is upstairs, soundly asleep, my lady."

Hiding a satisfied smile, Elizabeth hurried into the salon, closing both doors behind her. "Lionel."

He was facing the windows overlooking the gardens behind the house, and he turned. He studied her. "I received your message and left immediately. You look terrible. What happened?" He strode forward.

"This is my greeting?" Elizabeth murmured, standing on tiptoe and pressing her mouth to his. Even though he had made the same horrid journey as she, he was hardly disheveled, she noticed. But he barely returned the kiss, and she stood flat-footed again, eyeing him. "Olivia escaped, and she is with your brother. Arlen is certain they are on their way to Bedlam to rescue Hannah." She had kept both hands on his chest and was now rubbing them there.

His set expression did not change. As she slipped one hand underneath his waistcoat, he appeared not to notice. "This is intolerable," he said beneath his breath.

Elizabeth strained forward again and flicked his neck with her tongue. Her husband was upstairs, but he slept too soundly to cause concern. Her body pulsed and throbbed in favorite, hidden places as she thought of Lionel taking her in the salon.

He jerked, caught both her wrists, and held her away. "Do I seem amorously inclined to you?"

Her eyes widened. "No. You do not. But Houghton sleeps like a dead man." She did smile. "Pardon the pun."

His jaw flexed. His eyes were hard, and still he did not smile. "What the hell happened? Your damned servant failed to do as she was instructed, Elizabeth," he said, his tone cold and filled with anger.

Her own smile vanished. "Do not talk to me that way, Lionel."

He stared. She stared back. Finally he softened, pulling her into his arms and against him. "I apologize."

"Good." She turned her face and nuzzled his neck. "I dismissed the maid. And you are right, clearly she failed to do as she was told. Otherwise, your plan was brilliant, Lionel.'' Elizabeth pressed her mouth against his neck, sliding her hands slowly down his torso, to the waistband of his breeches. After hesitating only briefly, she slid them lower, caressing the soft bulge of his flaccid manhood. To her delight, it quickly began to harden. ''Put your mind at ease,'' she whispered, her breathing deepening now as she played with him. ''Arlen intends to meet them there. He will do our dirty work for us, darling.''

He gripped her hand, stilling it. ''Your brother is not infallible.''

She lifted her heated blue gaze to his. ''Let us not speak of Arlen now.''

Lionel stared, his chest beginning to heave, and then he cursed. He shoved Elizabeth away, so forcefully that she almost stumbled. ''Lionel!'' she exclaimed.

He was hurrying to the door. ''I have no time for this now!''

She caught him from behind by the arm. ''Halt! Why do you care about this so much? I do not think it is because you yearn for Olivia yourself! Why?'' she demanded, her mouth set, eyes flashing.

''Why did you wish to imprison and poison Olivia, my dear?'' Lionel returned coolly.

''I have many reasons. But do not avoid the question now.'' Yet Elizabeth smiled and did not allow him to speak. ''You are afraid of her, are you not, my dear? You are afraid of her and of her child.''

His gaze was hard, brilliant, unwavering. It was a moment before he spoke. ''You are jealous. You are jealous because Garrick is in love with Olivia—the way he never felt for you.''

''That is not true.'' Elizabeth released his arm. ''You did not answer me, Lionel. Why are you afraid of Olivia and her child?''

He smiled at her without mirth. ''I am hardly afraid of them, my dear.''

''The child is a witch, like her mother,'' Elizabeth said, her gaze riveted on his. ''We have already discussed this.

She is more powerful than her mother. You can confide in me. After all, I am carrying your child.''

He continued to smile. ''Please. Do not take me for a fool. The child might be Arlen's, and I am well aware of it.''

Elizabeth paled. ''Are you mad? Arlen is my brother,'' she began.

''Hush.'' He placed a finger on her lips. ''I know the truth. But your secret is safe with me.''

She trembled.

''Surely you do trust me, Elizabeth?''

''Perhaps,'' Elizabeth said slowly. ''Perhaps we must trust one another.''

His gaze slid over her. His smile, which did not reach his eyes, remained in place. ''And why should I trust you, my dear?''

''Because we are alike,'' she said simply.

He merely looked at her. ''We will talk later. I have work to do.''

She watched him throw open the doors, then followed him. ''You are going to Bedlam,'' she said to his rapidly departing back.

At the front door, he whirled. ''Be a good wife and take care of your husband,'' he said, bowing. Neither footman, as still as statues outside the door, blinked. ''Good day, my lady.''

She watched him hurrying away. ''Good day, my lord,'' she said. But she hugged herself, staring after him. He knew too much, and she was uneasy. But perhaps she knew as much about him. That last thought reassured her. In any case, he would take care of Olivia and Hannah, and their secrets would be safe. Elizabeth turned and stared up the stairs, thinking now about her husband and what she must do. Her eyes were hard.

Lightning cracked overhead. Garrick pulled Olivia closer to protect her from the driving rain, but it was no use: they were both soaking wet by now. He had purchased a small phaeton in Ashburn, and the wind drove the rain in upon them. Thunder cracked loudly not far above them.

He could not help but think that this kind of day was an omen, and he was not a superstitious man. "We are almost there," he told Olivia. "How are you faring?"

She looked out at him from under the hood of the mantle he had purchased for her, tendrils of wet hair curling about her face. "I am afraid," she whispered.

"I know. You have nothing to fear. I have no doubts about my ability to gain Hannah's release." His determination knew no bounds, but he was lying, because he thought it likely that Elizabeth had sent a warning to Arlen. He only hoped that, in this foul weather, the messenger was taking his time—if not ginning it up in front of a warm fire in some public barroom.

Bedlam loomed ahead of them. Garrick halted the phaeton, squinting through the gloom and the rain. The asylum was a low squat stone structure. Engraved in gray stone above the heavy wooden door were two words: Bedlam Hospital. In front of the building lay a small square empty courtyard, and an iron gate, closed and padlocked, barred the short, muddy drive. The low-storied, thrush-roofed tenements surrounding Bedlam belonged to the poor underbelly of the city. Smoke poured from numerous protruding chimneys, aromas abounded of onions and potatoes, but even with the wind and the rain, the odor of the sewage running in the streets was overwhelming. Not a soul was in sight, but somewhere not far from them, a couple could be heard shouting at one another from behind closed doors.

"Oh, God," Olivia whispered, clutching Garrick's hand as he helped her down to the curb. Treve jumped to the ground from the backseat.

Lightning flashed again, this time just beyond the asylum, illuminating it starkly. Garrick gritted his teeth and pulled her forward, crossing the dirty street. He rang the bell beside the closed gates ceaselessly. Treve whined.

The door to the building opened and a drably uniformed man came hurrying toward them. "Who be ye?" he growled at them from under his cap, glaring suspiciously.

"I am Lord Garrick De Vere," Garrick said, purposely

not identifying Olivia as the countess of Ashburn. "We wish a word with your supervisor."

The big burly man eyed him.

Garrick thrust a few coins in his hand.

They disappeared instantly, and then the key was turned in the lock and the gates were open. "Follow me, me lord, me lady," he said, ducking his head because of the rain.

They hurried across the courtyard. Garrick ordered Treve to stay, and he and Olivia entered the asylum. The guard closed the door behind them, the sound loud and somehow ominous.

Garrick looked around quickly, but there was nothing to see. The room was empty except for a fireplace and two scarred and rickety wooden benches. One single corridor led into the building's interior; at its end was a solidly closed, barred door. But light was spilling from another room just beyond the entryway.

The guard beckoned to them, and they walked after him to pause on the threshold of a small room. It was no larger than a maid's closet, but a fire crackled in the hearth. Across from the fireplace a man sat at a desk, a single oil lamp glowing. The room was dark and gloomy; the lamp hardly shed any light. "Mr. Hepple, ye have visitors, a lord an' 'is lady," the guard said.

Garrick stepped in front of him, throwing a warning look at Olivia to remain silent and where she was. "Sir. I am Garrick De Vere, the son of the earl of Stanhope," he said, bowing.

The tall, wiry, bewhiskered man rose, tugging at his stained frock coat. "Good day, me lord. What a surprise this is. I don't get high 'n' mighty visitors very often." He smiled, baring yellow teeth. An incisor was missing.

"I'm sure you do not." Garrick's smile was brief. "I have come for the eight-year-old blind girl recently brought to you," he said. "Her name, whether you know it or not, is Hannah."

"Hmm." Hepple stared into space as if thinking. "I know of no sich girl, me lord. Blind, did ye say? An' about eight years of age?" He shook his head. "Afraid I niver seen such a child—an' I interview every inmate meself.''

Olivia made a choking sound of despair.

Garrick sent her a look, stepping closer to the supervisor of Bedlam. He towered over the man. His smile was hard. "Perhaps this will help you, sir." He withdrew a personal note from his interior breast pocket and laid it flat on the desk, in the small circle of light cast by the single kerosene lamp burning there. Thunder boomed outside, just overhead. The sum of the note was completely visible—it was for ten thousand pounds. "Has your memory improved?" Garrick asked coldly.

Hepple looked from the note to Garrick, remaining silent.

Suddenly there was the sound of rustling cloth behind him, and Arlen Grey stepped out from the shadows behind the desk. "I'm afraid it does not," he said harshly. Then he looked at his wife. "You whore."

And in that single brief moment, Garrick knew the urge to do murder. It would be so easy now. But even as it flashed through his mind that he could strangle Arlen and hide the body, the burly guard stepped closer to Hepple and Arlen. It was enough for Garrick to regain his sanity. "I am hardly surprised to see you," he said, his breathing deep and uneven.

"Arlen, please let me take Hannah from this place! I will do anything, anything, please!" Olivia cried, dashing forward.

Garrick caught her and dragged her to his side before she could fling herself at her husband. "Stop. I will handle this," he cried.

She looked up at him, tears streaming down her face. "Will you? *Will you?*"

"I am afraid the child stays here, where she belongs," Arlen said coldly. "Your punishment, Olivia, for being such a loyal and loving wife."

"Punish me, but not Hannah!" Her bosom heaved. "How can you do this, no matter that you hate me? Hannah is your child—"

"No!" he roared. "She is not mine. And we both know it!"

Olivia's face was suffused with shock.

Garrick pushed Olivia behind him. "I will kill you, Ashburn, one day, some way, if you do not have your daughter released."

Arlen laughed and faced Hepple. "Did you hear that? De Vere has threatened my life. Is such a threat not against the king's law? You will have to do better, De Vere. Your threats do not persuade me."

"I am going to expose you for exactly what you are," Garrick said, low and furiously. "For an abuser of women and children, and a would-be murderer. You are the one who shall wind up behind bars when I am through."

Arlen laughed with real mirth. "Do you think your word could possibly be taken against mine? You, the savage from Barbados? The Stanhope black sheep? The seducer of innocence? A man even his own father despises? I am the earl of Ashburn. You cannot best me."

His pulse was pounding, his fists clenched. Garrick failed to find a suitable reply, because Arlen was right. No one would believe or support him. Except, perhaps, the earl of Stanhope—if he sold his soul to him first. In that instant, he knew that was exactly what he would do. There was no other choice.

"Garrick may not be able to best you, but I can," Olivia suddenly said very tersely.

Surprised silence greeted her words, and then Arlen laughed.

Olivia stepped forward, past Garrick, pulling off her hood. "If you do not release my child," she said, her tone low and hoarse but very, very succinct, "I shall tell the world about your liaison with Elizabeth."

Garrick whirled, shocked. Surely Olivia did not know of what she spoke!

Olivia did not look at him. She raised one hand; it was a fist. "I will tell everyone just how much you love your younger sister—how much—and how often."

Arlen stared. Garrick stared, the oddness of Arlen's relationship with Elizabeth suddenly becoming comprehensible. But how could anyone have guessed?

Even in the poorly lit room, Arlen's face was garishly white. "You know nothing, Olivia. This is absurd. Lies—"

"I have known since we were first wed. My God, the two of you carrying on like animals under my own roof, with me a newlywed. I pretended for years that I knew nothing. I pretended to myself. It was so ghastly! But I am not the only one who knows. The entire household knows, Arlen. And from what I have gathered, this has been going on for some time. When was it that you became Elizabeth's guardian?" Olivia stared.

Arlen did not reply.

"She was ten, was she not? Is that when you first took her?" Olivia asked harshly. But her tone was also tremulous.

No one spoke. No one stirred. Garrick finally roused himself, the shock subsiding. "So that is why you have hated me ever since we were children. She was always chasing me—you could not stand it."

Olivia touched him, silencing him. "Arlen, when I am through with you and her, there is not a door in society that Elizabeth will be admitted through. Not a single one. The world will know her for the despicable whore she is. And I imagine that everyone will rightly assume that you are the father of the child she now carries."

"You bitch," Arlen finally said.

"Give me my daughter. We will disappear. You will never see us again. Otherwise, your precious sister will lose everything. I will make sure of it," Olivia responded.

Garrick looked at her beautiful face, and he alone knew the immense courage and effort this cost her. "Well done," he said softly.

She did not look at him, her clear gray eyes focused only on her husband of the past nine years.

"We should have killed you!" he cried. "Very well. Take her. Take her and get out of this country, as far away from me and mine that you can go! I am annulling this marriage, Olivia. I shall find grounds, I promise you that. And I give you nothing!"

Olivia bit her lip, tears suddenly flooding her eyes. Garrick automatically reached out to steady her, but he spoke to the warden. "Take us to the child."

Hepple nodded, moving past them and into the hallway, the burly guard just behind him. Garrick kept a grip on Olivia as they hurried after him. He felt her body trembling with fear and exhaustion, and he could not blame her. No one spoke. Their footsteps rang hollowly in the hall. After extracting a ring of keys, Hepple unlocked and opened the barred door.

Olivia whimpered. Garrick held her more tightly. On each side of the corridor were barred cells, crowded with filthy, ragged, unkempt men. "Do not look," Garrick said as they followed Hepple toward another door. Chaos seemed to reign behind the bars. The inmates jabbered and fought, drooled and picked at ticks and fleas like monkeys. A man urinated through the bars. Another man was trying to kiss a fellow inmate. Someone wept loudly.

"Hannah." Garrick gripped Olivia and propelled her through the next doorway. But he knew he would be haunted for the rest of his life by all he was seeing.

They entered a rectangular room. There were no bars, no cells. The room was filled with women of all ages and all shapes, old and young, fat and thin, as unkempt and maddened as the men. Moans, jabbering, incoherent speech patterns, shouts, and raucous laughter made the din deafening. The air was close and foul. The corners of the room had chamber pots, but there was feces on the floor. Garrick could not spy Hannah anywhere.

Suddenly a filthy young woman with matted brown hair threw herself on the floor in front of them. "Gawd bless ye both, gawd bless ye," she cried, hands clasped in prayer, face uplifted toward Olivia.

Olivia stared down at her. "Oh, God."

Garrick quickly handed her a few shillings, moving Olivia aside.

"Mama."

Olivia froze.

Garrick whirled and saw Hannah sitting against a wall, her face strained, unmoving. "Hannah!"

But Olivia had seen her at the same time. She cried out, rushing forward, as Hannah slowly stood, arms outstretched. "Mama!" Hannah called, her face crumbling as she began to cry.

Weeping, Olivia grabbed her daughter and buried her in her embrace. "I will never forgive myself," she sobbed. "Please, please, tell me you are all right." She rocked her.

"Mama, Mama, I've been so scared," Hannah wept, clinging.

Garrick touched the back of Hannah's head. He had never in his life been more relieved. "We should go, now," he said. He pried Olivia's arms from her child and lifted Hannah into his arms. "Ssh," he said. Olivia gripped his coat. "Hepple, let us go."

They crossed the overcrowded room swiftly, ignoring the outstretched hands and the bodies pushing at them. The supervisor opened the door they had just come through, Garrick standing behind him. At the far end of the corridor, past the many barred cells and the insane men, the opposite door was opening to admit another party. Garrick froze, filled with sudden comprehension, filled with dread.

For it had been too easy, and he was well aware of it.

When that far door was fully ajar, Lionel stood at the opposite end of the hall, staring at them, his expression cold and hard.

CHAPTER TWENTY-NINE

For one stunning moment, the two men stared at each other across the length of the corridor. Garrick turned. He seized Hepple's arm, slamming the heavy door closed in their faces. "Is there a back way out of here?" he shouted.

"We niver use it, but there is—"

"Show us, now." Garrick shook him. "I left my note on your desk, damn it, man," he said. "For ten thousand pounds."

Hepple turned swiftly and pushed his way through the crowded room; Garrick, with Hannah in his arms, followed, Olivia right behind him. He unlocked another door, holding it wide open for them. "Just follow this hall," he said. "It comes out on the street behind the building."

"The key," Garrick said grimly.

Hepple hesitated, then slipped a key on a cord over his head from where it had been hanging about his neck. "Ye nobs are as mad as the rest of 'em," he mumbled.

But Garrick did not hear. He was already racing down the dark, unlit, and very narrow hall with Olivia. The air was fetid and close, as if the hall had not been used in years. The stones beneath their feet were rough and uneven. He heard the door slamming behind them. The sound echoed loudly, reverberating.

"What if this is a trap?" Olivia breathed from just behind him. "Lionel is the Stanhope heir, Garrick, and once Hepple finds that out, he will be more eager to help him than us."

"By then we will be gone," Garrick retorted as they reached the end of the corridor. A solid wood door confronted them. He let the key slip from his fingertips to Olivia's, still holding Hannah against his chest. For an instant he watched Olivia insert it in the rusted lock with trembling hands. "How are you faring, Hannah?" he asked softly.

"He wants to hurt me," she whispered against his neck, clinging with a shockingly strong grip to him.

"Your father cannot hurt you now," Garrick said.

"No. Your brother wants to hurt me."

Garrick stiffened. "He will not have the chance." But his eyes met Olivia's briefly. The man who had chased them to Bedlam was an impostor. Wasn't he? Garrick was shaken. Hannah did not seem to have any doubt about Lionel's identity.

The lock turned. Olivia pushed at the door and it opened, groaning in protest. Outside, the morning was almost black as it continued to pour. Olivia pushed the door shut behind them. Garrick whistled loudly for Treve. Olivia looked up at him fearfully as they waited for the setter, and then the dog was racing toward them from around the side of the building. He barked once.

"Come on," Garrick shouted, and they began running across the vacant street. Garrick looked back over his shoulder, but no one was in pursuit—yet. And a moment later, the three of them and the dog were leaping into the phaeton, Garrick whipping the gelding into a canter, the small vehicle careening away.

CAEDMON CRAG

The sky was gray and heavy with clouds. The ocean, just below the cliffs, appeared black and ominous. Whitecaps frothed viciously around the glistening black boulders strewn about the taupe-colored beach. The wind howled, buffeting them incessantly. Garrick was at the reins of the phaeton, in the front seat. Olivia sat with her daughter in the back, holding Hannah as she slept, Treve's head in Hannah's lap. Relief at finding and rescuing Hannah had long since given way to other, more turbulent, and more hopeful, emotions. If Arlen would really annul their marriage, and if Garrick could turn his back upon his family, then she would be free to marry him and become his wife and the mother of his children. The future beckoned so brightly that it was painful. But along with the joy, Olivia was aware of something else, a nagging dread, demanding her attention.

She must not entertain it now.

Garrick shifted in his seat to look back at her. Olivia smiled at him. "I can never repay you for this," she said softly, her tone harsh with the depth and power of all her emotions.

The wind chose that moment to howl like a banshee, and he waited until the huge gust had died down before speaking. "Yes, you can," he said. "When Arlen annuls the marriage, you will marry me."

She felt her eyes instantly becoming moist. "It is my dearest wish right now. But if he does not annul the marriage after all?" she asked softly. "Will it be enough for me to repay you with my love, from now until eternity?"

"Yes," he said hoarsely.

He turned, urging the gelding on, driving him into the wind. Olivia looked down at her sleeping daughter, trying hard not to cry. She was almost ready to believe in happy endings and miracles, and she was acutely aware that her heart was filled with love and hope and joy. Still, fear remained. She could not get rid of it. To counter the weightlessness of her happiness, there was a dark, depressing heaviness she could not shake off or drive away. She could not understand it—she was afraid to think about it. Garrick had just asked her to marry him, and maybe, just maybe, Arlen would annul her marriage and set her free, allowing a miracle to happen. In her heart, there should only be love, there should only be hope. So why this horrid, niggling, oppressive dread?

It was as if they had all not suffered enough. It was as

if, somehow, impossibly, being together now, her daughter miraculously safe and sound, had been accomplished too easily. But it had not been easy; it had been inhumanly cruel and torturously difficult.

She pressed a kiss to Hannah's forehead, wishing the dread would disappear. Her daughter did not stir. She was exhausted, and Olivia could understand why. She desperately wanted to know the details of what had transpired at Bedlam, and just as desperately, she did not. She knew that a part of her would never forgive herself for allowing Hannah to be incarcerated in the asylum.

She felt a tear slipping down her face as she stared at Garrick's strong back and broad shoulders. She must let go of the guilt. She must think now only of the future. But why was she afraid? Was it because of Lionel? She could not forget the odd, implacable look on his face as he had stared at them from the other end of the hall at the asylum.

And ahead, the rooftops of the manor at Caedmon Crag suddenly appeared, starkly etched against the dark, cloud-heavy sky. Olivia pushed strands of flying hair out of her face. The wind remained so strong that leaves and twigs swirled about the ground, and the few trees on the heath swayed eerily. Now was not the time to think about America. She trembled. "You are intending to expose Lionel for a fraud. If you are right, then you are the legitimate Stanhope heir, Garrick. Can you really walk away from your heritage?"

"Yes. I can." He suddenly halted the team of chestnut mares and turned around on the front seat to face her. "I have never wanted this. This place has never felt like my home. Where you and Hannah are, Olivia, that is my home."

She started to cry, nodding, holding Hannah tightly. She felt her daughter rousing. "I must tell you something," she whispered as the heaviness began to press itself upward from inside her body, her heart, her soul, infringing upon the hope and happiness.

"What?" He was grim.

She wet her lips. "It is not over. I have been trying to

tell myself that this horrible feeling I have is just left-over fear and natural enough, but it is not. I know this is not over. There is going to be more suffering, Garrick.'' To her surprise and dismay, tears slipped from her eyes.

He stared. After a long moment he said, ''Don't cry. We will finish what has to be finished, and together, the three of us will withstand anything. I promise you that.''

Olivia could not gaze at him anymore, and she bent over Hannah, stroking her daughter's hair, seeking comfort from an eight-year-old child; wanting to go to Garrick and be held by him as if she were the child herself.

''Mama?'' Hannah murmured sleepily.

''Darling, you are awake!'' Olivia exclàimed as Hannah sat up, yawning widely. She hugged her hard. ''My dear, we have some bread and cheese, are you hungry? We have fresh milk, too.''

Hannah suddenly faced her mother, her expression no longer sleepy but exceedingly alert. ''We are in Cornwall, near Caedmon Crag.''

''Yes,'' Olivia said, watching her closely.

''Mama!'' Hannah tensed, her sightless eyes wide. ''We must hurry.''

''I do not understand,'' Olivia whispered, searching her daughter's blank eyes for the truth. ''Why must we hurry, dear?''

Hannah faced Garrick. ''Lionel. He is coming. To stop us. But something is here—I am certain of it.''

For one moment Olivia met Garrick's gaze. ''What, Hannah? What is here?''

Hannah hesitated. ''He will show me.''

''Who?'' Olivia asked. ''Who will show you?''

Hannah's expression was strained. She did not answer. ''Can we go to the manor now?'' she asked instead.

Garrick, his jaw flexed, nodded and lifted the reins. But as the mares drove off, he said, ''Hannah. I have a favor to ask of you.''

And Olivia looked at him, dread mingled with dismay— and resignation.

*   *   *

Hannah did not pause. While Garrick and Olivia stood on the threshold of the bedroom Lionel had used as a boy right up until his death, she walked directly to the bed. She touched the bed coverings, which were faded and old and covered with dust. She lingered there, then walked across the room to a closed chest. Bending, she opened the lid.

Garrick's heart was beating hard, too much so for comfort. He hurried to her, afraid she might hurt herself if the heavy lid fell closed. Hannah slipped to her knees, her hands in the chest. Garrick peered down. The chest contained faded lawnshirts, breeches, stockings, underclothes. Lionel's old clothing.

His heart beat more swiftly now, and his vision blurred. There was a small stabbing of an ancient hurt inside of him, but now he faced it instead of trying to shove it away—or to run away himself. When Treve buried his damp nose into his palm, he did not even notice. When had he last been inside Lionel's room? Suddenly he remembered the two of them as little boys, sharing Lionel's bed until the governess caught them and chased Garrick back to his own room. It was difficult to breathe.

There were so many memories, and as clear as if it had been yesterday, he remembered standing with Lionel on the cliffs by the ruined keep, talking about smugglers, Lionel trying to give him the Spanish coin. What had happened? And why?

Was Lionel dead? Or was he very much alive?

Hannah suddenly stood. "There is nothing here. I do not feel anything," she said tersely.

Garrick felt relief—he also felt dismay.

Olivia came forward. "Let's go downstairs and sit in front of the fire for a while. We are all very tired." She smiled, clasping Hannah's thin shoulder, but she gazed at Garrick.

Treve turned suddenly and faced the door, whining.

Simultaneously Hannah stiffened. She had also turned toward the doorway. Olivia was as frozen.

"What is it?" Garrick asked, aware that something in the room had changed. A heaviness had infused the atmosphere. It was tangible, but not frightening. He was not gifted, but . . . something was present. Or someone.

He felt as if they were all being watched.

"We are not alone," Olivia said quietly.

And before Garrick could demand elaboration, Hannah rushed past her mother and into the hallway.

"Hannah!" Olivia cried, running after her. Garrick followed. Hannah hurried downstairs and through the dark, vacant front hall, Treve on her heels. She did not hesitate. She easily navigated her way around the table and few chairs there. Garrick wanted to ask a dozen questions, but he did not dare. The look on Olivia's face told him not to. He was afraid to interfere with whatever was happening now. He sensed that the moment of truth was at hand.

The front door was open. Garrick was certain he had left it closed, as he had their very first night at the manor a few weeks ago. Hannah stepped outside without pausing. If the wind gusting in her face bothered her, she gave no sign. Her strides increased in pace. She started running across the courtyard, Treve bounding at her side.

Garrick and Olivia also broke into a run, in order to keep up with her. They followed her and the dog through the barbican and across the drawbridge. Hannah suddenly veered off the road. Far ahead of her, a portion of the jagged top of the ruined keep could just be seen, barely emerging from the gray, cloud-swept sky.

Garrick heard it first. He faltered, the sound of pounding hoofbeats drawing his attention from Hannah and the dog. He spun around, searching the landscape for an approaching rider—and saw a horse flying down the road toward them. He stiffened.

"Garrick!" Olivia cried, seizing his arm.

And Garrick did not have to be told to know who it was. The rider halted his gray mount violently, causing the animal to rear wildly. But Lionel dismounted before the gray was even standing still. His strides long and hard, his cape whirling about him, he came running forward.

Garrick braced himself, mentally as well as physically. "Step back, Olivia," he said, low, so only she could hear.

"What if he is armed?" she cried.

"Step back," he snapped. They both knew why Lionel had chased them to Cornwall.

She moved away from him. Garrick could feel her fear.

Lionel slowed to a walk only a few yards from him. "You left Bedlam in such haste, Garrick."

"Obviously we were in a rush," Garrick said smoothly.

Lionel halted. "To return to this dismal place?" He smiled, but it did not reach his eyes. Then he glanced at Olivia. "My lady. Where is the child?"

"What do you want with my child?!" Olivia cried, suddenly coming forward, the wind tearing at her cloak and skirts.

Garrick stepped in front of her, blocking her way. He did not allow his eyes to roam the countryside in the direction Hannah had disappeared. "Hannah is far away, in a very safe place," he said softly and with a menace he had no wish to disguise.

Lionel's gaze slammed to Garrick and remained there. "I do not believe you," he said harshly. "She is here. Where? At the manor? But you would not leave her there alone."

"And why, my dear brother, are you so concerned over the whereabouts of a little blind girl?" Garrick asked.

Lionel stared. "She is a mad child, with mad thoughts. I do not like being the target of her unruly tongue," he finally said. "She should have been left in the asylum."

Olivia cried out. Again Garrick stepped in front of her to prevent her from stepping forward and perhaps lunging at Lionel. "Perhaps you are afraid of her—as you should be," he said grimly. "And perhaps, now, you should be afraid of me."

Lionel's stance changed, became aggressive. Suddenly the two men were circling one another warily. Olivia gasped, but neither man paid her any attention. "I am not afraid of you. I am the Stanhope heir. Father has publicly declared it. It is you who should be afraid of me," Lionel said.

Garrick laughed. "Not for very long. Let us do away

with all pretense," he said with sudden heat. "You are not Lionel. You cannot be Lionel. And we both know why I am here—and why Hannah is a threat to you. We shall unmask you, you bastard."

Lionel smiled, but it was more of a snarl. "Never," he said.

"Admit the truth," Garrick demanded, becoming motionless, his entire body tensed to spring and attack. "Because I have had enough."

"I am your brother. That is the truth," Lionel cried.

Garrick smiled. "Tell me about Margaret MacDonald."

Lionel's expression remained implacable. "What is it that you wish to know?"

How cool and contained he was, Garrick thought. "Tell me about your relationship with her."

"Why?" It was a demand.

"Because if you are truly Lionel, then you know that she was the most important woman in your life," Garrick said.

A light—of relief?—flickered in Lionel's eyes. "I loved her very much."

Garrick did not respond.

"As you well know."

Garrick held himself still.

"What more should I say?" Lionel's temper was evident. "Clearly you are testing me—and clearly your machinations fail."

"She was your mother," Garrick said.

And for one instant, Lionel's eyes went wide with surprise.

"Father told you the truth when you were eight years old," Garrick cried.

Lionel shook his head. "But you? How did you find out?"

Garrick froze, because for one moment he had been certain that Lionel was a fraud—that he had not known about Meg MacDonald. And Lionel, sensing Garrick's doubt, laughed. "You cannot win, Garrick," he said.

Garrick saw red. With a sound that was more animal than human, he threw himself at his adversary, his rival.

Lionel jumped forward to meet him. "No one will believe you!" he shouted as they grabbed hold of each other and wrestled back and forth.

"No?" Garrick laughed as his superior size and weight drove Lionel backward. "Olivia is my witness." He finally shoved him violently, and Lionel went flying to the ground on his back. Garrick launched himself at him. As he did so, he saw Lionel drawing a dagger from beneath his cloak. Olivia must have seen it, too, because she screamed.

But it was too late. Garrick landed on Lionel as he thrust up with the blade. But, miraculously, Lionel missed, merely slicing through Garrick's coat.

With a roar, Garrick pinned him to the ground, gripping his right hand until he felt the bones there being crushed. Lionel screamed and released the knife.

Garrick reached for it, grabbed it, and flung it as far away as he could. For one instant, they were eye to eye and nose to nose, face to face. "No one will ever believe you and your whore," Lionel shouted, panting. "The earldom is rightfully mine!"

Garrick slammed his fist into Lionel's face.

Bone and cartilage smashed. Blood spurted from his nose.

Garrick stood, hoisting Lionel up with him. "Confess." He held him by his throat. "The truth! I want the truth!"

Lionel smiled at him. Ugliness and hatred had appeared in his eyes. "No."

Garrick hit him again savagely, this time in the stomach. He watched Lionel double over with real satisfaction. "Confess," he cried. "Or I will beat a confession out of you."

Lionel straightened, only to meet Garrick's fist a third time—and this time it was a blow to his face. His head snapped back, and the force of the blow sent him hurtling backward, and he again landed on the ground. This time he lay curled on his side, panting, bleeding. Garrick towered over him. "I will rip you to pieces," he said. "With real pleasure."

Lionel looked up at him from where he lay in the dirt

and mud. "Then you shall be hanged for my murder," he
snarled.

The dog barked.

Garrick straightened and met Olivia's gaze. Treve barked
again, the sound high-pitched and adamant.

Garrick grabbed Olivia's hand, forgetting all about Lionel, alarmed. They turned and ran through the gorse toward
the ruined keep. The stone shell came into view as soon as
they topped the first rise. Garrick spied Hannah's small
form immediately—she stood in the corner of the shell,
Treve dancing around her. He thanked God that she was
all right.

"Come on," he said as he and Olivia half-ran and half-
stumbled down the hill, kicking up dirt and stones as they
did so. Hannah turned toward them with an expectant look
upon her face.

"Hannah!" Olivia cried as she caught her daughter in
her arms. "What is it? Are you all right?"

"Mama, he is here," Hannah said.

Olivia frowned, brows furrowed.

"No. Here." Hannah pointed at the ground. "This is
where the body is. My lord, this is where you must dig."

Garrick stared at the grass-covered earth in the corner of
the keep, a chill sweeping over him. And then instinct made
him look up.

Lionel stood atop the hill, his pale, fawn-colored cape
stained with dirt and blood, staring down at them.

CHAPTER THIRTY

Garrick glanced at Olivia, who had also spied Lionel. She put her arm protectively around Hannah as Lionel began coming down the hill. He moved awkwardly, with a limp.

Garrick looked at Hannah. "Say nothing. And do not be afraid," he said.

Hannah nodded, but she moved even closer to her mother.

Garrick did not move, staring as Lionel approached. It took him many minutes to hobble across the interior of the keep. Finally he halted, gazing with open sarcasm at the three of them. "So? What is all the fuss about?" But his gaze was sharp, belying his tone.

Garrick stared. If Lionel's body was buried here, it did not seem that this man knew about it—and he felt a tremor of doubt. On the other hand, this man was not necessarily a murderer. Someone touched his back. He turned, and was seized with confusion. It had not been Olivia, for she remained out of reach. It must have been his imagination, but the hairs on his nape prickled. His glance found Olivia. Her eyes urged him to believe.

"My brother is buried here," Garrick said slowly. And the certainty began to build.

At first Lionel started. Then he laughed.

"If you have nothing to worry about, then you should

not object when we dig up the body?'' Garrick queried coolly. But he was trembling.

"If there is a body buried here, how will you prove it belongs to a boy dead for fourteen years?''

"So he is dead.''

"That is your supposition, not mine. I know who I am,'' Lionel said.

His adversary had a point, a damn good one. But he was compelled. There was no going back now. And freedom awaited him on the other side.

"Yesterday I sent a message to Stanhope, asking him to meet me here. I am expecting him at any moment. We will dig up the grave when he arrives,'' Garrick stated.

Lionel's eyes narrowed. "You are a fool,'' he finally said. "There is no grave.''

Garrick sincerely hoped that he was wrong.

It was raining, but lightly. Still, it was not an ideal day to dig up a body—if a body was truly interred there in the corner of the keep.

They had gathered there within an hour of the earl and countess's arrival at the manor. Garrick had been surprised to see his mother, and worried, too, by the sight of her— she was pale, red eyed, visibly distraught. She was not with them at the ruins, having begged to retire to her rooms, pleading fatigue from the journey.

"I do not understand the logic of this,'' Stanhope said grimly. But there was something in his eyes Garrick could not decipher. It was not fear. Was it resignation?

Garrick stood beside Olivia and Hannah, not far from his father and Lionel, everyone cloaked in hooded mantles to avoid the damp mist. Two villagers were using spades to dig up the stony earth. Garrick watched clumps of wet dirt flying backward from the spades. He shifted. "I have asked for your patience, Father. If Lionel is truly buried here, can you not give me that much?''

The earl skewered him with wide, grave blue eyes. "You base your theory upon the ramblings of a blind child. Some might say you have gone mad yourself, Garrick.'' But his tone was not as caustic as usual.

Garrick's jaw tensed. "We have been over this before. But I will say it again. If Lionel were alive, he would have come home many years ago. He would have never hurt us this way.''

Stanhope stared, shifting his weight from one foot to the other. Garrick again thought he saw a flicker of something he could not identify in his eyes. Then he watched the earl glance at the tall, somewhat husky blond man standing beside him. How relaxed the impostor was. How confident. What if he, Garrick, were wrong?

"My lord," one of the villagers said, pausing to lean on his spade, "there ain't nothing here, my lord. We've dug deep enough for any grave.''

Stanhope gave Garrick an enigmatic look and walked over to the hole in the earth, gazing down at it. Lionel followed him, then turned and grinned at Garrick. There was nothing mirthful or endearing about his expression. Garrick had the urge to knock him into the ground and bury him alive.

Olivia plucked his sleeve. "Do not.''

Stanhope and Lionel turned away from the dark, wet hole. "You may go," the earl told the two young men. Suddenly furious, Garrick strode past them, pulling a spade from one of the boy's hands as he started walking away with his partner. Garrick began digging furiously.

"Give it up, Garrick," the earl ordered.

Even angrier, Garrick thrust the spade into the ground again and pushed up hard on a clump of dirt. And again. And again.

"He is mad," Lionel said very clearly. "Let's have a drink, Father. And tell poor Mother what has happened.''

Garrick gritted his teeth, sweat pouring down his face, and slammed the spade into the earth, ready to give up and shout in frustration and rage. Then the spade hit something hard. He slammed it down again and felt it break through something, an object that was neither as hard as stone nor as soft as the wet, condensed earth.

And when the spade came up, he saw what appeared to be a tattered piece of blue rag on it. "Wait!"

He dug again, carefully now, repeatedly hitting the buried object, a sick, ill feeling, almost of dread, rising up within him—competing with certainty and anticipation. His pulse drummed deafeningly in his ears. Everyone had gathered around him.

He knew what he was digging up.

"Oh, my God," Olivia said as something dirty and white and covered with pieces of blue rag appeared before their eyes.

"Jesus." Garrick dropped to his knees, moving the earth with his hands now, recalling that Lionel had been wearing a blue coat the day he had disappeared. The earth gave way, revealing pieces of bone. An arm, a shoulder, and part of a torso was emerging, the flesh having long since rotted away. Tatters of fabric, blue and discolored gray, remained. Garrick realized he could not see. His tears blinded him.

"Dear God," Stanhope cried, stepping down beside him. And he was on his knees, staining his once immaculate stockings and breeches, beginning to claw the dirt with his own bare hands. "But this could be anyone," he gasped.

Garrick wiped his eyes with his fingers. "This is not an adult. Look, damn it, look!" The urge to vomit was strong, but he pushed more dirt off the skeletal corpse, revealing his chest and other shoulder, his neck and head. And when faced with those sightless eyes, the gaping sockets where the nose and mouth had been, Garrick turned and wretched violently.

"This is a boy," the earl whispered, kneeling in the dirt, unmoving. "A boy . . . oh, God."

Garrick felt Olivia touching him from behind. His tears halted and his vision cleared. And hanging on a fine gold chain about the skeletal neck amid the dirty faded rags was the Spanish coin.

The earl saw it, too. "The coin," he cried.

Garrick suddenly lurched to his feet, turning. "You!" he screamed.

"I had nothing to do with this!" Lionel said, his face

devoid of all color, fear finally evident in his eyes. "I am not a murderer—I would never murder my own brother!"

Garrick froze.

"Yes, Garrick," Lionel said, unmoving and ashen. "He was my brother, too, not that he knew me or I knew him. I wasn't good enough to be a part of the family." His tone was caustic. "Am I not right . . . Father?"

The earl was bowed over the body. He did not move.

"You're a bastard," Garrick said, shocked. "That's why you look like a goddamned Stanhope."

Lionel nodded. "And my name is Richard," he said. His gaze turned ugly. "My mother named me after him." He pointed at the earl. His hand was shaking.

Stanhope was rising heavily to his feet. He stared at his bastard son, still stunned by the discovery of Lionel's body.

"Did you know the truth about him?" Garrick accused his father.

And in that instant, Stanhope appeared confused and very, very old. He looked at Garrick. Then his expression firmed, and he was the earl of Stanhope once again. "A very long time ago," he said heavily, "just before Lionel was born, a housemaid came to me and told me she was pregnant with my child." His gaze was now on the pretender. "I did not believe her." Suddenly his face became taut, his nostrils turning red. He stared down at the skeleton in rags. "Oh, my God. My dear, dear Lionel."

"You knew," Garrick said, and it was an accusation.

The earl inhaled, fought for his composure, and faced his son. "I suspected from the start that this man was a by-blow."

Garrick shook his head in disbelief.

The pretender stepped between them. "Do you even remember her name, Father?" His tone was bitter, scathing.

"Frankly, I do not. She was a tart," the earl said flatly.

Richard lunged forward, but Garrick caught him, restraining him. "You turned her away penniless!" Richard shouted at the earl. "She was pregnant, with your son, *with me*, and you sent her packing with nothing but the rags on her back. And her name," he spat, "was Molly Nelson."

"She was not a virgin when she came to me," Stanhope said flatly. "I did not believe she was pregnant, nor did I believe I was the father if she was." He stared. "Of course, all of that changed. The moment I saw you I knew you were my flesh and blood."

"That is right. I am your flesh and blood," Richard said. *"I am your son."*

"But you are illegitimate," Garrick said, looking from one to the other. "How is it that you knew so much about me and Lionel, so much about the family?"

Richard faced him. "I grew up in Carston. Mother never even considered leaving. You were practically raised at the Hall, you and Lionel. I watched the two of you, playing, riding, even taking your lessons—all the time. I spied. I used to sneak around the grounds, just to see what the real brothers were doing. I even stole into the house on several occasions. Once, a servant caught me—but I escaped." His face was flushed now. "Do you know what it was like, to go to bed night after night, starving and cold, knowing that just down the road my brothers had full bellies, down comforters, dozens of clothes, hundreds of toys—and a father?"

"You hated us," Garrick said. "You still do."

"When I was older, I followed you in the summertime to Caedmon Crag. When you and Lionel finished playing in the smuggler's caves, I would play there myself—pretending I was legitimate." He stared, hatred in his eyes. "Pretending I was Lionel, the brother I resembled. I have rights, too!" he cried.

"You have no right to the earldom." It was Stanhope, speaking decisively for the first time. "You are a bastard, not the heir. Garrick is my heir."

Richard's fists were clenched. His entire body was shaking. "So now you disown me?"

"No. I will not disown me. I will provide for you, and well. But you are not the heir to my title, my estates, my fortune." Stanhope looked at Garrick.

"If you knew all along that Richard was a fraud, why did you pretend to believe him to be Lionel?" Garrick asked. "Why did you declare him to be your heir? I am sure you have a clever reason, but good God, look at what you have done to my mother!"

"It was a way to bring you to heel. Considering that you have no filial sense of duty, I had no choice but to use whatever advantage I had."

Garrick opened his mouth, an unkind epithet on the tip of his tongue, but Olivia suddenly took his hand and the curse died unspoken. He put his arm around her. Hannah was on Olivia's other side. "Well, Father. Your stratagem has failed. I am not a puppet, to dance upon your strings. I am not accepting this earldom. I am leaving the country, with Olivia and her daughter. And I don't give a damn what happens to the earldom," Garrick said.

"Garrick!" the earl cried in shock.

But Garrick turned his back upon him. He faced Richard, his bastard brother. "Tell me the truth. Did you and your mother kill Lionel?" But he knew that the answer was no. It made no sense for them to have done the deed and then wait so many years to perpetrate such a sham.

Richard returned his regard unflinchingly. He did not look away, and his eyes were not opaque. "No. We are not murderers. I don't know who killed him, or what happened," he said without hesitation. "It was only when you returned from Barbados that I realized I should come forward and claim the earldom for myself. I am telling the truth. If I had murdered him, I would not have waited fourteen years to do so. In fact," he said, "I would never have let you dig up the body, either."

The two half-brothers and the earl entered the manor, everyone strangely silent. No one had spoken since they had left the keep, with servants bringing back the body on a sledge for a proper burial. Olivia and Hannah had returned to the manor earlier. Garrick now watched as Lionel stood in the front hall, unmoving, while the earl walked through it, heading toward the study, or so Garrick suspected. Stanhope's shoulders were slumped. He appeared old, even defeated, and for one moment as he watched his father disappear, Garrick felt sorry for him.

"Now what?" Richard asked.

Garrick turned. This impostor was his half-brother; finally the circumstances of the past months made so much sense. But the answer to the question "Why?" still eluded everyone. Perhaps, Garrick thought, the answer to Lionel's disappearance and murder was not meant to be found.

He thought about his dead brother with sadness, but it was a brief feeling, and it was no longer intense. "Now we bury Lionel as he deserves," Garrick said, heading decisively toward the stairs.

"Wait." Richard rushed after him. "What will Father do?"

Garrick met his blue gaze. The impostor was no longer confident; there was anxiety in his eyes. Garrick did not want to feel any sympathy for him, and he refused to think about a young bastard boy abandoned and unclaimed by his real father, denied the privileges of wealth and station, growing up poor and hungry and angry. "He will come around, I think, because you are his son, and I am not ever returning."

He bounded up the stairs and hurried to his mother's apartments, dreading telling her what he must. He raised his fist to knock on her closed door, then hesitated. He could clearly hear her weeping.

Garrick knocked, filled with tension. Straining to hear, he realized she had ceased crying, and suddenly the door opened. Eleanor forced a smile.

"Why are you crying?" Garrick asked simply.

Her face crumpled and she turned away, weeping anew.

Stricken, Garrick went to her and put his arm around her. "Please, do not cry. Mother, I wish you had not come to the crag."

She sniffed into a handkerchief, nodding, and finally looked at him. "I also wish I had not come." She walked away, and to his dismay, he saw it was to refill an empty port glass. The bottle, he remarked, was already a third empty.

"Are you so unhappy that you must drink before dinner?" he asked gently.

She sipped and faced him. "Yes."

He did not know what to say to that.

"What happened?" she asked.

He removed his wet mantle and sat down. "We found Lionel's body. He is dead. He died when he was just a boy. There was proof, that old coin he wore around his neck."

She stared at him speechlessly.

He wet his lips, standing. "The impostor is Father's by-blow. Apparently before he married you he got a housemaid pregnant. His real name is Richard Nelson."

She continued to stare at him, having lost all of her color.

Worried, Garrick went to her. "I am sorry to be the one to tell you this."

Breathing harshly, she turned away. "I knew. I knew he was dead. Dear, dear God."

"How could you know?" Garrick asked. "Do not blame yourself—"

She interrupted him by running across the room, bending, and unlocking the doors to a sideboard's cabinet. He glimpsed the empty bottles hidden there and winced, determined to end his mother's drinking once and for all. Then he stared. She had straightened and was holding a leather-bound book. "Take this," she cried. "For I can no longer bear the guilt!"

Confused, Garrick took the volume. "What is this?" he asked, flipping it open. Quickly he realized that it was his mother's diary. And suddenly he had the urge to dispose of it—before he or anyone could see the contents.

"My journal," she said, her face distinctly gray. "I stopped writing in it fourteen years ago."

Garrick froze. Dread filled him, and with it came a vivid recollection of Olivia's warning, that the suffering was not over yet. His fingers moved of their own accord, against his will. He found the last entry. It was dated April 23, 1746—two weeks after Lionel's disappearance. He had no wish to read the entry, but the name MacDonald leapt off the page at him. Startled, his gaze slammed to it again. He read, "The new laird, Ross MacDonald, Meg's little brother, now a man bent on vengeance."

Frightened, Garrick slammed the book closed and jerked his gaze to his mother. She was crying soundlessly as she gulped down the port, her tears spilling into the glass.

"Stop!" he shouted, suddenly enraged. Before he knew what he was doing he tore the glass from her hand and threw it across the room. It landed on the carpet without breaking. The port wine was darkly red against the pale rug.

He inhaled. "I am sorry. My God. What is in this diary?"

She looked at him, and it was an eternity before she answered. "They did not know. He did not know. Meg's brother never knew that Lionel was his own flesh and blood when he abducted him and—" She broke off. "He never knew when he killed him," she whispered hoarsely.

Chills swept over him. Suddenly he was gripping his mother, shaking her. "I don't understand any of this!" But he did. Oh, God, he did.

"Ross MacDonald loved Meg and he abducted Lionel to avenge her death, thinking him to be my son—not hers! There was a note that told how Lionel had been abducted, and why. I destroyed it." She trembled violently in his arms.

He stared, sick with shock, unable to believe what he had heard—unable to believe his mother's duplicity, her guilt. "But why?" he asked numbly. "Why? You could have saved his life!"

"I hated your father," she said, and as he released her she slumped, becoming as old and ugly as his father. "I hated him because of you. Because he favored Lionel and made you so unhappy all of the time. I never thought the MacDonalds would kill him. Oh, God, I was *glad* he took Lionel. I was glad because, with Lionel gone, maybe, one day, he would treat you fairly, maybe, one day, he would start loving you, Garrick." She lifted her wet eyes to his.

He was in shock. He could not speak.

"I didn't even know until today that he was truly dead,"

Eleanor cried. "I had been hoping so much that Lionel had truly returned—as if that could redeem me for the past!" Briefly she closed her eyes. "I destroyed the note. I was foxed most of the time. I could not think clearly. And what if they had taken you, instead? Don't look at me that way!" She suddenly flashed. "I have more than paid for my crime! I have lived with a hideous guilt every day of my life—I have lived with nothing but regrets!"

Garrick had never been more ill. He turned away from her, trying desperately to understand. He realized he had dropped the diary, and he bent to retrieve it. He would not give it to the earl. Not ever.

"I am sorry," she said, walking away from him.

He did not turn. More suffering. He crossed the room slowly, very tired now, feeling like an old man himself. How right Olivia had been.

Then came the wave of grief, astonishing in its intensity. *Mother. How could you!* If she had spoken up, Lionel might not be dead.

When he reached the door he abruptly felt a blast of frigid air, and suddenly, too late, he realized she had opened the window and he knew. He whirled.

Screaming, "Mother, don't!"

Eleanor slipped onto the windowsill, not looking back, and launched herself to her death.

STANHOPE HALL

She had known where she would find him. Olivia paused, clasping a bouquet of daffodils in her hands, gentle, early spring sunshine washing over the family cemetery, casting the pale headstones, the larger white marble crypt, the grass and trees in a warm, mellow light. Garrick stood before the high marble vault with his back to her, his head bowed. She ached for him, sharing his pain and his grief.

She had not moved, and the countryside was stunningly silent, lacking even birdsong, but slowly Garrick turned, sensing her presence. He smiled slightly at her.

Her heart leapt a little as it always did at the sight of

him, because she loved him so and he had given her the miracle of freedom and hope. She started toward him.

When she came abreast of him, he accepted the flowers, laid them down at the foot of the crypt, and he put his arm around her. "How are you?" she asked softly.

Their gazes met. "I have you," he said, after a pause. "You, and Hannah."

Tears filled her eyes. "Yes, you do," she said. "How was the funeral?" It had been a private ceremony, held just yesterday—three days after the countess's suicide.

"Horrid."

She pressed closer to him. "I wish there is something I could say, or do, to make you feel better," she began.

He turned fully toward her. "Having you here, with me, is all that I need." He cupped her face in his strong hands. "Are you all right?"

She nodded, smiling at the irony of his asking about her welfare. "Hannah and I have taken lodgings at the Mayfair, but nothing could keep me away from the Hall today. Garrick, I am so sorry this happened."

Tears shone in his eyes. "Although I will always miss her, and although I will never understand how she could have destroyed that note, in a way I am glad that she has finally found her own relief, and her own freedom. She wasn't bad and she wasn't evil."

"She was human," Olivia said gently. "And she loved you with all of her heart and her entire soul." Olivia smiled and touched his lips with her forefinger. "And I love you, Garrick. I will always love you."

He held her hard, then, burying his face against her hair. "How soon," he whispered roughly, "can you and Hannah be ready to depart?"

Olivia was surprised and she met his regard. How serious he was. "If you wish to leave within the hour, we would be ready, Hannah and I."

He smiled. And the dull light in his eyes changed, warming, becoming vital and alive. "Only you," he whispered, "would make such a reply."

Olivia did not hesitate. "I have waited an entire lifetime

to find you, Garrick. I am tired of waiting.''

''I am tired of waiting, too,'' he said simply. ''Can you manage, even though it will be some time before your marriage is annulled?''

She nodded. ''Arlen is perverse and unpredictable. It has crossed my mind that in the end he might not annul our marriage, just to spite me and prevent me from marrying you. But I no longer care. I only care that we are together, you and I and Hannah.''

He studied her. ''That is all that I care about, too, at this point, Olivia. There has been so much suffering, but I can feel that we are on the verge of so much happiness. I have given this a great deal of thought. I want to take you and Hannah to America.''

Her eyes widened. An image of the colonial land she had never actually seen appeared in her mind, drawn from etchings and watercolors so often displayed in the newspapers and journals she read. Olivia imagined a land filled with thick forests and red-skinned natives, but the beaches were the color of pearls, the lakes emerald-green, the skies impossibly blue. Her heart raced. Excitement swept through her. And it was joyous. ''A foreign land, where no one knows anything about us. The perfect place to begin a new life,'' she said, suddenly overwhelmed.

''Those are my thoughts exactly,'' Garrick said, tilting up her chin. His lips on hers were soft and tender and gentle. ''It is a land, they say, of infinite opportunity.''

''Oh, Garrick.'' She clasped his hands. ''America. How perfect.''

''No, Olivia,'' he said, smiling. ''*You* are perfect.'' And he pulled her close again.

ONE MONTH LATER

The day was perfectly placid, warm with a soft breeze, mellow clouds drifting in the sunlit sky; in short, it was the perfect day to set sail for a foreign land.

Garrick stared up at the frigate that was bound for the American colonies, specifically for the port of Jamestown.

He quickly spied Olivia and Hannah standing at the railing, in spite of the other passengers crowding there and the sailors preparing to disembark. Olivia was lovely in a pale green dress and mantle with a white hat, while Hannah, in a yellow-flocked ensemble, restrained Treve on a leash. Mother and daughter were waving at him, smiling widely.

He was smiling, too, not just with his mouth, but with his heart and his soul. He lifted his hand and waved back at them. How beautiful they were. How he could gaze upon them this way for an eternity—for the eternity Olivia had promised him.

"Garrick."

The moment broken, his smile fading, Garrick turned to the earl of Stanhope, who stood at his left side. His half-brother, Richard, was beside him.

"How can I convince you to change your mind?" the earl asked. As usual, he made a splendid figure in a boldly blue frock coat and immaculate white breeches and stockings. He no longer appeared his age, but a dozen years older, at the least. The discovery of Lionel's body and his own wife's death had taken their toll. Garrick was beginning to understand that he had loved Eleanor, in his own way.

"I am not changing my mind," Garrick said firmly. "There is nothing here for me."

The earl stared, absorbing that. Glancing at Richard, Garrick saw satisfaction in his blue eyes. "Will I ever see you again?" Stanhope asked.

"I doubt it," Garrick said truthfully.

The earl made a face, partly resignation, partly dismay. "I do love you, you know."

Garrick blinked in shock. Then he said, "Father, actions speak louder than words. And your words are a bit late—twenty-six years too late, in fact."

"Very well. But know this. If you ever decide to return, you are more than welcome—and I will tell the world the truth about Lionel and make you my heir."

If hope flickered in his father's eyes, Garrick did not see it. "Leave society to its delusions," he said. He spoke about the fact that the earl had kept the truth about Lionel a secret, and to this day, the peerage believed Richard Nelson to be Lionel De Vere. The pretender had not been unmasked after all, although rumors were running wild in Cornwall, but Garrick no longer cared. Let Richard take the title and the earldom. He himself was free at long last.

"It is time for me to go," Garrick said. He looked at Richard, the man still calling himself Lionel. He nodded. "I wish you no ill," he said.

Richard shrugged. "Bon voyage," he said. "I am sorry you shall not be present at my wedding." But his tone made his feelings obvious—he did not give a damn.

"I do wish you and Elizabeth a very long and happy union," Garrick said, careful to keep any mockery out of his tone. How they suited one another—how they deserved one another. And how it would torment and agonize Arlen—deservedly so. Garrick faced his father. "I will write, when it is time to do so," he said. "After we are settled."

The earl hesitated. Then he glanced from Garrick to the frigate and back again. "I owe you this much," he said. "I will make sure Arlen Grey annuls the marriage so you can marry Olivia."

Garrick stared, amazed. When he had recovered he said, "And when you ask for repayment of such a debt?"

The earl smiled. "Then you shall owe me, shall you not?"

Garrick knew that one day that day would come. "You will never change," he said, but without rancor.

"No. I am too old to change. But I am not a bad man, Garrick. Difficult, perhaps, but that is all." The earl smiled. "I will get my heir," he said flatly. "For there is nothing I want more."

"For once, we are in complete agreement," Garrick said, knowing his father would succeed, for the stakes meant everything to him. And he thought about Olivia one day soon carrying his child and being his wife. Wonder and awe filled him. Garrick bowed. "Good-bye, Father."

The earl nodded gruffly, not reaching out to embrace him. That would have been awkward for them both.

Yet as Garrick turned away, he knew he had glimpsed tears in his father's eyes, and he was moved in spite of himself—in spite of the huge gulf of the past that would always remain between them.

And then he saw the future.

Olivia, beaming, continued to wave from the railing where she stood, urging him now to come to her. Hannah jumped up and down, unable to restrain her excitement. Treve barked, wagging his tail wildly. His heart melted, and he began to run up the gangplank, his strides coming faster and faster still. Garrick bounded onto the deck, and a moment later, he swept Olivia and Hannah into his arms. He swung them around and around, his setter barking madly at them.

The future—Olivia and Hannah and a new, wild land.

A land filled with hope and promise, land with no past to hold anyone back. The joy that had lurked on the horizon overcame him then—and forever—as the lines were cast and the frigate inched away from the berth and out of the harbor, sailing to that faraway place called America.